More praise for BAD MEDICINE

"[Ron Querry] has established himself not merely as successor but as rival to Tony Hillerman."

—*World Literature Today*

"A story that needed to be told—and Mr. Querry tells it brilliantly."

—Diana L. Ossana

"A good read for anyone interested in Native American culture and beliefs. The characters are authentic and realistic; the healers, both traditional and non-traditional, will have you pulling for their cause. And the 'bad medicine' man will scare you half to death."

—*The Advocate,* Baton Rouge

"[Querry] manages to mix Indian mysticism and suspense in an entertaining fashion . . . giving readers an in-depth look at life on the Navajo reservation. . . . A novel to enjoy."

—*Sunday Albuquerque Journal*

"Entertaining reading."

—*Tucson Weekly*

"[Querry has] the ability to create lifelike, sympathetic characters. And some critics feel he has 'the best ear for dialogue in the business.' "

—*The Arizona Daily Star*

BY RON QUERRY

From Bantam Books

The Death of Bernadette Lefthand

New York Toronto London

Sydney Auckland

BAD MEDICINE

Ron Querry

BAD MEDICINE

A Bantam Book

PUBLISHING HISTORY
Bantam hardcover edition published April 1998
Bantam trade paperback edition / May 1999

Book design by Dana Treglia.
Map by Jeff Ward.

Library of Congress Catalog Card Number: 97-24069.

ISBN 0-553-37799-X

Published simultaneously in the United States and Canada

Bantam Books are published by Bantam Books, a division of Random House, Inc. Its trademark, consisting of the words "Bantam Books" and the portrayal of a rooster, is Registered in U.S. Patent and Trademark Office and in other countries. Marca Registrada. Bantam Books, 1540 Broadway, New York, New York 10036.

PRINTED IN THE UNITED STATES OF AMERICA

BVG 10 9 8 7 6 5 4 3 2 1

This book is for Elaine . . .

but for her, I might never

have seen the dance

What follows is a work of fiction inspired by a series of events that are a matter of fact and that took place on and around Navajo and Hopi lands in northern Arizona and New Mexico over a period of weeks in May and June of 1993. The author would have you know, however, that the places and characters in this account—as well as the names ascribed to them—are fictitious or are used fictitiously.

And perhaps the day will come when, to the bane and
enlightenment of man, the plague will rouse up its
rats again and send them forth to
die in a happy city.

—ALBERT CAMUS
The Plague, 1947

Thou shalt not be afraid for the terror by night;
nor for the arrow that flieth by day;
Nor for the pestilence that walketh in darkness;
nor for the destruction that wasteth
at noonday.

—PSALMS
91:5–6

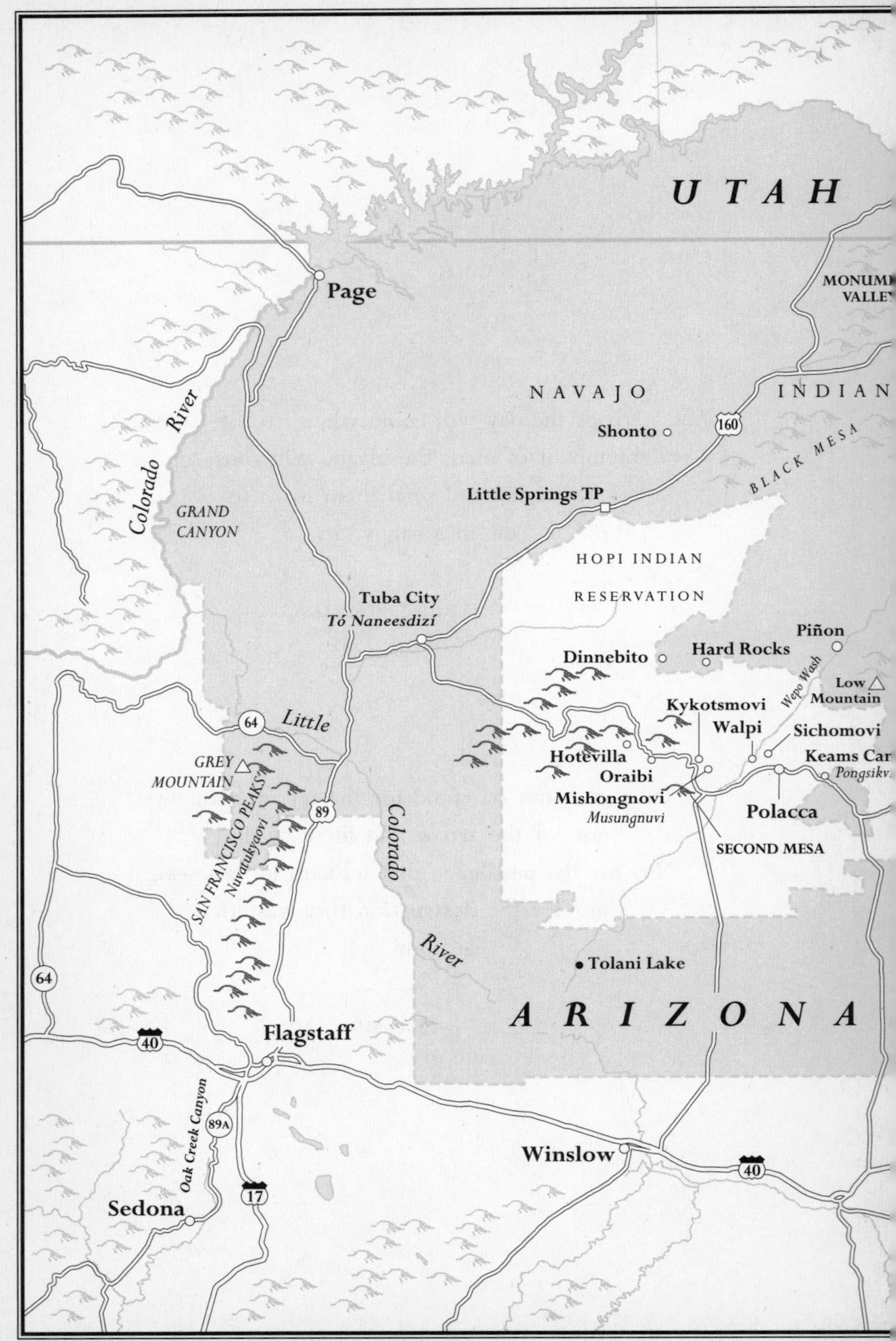

UTAH
Page
MONUM
VALLE
NAVAJO
INDIAN
Colorado River
Shonto
160
BLACK MESA
GRAND CANYON
Little Springs TP
HOPI INDIAN RESERVATION
Tuba City
Tó Naneesdizí
Piñon
Dinnebito
Hard Rocks
Wepo Wash
Low Mountain
Kykotsmovi
64
Little
Walpi
Sichomovi
GREY MOUNTAIN
Hotevilla
Keams Ca
Oraibi
Pongsikv
SAN FRANCISCO PEAKS
Nuvatukyaovi
Mishongnovi
Musungnuvi
Polacca
89
Colorado
SECOND MESA
River
Tolani Lake
64
ARIZONA
40
Flagstaff
Oak Creek Canyon
89A
Winslow
40
17
Sedona

COLORADO
FOUR CORNERS
191
160
Teec Nos Pos
T'iis Náabas
San Juan River
666
Shiprock
Farmington
Mexican Water
RESERVATION
Chinle Wash
Round Rock
12
Lukachukai
Tídááchiid
NEW MEXICO
Many Farms
Two Grey Hills
Tsaile
Canyon del Muerto
'Ane'é tséyi'
Massacre Cave/Two Fell Off
Adah Aho'doo'nílí
Chinle
Ch'ínílí
Canyon de Chelly
Sheep Springs
Hashké
27
Kinlichee
Round Top
Cross Canyon
Two Story TP
Fort Defiance
Nazhoni
Coyote Canyon
Twin Lakes Bahastl'ah
Hubbell TP
Ganado
St. Michael's
Window Rock
Tségháhoodzáni
3
Gallup Na'nizhoozhi
RED ROCK ST. PARK
Wide Ruin
40
Ft. Wingate
Army Depot
Shash bitoo'
0
25
50
Scale of Miles
© 1997 Jeffrey L.Ward

BAD MEDICINE

Prologue

In the high desert landscape that is typical of the vast Navajo Reservation in northeastern Arizona there is, in an area otherwise remarkable only for its low mountains and mesas and relatively shallow dry washes, a spectacularly and indeed startlingly deep and rugged system of canyons that spreads from its mouth near the town of Chinle like fingers to the north toward the Lukachukai Mountains and on east toward Two Grey Hills. And while the northernmost of these canyons is most widely called by its Spanish name, Canyon del Muerto, traditional Navajo know it by its Navajo name, *'Ane'é tséyi'*, which means, literally, "The Canyon Behind."

And there is a place known as Massacre Cave on what is the far-north rim of this particular canyon where, in the winter of 1805, a Spanish soldier—a lieutenant by the name of Antonio Narbona—led a force of some three hundred troops on a murderous assault against a group of Navajo, women and children for the most part, who had sought to hide from the well-armed soldiers on a shallow ledge some six hundred feet up the side of the sheer eight-hundred-foot-high rock wall. Nearly two hundred years have passed, and still the Indians tell of how the first soldier to climb over the rock parapet that day was met by a fierce young woman wielding a knife, and how, in the struggle that ensued, the woman and the soldier fell over the side and plummeted to their deaths. And they tell about how in the hours that followed there were more than 115 mostly women, children, and old men slaughtered by the Spanish troops.

And they tell us, too, that to this day the place the whites call Massacre Cave is known among the Navajo as *Adah Aho'doo'nilí:* "Two Fell Off."

ADAH AHO´DOO´NILÍ

This is the way the story begins: Early on a certain morning in late April—the year is 1993—there is a solitary figure standing smoking a cigarette at the Park Service overlook at Two Fell Off.

Already there is a brisk breeze blowing from out of the west and the figure standing looking down into the canyon holds tightly to the green iron railing placed there to protect the unwitting tourist from approaching too closely the edge and falling over the side. And now the figure—and this figure is plainly that of a man—stubs out the half-smoked cigarette butt on the red rock ledge before he turns and walks quickly back up the trail that has brought him to this spot. And at a place about halfway along this quarter-mile-long path that winds its way back to the visitors' parking area, a place where the narrow dirt trail veers sharply away from the rocky precipice, the man stops to listen for any sound that an approaching vehicle might make. When he feels certain that he's alone at this place—that it is still too early for tourists to have yet begun arriving at the overlook—the man ducks off the path and into the shadowed mass of sunflowers and snakeweed that is here so thick and tangled that, before he's gone more than a half-dozen paces, he is effectively obscured from view.

And then, a couple of hundred yards from the windswept ledge, about half or three-quarters of a mile north of the Two Fell Off overlook, the man comes at last upon the crude eight-sided dwelling that he has been looking for—that he has been told he would find here. Set well back from the path, this hogan is mostly hidden from view by dark blue-green greasewood bushes, pungent scrub juniper, and by abundant, full, verdant piñon, their branches drooping uncharacteristically low under the weight of swollen, nut-filled cones. It is a traditional Navajo hogan, this place, fashioned from rough-hewn cribbed logs chinked with mud. The man hesitates only a moment before he walks directly up to the unpainted and weathered plank-wood door and raps sharply on it with his knuckles. He listens for some noise from within the place, but there is, except for the sound of wind in the pines, only the deadly quiet, and so he raps again, this time more loudly, and he calls out: "Hullo? Anybody there?" And when still there is no response he first pushes and then leans his shoulder hard against the door. It is neither latched nor locked yet it is only with some effort that the man is able to push open the door with his shoulder and then stoop slightly to step into the relative darkness of the place—the floor of which is hard-packed dirt, as is the roof.

Inside, there are the spare furnishings common to such a structure; near the center of the single room there is a small cast-iron stove and beside that a low plank table upon which are arranged various bags and cans of foodstuffs—some unopened, others nearly empty, the remains of their contents—coarse-ground coffee and sugar, stewed tomatoes and sweet pork and beans, mostly—long since dried out or gone bad. Along the wall to the right of the door there is a narrow bench for sitting or perhaps for lying down, and beside this bench an old wooden box that has been set upright on its end, and there are on this box a dented blue-green can of Bugler-brand cigarette tobacco and some blue-tipped wooden kitchen matches alongside a small packet of papers for making cigarettes. A smaller wooden box has been nailed to the wall above the table to serve as a crude cabinet for several dusty brown bottles of liniments and small tins of salves. And here and there, protruding from the wall of the structure, nails that have been halfway driven into logs hold various items up off the dirt floor: bits of rope and twine, a rusted iron cooking pot, a cracked and brittle-dry horse bridle.

And in the center of this single room, too, near the small stove, there is an open firepit that seems larger than one would expect to find in a room of this size. The smokehole in the roof directly above the firepit admits what little light there is, and dust specks float slowly in the single beam of sunlight that falls from the smokehole to the place where it strikes the floor. And beside the firepit there is a moderate-sized stack of firewood . . . not rightly a stack, it is, rather, a disordered jumble of twisted pitchy pine roots and piñon knots. And there, on the floor, directly opposite the single east-facing door, lies a stained and filthy sheepskin pad that has served as the ragged sleeping pallet in this place. And there is throughout this room a heavy layering of dust . . . dust covers everything . . . and cobwebs . . . and greasy black soot and the powdery gray ash from who can say how many fires. . . . And it is clear to the man, too, from the muffled scuttling noises he hears and from the black pellet-droppings and emptied piñon-nut shells that he can make out where they lie scattered about, that more than a few pack rats and field mice have made themselves a home here.

Oh, but the interior of this hogan is dark and filthy from neglect. More than simply neglect—and neglect is a condition not common to the clean and tidy homes that are the tradition among the *dine'é*—for this is a suffocating place, an evil place even, that no good person would dare to enter.

For finally, there is this: Lying on the floor, close up beside but not quite upon the filthy sheepskin sleeping pad, are the shrunken and dried remains of what was once a human being.

It may seem odd that the man is only slightly startled by the fact that there is a corpse in this room. But while it is true he has come expecting to find someone *living* here, he has come in search of some *thing*, and the fact that there is no living person to interfere with his search means that what might otherwise have been uncomfortable and complicated will now be easier. The room smells musty. It is clear that this corpse has been here, undisturbed, for some time now. The thing is dried out and grotesquely leatherlike, mummified, in fact—the effect of the suffocating heat and the dry air that characterize the lower Sonoran steppe terrain of this isolated region of the reservation. This thing is lying on its side, its knees are awkwardly bent at surprising angles and its arms are drawn up in front of its chest as if in some ghastly caricature of prayer. And hideous, clawlike hands that are remarkable for the long nails, yellowed and filthy, at the ends of blackened, misshapen, dry-shriveled fingers clutch at a medicine bundle—a leather pouch the size of a child's hand, laid flat. The man can hardly believe his good fortune, for it is just such an old Navajo man's medicine bundle that he has come in search of.

What had once been the flesh of lips of this thing are pulled back in a ghastly grimace of death from rotted and broken teeth—pulled back in a sardonic and distorted grin, or more precisely, perhaps, frozen forever in an expression of surprise at the awful realization of what must have been a final, horrible moment of life. And what had been, in that life, a man's eyes, are now half-closed and sunken orbs—empty black holes, really, behind dark leather lids. Wispy ash-gray strands and matted tufts of hair stick awkwardly out from the skull—a frayed and filthy purple scarf that had once been knotted in the traditional way above the corpse's left ear is now fallen almost comically askew across the right eye and the bridge of the nose—of what is left of the nose, rather, for it has been chewed and mostly eaten away by rats and mice.

The man reaches down. The clawlike fingers of the corpse have no real grasp on the pouch, and the thin leather thong by which it has been attached to the thing's neck fairly crumbles to dust at the touch.

Holding the pouch now, still marveling at his good fortune, the man casts a final look around the dark room before stepping out into the morning sunlight. He pulls the wooden door shut tightly behind him and squats on his heels beside the warm and sunny exterior wall to examine the contents of the medicine bundle. Fashioned from crudely tanned leather hide, the pouch has been painstakingly stitched with a single length of sinew and knotted tightly closed. He takes a jackknife from his pocket and cuts the lace stitching in several places. Carefully unfolding the leather pouch, he discovers inside, wrapped in an oily black cloth, a single object—a small stone tablet, measuring perhaps four inches square and half an inch thick. Turning the stone over in his hands, he sees where a pattern of marks has been etched on the stone's surface. On one side there is a strange series of broken and solid lines, and on the other, he can make out what appears to be a pair of stylized animal tracks . . . bear prints.

He wraps the tablet back up in the black cloth and places it and the now-empty leather pouch deep into his pocket. Pushing open the door, he glances once more around the dark interior of the hogan. As he pulls the door closed and turns away from the place, there is an odd smile on the man's face. His heart is pounding in his chest and he is whistling softly now . . . he lights a cigarette and begins the short hike back down toward the Two Fell Off overlook.

TÍDÁÁCHIID

Something is terribly wrong.

In the dim, still quiet the young woman's breathing has become now even more shallow and labored. From deep within her quick-rising and falling breast there comes a rasping, rattling noise, and by the pale yellow glow that spills from the single kerosene lantern, which provides the only light inside this place, any one of those present who might dare to gaze directly into this young woman's face—and none will, it seems—would see plainly the look of fear in her frantic-wide eyes . . . darting eyes that are reddened and angry-looking with inflammation . . . eyes that have taken on the look of something wild.

The air in the hogan is oppressive, heavy with the smell of smoke and herbs, of burning wood and sharp sage. Along one side of the nearly dark room five women are seated with their backs pressed against the wall. One cradles an infant wrapped in a thin blanket . . . it is the child of the sick young woman. Directly across from the women and the child—seated cross-legged against the opposite wall—are three men. The men sit quietly—all three are smoking cigarettes. The young woman is sitting on a brightly colored woven saddle blanket in the very center of the room, her legs are stretched straight out in front of her, her arms are crossed loosely across her stomach and her shoulders are slumped forward. Her hair is tied up with white yarn in the traditional manner of the Navajo and she wears a broomstick-style skirt that reaches her ankles. Her feet are bare and, as is the way of her people when one is the patient in a ceremonial procedure such as this, she is naked from the waist up. Her cheeks and forehead are flushed red and her lips are cracked and dry from the fever that rages within her—yet her hair is moist and tangled. Her whole body aches and she coughs sporadically.

An old woman is kneeling beside the sick girl. Leaning in close, the woman can be heard to be speaking to the girl in a low, halting voice—speaking to her in the language of the *dine'é*—in the Navajo language.

"T'áadoo bee níldzidí," she says. "Don't be afraid, child . . . we got to try to find out what it is that's causin' this hot, choking sickness in your body."

The old woman's clothes are of the traditional Navajo sort—a purple velvet blouse that is dull with age, a full skirt and brown leather moccasins. Around her neck hangs a heavy silver squash-blossom necklace, and on her left wrist there is a large needlepoint bracelet. There are turquoise rings on both the old woman's hands—hands that are constantly and gently moving over and across her patient's shoulders and hair, touching the girl much as a blind person might explore some unknown surface. And as she does so she is chanting softly . . . intermittently . . . the chanting interrupted now and again by questions directed at the younger woman.

"Where have you been walking?" she asks. "Have you been careful about not steppin' on one of them tracks left there by a snake or maybe in the footprint from a coyote?"

"Yes, grandmother." The girl's voice is hoarse—her words are dry and raspy—and there is real fear in her words. "I've been watchin' where I walk."

The old woman is now sprinkling corn pollen from a small leather pouch she carries . . . sprinkling pollen on the girl's breast. ''Have you been hangin' around over there at that trader's room where he keeps that stuff from the old ones? You been picking up pieces of them old broken pots or goin' around them *ch'íidii* hogans over there?'' She points with her chin and lips toward the south—toward Canyon de Chelly. The young woman is shaking her head. There are tears on her cheeks.

''You got to tell me so I can help you, child. Have you been drinkin' that wine and beer and goin' around with those good-for-nothing drunk Indians or them *bilagáana* boys in them towns when you ought to be back at home with your own baby?''

''No, grandmother. I haven't done none of those things.'' And she is racked with coughing—the burning pain in her chest is sharp and terrible.

Still talking low and singing, the old woman has begun to rock back and forth rhythmically. ''And what about dogs,'' she says. ''Have you been seein' any strange dogs that don't belong to your outfit comin' around there lately?''

The girl shakes her head feebly, a look of resignation on her face now, if a look of resignation can be said to show through on a face at once rigid with pain and fear. ''No.''

''Or how about strangers that might have some kind of evil on their mind?'' The old woman is rocking more vigorously now.

''Nobody, grandmother.''

And now the old woman is silent—rocking still, but without speaking or singing. To those watching in the dim light her eyes appear to have closed and her mouth to have gone slack—not moving now but partly open, it seems. She makes no sound.

Slowly now, the old woman's arm—her right arm—has begun to twitch and the fingers on her hand to quiver. The movement of the arm and hand is only slight at first, but very soon the movement becomes more pronounced. And still the old woman's eyes remain closed—it is as though she is asleep, or in that state of dreaming that precedes sleep, perhaps. The movement of the arm becomes almost violent for a brief moment—uncontrolled and convulsive—and then it seems to relax and it is only the hand that trembles and shakes.

The woman begins to mumble sounds: ''*Jį'ani'įįhí*,'' she says softly—

though barely audible, it is an odd word that means, literally, "day thief."

The others in the room look on quietly, their faces exhibiting not the slightest sign of surprise, for they have watched *ndilniihii*—hand-tremblers—at work before . . . seen the workings of the traditional Navajo diviner who is called upon, not to heal—it is the *hataałii,* the singer, that is the healer in the Navajo Way—but rather to diagnose, to divine by hand-trembling, just what it is that has caused the illness or the unbalance in one's life and so, by means of this gift received from the Holy People, to determine what Way or ceremony may be required to return this patient to her previous state of health and well-being . . . to the Navajo state of *hózhǫ́*.

Several minutes pass and the only sound in the dark, smoky hogan is the occasional coughing of the girl.

When the trembling in the old woman's hand has stopped completely she sits silently for what seems a very long time—not moving at all. Her wrinkled brown face glistens now with sweat, and although it is warm inside this room, it is not so warm that one would normally perspire. Her eyes remain closed and her mouth is still partly open. Then, with a start, her head jerks back and her eyes open wide. The old woman takes a deep, gasping breath of air—it is as though she has been holding her breath for a long time, which she has not.

"*Baa ha'aldéé́,*" the old woman cries out. "It is beginning!"

And just then the girl is racked by a torturous fit of coughing that leaves her gasping and fighting for breath. And there is a gurgling—a rumbling noise almost—from within her chest, and struggling now desperately for air, she slumps even farther forward.

And then in a frantic instant she gathers what air she can and manages to gasp one last exclamation:

"*Binásdzid!*" she cries: "I am afraid!"

She is unable now to make another coherent sound; her face is wildly contorted with the terror she most certainly feels—her hands clutching and clawing frantically at her throat. And the women in the room move quickly to reach her side. It is clear that this girl can no longer breathe, that she is suffocating. It is as though—and this is what is most appalling—she is utterly conscious of the fact that she is suffocating, that she is dying, in fact, and she is very nearly mad with this horror that has taken hold of her so completely.

And now her eyes roll back in her head, her arms flail about and then become rigid . . . the women hold her down so that in her thrashing, seizurelike movements she will not further injure herself. And all the while the old hand-trembler seems totally unaware of what is going on in the room—seems disconnected, in fact, from all that is happening around her. It is as if she herself is in a trancelike state. Unable or unwilling to open her eyes, she is swaying back and forth.

"*Jį'ani'įįhí,*" she says again.

And just now there is a coldness that comes suddenly into the darkened interior of the room. And the air inside this closed place that has smelled so sharply and so strongly of burning sage is at once musty and stale. The door to the hogan has remained tightly shut, to be sure—for it could not have been opened, even for a moment, without those inside knowing it. And yet there is all of a sudden in this room—standing in the darkest place within, near to the door but apart from the others—a twelfth person: A stranger, it is a woman who has appeared. A woman whose clothing is worn and soiled and who is herself dirty and barefooted. The woman's long dark hair is matted and dull and although she makes no sound, it is obvious that she is weeping. Her face is hidden—buried in her hands. And the old hand-trembler's eyes have opened now, and are staring—fixed and remarkably unsurprised—at this strange woman who has so suddenly appeared.

And the dying young woman, her eyes, too, have settled on the apparition that has appeared beside her. . . .

The men in the room look on still in silence. To a man, their eyes have widened now in a look that is more precisely curiosity than alarm or fear, and yet not one of them makes any movement toward the strange woman, nor is there any attempt by any one of these men to assist or touch in any way the dying girl.

• • •

And as quickly as it had appeared, the apparition is gone and the old hand-trembler looks to have wakened from her reverie. Her eyes are wide now and her voice takes on a determined, somber tone as she turns and speaks softly and directly to the woman who sits cradling the infant—the woman who is the patient's mother: "You have to take this girl to the *bilagáana* clinic over there to Lukachukai."

And then, because the mother holding her grandchild there in the darkened room looks frightened and helpless and unable, even, to move, the old woman says to her in a voice that is louder now: "Listen to me. You got to go and take this child over there now. . . . Do it, before your girl winds up dead!"

LUKACHUKAI

He's taken the long way this morning for this first trip to the Lukachukai Health Station. It was just a little after seven when he left the village of Hashké to drive south to where Navajo Route 3 heads west past the towns of Ganado and Round Top before turning back north up through Chinle and Many Farms, across Chinle Wash and to the Round Rock Chapter House where he now turns back down toward Lukachukai.

"Loo-ka-chewk-eye, Loo-ka-chewk-eye." Dr. Push Foster is repeating the word aloud to himself as he drives. He loves the sound of the Navajo language—when it's pronounced properly, anyway. He's determined to embarrass himself as little as possible and so whenever he finds a spare minute he practices the terms he expects might prove useful from the *Navajo Dictionary of Diagnostic Terminology* and the *Conversational Navajo Dictionary* that the Health Service provided him along with the Oath of Allegiance and a government-issue stethoscope:

"*Where does it hurt?*" he says . . . *"Háadish neezgai?*

"Take this medicine . . . díí azee'niyá . . . díí azee'niyá."

The words look impossible on the page, to be sure, and Push has never had any particular aptitude for languages. But this Navajo . . . why, it might as well be Sanskrit. And just seeing the words written on a page is no help at all . . . unless he can hear the words spoken, he can't even begin to imagine how they're supposed to sound, let alone how to say them himself. Even back in his room, when he can turn to the front of the book and pore over the guide to pronunciation, when he can read that

> The slashed *l*, or *ł* as in *hataałii*—"medicine man" or "singer"—is an unvoiced *l*. The sound is like "th" except that the tip of the tongue is placed not on the teeth but rather on the upper palate. Air is expelled between the sides of the tongue and the palate, and no voicing comes from the throat. An accent mark over a letter indicates a high tone and the absence of the mark a low tone . . . the two together indicate a higher tone dropping to a lower one. Double letters indicate a drawing out of the tone. . . .

But the Navajo staff at Hashké Indian Hospital are friendly and patient and seem genuinely eager to help: *"And hello to you, too, Dr. Foster—except it's not* Yah-ta-hey *. . . that's how some of the white people say it. We Navajo people say:* Yá'át'ééh."

Push is barely a month into his two-year stint as a commissioned officer in the United States Public Health Service, and this is to be the first in what will be his regular rotation as medical attendant at one of what can only be properly called the far outposts of medical care on the Navajo Reservation. The Lukachukai station is one of a dozen or so outposts scattered across the reservation that are staffed seven days a week by one or two Navajo Public Health workers—sometimes a registered nurse, more often a practical nurse or a nurse's aide—and where a graduate physician or a licensed physician's assistant shows up to examine patients on one or sometimes two days each week on a rotating basis. That's the plan, anyway. In truth, only at the best of times has there been a real doc at Lukachukai two days a week, and lately the Public Health Service has been even more shorthanded than usual.

The Health Station in Lukachukai isn't difficult to find. Push hadn't imagined it would be. Public Health facilities have a certain look to them—which is to say they look strikingly like Public Health facilities.

A young Navajo woman in a white lab coat is sitting at the reception desk sorting through a stack of forms when Push walks in. It is half-past nine.

''I'm Dr. Foster,'' he says. ''From the Hashké IHS. I'm supposed to check in with a Mrs. Hoskie, I believe it is, and see any patients that might present themselves. I'm afraid I'm a little late, but I didn't judge the drive quite as accurately as I'd meant to.''

''They been waitin' for you to get here,'' the young woman says. ''Gettin' pretty anxious, too.'' And she leads Push back down a short hallway to a door marked Patient Ward. She stands on her tiptoes to peer through the glass window in the heavy wooden door and gestures with her chin to where a group of Indian people are huddled around one of the three beds—the other two beds in the room are made up but empty. ''That's Mrs. Hoskie there, the short lady wearin' the white coat like this one I got on.'' And with that, she turns and leaves Push Foster standing alone in the quiet hallway.

As he enters the room, the short, heavy-bodied, middle-aged woman in the lab coat leaves the bedside and steps forward to meet Push. ''Are you the doctor that was comin' up here today?'' she asks. And when he replies that he is and introduces himself, the woman looks relieved.

''I'm Betty Hoskie, Dr. Foster. I'm the Public Health Nurse for this station. That lady doctor from over there at Hopi who came here last week said that a new doctor would be comin' today . . . I was sure enough hopin' you'd get here soon,'' she says.

''Yes, Dr. Blair from Keams Canyon . . . I take it she and I will be alternating visits here for a while—until the Health Service can fill some vacant slots, anyway. Sorry I'm late, what's on the schedule?''

Betty Hoskie turns toward the half-dozen Navajo people standing beside the hospital bed. ''This family brought their girl in early this mornin' with terrible breathin' trouble. The mother there says that Birdy Tooclanny told them they should bring her.''

"Birdy Tooclanny?"

"Yeah, she's a hand-trembler from up there around where they stay, at Tídáachiid."

"A hand-trembler?" And thus Push is plunged directly into the culture shock he had anticipated might come along sooner or later—it's just that he hadn't anticipated it coming along quite so soon. "You're saying that this patient was referred here by a hand-trembler?"

"Yeah. So I guess it must be somethin' pretty bad that's wrong with her. Otherwise they would have had a traditional sing."

Push Foster approaches the bed and sees that the young Indian woman lying there is pale and listless. Her eyes are glassy—rimmed angry red and half closed with swelling—her lips are cracked and dry from the fever that rages within her pitifully frail-looking body. And he can hear that she is nearing total respiratory arrest. Her breathing comes in short and shallow-jerking gasps, her hair is matted wet from sweat and yet her skin is sallow and dry. A large green tank of oxygen stands beside the bed and a coil of thin plastic tube stretches from the tank's regulator to the pillow and then up to a two-pronged cannula that passes beneath the girl's nostrils.

"How long has she been like this?"

"The family was waitin' out front when I got here this morning. The girl was at least able to walk in when we opened at seven, but she's gotten worse. . . ."

Push takes the girl's wrist and finds only a flutter of a pulse. He touches his stethoscope to her chest—the gurgling sounds tell him that her lungs are filled, that they are sodden, almost, and her heartbeat is weak and erratic. This is serious—*very* serious.

"Mrs. Hoskie, can you crank the head of the bed up—this girl is not just congested, she's literally drowning in her own fluids." His heart is racing but he struggles to keep his voice steady—there are other people in the room, the girl's family members, presumably, and apparently they are not inclined to leave. "I'll need suction. . . . Is there a respirator here somewhere . . . a ventilator? We've got to help her breathe. . . ."

Without answering, Betty Hoskie motions toward the next bed and then turns and hurries from the room. Push hopes she has gone to fetch a ventilator and is not simply deserting him. He sees a portable suction machine standing beside the bed she's indicated. He flips the toggle switch on the side of the unit and is relieved to hear the small electric motor purr to life. Sliding the thin nasogastric tube down the girl's throat, Push can hear the bubbling sound of mucus being sucked into the vacuum jar. And just as he finishes suctioning the girl's throat, Betty Hoskie comes hurrying back into the room rolling an older-model Byrd Positive Pressure Respirator before her.

"Oh, thank god," Push says. "I was afraid you'd . . ."

"I didn't know what size trach tube you'd be needin', doctor," Hoskie says, and she offers him three options.

With the airway taped in place and connected firmly to the respirator unit, the young woman's chest begins to rise and fall along with the steady mechanical motion of the cracked black rubber accordion bellows. A low-pitched whistling sound comes from her chest, and the too-loud noise of the machine is cold and impersonal. Push looks up to see the Navajo people, who have stepped back away from the bed as he works, staring at the girl with eyes that are wide and frightened-looking.

"How long has she been sick?" Push says, to no one in particular. When no one answers, he looks to Betty Hoskie.

"They say she started feelin' bad a couple of days ago," Hoskie says, and she leads Push away from the bed and over to the window. The family moves back in closer to the sickbed—once again they surround the girl and stand silently watching her.

Hoskie speaks in a low voice now: "The girl's name is Yvonne Tsosie. Her mother says that she started off by complaining of general achy feelings with a headache and a bad cough and that they figured she had a bad cold or else a case of the flu and were giving her aspirin and cough medicine that they got from the grocery store. But then when she went downhill so fast and started having real trouble getting her breath, they got very worried and so arranged for the hand-trembler to try to see what was wrong and maybe tell them what they should do. I guess she was pretty far past any kind of traditional help by then, though, and so they brought her over here early this morning just as soon as they could arrange for somebody to carry them over in their pickup truck. Evidently that's about all they can tell us about it. . . .''

''Well, we'll need to get some blood work done . . . and some chest views. There *is* an X-ray unit here, I hope?''

''I drew some blood before you got here, thinkin' you might want to get some routine lab work, but I was waiting to see what exactly you'd want me to order. And I did go on ahead and get a chest X ray, too. I should tell you, though, our machine isn't the most modern, but I figured with all that gurglin' in that poor girl's chest . . . and she's a whole lot worse now.''

''That's good that you did . . . where could I see that X ray?''

''It's up on the light box in the workroom next door—I'm not sure how good the image is, though, it's mostly just all white and cloudy-lookin'.''

''I'll take a look. And while I do, how about we get another lateral view—so that I can compare the two . . . see what kind of progression is going on.''

While Push goes next door to study the original image, Betty Hoskie sees to it that another X ray is taken. When he returns to the ward, she tells him that the film is being processed and should be available for him to see in ten or fifteen minutes.

''Good. Now then, what sort of IV fluids do you keep on hand? Have you got . . .'' At that moment Push is distracted to see that all of the Navajo family members who have earlier surrounded the girl's bed are now walking past him and Hoskie and filing out of the room. They do not look at Push or at Betty Hoskie and neither do they say anything. Indeed, the only sound they make—and it is the first sound he has heard from these people—is that coming from the two older women, both of whom are moaning softly. The sound is a mournful keening that causes a chill to pass down Push's back.

''What's this?'' Push is confused at first. ''Where are they going?''

''Uh-oh.'' Betty Hoskie's eyes widen and she starts toward the girl on the bed. But even before he can join her at the bedside, Push Foster knows what it is that has caused the family to leave the room. He knows that, even though the young woman's chest is still rising and falling regularly—and that the ventilator is forcing air into and out of her lungs—Yvonne Tsosie is dead.

From force of habit he looks at his watch to note the exact time of death—it is not quite ten-thirty.

Push Foster has been in the Lukachukai Health Station for slightly more than forty-five minutes.

WEPO WASH

And at the same time, some seventy-five miles to the southwest of the village of Lukachukai, a white man and a white woman who have been camped here for several days are digging for artifacts at a remote site on the rough, dry bank of Wepo Wash, near the far southern edge of Black Mesa, not far from the place where the fingers that form First and Second Hopi Mesas might be said to be joined in a web.

From the moment they first arrived and set up their camp, the pair have believed themselves to be completely alone and their presence utterly unnoticed, so remote is this place. Yet for much of the time that they've been here, something has been watching in silence as these two have gone about their work. From the scant shade cast by a scrubby juniper tree growing out of the dry, rocky soil three-quarters of the way up the side of a low mesa not three hundred yards from the diggers' campsite, black eyes have watched with keen interest the whole of the scene spread out below. And it is this that the black eyes have witnessed:

Each day the white woman wears starched khaki trousers and long-sleeved khaki shirts. Invariably she keeps a brightly colored scarf tied loosely about her neck and she wears lightweight cotton garden gloves whenever she is at work—gloves of the sort that have raised black dots on the palm sides. A wide-brimmed pale yellow straw hat with a black ribbon band shades her face, and on her feet she wears low-cut leather work boots—expensive waterproof boots with heavy lug soles. On those not-infrequent occasions when the woman removes her hat—to wipe perspiration from her brow, or to use it to fan herself against the heat from the broiling sun—the eyes that are watching can see plainly that her hair is yellow-blond and that it has been cut straight across her forehead and evenly around the back of her neck just below the level of her ears. Can see that, except for the startlingly bright red smear on her mouth, this woman's complexion is as pale and as colorless as any might be. Can see, too, when she removes the cotton gloves, that she wears silver and turquoise rings and that there is bright red lacquer on the tips of her fingers. And there are silver disks dangling from her ears—disks that shine and glint in the glaring, white-hot sunlight.

The woman's companion, on the other hand—and it appears that he is older than she, though not as much older as she would have other people believe—dresses in loose-fitting hiking shorts and T-shirts decorated with pictures and writing. Sometimes he wears a cap . . . a baseball-style cap that is colored maroon and yellow-billed, with a stitched-on emblem of the stupidly grinning, long-toothed, cartoon Indian from Cleveland with its mawkish feather sticking up from its head. And when the man wears no hat, and often he does not, he ties a red bandanna across his forehead. His close-cropped hair is sun-bleached white on the tips and melds easily into the similarly close-cropped gray of his beard. On his feet he wears not sensibly sturdy hiking boots like his companion's, but rather worn-looking brown suede sandals—open-toed. He wears no socks. The man's complexion—while not nearly so fair as that of the woman—is weathered-looking, sunburned-peeling and freckled . . . his lips are cracked and chapped.

It may be said that these white people are not here, precisely, as grave robbers—certainly the woman does not consider herself to be a grave robber. In fact, she is a university-trained field archeologist whose excavation work is carried out with the required permissions of the appropriate agencies—the Department of the Interior, the Bureau of Indian Affairs, and the Hopi Cultural Preservation Office—and with the financial support of a privately endowed research foundation. On the other hand, the woman's companion—and he is just that: her *companion*—would rob a grave in a heartbeat if he thought it might be to his advantage. This is a fact . . . a fact the woman will not likely admit to herself, much less to others, although she very likely knows it to be true.

From the place where it watches, black eyes can see that the white couple's campsite, and it is neatly laid out, is made up of two tents—one for sleeping and the other, presumably, for work and for storage—and a lean-to nylon shade arbor beneath which there is a low table where the two sit to eat their meals and to read and to make their notes and to clean and examine the potsherds and other items they excavate from the wash. Beside the working tent is parked an early-model four-wheel-drive utility vehicle—the two-door, boxy model of Land Cruiser with its wide, knobby tires and oversized roof rack and heavy iron bumpers and roll bar. The vehicle is somewhat beat-up—weathered and scratched—and what dark green paint still manages to show itself through the hard, caked-on mud and dust is badly sun-faded. The doors to the rear compartment have been removed, and a single orange insulated water barrel and two large blue ice chests occupy the cargo space. A battery-powered radio/tape player—a boom box, really—sits on the table beneath the shade arbor alongside a green two-burner Coleman gas stove and a gas lantern. Usually there is music coming from the boom box—an odd mixture of country-and-western tunes and jazz, mostly. The music, no matter which type is playing, seems remarkably out of balance here in this almost deathly silent place.

The two rise early each morning. At first light he sits smoking cigarettes as he waits for the water to boil in a white-speckled blue enamel pot on the Coleman stove. Then together they eat fruit and bread with jam while they talk over steaming cups of instant coffee. They are at their separate places digging through the soil with small trowels even before the sun is fully risen. And then, as surely as if there has been some signal, sometime around midmorning the two will stop whatever it is they're doing at the time to sit on folding chairs across from one another at the shaded table and write and sketch in notebooks. They will talk and gesture excitedly sometimes, and nearly always they will peel and eat oranges as they write . . . he will chain-smoke cigarettes and drink beer from aluminum cans that he retrieves from one of the ice chests in the Land Cruiser. She will dampen a white handkerchief in the icy-cold water at the bottom of the chest and wipe her face and neck. And she will rub cooling slivers of ice on her lips and on her wrists—on that place on the inside of each wrist where the veins show blue through translucent white skin. And she will sip cold, clear mineral water from a small plastic bottle.

And after a time, the two will go back to their tasks of digging and sifting. She will stop for short periods now and then to rest in the shade and to drink and to write and sketch—her record keeping is precise and detailed. And occasionally she will fetch a camera from the work tent and take photographs of the site, often calling for her companion to come and stand or sit in the frame so that there might be a ready reference as to scale. One of her cameras is a typical Nikon 35mm model with black-and-white film, the other a Polaroid instant camera. As quickly as they are dry, the Polaroid color prints are attached to corresponding pages of description and measurement in the field notebooks, later to be joined by—or sometimes replaced with—the processed 35mm black-and-white images.

When the sun climbs high overhead, the pair will stop their work completely. And although it will likely be well past the noon hour, they will sit together in the shade and talk quietly as they eat a lunch of fruit and cheese and share a bottle of not-inexpensive white wine before retiring to the darkness of their sleeping tent in an attempt to escape the stark dry heat of the afternoon sun. There to doze on their cots or perhaps to read—for sure there will be music playing.

Later in the afternoon, once they have rested, they will again undertake their tasks—now less-arduous work: cleaning, recording, and photographing their finds, and perhaps sharpening their trowels. Invariably she will check her field notebook and her sketches, and inevitably she will revise and redraw them.

Then, when the sun sinks below Second Mesa to the west and the air cools ever so slightly, it is nearly always the man who prepares the evening meal. The woman will sit alone, reading, and then she will join her companion at the table and together they will drink wine—certainly they will listen to music. And at dinner they will engage in animated conversation—at times they will argue, at other times they will laugh. Later, by the light from the Coleman lantern, the woman will read aloud to the man as he sits smoking and drinking whiskey now. She will read pages from her notes or passages from one of the several books she carries and to which she seems constantly to refer—ethnology and anthropology texts, most frequently. And then, after a time, she will get up from her place at the worktable and retire to the sleeping tent. And before long he will follow, and the lantern will go dark and the music will stop. And then the only sounds at that place will be the anxious yip-yipping song of coyotes far off to the north and the low moan of the wind in the scrub vegetation and the soft flutter of nightwings.

And so it is that for several days, at this remote place on the dry banks of Wepo Wash, each day has proceeded in much the same routine: Two white people—an archeologist and her male companion—believing themselves to be alone, and for much of the time black eyes have watched their every movement from partway up the side of the nearby low mesa.

Listen! This is a dream . . . a dream that a man is having at this very moment:

It is a dream like none this man can recall ever having had before. It's a dream in which he finds himself alone in a pickup truck . . . traveling on an unfamiliar road. It's nighttime and it's raining. And then all of a sudden—in that curiously abrupt way in which the focus of dreams can shift—it is no longer raining . . . the man is no longer driving . . . he's no longer even in a vehicle. Rather he is standing all alone in darkness near the edge of a high stone ledge, and the next moment there is a tall young woman standing before him. He doesn't recognize this woman. She is dressed in a torn and badly stained garment fashioned from what appear to be animal skins, and on her feet there are scuffed-worn moccasins. He cannot recall ever before having seen this young woman . . . her hair is a dull black and it is long and scraggly—dirty and matted. He can see that she's been hurt somehow . . . very badly hurt. At first he sees only a trickle of dark blood running down the woman's cheek. But then, as he leans in to look more closely, he can see plainly that there is a lot of blood, and that this blood is coming from an awful, gaping wound that begins at the point of the young woman's jaw, runs jagged up across her temple, then crosses above her left ear to disappear into her hairline . . . he can see, too, that blood is now running—dripping, really, from the young woman's chin—down and onto the front of her tattered dress. And from the ashen paleness of the young woman's face—and it is ghostly-white by now—he is certain that this wound is deadly serious. And while dreams do not, as a rule, seem remarkable to a dreamer as the dream is happening, *there is much about this dream that does seem remarkable to the man: There is just a whole lot of blood—way too much blood. And this pale woman who is standing there before him is ghostlike . . . she is standing there and she is moving, yet it is as though she is dead—her eyes are black and sunken and there is, overall, a look of absolute and unknowable fear about her. And her face is not just gashed, it is battered—her features are broken and bruised and she appears to be in great torment as she desperately tries to say something to the dreamer. But he can't make out what it is that the woman is trying to tell him, and he can't concentrate on listening because suddenly there are people standing all around the woman—standing beside her and behind her—they are women and children mostly, these people . . . dozens of women and children and every one of them is terribly hurt, with horrible deep cuts and awful bleeding wounds . . . and all together they are making a dreadful noise. The children are crying and making heart-wrenching sounds, really . . . sounds as mournful and as sad as the dreaming man thinks he has ever heard. And the women, they are uttering a low wailing now, a weeping and crying so sorrowful and so forlorn . . . so terrible that, in the dream, the dreamer is unable to make out what the disheveled woman who had first appeared to him is trying so desperately to say because he is so wholly distracted by the terrible sounds the mutilated women and children are making.*

And then, it is at this place that the man awakes from his dream.

HASHKÉ

"Jesus!"

With a loud gasp, Push Foster sits bolt upright in the narrow single bed. His heart is pounding in his chest and sweat drenches the sheets despite the refrigerated air pumping out from the rust-pocked vents on the small, clattering air-conditioning unit mounted in the window of the second-story room in the bachelor-quarters wing of the Indian Health Services Hospital in Hashké, Navajo Nation, Arizona. The worn-thin bedsheets smell of strong laundry soap and undiluted bleach and the cold air of still-stronger disinfectant. The air in the room is wet and heavy—and at the same time, it is stale—suffocating somehow.

Swinging his legs over the side of the bed and onto the worn brown-carpeted floor, Push fumbles for the tiny button on his wristwatch—the button that, when depressed, should light the tinier-still bulb that is supposed, in turn, to illuminate the boxy digital numbers displayed on the black plastic face of the timepiece so that the wearer might be able to see, even in the dark, what time it is. But even if this procedure had worked—and it hadn't, and he supposed he'd probably pushed the wrong button and instead of light he'd started that frenetic blur of numbers that indicates, presumably, that the instrument is in its stopwatch mode, that mode that he can never really imagine anyone, even the most obsessive marathon runner, actually using anyway—even if the tiny, dim light *had* come on he likely wouldn't have been able to read the numbers.

This room is very small. And so Push stands and, without having to take so much as a step, reaches his hand into the bathroom, finds and then flips the light switch.

It is 4:45 A.M.

Standing over the sink now, Push splashes water onto his face, cups his hands beneath the tap, and sucks a mouthful of the lukewarm liquid. He swishes it around and spits it back into the chipped porcelain bowl. Nasty, he thinks . . . the water tastes metallic and rusty, like old plumbing pipes.

He walks around the bed and stands beside the north-facing window. Reaching up, he hooks a finger into the blinds and pulls open a three-inch gap. Looking out into the predawn light, Push at first sees no sign of life—no people moving about at this hour and no cars traveling the blacktop road that runs past the deserted parking lot beneath the window. But just now Push does make out something moving in the trash-strewn weeds beside the road. A large white cat is stepping carefully—daintily, almost—as it makes its way across the asphalt and on toward a dark hole that is the opening to a culvert passing beneath the raised berm of the bar ditch. The cat has something dangling from its mouth . . . a mouse, probably? Or a lizard? Push can see only that there is something in its mouth in that moment before the animal disappears into the blackness of the culvert.

And now Push has had this dream—and it's a bad dream—it's a terrible dream, is what it is, and Push hates it that he's been dreaming. *Get your mind on something else,* he thinks.

And so he reminds himself that this is going to be a grand adventure. Two years in Indian country are sure to be more satisfying than time spent on some military base somewhere. There's no draft anymore and so he isn't *required* to serve, but it had seemed like the right thing to do—at the time, anyway—to pay back a little for the government handouts he'd received while in medical school. The volunteer work in the free clinic in Atlanta was as much public service as most people in his position would feel obliged to do, but Push had felt like taking some time out before settling into the rut he knew was ahead of him. Spending two years on a reservation—two years of near total immersion in Indian culture—was not something he'd likely do once he'd established himself in private practice somewhere. If he was ever to do this, now was the time.

Push is remembering how as a kid he used to make summertime trips with his mother and his grandmother, and how sometimes his aunt Boolah and her two boys would come along. He's remembering how they would drive in his grandmother's big Buick from Oklahoma out across the Panhandle of Texas—he always loved the idea that people referred to parts of Texas and Oklahoma as the Panhandle. And even though he had never once visited that part of Oklahoma, he'd often stared at it on maps and could readily see how that narrow strip of land that jutted out toward the west resembled nothing so much as the handle of a pan. But it was harder to try and imagine how Texans had the nerve to call a panhandle that part of their state that looked more like a chimney to him. He's recalling how they'd pass through the flatlands of Shamrock and McLean ("The Up-Lift Town," or so the billboard on the outskirts of McLean said, on account of the brassiere factory of which that town's residents were apparently quite proud) and then on to the sprawling city of Amarillo and then tiny Wildorado with its eye-watering stench of cattle feedlots—"Smells like money," his grandmother would invariably announce—and on into New Mexico. And how his grandmother always rolled down her window the moment they crossed the state line and insisted that everyone in the car agree with her as to how different the New Mexico air smelled—how much *better*. And although Push could never actually distinguish even a subtle difference, he always did agree. They were going on vacation, his mother said—to the cool of the pine-covered mountains, to escape the sweltering summer heat of home. But to Push's mind, they were really going to see Indians. He smiles now at the memory. Hell, there were way more Indians in Oklahoma than there were in New Mexico. But in Oklahoma, Indians were common—just like everybody else. They dressed like farmers and cowboys . . . they *were* farmers and cowboys. And gas-station attendants and schoolteachers. To young Push's eye the Indians the tourists saw in New Mexico dressed up like Hollywood Indians in feathers and bright-colored blankets and they played drums and danced on the green lawns of the tourist courts. Danced, that is, when they weren't sitting around on the Santa Fe sidewalks in front of the Governor's Palace selling jewelry. And they talked funny, Push remembers thinking—talked among themselves in grunting and halting-sounding languages. In Oklahoma, the Indians always spoke English. In Oklahoma, schoolchildren were taught that the state's Indians belonged to the Five Civilized Tribes. As a boy in Oklahoma, Push had learned to recite with his classmates in singsong fashion the names of those five tribes—*Choctaw, Chickasaw, Cherokee, Creek, and Seminole*—even before he'd fully committed to memory the Pledge of Allegiance to the flag. He was proud that *Choctaw* came first, and he remembers being puzzled that the last one in the litany—*Seminole*—broke the chain of alliteration by starting with an *S*.

Now a shiver passes over him, and even though he is cool, standing as he is in front of the clattering air-conditioning vents, Push can feel that sweat has begun to trickle down the hollow of his back. He turns from the window and walks around the bed and into the bathroom—into the cramped shower stall. He turns the cold tap on full force and lets the lukewarm, metallic-tasting water trickle over his head.

It is 5:07.

Push Foster is a mixedblood, a "breed" Choctaw on his mother's side. It was a very white man who left him with these blue eyes and the fair skin that sometimes burns and freckles in the sun. The man who fathered Push had been little more than a rumor in his son's mind—a shadowy legend about whom he'd never asked and his mother had but rarely spoken. He was fully grown and his grandmother's long black hair gone all white and her once-smooth brown skin turned leatherlike when she had finally, one rainy afternoon not long before she died, told him stories of his father's white-boy prettiness and of his eye for dark-skinned girls—told about the man's taste for cheap whiskey and how it was that on a hot summer night in a drunken rage he'd broken her daughter's nose and kicked the girl whimpering from corner to corner of the large kitchen room in the big old log house that stood on Adella Foster's allotted homestead in south-central Oklahoma—the house and buildings and the 110 acres of rich river bottomland she called Choctaw Place—and how she'd taken the heavy antique German 10-gauge shotgun from its place beside her bed and would surely have shot and killed on the spot this crazy drunken man who dared to hurt her child had not the sobbing young woman begged her not to do so. Told how that pretty white man had taken but a single look at the tiny brown woman there where she stood in the kitchen doorway, her hip cocked forward as she strained to aim the heavy long black shotgun full into his face—how he had understood completely in that brief moment that this small woman meant surely to kill him, and so had turned to run headlong into the black Oklahoma night, never to be seen or heard from again.

''Oh, I might not have *killed* him,'' she said. ''He might even have gotten better, I suppose.'' His grandmother smiled at the memory now, after all the years. ''But he would never have gotten well.''

And then, seven months later, when the pink-skinned baby boy had arrived loud-crying and wet into the world, Patsy Foster—although herself of mixed blood, a fiercely proud woman—in a moment of what must have been unbridled cultural pride aimed to fly in the face of any who might dare to focus on her bastard baby's fair skin and blue eyes, named her son Pushmataha, after a famous Choctaw headman she'd read about in her mother's books. Or perhaps, Push sometimes thought, it was really only a joke, her naming him that. Like most Choctaw women—indeed, like most *Indian* women—his mother had loved a good joke. Still, growing up with a name like Pushmataha—even in Oklahoma, in the Choctaw Nation, where names are oftentimes astonishingly *un*common—was not an easy thing for a boy. And only later in his life did it occur to Push to appreciate the fact that that good woman had not instead been moved to name him after one of old Pushmataha's fellow chiefs: Moshulatubbee maybe, or worse yet, Apukshunnubbee. Now *that* would have been a good joke.

And so Push Foster is mixedblood Choctaw. Indeed, were he asked—and he has on more than one occasion been asked—he could produce a card issued by the Department of the Interior, Bureau of Indian Affairs, certifying that he, the bearer, possesses one-quarter-degree Choctaw Indian blood. Having that card means that he can sell any artwork he produces and label it ''Indian made''—except, of course, he doesn't produce any artwork—and it means that he can go to the Indian hospitals for medical care, and it means that, as long as he brings his own container, he can stand in line to pick up the surplus commodities—foodstuffs like bright orange cheese with green and white spots and pears and peaches and fruit cocktail in thick, heavy syrup and instant mashed-potato flakes and canned peanut butter with an inch of yellow oil floating on top—surplus commodities that the Great White Father in Washington hands out to those of his children whom he officially recognizes as ''Indians''—no matter whether or not they are indigent.

The phone in this small room is one of those heavy, black types that Push didn't think were even made anymore. Probably they aren't—it's just that this phone's been here a very long time.

''Dr. Foster?'' The voice is that of a woman. Push is sitting on the edge of the bed, drying his hair with a towel. Like the bedsheets, the towel smells strongly of bleach. ''This is Leslie Blair . . . over at Hopi? Oh, darn it . . . I called too early, didn't I? I'm sorry.''

''Hey, Leslie Blair. Of course it's not too early, I've been up for several minutes, now. What, you think I'm some kind of lay-around lazybones or something?''

''Not at all,'' she says, and she laughs. She laughs easily, Push thinks. ''I'm afraid that my time out here has put me in the habit of early-to-bed, early-to-rise, and it wasn't until I'd already dialed your number that it dawned on me I shouldn't presume you've fallen into that mode yet—I don't mean to be rude, you know.''

''Not at all . . . To be honest, I didn't have the best of days yesterday, and I didn't sleep all that well last night . . . but I'm all showered and shaved and feeling refreshed and ready for whatever's in store for me today.''

''Yeah, I heard that your introduction to Lukachukai wasn't all that great. . . .''

''Oh, you heard about it, huh?''

''Well, it's a big reservation, Dr. Foster, but word travels fast out here—Moccasin Telegraph, we call it. . . .''

"Yeah, I know. Say, but I wish you'd call me Push so I won't have to call you Dr. Blair."

"Okay . . . Push. Listen, I'm sorry, but can you hold on just a second? I forgot I'd put water on to boil and now I've got a teapot screaming at me from in on the stove and it's about to drive me crazy."

"Sure . . ."

Pulling the frayed cord that raises the sun-yellowed blinds and cranking the window open, Push looks out across the parking lot while he waits for Leslie Blair to come back on the line. He recalls how she looked when he first met her in Gallup during the quarterly medical-staff meeting shortly after he took the post at Hashké.

She was, like himself, a "two-year man," although she was nearing the end of her second year. A strikingly attractive woman—he'd guessed her to be about thirty—she'd been dressed in a stonewashed chambray shirt and faded Levi's and he'd noticed that she was wearing fine beadwork earrings and handsome handmade silver bracelets on both her wrists. The jewelry had looked perfectly natural on her—never mind that she was wearing heavy, lug-soled hiking boots. He'd liked her right away and was looking forward to seeing her again.

Now Push can hear a whistling teapot over the sound of a radio playing from somewhere in her place. Across the way he sees again the white cat that had earlier disappeared into the drainage culvert—this time the animal is sunning itself lazily and washing its face in that fanciful way that cats do . . . stopping now to prick its ears cautiously when the occasional car passes or there is some other unexpected noise. Push hears Leslie Blair pick up the receiver.

"There," she says. "So, got any idea what killed your patient up there?"

"Hard to say, the history was pretty sketchy. . . ."

"You'll be seeing a lot of that here on the rez, I'm afraid."

"Yeah, well, it's not just a reservation thing—I saw a lot of that in inner-city Atlanta, too. Anyway, I'll need to see the blood-work results on the girl before I can begin to rule out things. Mrs. Hoskie told me she'd ask the lab to call the results directly to me here. For now, though, it goes down as a case of unexplained respiratory failure—Adult Respiratory Distress Syndrome.''

''Sudden Infant Death Syndrome for grown-ups, huh?''

''Yeah, which just means I don't know why the girl got so sick so fast.''

''Well, I guess maybe the folks at Lukachukai wanted to give you a special welcome. Remember to call me if there's anything I can help with—and stop in for coffee if you get a chance.''

''I will. Thanks for calling, Leslie.''

''Push?''

''Yeah?''

''Did I understand you to say you're from Atlanta? I thought you were from Oklahoma.''

''I'm not *from* Atlanta, I did my residency there—spent the past three years in Internal Medicine at Emory University's Crawford Long Hospital.''

''Well, bless your heart . . . I'm an Alabama girl, myself, you know—Tuscaloosa, to be precise.''

''I didn't know, but I suspected as much . . . that's quite a southern drawl you have. Small world, huh?''

Push says good-bye and hangs up the receiver. The morning sun is shining brightly now, and already the day threatens to be hot and dry. And probably windy, he thinks. He's been warned that it's nearly always windy in this country, and that dust swirls almost constantly here, especially in the spring. He glances out the window, toward the spot where the white cat had earlier been sunning itself. There is no sign of the animal.

Push switches on the small black-and-white television set on the bedside table. The early-morning news show from Albuquerque features segments on a manufacturer's recall of automobiles with faulty parking brakes, an undercover investigation of food-stamp fraud, and a five-day outlook calling for dry air and seasonably warm temperatures.

There is no mention of a mysterious outbreak of illness on the Navajo Reservation.

It is 6:12.

LITTLE SPRINGS

The Little Springs Trading Post is housed in a small cut-stone building set back several hundred yards off the paved surface of Highway 160 at a desolate place where that road passes closest to the farthest northwestern border of the Hopi Reservation.

The white trader and his Navajo wife have been at Little Springs for seventeen years. Before that, they were at his father's trading post at Teec Nos Pos, a hundred miles to the north and west. Both the white man and his Indian wife were born and have lived their entire lives on Navajoland.

On this particular morning Travis and Lizbeth Austin are seated at the yellow Formica-topped kitchen table where they sit every morning, listening to the radio and drinking coffee and talking.

More specifically, on this morning the trader and his wife are measuring and bagging roasted piñon nuts to sell to the tourists who stop at the Little Springs Trading Post on their way to Monument Valley from the west or to the Grand Canyon from the east.

And as they work, they are talking about the piñon harvest and how unusually plentiful the sweet nuts are this year. The Navajo families who gather the nuts to roast and to sell and trade at Little Springs have been coming much more frequently, it seems, than in any other year either can recall. The piñon gatherers maintain that the really good harvests come but once every seven years . . . but *this* year, this is a year for piñons like not even the old people can recall having seen. Only three times in this century, they say, have the sweet nuts been plentiful enough to harvest all year round.

And another thing, the trader tells his wife, there are fewer hawks than usual, he believes. And fewer owls and other raptors. Oh, the field mice and the pack rats are having themselves a fine feast . . . they're breeding and multiplying like rabbits and all the while growing fat and shiny. And so, it would seem, should be the owls and hawks and coyotes . . . and anything else that eats the fat rodents that eat the plentiful nuts.

There are just way too many pack rats around here this year, Austin is saying. The cinder-block storage shed that stands out back by the windmill is being taken over by the gluttonous little beasts. After lunch she can maybe help him for a while . . . together they can turn to and clean out the nests and the litter in the shed . . . spread some poison around the cracks and in the dark corners. He means to store the bulk of the piñon nuts in there till wintertime.

''Those pampered cats of yours can't keep up with their jobs, it seems to me, and we sure can't afford to have the rats and mice helping themselves to our stock of nuts just because there's plenty of them this season,'' he says. ''Let the wild critter population go out and gather its own supply.''

''We'll need to be kind of careful, though,'' Lizbeth says. She is remembering how, more than thirty years ago, when she was just a little girl, her grandfather who lived over by Red Mesa used to caution her and her brothers that if a mouse got on their clothing—just *touched* their clothing, he told them—they were supposed to get rid of the garments—to *burn* them, he said.

''Old-time Indian superstition,'' he tells her. ''That's just on account of your grandparents didn't have themselves a washing machine, I figure. . . . In any case, clothes are a little too expensive to be burning just because of a few mouse turds."

"Maybe so," Lizbeth says. "But you know, the old people used to know a lot of things that we've gone and completely forgot all about."

"Well, that may be, but all the same, don't you go burning any of *my* clothes on account of mice getting in the clothes hamper."

"And maybe if we'd stop feeding those cats that expensive feed-store cat food they'd develop a taste for mice like nature intended," he grumbles. "Why heck, Lizbeth, that blue dog of mine out there makes a better mouser than those two pampered house pets . . . and he doesn't do all that much except lay around sleeping and snapping at flies."

HASHKÉ

Nearly a week has passed since Push Foster's drive up to the health station at Lukachukai, and as he steps out the main entrance door and into the bright morning sun he's trying to recall if he's been outside the hospital even once during that time.

At this hour of the morning there are very few customers in the Short Mountain Cafe. Except for a convenience store that sells precooked fried chicken and microwave-heated burritos, the Short Mountain is Hashké's only eating place. In all the time he's been here, Push has previously eaten only in the hospital's employee cafeteria. On this morning, however, he feels the need for a change.

Push has been called to a meeting in Window Rock—the capital of the Navajo Nation—to discuss an alarming number of incidents of a strange illness that have been reported in the past week or so. Push has been called to this meeting by an old friend from his days in Oklahoma. Sonny Brokeshoulder is the head of the Health and Human Services Agency for the Navajo Nation, and although Push hasn't seen him in several years—since the two graduated from medical college—they have kept in touch and, in fact, Sonny Brokeshoulder is a good part of the reason that Push requested to be assigned to the big Navajo Reservation in the first place. And not surprisingly, Public Health Service officials were more than willing to accommodate such a request. Most of the graduate physicians who volunteered for IHS duty—and certainly those, like Push, who had completed residencies in specialty fields that were sorely needed in the service—preferred assignment to the more glamorous places: Santa Fe or Taos, New Mexico, say, or even to the more glamorous-*sounding* places . . . like Wounded Knee, South Dakota.

The Short Mountain Cafe's lone waitress is occupying herself by rearranging the sugar substitute on all the tables according to the color of the small envelopes: pink or blue. The ''real'' sugar is in white envelopes, the unrefined, ''natural'' sugar is packaged in brown. The waitress wears a black apron. There is a cigarette dangling from her lips. Here's a woman who is too-colored, Push thinks: Her lips are too-red, her cheeks too-pink, her eyelids too-green and sparkly—too-green and sparkly, anyway, for so early in the morning—her stiff-brushed hair is too jet black. Nothing about her colors seems real. She doesn't look up as Push stands surveying the near-empty room from beside the Please Wait to Be Seated sign.

Behind the cash register a puffy-eyed, dyed-black-haired woman in tight-fitting plum-colored jeans and an electric-blue western-cut shirt sits perched on a high stool, talking into a telephone while she scrutinizes her fingernails. When she's not actually talking into the receiver or yawning, she's busily chewing gum with a loud popping sound. The pile of souvenir newspaper print menus in front of the gum chewer suggests that she is the dining-room hostess. Push is standing almost directly in front of this woman, waiting for her to finish her conversation or in some other way to take notice of him. When, after a reasonable amount of time, she does neither, Push takes a menu from the stack and makes his way to a table near the coffee bar.

The lone waitress pauses in her sugar sorting when she notices Push seated at the table, studying the menu.

''I'm sorry, honey, can I help you?'' she says.

Push smiles. ''Excuse me . . . but I was wondering if I could maybe get a little breakfast?''

The woman stubs her cigarette out in an already-filled ashtray and takes a glass of water from a tray with several filled glasses. ''Have you been sittin' there long? My mind has just been wanderin' to beat the band this mornin'. . . . As you can see, we ain't exactly overrun with business yet.'' When she says the word *business,* it comes out ''*bid*ness.'' The waitress's plastic nametag reads *June*.

''The tour-bus crowd has apparently elected to dine in Gallup and the local Hashké coffee klatch don't generally start showin' up till around seven or so.'' She leans over and whispers conspiratorially as she places the water in front of Push: ''I'm surprised Yolanda over there could find time to interrupt her personal phone conversation long enough to notice you come in.'' She nods toward the hostess, who is still talking into the telephone and inspecting her nails. ''She generally only gets off her big fat butt for some of the hornier regulars who'll pinch it for her and then grin like idiots and try to look down her shirt—out-of-towners usually just get the phony smile and maybe shortchanged on their way out.''

Push smiles. ''Yes, I gathered she wasn't all that interested in me. How does she keep her position?''

''The way I figure it, her 'position' is most probably what the big boss likes best about Yo-Yo—if you know what I mean.'' And she winks at Push.

''Is this the smoking section?'' he asks.

''It's *all* smokin' in here, darlin'—we're an equal-opportunity establishment. Don't tell me you're one of them tree-huggin' environmentalist types who's bought into the liberal secondhand-smoke'll-give-you-lung-cancer routine?''

''Well, I don't smoke myself, but I try not to make a fuss about it.''

''Coffee?''

''Please.''

''My name's Georgia, and I'll be your waitress.''

''Well thanks, Georgia.'' Push smiles up at the woman. ''I'd sort of expected that June would be waiting on me, but what the heck. . . .''

Georgia looks puzzled and starts to say something. She thinks better of it, shrugs, and turns to get the coffee.

By the time Push has finished eating breakfast Georgia has discovered she's wearing the wrong nametag—that Push was, as she says, ''only funnin' '' her.

The hostess in the tight plum pants cradles the phone against her shoulder with her fast-moving, gum-chewing chin so that her long-nailed hands are free to take Push's money when he goes up to the register to pay. As he places the twenty-dollar bill into the woman's outstretched palm, Push sees that each of the fingernails that have so intrigued her is decorated with a tiny decal of a sign of the zodiac.

''Ever'thing okay?'' she asks and, without waiting for an answer, immediately returns to her conversation. When he's counted his change—Georgia *did* say Yo-Yo was inclined to short strangers, after all—Push becomes aware that the cafe is now nearly filled with customers. At several tables there are couples—tourists, in all likelihood, uncomfortable in their stiff new stone-washed blue jeans and brightly colored western shirts and too-new cowboy hats with cheap silver concho and bird-feather hatbands, none of which look even remotely natural. And expensive, yet still gaudy-looking, silver and turquoise jewelry—it is as though some jokester Navajo silversmith, in a kind of diabolical turnabout prank, has painstakingly fashioned fine stones and rare metals into counterfeit replications of Taiwanese dime-store costume jewelry.

At the table nearest to the cash register, two rosy-cheeked, blond-haired men in their mid-twenties poke suspiciously at their breakfast burritos and speak to each other in what Push takes to be German. At another table—this one meant to seat six—four people are seated, while two others sit, each alone, at nearby tables laid out for four—six diners where there might be fourteen. All are men and among themselves they talk familiarly back and forth—the men at their different tables—of weather and other small matters. These six are, no doubt, the local crowd about whom Georgia had spoken earlier.

At the machine by the front door Push stops to buy the morning edition of the *Albuquerque Journal*.

As he walks across the hospital grounds to where he's parked his truck, Push scans the morning paper. Not much new from the day before. He shakes his head over a feature article that explains that the governor of the state of New Mexico is traveling in Florida on a boosterism junket trying to talk the tourists in the Sunshine State into dropping everything except their wallets and coming to the Land of Enchantment.

Push reckons it will take him half an hour to drive to Window Rock—his meeting is at nine.

NAVAJO ROUTE 3

Chicken boxes . . . damn. Those are chicken boxes.

It's only after he's driven a couple of miles past what must have been a dozen of them that it dawns on Push what he's seeing are discarded Kentucky Fried Chicken takeout boxes.

Sure enough, it's the Colonel, with his natty goatee and his southern-gentleman string tie, grinning up at passersby from the trash-strewn bar ditch alongside Navajo Route 3. At the Kinlichee Chapter House the road forks and Push has taken the left fork east toward Cross Canyon where it joins the main road to Window Rock. The waxy red-and-white cardboard boxes are everywhere . . . they outnumber even those awful plastic grocery sacks that he remembers having seen hanging snagged on the bushes and barbed-wire fences that border that stretch of highway that runs between Gallup and Window Rock. Red and white and blue plastic sacks, and red-and-white cardboard boxes, and broken glass—the shattered green glass the remnants of broken wine bottles, mostly . . . scattered there like ancient potsherds strewn on an Anasazi trash heap. Push wonders if in a couple of hundred years Park Service officials will post warning signs and lecture tourists about how taking even very small pieces of broken glass as souvenirs from these sites is vandalism just as surely as is removing the rarely discovered entire and unbroken wine bottle—that archeologists and other scholars need to know exactly where, in relation to this ancient roadway, that particular twentieth-century wine bottle might have been thrown. Will the Kentucky Fried Chicken boxes hold up over the ages? Will those white Styrofoam cups from the Sonic Drive-Inn hold fast the traces of lipstick and brown coffee stains so that archeological investigators might one day marvel over them? And all those sacks from Albertson's and Basha's grocery stores—what will become of them?

For some time now he has passed walkers going, he imagines, home after a night begun in bordertown bars and finished in doorways and alleys or perhaps in the Gallup jail drunk tank. He thinks how he's always been struck by these walkers—their shoulders stooped, their eyes downcast on the littered right-of-way stretching before them—how they rarely if ever seem actively to seek rides, don't stick out their thumbs like Interstate hitchhikers. But if you should stop for any of them—and Push has, on occasion, stopped—they will likely as not climb into the vehicle beside you without a word and sit staring straight ahead until you reach your destination and let them out, or else they will silently nod toward some side road as you approach to indicate that this is where they want to be left off.

And Push passes Two Story Trading Post and the village of St. Michael's.

Thinking that this landscape reminds him, curiously, of Oklahoma, Push wonders at how it is so much greener than he had expected it to be around here. East of Window Rock, where the Pittsburgh Mines are located, coal-company officials boast of their ecologically correct efforts to cover up the ugly scars left after their enormous hydraulic shovels have churned and ripped and dug the ore from the earth, when really all they've ended up doing is making the land there resemble parts of Oklahoma or the Texas panhandle more than the rugged scrub-mesa it was before they came. They've transformed the area into foreign-looking hills of gently rolling machine-sown grasslands enclosed in tightly strung barbed wire stretched on green iron T-posts—shiny new barbed wire hung with the always-present frayed plastic grocery sacks snagged, flapping in the near-constant winds.

Slowing now, Push passes the Navajo Nation Fairgrounds and approaches an area of roadside businesses that marks the western edge of the town of Window Rock. He drives past the car washes and the fast-food outlets. At the stoplight in front of the FedMart grocery store, he can see the Navajo Nation Inn and the Tribal Museum and Crafts Center. He turns north for a couple of hundred yards and then into the main entrance to the Navajo Tribal Headquarters complex. Making his way past the ugly concrete administration buildings that resemble federal buildings everywhere, Push heads for the older and so more handsome red-stone structures—the hogan-shaped Council Chambers and the single-story offices of the president and vice president and the various other officials of the Navajo Nation.

At the circle drive in front of the Council Chambers, Push sees that there is parked a brightly painted but still decrepit-looking school bus that—from the look of the stovepipe sticking up through its roof and the bold-patterned curtains hanging over its windows—has been converted into an approximation of a house on wheels. Parked beside and behind the bus are two vintage Volkswagen Campers, and a beat-up Ford van. All four vehicles have been decorated with painted flowers and peace signs and slogans, and the bus sports two remarkably tall flagpoles—one mounted at the front and the other at the rear—with bright-colored tie-dyed banners that wave and flap in the stiff morning breeze. There are a dozen or so children perched on duffel bags and boxes tied haphazardly to a rust-pocked chrome rack mounted atop the bus—the children are waving small flags and chattering noisily. Most of the youngsters are pale blond or white-haired, most are barefoot, and not a few appear to have had bright orange and red and green Day-Glo streaks and stars and what look to be flowers painted on their cheeks and foreheads. From their perch atop the strange-looking bus, the children are watching with interest if not animation a band of oddly attired people who are enthusiastically beating handheld drums and clanging small brass cymbals as they chant and hum and dance gaily around and about the flagstone entryway leading into the Navajo Nation Council Chambers.

"*Jesus,* it's a whole little band of crystal huggers." Push says this out loud. If he didn't know better, he'd think this was Santa Fe. . . . Damned if it didn't feel like the seventies all over again.

Several Navajo people stand around, watching this spectacle, their faces void of expression. They seem bewildered to see the sandal-clad, wispy-bearded men with their long, pale hair twisted and matted into a white-boy approximation of dreadlocks, wearing wildly colored balloon-legged pants and wilder still tie-dyed tunics or chiffon shirts, slapping drums and blowing on flutelike instruments and squawking out what they presumably imagine to be Native American chants as they leap and twirl like awkward birds. And the women . . . barefoot women dressed in flowing, sheer print skirts and tiny pastel tank tops and long dangling beadwork earrings. Some of these women have shaved their heads, others have close-cropped hair dyed orange and purple, while still others wear their hair long—at least two have feathers and bright red ribbons woven into long, thin plaits. The women, too, are singing and chanting shrilly; some wear bells attached to their ankles. And even from a distance, Push can see that the eyes of these dancers, while heavy-lidded, are yet brightly glazed with pupils that are overly large and utterly vacant.

Whew . . . The lights may be on in there somewhere, he thinks. *But I doubt seriously if anybody's home.* Push is shaking his head in wonder at what all he's seeing.

TSÉGHÁHOODZÁNI

When he's managed at last to find a parking space in front of the Navajo Nation administration offices, Push walks into the pink stone building through the door marked Health and Human Services.

A dark-skinned, middle-aged Navajo woman dressed all in purple is sitting at what he takes to be the reception desk. A carved wooden plaque of the sort one might have made at booths at state fairs and flea markets is propped against a computer monitor and announces that this desk is that of the administrative assistant. Just now, the woman is gazing intently at a computer screen upon which appear bright neon-colored fish and cartoon-character sea horses swimming back and forth in the jerky, computer-pixel way that seems exaggeratedly unrealistic to Push.

"Good morning." The woman doesn't look up when she speaks, but her voice is warm and friendly. "How do you like my new screen saver? The manual that came in the box with it says that it's supposed to be real soothin' and that it will help to cut down on some of the stress in the workplace.''

''And good morning to you.'' Push smiles. ''Looks pretty fancy to me. I remember I saw one at the Federal Building in Atlanta one time that was supposed to make it seem as though you were driving in a car and that there were bugs hitting the screen—you know, like the screen was the car windshield and bees and grasshoppers and things like that were splattering into it.''

''*Yuck!* Squashed bugs don't sound all that soothin' to me,'' she says, turning in her swivel chair to smile up at Push. ''No wonder those government workers always sound so disgruntled whenever I talk to them on the telephone, it seems to me like that sort of screen saver could even wind up *causin'* stress instead of cuttin' down on it. I think I like these pretty colored fish better.''

''And I think you're probably right. My name is Push Foster, and I'm scheduled to have a meeting with Dr. Sonny Brokeshoulder someplace around here at nine o'clock, but I'm not sure just where I'm supposed to be. I was hoping maybe you could point me in the right direction.''

''Oh, thank goodness, I was afraid you might be one of them weird drum-beaters that was raisin' all that commotion out there in front when I came in.''

''Lord, no.'' Push grins. ''If you ask me, you all are just way too polite. Most people I know would've run those freaky folks off before they could even unpack their flutes and incense burners.''

''Yeah, I know . . . they're claiming that they're on a *vision quest,* but I think that whole notion of the vision quest was really just something that started out as a big joke . . . maybe a bunch of guys was hangin' around chewin' on peyote cactus one day and came up with the idea of sayin' if you go sit on top of a mountain and stare at the sun you can get in touch with the Great Spirit,'' she says, shrugging. ''You know, something to pull white people's legs. It just seems like Indian ways are getting more and more popular every day—especially with those *tsiiyog* out there . . . those hippies.''

Push is trying to remember the last time he heard someone use the word *hippie*.

''Sonny's office is in this building, all right, but whenever he has meetings they're usually in the Annex out there in the back.'' The woman stands and walks over to the window and points outside.

''Ever'body calls it the Annex . . . but I don't really know why. It's just that ugly pink house trailer sittin' over there kind of all by itself . . . see . . . that one over there that's the color of Pepto-Bismol?''

Push nods.

''You're a little bit early, though—I haven't noticed much action over there this morning. I'm pretty sure Sonny still hasn't come in yet, but he should be along any time now. We got hot coffee if you'd like to have some—it just finished perkin' a couple'a minutes ago.

''Did you come all the way up here from Atlanta?''

''No, I just came over from Hashké. . . .''

The woman is looking for something in a green four-drawer metal file cabinet.

''So, you're from Hashké, huh?'' she says, as she rummages through the contents of yet another drawer. ''It's funny that I don't remember seein' you around before.''

''No, well, I'm new to the area—that is, I'm the new Public Health staff doctor at the IHS Hospital over there.''

''Oh yeah, Sonny's been talkin' about you . . . I didn't know you were comin' over here today, though. You guys used to go to school together, huh?''

''Yes . . . some years ago. But we haven't seen one another in a while.''

''Aha!'' With a broad smile now, the woman holds up a rare not-yet-discarded plastic Basha's grocery sack containing a stack of bright red Hot & Cold Dixie cups. ''I just *knew* I remembered that these were around here somewhere. They're left over from one time last year when we had a busload of tourists who came from over in Japan, I think—or maybe it was China. I never *can* keep those two countries straight, for some reason.

''Hey, did you know that the Navajo word for Japanese and Chinese people is *nááts'ózí*?'' She says the word again, for emphasis, more slowly this time. ''*Nááts'ózí* . . . In English that would mean something like,

'Their eyes are skinny.' To tell you the truth, I always thought that was sort of a funny thing—to be calling somebody somethin' on account of the way their eyes look. Especially since so many Navajo people have skinny-lookin' eyes, too.''

The woman is unwrapping a fresh stack of cups.

''I'm a Navajo, by the way. Some people can't tell the difference—they figure all us Indians look alike. And a lot of people think that the Navajo language is hard to make any sense out of, you know, but it really isn't. As a matter of fact, I'm of the opinion that it's just a whole lot more logical than most languages, which just seem to make up words whenever the people figure that they need a new one. Like that word 'computer.' What is that word supposed to mean, for goodness' sake? In Navajo when we want to talk about one of those things we say *béésh nitséskees*. Do you know what that means, Dr. Foster, *béésh nitséskees*?''

''No, I don't believe I do.''

''Well, it means 'thinking metal'—and I'd say that's a pretty good description of what those contraptions do,'' and then she smiles at Push. ''At least that's what they do whenever they happen to be workin' right, that is.

''But anyway, those Chinese people were travelin' all around New Mexico and Arizona looking at Indians and they stopped off here to gawk at some Navajo Indians.''

Handing Push one of the waxed paper cups—the bright red cups with handles that fold out are emblazoned with green holly leaves and the words *Happy Holidays*—the woman gestures with her chin toward where a large aluminum coffeepot sits on a low table next to the copy machine.

''You know, I had completely forgotten that it was around Christmastime when those skinny-eye tourists were here. I guess we need to get us some new coffee cups for visitors that don't wish you Merry Christmas in the middle of the hot summer.'' She laughs. ''I can remember that those little guys were very polite—you know, smilin' at everything and bowin' even—but I was surprised that they didn't take much to coffee . . . didn't like it, I guess. Mostly they liked to drink tea or Pepsi-Colas instead.

''There's some sugar and imitation creamer in those two Tupperware bowls there by the pot.'' She makes a face when she says ''imitation creamer.''

She fills her own cup—a large black ceramic mug that bears the Great Seal of the Navajo Nation and the name *Priscilla Yazzie* in swirly gold letters.

''You like livin' over there in Hashké?'' she asks. She is spooning sugar into her coffee.

''Uh-huh . . . everyone's been very nice to me.''

''I guess it must be kinda different for you—livin' out here, and all. Didn't you come from one of those big cities? Alabama or something?''

''Atlanta,'' Push says. ''I came here from Atlanta, Georgia.''

''You probably miss all the big doin's that goes on in a city like that, huh?''

''You know, I can't honestly think of a single thing I miss about it.''

There is only one plastic spoon on the small table next to the copy machine—Push stirs creamer and sugar into his coffee and then wipes the plastic spoon on a brown paper towel that he takes from those stacked neatly beside the pot. The smell of the wet paper reminds him of the towel dispensers in the boys' rest room at his high school back in Oklahoma, and he wonders why whoever is in charge of stocking the coffee bar doesn't use the odorless white paper towels instead.

''What do you think is goin' on?'' Priscilla Yazzie asks. ''With all this weird stuff that's happening?''

''What do you mean?''

''You know . . . with these young people gettin' so terrible sick and all . . . To tell you the truth, I'm gettin' pretty worried about this business. It's not like we've exactly got what you'd call the best health-care system in the world around here, and it seems like it's not all that unusual for Indian people to get sick and even to die from things that white people in big cities don't particularly consider all that serious. But I figure whenever young, healthy kids start gettin' sick and dying, well . . .''

And just at that moment there comes a quiet but strong voice that speaks from behind Push almost into his ear:

''Well, would you look at what we have here.''

Startled, Push turns around to see that the voice belongs to his friend, Sonny Brokeshoulder, who is standing smiling at him from the doorway that leads back into the interior offices.

''This is the famous Dr. Pushmataha Foster that I've told you so much about, Priscilla.'' Sonny Brokeshoulder's shining black hair is parted straight down the center of his head and has been woven tightly into braids that hang down his chest, three-quarters of the way to his waist. The last four inches of each braid is wrapped in bright red ribbon. His friend has come quietly into the building through some back entrance, Push thinks, surely he could not have come through the front door without being seen.

Sonny Brokeshoulder was born to a very young Navajo girl in a dirt-floored hogan at a place called Coyote Canyon some thirty miles northeast of Gallup—a place, like much of the Navajo Reservation, where there is neither electricity nor running water.

If he'd ever known his mother's name, he'd long since forgotten it, and try as he might—and he did try, early on, at least—he could never recall the look of her face. The past-middle-aged Pentecostal missionary couple who took him away from the girl when he was only three years old and then away from the Navajo country altogether when he was five spoke but rarely of either, and then only during those times when the Reverend Ephram Brokeshoulder and his wife, Ida, were attempting, in ways that were unkind and ugly, to strike, as they put it, the fear of god into a very frightened and confused young boy. Sonny Brokeshoulder could recall with unsettling clarity that it was during those times that they would ball their blue-veined white hands into hard, bony fists to shake before his face—could recall how they would screw their own pale, bloodless faces into scary, angry masks, and lean close in so that the boy could not avoid the stinking smell of their foul, sour breaths, recall how it was that they would beat him down—not with those fists, but rather with their hissing, ugly voices. Voices that sometimes spoke in strange and incomprehensible sounds—speaking in tongues, they would later say—voices that other times told him over and over again that his blood was bad . . . that it was dirty . . . that his own mother was nothing but a wine-soaked whore.

''She was one of those Chee girls,'' they would say—as if that phrase could possibly mean anything at all to the young and frightened boy. And they would tell him, too, that his mother was one of those sinful, godless Chee girls, who were not Christians, but rather were heathen animals who drank devil's wine and liquor and spoke blasphemies and lay down with worthless drunken men to fornicate like reservation dogs. Tell the boy that he himself should get down on his knees—sometimes forcing him to his knees, in fact—that he should fall to his knees and thank God and them that they had been so kind and generous as to have saved him from that godforsaken hell where the Navajo live in their own filth and their vile ignorance. Saved him from that miserable dry place where they themselves had toiled and preached God's Word for seven long and thankless years before finally giving up and going back to Oklahoma, there to minister, they said, to good white Christian people who knew to bathe and to eat clean food and to pray and to speak English as God would have them do.

Sonny Brokeshoulder was in his last year of high school before he chanced upon the surname Chee in a book in the school library . . . until then he'd always assumed that Chee was an adjective—a descriptive term rather than a surname—that a Chee girl was something unclean and that, according to Reverend Brokeshoulder and his wife, his own mother had been one. The question of who Sonny's father might have been was never even considered.

And so it was that a Navajo boy came to be raised in southern Oklahoma—close up beside the Texas border—far from his own people and farther still from the ways of his people, raised up to be a white boy—a brown white boy, to be sure, but a white boy nonetheless. And all the while this Pentecostal preacher who had adopted him claimed that he himself was part Indian—"too much Indian," he'd always add, with venom in his voice—as the burden of his name, Brokeshoulder, implied. It was strange, or so it seemed to Sonny, that a man who publicly professed such love for all of mankind as did the Reverend Ephram Brokeshoulder could feel such animosity toward Indian people—such contempt. But as he grew older Sonny came to see the sad truth in at least one thing that this man had told him over and over again: that in the relatively redneck part of the United States of America where Sonny

Brokeshoulder grew up—in southern Oklahoma—one is generally far better off if he is white.

"If you're white," the vile old man would repeat ominously, "then you're right—if you're red, you'd be better off dead."

Growing up, Sonny Brokeshoulder attended church-run boarding schools, mostly. Always he attended church services. Then, as soon as he was able, Sonny left the Brokeshoulders' house and their church and their Holy Roller boarding schools and went off on his own to college. And though he thought at times to take the name Chee as his own, he never did.

Brokeshoulder may not be my Navajo name, he thought, *but it is a fine name just the same—an Indian name. And I won't deny it like that awful old man has done.*

Still, try as he might, Sonny Brokeshoulder could not recall his own mother's face—could not stir from his memory so much as a shadowy image of the face of that Chee girl. In the years he'd been back on the reservation, he often found himself looking directly into the faces of women whom he knew or guessed to be in their mid-to-late forties . . . looked into their faces even though the Navajo culture is one where to look directly at another is considered impolite, if not downright rude. He simply could not help but wonder about his mother. On those occasions when the women he came into contact with were named Chee—and they were by no means rare, the name is not an uncommon one among the Navajo—his curiosity was sometimes close to unbearable. Still, he never directly asked the women questions that he knew to be improper. Rather, what he always kept foremost in his mind was that his mother was Navajo. And because she was Navajo—because what your mother is, you are—Sonny Brokeshoulder knew that he was Navajo, too.

"You remember me telling you about this guy, don't you, Priscilla? This here's one of those *civilized* Indians from Oklahoma." Sonny Brokeshoulder stands grinning, his right hand extended toward Push. "But you ought not to hold that against him."

The two men shake hands warmly. They have been fast friends ever since their undergraduate days at the University of Oklahoma.

"You practicing to do the sneak-up, Sonny? You know, you could about cause a guy's heart to attack him, what with the way you just appeared out of nowhere like that—standing there grinning so big and looking so ugly."

"Hey, that's the Navajo way of doing things—coming into a place all quiet-like, so as not to disturb the air. We're not like all you civilized Indians from back east who make it a point always to be whooping and hollering to announce your whereabouts to everybody within earshot. . . . Man, it's good to see you, Push. I can't believe you've been within a couple of hours of here for something like a month now and we haven't gotten together."

"I tried to see you when I came through a week or so ago on my way back to Hashké from Gallup, but they said you were over in Flagstaff. . . ."

"Just like the old days, huh?—me calling on you when I have a problem or something I don't understand . . ."

"You sounded pretty worried on the phone. . . ."

"Well, I *am* a little bit worried. When I talked to you yesterday I told you I had a couple of strange cases around here—cases like the one you saw in Lukachukai last week. But now it looks as if it's more than just a couple. I've asked some other folks to come over this morning, too. I'm hoping that you big-time city docs can maybe get your heads together and put my mind at ease. . . ."

At her desk Priscilla Yazzie has been talking on the telephone and listening to the conversation in the room at the same time.

"Sonny, that was Dr. Blair," she says, hanging up the receiver. "She was callin' from the phone at the Council building to say I should tell you that her and Mr. Slowtalker and Wiley Bigboy are over there at the Annex. And they also called from Gallup to say Dr. Pierce had some kind of emergency come up but that he'd try to make it over here as soon as he could get loose."

"Okay, I guess we can go on over and get started . . . and you might as well bring that coffee with you, Push." Sonny's voice has taken on a more serious note. "This may take a while."

Sonny holds the door for Push. "You Choctaws work on Indian time schedules, too, Foster? Or is this just a Navajo thing?"

WEPO WASH

Sabine had started back to work at Site #3 at five-thirty on this still, bright morning . . . five-thirty and the temperature *already* in the mid-to-high eighties. The air is clear and dry, with no sign of clouds. Peter had agreed to resume work at Site #4 as soon as he'd finished having his coffee. Sabine felt that there might still be more samples to uncover, even though she'd trowel-excavated to twenty centimeters gravel deposits that appeared culturally sterile. The previous day's finds of sizable exposed and near-surface potsherds had been especially encouraging, and she wanted to take the morning, at least, to finish up at the mound before moving over to Site #4 to prod Peter along with the work on the pit house.

She's surprised—and at the same time delighted—at how secluded it is in this place. It's funny, she thinks, but her previous experience has been that the Navajo are extremely curious about archeology, and whenever she's been on digs in Navajo country she's come to expect that local people will show up even in the most remote places and stand around for hours at a time just watching. That doesn't seem to be the case here with the Hopi, however. And she wonders—is it indifference, or aloofness, or what? Surely *some*one's aware that they're here. Maybe the Hopi just have more sense than to spend the day out in the hot sun.

Last night at dinner Peter said that the weather today would likely be hotter even than it had been. When she asked him if he'd heard a weather report on the radio, he said he didn't need a radio to tell him it was hot. Peter's getting more and more grouchy. He thinks this dig is a bore. She's tried to tell him that they can't always make the great finds, but he's impatient.

She tries not to think about the growing sense of unease she feels with the way her companion has been acting lately. He seems restless and more and more frequently he gets angry with her over the silliest of things. What does she really know about him, anyway? Or is she just imagining things? . . .

She can hear plainly the tape that is playing on the table where Peter is working: The song is James McMurtry's "Too Long in the Wasteland."

Perhaps that's it, she thinks—Peter's just been too long in the wasteland. A trip to Santa Fe will be good for him—maybe brighten him up a little.

And now it is midmorning, and as she walks back to the campsite to refill her water bottle, Sabine stumbles and nearly trips over a greasewood root. And as she reaches out her hand to break her fall, something catches her eye: It is the exposed mouth of a clay jar—an *olla*—that protrudes from the side of the wash at just about the level of her knees. When she has regained her footing, Sabine bends down to examine the jar, which she sees now has been very nearly obscured by brush and so had escaped earlier detection. Although it is partly buried in the dry, caked clay of the wash, the jar appears to Sabine to be both entire and intact. Her eye is practiced, and she judges her find to be approximately twenty-five centimeters in overall length and eighteen centimeters around. And now she feels a shiver of excitement stirring in her as she sees that the jar is not broken, so far as she can tell. And peering into the dark interior of the vessel, she's especially happy to see that it is *not* filled with silt—which is to say the jar is, for the most part anyway, empty.

TSÉGHÁHOODZÁNI

The cloudless blue sky over Window Rock is painfully bright as the two men walk up the cracked concrete sidewalk that leads away from the pink stone tribal building and toward the two-lane asphalt drive.

Curving around past the parking lot situated beneath the great natural stone formation that lends this place its name, the asphalt runs out and the driveway becomes a dirt path that dead-ends at the pink trailer that Push had seen from the office window.

''Any idea what this might be, Push?'' As they approach the shabby-looking outbuilding Sonny's voice sounds worried. ''I mean, since it's looking more and more like the sickness I'm hearing about is the same as what you saw last week?''

''I can't say for sure.'' Push steps up onto the wooden deck of the Annex. ''I'd be inclined to think along the lines of pneumonia—except for the fact that it's so fast-moving.''

''Yeah, at first pneumonia seemed like a possibility to me—although I'm thinking now it's more likely we're looking at something like pneumonic plague. But I agree that whatever it is moves faster than anything I can remember having seen. I've got Priscilla trying to get hold of a good young veterinarian I know who's working at the Western Navajo Agency over in Tuba City.''

''A veterinarian? . . .''

''Yeah, that way we can be better prepared in the event it turns out what we're seeing is zoonosis . . . some disease transmitted by animals. If it is an outbreak of some strain of plaguelike bacillus, we'll need to institute a massive program of flea control.''

''The current thinking on infectious disease is that *containment* is the highest priority, Sonny. How widespread does this seem to be? Are the cases geographically localized?''

''I don't have all the details yet, Push, but the fatal case Ed Pierce had in Gallup on Friday came from up at Tídááchiid—where your girl who died at Lukachukai lived.''

''There you go . . . I suppose it could be coincidence, but it's not likely.''

''A couple of the cases are from the other side of the rez, though. . . . But like I said, I've called on you *real* docs to come help ease my mind.'' Sonny is smiling now. ''I can't afford to let my people around here start getting all nervous over this . . . nothing much worse than a bunch of worked-up Indians, you know.''

''I'd say your assistant back there seemed worked-up enough already.''

''Priscilla? Why, she figures worrying is the number one duty of an administrative assistant.'' Sonny is smiling more broadly. ''She's kind of talkative, too, isn't she? And when she isn't talking your leg off, she has this way of listening to everything that goes on around here and only hearing about a third of what's actually being said. And she generally ends up reaching some pretty far-fetched conclusions based on that third of the story that she's heard.''

''She seems nice.''

Sonny stops and looks at Push. ''*Nice?* That woman is priceless, Push—she's my right arm. You know, she's been with me since day one. The very first day I was hired on here Priscilla Yazzie came walking through my office door lecturing me on how she understood the way it usually works around here—how a new broom sweeps clean and all, and that even though she'd been the previous department head's assistant, she figured I'd probably be asking her to step aside to make way for my own person. She told me she needed this job in the worst way—said she was a single mother.'' Sonny smiles at the memory. ''As soon as I could get a word in edgewise, I told her I was *hoping* she'd stay on and help keep me out of hot water with the big chiefs. I had a hunch they'd be looking at me as an outsider and I figured she knew the way things really work around here.'' Sonny steps up onto the wooden porch of the Annex.

''And I was right, too,'' he says. ''I've never regretted it for a minute.''

To the left of the sprung aluminum door that is the entrance to the trailer, Push sees that someone has spray-painted the aluminum siding with the letters *FBI* in the fat, balloonlike characters of what he thinks of as urban-gang graffiti.

''I've been seeing this crap all over out here,'' he says, nodding toward the scribble. ''For some reason I think of this as being more a big-city thing.''

''Yeah, disgusting, isn't it? That *FBI* there? They tell me that stands for 'Full-Blooded Indian.' Like we really *need* people spray-painting their blood quantums on the walls. We're seeing this kind of stuff everywhere lately—it's like kids have no respect for anything anymore. I guess they think they've got to mark everything—like a pack of mangy reservation dogs that go around lifting their legs and peeing on anything that'll hold still long enough, you know? I'm just waiting for the morning I look up to see where they've managed to tag the big rock up there.'' He gestures toward the sacred sandstone formation. ''It won't be long now . . . just a matter of time, I figure.'' He shrugs as he holds the door and waits for his friend to enter.

WEPO WASH

Sabine Vogel has spent the late morning and early afternoon painstakingly excavating her find. The air has grown increasingly stifling, but so elated is she at her good fortune in having literally stumbled upon an entire and intact Anasazi utility jar that she hardly notices the heat. Once she has extracted the vessel from the wall of the wash, she's made careful sketches and photographed the exact site of discovery. She's pleased to know that her perseverance has paid off, for this is as excellent a specimen of an undecorated, utility-type storage vessel as she has ever seen. It is of the finest museum quality.

After a hurried lunch, Sabine meticulously inspects and cleans the jar of all traces of gross exterior particles by gentle brushing. And then, using her fingers and quick bursts of canned air, she cleans the interior of what she is able to identify—judging from the strong, foul odor of urine and the presence of piñon-nut shells mixed with both dried and fresh droppings—as rodent nesting materials.

It's obvious to Sabine Vogel that this ancient ceramic jar, positioned as it has been, on its side with its narrow open mouth exposed, has for some time been used as a nesting den for small rodents—field mice, most likely.

TSÉGHÁHOODZÁNI

The interior of the trailer is even smaller than it had appeared from the outside. Off-white walls of cheap particleboard panels are stapled directly to wall joists. Yellowed plastic strips do little to hide, and in fact call attention to, the flimsy construction where seams of the four-foot-wide panels are joined haphazardly. Ugly avocado-green shag carpeting is worn thin and the floor creaks and moans . . . gives way with the weight of each step. This unit has clearly been constructed originally as a mobile *home* and not as the tribal-office annex into which it now has been pressed to serve.

Two brown conference tables practically fill the interior of the small room. The tables—and they are of the folding type seen most often in school cafeterias and in VFW and church bingo parlors—have been pushed together to form one long table. A dozen metal folding chairs are situated around the table; some are brown, some gray, a couple are of the sort that have padded seats meant to suggest a comfort that is in fact absent . . . all are scratched and old-looking. There is a long, broken-down couch pushed up against one wall and although the material that covers it is a threadbare plaid, it is basically the same tacky avocado-green color as the carpeting, and it is certainly as dingy and as worn as the carpeting. And finally, a tired-looking La-Z-Boy recliner adds to the overall gloominess of the room's furnishings, although at least it isn't avocado-green.

Altogether there is cramped seating for what? . . . sixteen . . . seventeen people? But when Push Foster and Sonny Brokeshoulder enter the Annex, they bring the total number present to five.

''Okay.'' Sonny looks at the three faces that have turned toward them. ''I see we're all here except for Pierce,'' he says. ''But I guess like most of our outfits, the Gallup unit's shorthanded and so it looks like the boss is having to fill in some gaps in staffing in their ER. Anyway, I'm hoping he'll be able to shake loose and come over, but since there's no telling when that might be, we might as well go ahead on and get started.''

Sonny introduces Push first to the younger of two Navajo men who are seated at the makeshift conference table alongside Leslie Blair: Wiley Bigboy is a short, heavyset, middle-aged man wearing thick eyeglasses and sporting a flattop haircut. Wearing khaki trousers and shirt and black tennis shoes, the man is dressed, Push thinks, like a maintenance worker. He is fidgeting in his seat—he looks as though he is about to get up and leave the room.

''Shorty, could you say a little something about yourself and what you do in Gallup?''

The man with the flattop is extraordinarily nervous—Push imagines that he is probably unused to being the object of such direct attention and so is uncomfortable in that role.

He clears his throat. ''Okay, Dr. Brokeshoulder . . . my name is Bigboy—Wiley Bigboy, Junior. But most people just call me Shorty. I'm a medical technician on the staff at the Indian Hospital over there at Gallup, New Mexico. I was workin' in the lab whenever they brought in that boy who died on Friday, which I guess is why we're here . . . but he was already DOA when I first seen him down in the ER, so what I seen was, like they say, *after the fact*. They called me down there to draw some blood and get some cultures, is all. He was already gone when he got to the hospital . . . there wasn't anything I could have done to change that, so I don't really know how anybody can expect me to be of any help in this thing now anyhow.''

''Okay, Shorty, that's okay . . . let's get it straight now, that we're not here because of any kind of suspicion on anybody's part that a patient didn't get good care,'' Sonny says. ''The problem is, we don't yet understand what's going on and we're trying to get all the information together that we can. Nobody's saying that anybody else is to blame.''

Wiley Bigboy sits back down in his chair. ''And I also helped Dr. Pierce out with the autopsies on both those people on Saturday morning—but you'll have to wait for him to tell you what the results of those and all the other tests were. Like I said before, I'm just a med tech, is all.''

''Mr. Bigboy here works closely with Dr. Pierce, Push,'' Sonny adds.

''I came over here because Dr. Pierce told me I was supposed to just meet him this morning,'' Wiley Bigboy rambles on. ''I probably shouldn't even be here at all if he doesn't show up, I sure as heck didn't know he was gonna get delayed. . . .''

''It's okay, Shorty,'' Sonny says. ''Nobody's going to put you on the spot.''

Then Sonny addresses the older Navajo man: ''*Hastiin* Slowtalker, would you maybe like to say a few words?''

A tall, slim man Push guesses to be in his mid-to-late sixties, dressed in stiff new blue jeans belted on narrow hips—the cuffs of the jeans are turned up neatly over scuffed boots—and wearing a faded green plaid western-cut shirt, stands to speak. Although he is thin, the old man's body looks wiry—muscular, almost. His graying hair has been combed straight back and tied neatly with white yarn in the traditional chignon at the back of his head. The deep chiseled lines of craggy-dark features set firmly in the man's bony face and the roughness of his movements are underscored by the rasping sound of his voice as he begins to speak.

''Okay, *Tsii'yishbizhii* . . .'' The tall man acknowledges Sonny Brokeshoulder by his Navajo nickname and then turns and faces Push Foster directly. The old man will not likely call Sonny or anyone else in the room directly by name—the traditional Navajo consider it discourteous to speak another's name in that person's presence and so rather speak of "this one" or "my friend" or refer to another by kinship or by nickname. As is the case in some other cultures, names are very powerful to the Navajo way of thinking, and to use a name too often—sometimes to speak aloud one's name at all—is to weaken that power.

"I am *diné*—a Navajo Indian—born into *Tó dích íi'nii*, the Bitter Water Clan, for *Tsé Njíkiní,* Honey Combed Rock People." And the man is dead silent. It becomes apparent that he is waiting for some kind of a response from Push—from the one person in the room that the older man does not know.

"I'm very pleased to meet you, sir," Push says. "I am *Chahta*—of Choctaw descent—of the Sixtown Clan . . . we say *Oklahannali*."

And now it is Push who is silent. He is wondering at the way he has so effortlessly spoken these words to this man . . . as if his normal way of introducing himself is in any way like that of a Navajo, who will invariably say his mother's clan—that one *into* which he is born, or belongs—and then his father's—that clan *for* which he is born. The day-to-day nature of these people's traditional ways is a revelation to Push, for while he knows intellectually about much of Choctaw culture and the mostly forgotten life-ways of that culture, that which might be called the *traditional* extent of his own upbringing was limited to some foods, which he just naturally assumed everyone ate, since everyone he knew did, and some words that people in Oklahoma used—the very name of the state is, after all, a Choctaw-language term for "red people"—and the stories about the "Little People" who played tricks on folks and tended to bad little boys and girls. But of course, he also remembers hearing the Uncle Remus stories of Brer Rabbit and the Tar Baby from the Deep South, and those of the brothers Grimm, and he can still recall the Russian folktale about Peter and the Wolf and Sasha the duck. And so Push grew up with little conscious sense of what might be called Choctaw heritage and is aware of very little impact that heritage may have had upon him. It was really only as an adult that he began to develop a curiosity and to look into and to learn about his mother's people. It wasn't something that the people around him gave much thought to, after all. The faddish focus on things Indian is much more recent, even among the older people back in Oklahoma.

Push hopes that this formality of introduction is what is on the other man's mind—is what the older man expects.

It is.

"Choctaw, huh? That's good. I was afraid maybe you was gonna say you was one of them Cherokee Indians."

"No, sir, I'm Choctaw." Push smiles.

Slowtalker continues. He holds a dusty black cowboy hat as he speaks. Push studies the way the man holds the hat—not as if in deference to the others in the room. The old man's eyes are shrewd and dark—*piercing,* one might say—and he gestures with his hands and with the hat as he speaks.

"I'm what Navajo people call *hataałii.*" He looks at Push. "That word means that I'm a singer, or what some white people might maybe call a medicine man, even though I never did like that name, 'medicine man.' " And again, the man is silent for a long moment—it is as though he is studying his words very carefully. "Anyway, I stay over there at Chinle," and he points with his chin and lips toward the northwest. "I am a council delegate for that Chinle Chapter, too. I have come over here today to represent the people of the Fort Defiance Agency and all of the *Dinétah.*" After another long pause, he turns once more to speak to Push directly. "I figure this person decided to have me here this mornin' on account of he knows that the medicine they do in them government hospitals ain't always much good," and he nods in the direction of Sonny. "And he knew he better get a *hataałii* to listen to this talkin' today."

"We know that peoples die sometimes," Slowtalker continues. "That's just the way it happens in this life. But it seems like we're used to you government doctors always having some kind of answer about how come a person to die. Of course, we don't always think that you are right about what you're saying, but then we start getting pretty worried when you doctors come right out and say you don't know *what* it is that's goin' around. Seems like you government people almost always allow as how you know everything. A lot of us are gettin' worried about this stuff that we're hearing about that is happening over there around Tídááchiid and up there at Shonto. So it's good that I'm here today to find out what it is we're supposed to do about this thing that's goin' around and threatening our people over there."

And then Silas Slowtalker starts to sit down. But again he hesitates, and instead, turns once more to speak directly to Push.

"You know what Navajo people call them Cherokee Indians?"

Push is caught off guard by the old man's question. "No, sir, I don't."

"We say that Cherokees are like *bizhéé 'hóní bizis*—that they're like them beer cans you can see on the side of the roads all over the place." The tall man's dark eyes are fixed on Push's.

"Oh?" Push waits.

"We say that they're like them beer cans, 'cause of how they're just about everywhere you look."

Push smiles—is it a joke that the man is making? "Yessir, they sure are that."

The old man shifts his glance momentarily to Sonny Brokeshoulder and then back to Push. "I thought you ought to know that," he says. "Of course, there are even some people who would say that Choctaw Indians are almost as popular as them Cherokees."

Push studies the tall Navajo's lined face for a trace of the smile that he wants to hear in the man's voice. There is no hint of a smile.

"Yessir, I imagine there are those who would say that." Push looks quickly at Sonny. Sonny winks at his friend.

As Silas Slowtalker sits back down, he adds, "I will be listening to what you gentlemens and this woman from the *'Ayahkinii* hospital have to say here today." The old man sets his dusty black hat on the table before him and sits back in his chair.

LITTLE SPRINGS

The Land Cruiser's brake pads are badly worn and so there is the grating squawk of metal against metal as the chunky green vehicle jerks and grinds to a halt in a choking cloud of red dust. It stops in front of the lone gas pump that stands outside the Little Springs Trading Post. The driver gets out and begins at once to serve himself gasoline, topping off the large green-and-brown military-surplus-style jerry cans mounted on the rear bumper. A neatly dressed, yellow-haired woman climbs down from the passenger-side door and makes her way toward the store. There is a large blue-mottled dog lying still near the door. The woman stops for a moment and peers down at the animal—she is checking to see that it is breathing. Satisfied that it is, she pulls open the screen door and steps inside.

"Hullo," she calls out. "Mr. Austin? . . . Lizbeth? Is anybody here?"

The muffled voice of a man replies: "Be right with you." The voice comes from within the large walk-in vault where the silver and turquoise jewelry and the finely woven Navajo rugs and various other items of value are kept. On this morning the trader is checking the dates on the saddles that have been pawned for cash and credit at Little Springs.

A tall, darkly tanned, bearded man in blue jeans and a faded blue denim shirt, Travis Austin appears in the doorway leading from the vault. ''Well now, good morning, Dr. Vogel. And just how are things in the grave-robbing business?''

''Good morning to you, Mr. Austin.'' Sabine Vogel is inspecting the glass case that holds the dead pawn that—unclaimed after the agreed-upon period of time—is offered for sale. ''And perhaps I should inquire of you about prospects in the loan-sharking business . . . that *is* what you do, isn't it? Loan the local sheepherders money at exorbitant—no, let's agree right up front that they are scandalously *usurious*—interest rates?''

The trader laughs. ''Ah, you're a tough one, you are, Dr. V. But I guess I had it coming, at that. It's just that they used to say around here—and they were only about halfway joking when they said it, mind you—that the typical family on the Navajo Reservation consisted of six and a half people: a man, a woman, three-point-five-oh children, and the *bilagáana* anthropologist who happened to be studying them at the time. Now it seems like it's you fair-haired archeologists who've taken up the study of the native population . . . or of their *remains,* I guess I should say.''

''Very funny, very funny,'' the woman says, and she smiles at the trader in a way that shows she recognizes that he's really not as hard as he likes to sound.

Austin opens the cooler and takes out a can of iced tea. ''Hot and dusty today . . .''—he offers the can to the woman—''as usual. Come across anything of interest out there at your dig?''

Sabine takes the tea and pops the ring on top. ''Why, thank you, Mr. Austin.'' She takes a long drink and dabs at her mouth with a corner of her scarf. ''As a matter of fact, I found an exceptionally fine Pueblo III–era pot just the other day that wasn't so much as cracked . . . not something you'd loan money on, I don't suppose, but it'll make a great museum piece.''

"I don't have to remind you that I'm of the opinion that it would've been better off left where it was, but if it's going to be removed, I guess a museum case is a better place for it than some collector's trophy room in Dallas."

This is not the first time Sabine Vogel has had this conversation with Travis Austin—she doubts that it will be the last. But the two understand one another's positions and so the subject is not usually dwelt upon. Or, when it is, it is most generally done with a modicum of good humor and even grudging respect.

"Is Lizbeth around?" Sabine asks. "I'm interested in seeing what she's been working on."

"Of course she's here." As a matter of habit Austin's tone of voice takes on the hard edge again. "Where else you think she'd be? Shopping at the Little Springs Wal-Mart? She's around back working at her loom . . . when she heard you pull up she probably figured you to be a carload of out-of-state tourists stopping by to watch a real Indian work at making an authentic Navajo rug like the sign says. When you go back there be sure and announce who you are right up front, or she'll more than likely pretend she's in some kind of peyote-induced Native American rug-weaving trance and go on working and not even look up at you." And then, as if to reinforce the image, he calls out loudly, "Hey, Lizbeth! It's not a busload of eastern tourists after all, it's our local archeologist come to town on a shopping spree from her boneyard dig over to Hopi . . . you can quit acting all stoic and go back to talking in English if you want."

And at the same time the yellow-haired woman goes out the side door leading to the place where Lizbeth Austin is working at her loom, her companion comes in, slamming the front screen door behind him.

"You ought to chain up that goddamned dog of yours, Austin. The way that sorry cur snarls and growls at white people—hell, the sonofabitch is a menace."

"Dog's got good taste in individuals, is what that is." Austin is pleased to know that the animal dislikes this man. "He's no menace to honest people. But then again I'd be careful about calling him a cur where he might overhear you unless you're looking to lose a big chunk out of your leg. Why, Punk's a damned fine working dog, is what he is—a Queensland Blue Heeler . . . an Australian Cattle Dog.''

''Yeah, I might've known it wasn't an American breed—I still say the sonofabitch is a menace, though,'' the man grumbles.

''I don't know where you get off talking about a man's dog that way. And besides, those are strangely patriotic words to be coming from the mouth of somebody who drives around in a Japanese vehicle, I'd say.''

''Isn't mine, actually—it came with the woman,'' he says. ''Your pump out there seems to think I owe you eighteen dollars for that little bit of watered-down fuel I put in my tanks,'' he adds. And he hands the trader a twenty-dollar bill—his hand remains extended until the two bills in change have been placed into it. ''When was the last time somebody with good eyesight checked the flow on that gauge? I figure you're probably cheating the public by about half.''

''Those gauges are flowing just fine, and the gas is by-god good—as if that piece of shit you drive could tell the difference if it wasn't.''

Travis Austin gives Sabine Vogel a hard time, but in truth, he likes and even admires her, and he considers their banter good-natured. On the other hand, Austin very much *dis*likes Peter Campbell, and it is not a part of Travis Austin's nature to conceal his dislikes.

''You know, I never have understood what it is that attracts people to live way out here in the middle of nowhere, Austin.''

''It's in the blood, Campbell—this is probably the last good place on earth. But I don't suppose people like you could ever understand.''

''In the blood, my ass . . . I figure every one of you wannabe white people who live out here full-time have to be either born-again crazies or on the run from the IRS,'' Peter Campbell says. ''Then again, in your case I suppose it could be nothing more than a lack of ambition.''

Austin glares at the man. ''All right, you've paid for your goddamned gasoline—do you have any more business here, or are you just wasting time, mostly mine?''

The other man smiles insincerely. ''Listen, I came across something awhile back I thought you just might be interested in taking a look at,'' and Peter Campbell lays a small, dark bundle on the scratched glass-topped counter.

''It's a little play-pretty that I swapped an old man out of the other day.'' He nudges the object toward Austin. ''You understand, I don't figure it's worth much if anything, but I was wondering anyway what an experienced Indian trader like yourself might make of it.''

Austin reaches across and picks the bundle up. He carefully unwraps the oily black cloth from around the hard stone tablet. He turns the thing over, examining each side closely—it takes only a moment for him to recognize just what it is he's holding. And even then he can hardly believe it.

''Where did you get this, Campbell? Did you steal it?''

''I told you, I got it from an old Navajo over by Chinle—traded him out of it.''

''Pretty much the same thing with you—your trading and your stealing . . . who was this Navajo?''

''I'm not at liberty to tell you his name. It looks to be pretty old, though, wouldn't you agree? Say, but I'm right in thinking it isn't worth any *real* money, aren't I?''

''What'd you trade for?''

''Would you believe it, this old man over there said he wanted some dirt from a grave . . . I mean, he didn't want cash money or anything of value, just some dirt from a goddamn burial site.'' Campbell is shaking his head in disbelief. ''Said it had to be Hopi, was the only stipulation.''

''Hell, it wasn't *dirt* he was after, you fool, it was *corpse powder,* which is about as strong a medicine as a Navajo can have . . . *bad* medicine, is what it is, too.''

Austin fumbles with the cloth. Rewrapping the stone, he places it back down on the counter. ''If this is what it looks to me to be, I sure as hell don't want anything to do with it, Campbell.'' His voice has taken on a strange timbre—it is a shaking, hissing sound, almost. It's as though he is angry—or frightened, maybe. ''I don't know how you came to get hold of this, but it's not right . . . in fact it's downright *dangerous,* and I think you know good and well that it's dangerous. And there's also something wrong with your whole story, Campbell. Anybody who's spent any time at all around these people knows that there's no way in hell that a Navajo who's traditional enough to want to get his hands on corpse powder could bring himself to even *touch* this kind of thing . . . it would be the last thing he'd do, in fact. So it's clear to me that somebody here's lying through their teeth, and I've got a hunch it's you.''

''Now just you hold on a goddamned minute, Austin. I never said that the old guy I traded with actually had this thing *on* him—he traded me the information as to exactly where I could find it, is what he did. Pretty much the same thing, if a fellow wanted to get real picky, I suppose, but like I say, the Navajo didn't actually have the tablet *on* him. . . .''

''It doesn't matter—either way my advice to you is to get it back to where it came from . . . where it belongs, and fast. But in any case, I'm telling you to get it out of here!''

I *knew* it, Sabine!''

Peter Campbell is pounding the steering wheel in excitement as the Land Cruiser speeds rattling and bouncing over the washboard red-dirt road that snakes its way south from Little Springs toward Dinnebito.

''I just knew what that old Indian was telling me was the truth!''

And he is shouting to make himself heard over the road noise.

''You should've seen the look on Austin's face—I mean, I thought that sonofabitch was actually going to choke when he saw the bear tracks and realized what it was he was holding in his hands! He knew right away what he was looking at, all right . . . and there's no doubt about it! Oh, man, but this is it . . . the big find . . . and we are fixing to get ourselves rich and famous!''

Sabine Vogel is clinging to the dashboard handle with one hand and holding her scarf across her mouth and nose against the swirling, choking dust with the other.

''It has got to go to a museum, Peter,'' and now she yells to make certain he can hear her. ''I will not have you trying to sell it to some private collector. . . . I *mean* it! I will not stand by and watch while you destroy what little reputation I may have left . . . the very fact that you've gotten your hands on an object that's sacred to an entire people's culture is bad enough, but if you intend trying to sell it to some of your shady contacts who deal in stolen relics, I swear to you I'll . . .''

''You'll *what,* Sabine?'' his voice is hissing. ''Go running back to your cushy job at the university? . . . Tell the big shots there that your amateur assistant is the one who's finding the real treasures while you're still just digging up old cooking pots? Remember that it was you who brought me out here to this shitty country in the first place, goddamnit. It was you who taught me all that crap about the Hopi tablets.''

''Don't talk like that to me, Peter . . . you frighten me when you talk that way.'' Sabine feels the blood drain from her face. She hates whatever it is about her that causes her to feel so weak and helpless where Peter is concerned . . . hates it that she can't find the strength to stand up to this man . . . despises it that she's afraid of being alone—that she can't summon the courage to tell him to go to hell.

''You know that I've always insisted that cultural artifacts be properly preserved. You promised me that if you got it you'd take the tablet to a *museum,* Peter,'' she says again. ''A *museum.*''

''Yeah, yeah . . . whatever,'' and he is laughing now. ''Any museum that can come up with a truckload of cash can sure enough have it.''

TSÉGHÁHOODZÁNI

Sonny Brokeshoulder shifts attention to the woman doctor from Keams Canyon Indian Agency: "I realize you had a long drive over from Hopi this morning, Leslie, and I want you to know that I appreciate it that you made the trip."

"Glad to be here, Sonny," Leslie Blair says. "I just hope I can be of some help."

"Well then, I guess you all probably know that besides being the head of Health and Human Services, I'm also tribal medical examiner for the Window Rock/Chinle District," Sonny says. "Which just means that I'm supposed to get fairly regular reports from all the medical facilities located on the rez as well as from those in bordering areas. By fairly regular, I mean that I hear from them anywhere from daily to once every few weeks or so as a rule. Just in the past week, though, I've been getting an unusual number of reports about some undiagnosed, nonspecific respiratory incidents that have occurred in young and otherwise healthy individuals in the area."

''What sort of numbers are you hearing about, Sonny?''

''As of this morning, there have been eight cases reported to my office in just the past seven days, Leslie, and of those, four have resulted in death and three of the other four are hospitalized on supportive therapy—one of those on life support.''

''That's seven—what about the eighth one?''

''There's a question, it seems, of whether that eighth case wasn't maybe something else—flu, or even just a really bad cold. Anyway, that patient has apparently recovered.'' Sonny looks around the room. ''I know what you're probably thinking—that these numbers aren't particularly high given the fact that the Navajo Reservation encompasses an area the size of the state of West Virginia. But still . . . an average rate of a new incident for each day that passes, plus a case fatality rate of fifty percent, *is* significant, I'd say.''

''Not just significant,'' Leslie says. ''That's pretty scary.''

Just then the door to the outside opens and Priscilla Yazzie appears. All five of the faces in the room turn expectantly toward the bright light that the open door admits. Priscilla looks slightly embarrassed as she motions to Sonny Brokeshoulder.

''Come on in, Priscilla,'' he says.

''I'm sorry to interrupt you guys.'' She smiles. ''But they called from Gallup to say that Dr. Pierce is on his way over here.''

''Good, thanks Priscilla . . . any other calls for me? Any word yet from Tuba City?''

''No, not yet. But I'm holdin' down the fort, and just as soon as anything comes up you ought to know about I'll be sure and come on over to let you know.''

''Okay, thank you.''

Priscilla Yazzie backs out, closing the door. And then, almost immediately, the door opens wide again and Priscilla's face reappears at the exact spot where it had just disappeared. ''Sonny, I think Dr. Pierce is here already,'' she says. ''Anyway, a government car just drove up and it's drivin' around like it might be lost . . . I'll go check to see for sure if that's him.'' And she backs out, closing the door once more.

''Ah, the boss man,'' Leslie says, rolling her eyes.

Sonny grins at Push. ''What can I say? Ed Pierce is a career man—been out here for fifteen or twenty years—and still he's been known to get lost driving the six blocks between his house and the hospital.'' He shakes his head. ''And coming over here to Window Rock? Why, it's like a whole new world to him.''

In fact, Dr. Edward Pierce has been based in Gallup since the fall of 1974—nearly twenty years. During those years, he'll tell you, he's seen every kind of medical situation known to man. He's pronounced dead or pieced back together scores of victims of Interstate car and truck accidents, he long ago lost count of the number of suicides and beatings and knife and gunshot wounds he's seen, and he's grown almost accustomed to seeing the solid-frozen drunks—popsicles, the cops call them—who've passed out in alleyways and culverts in the dead of winter or who, in warmer weather, have fallen facedown and drowned in inch-deep irrigation ditches as they've tried to make their ways home after a night of drinking rotgut Garden De Luxe Tokay in bordertown bars. And he's no longer much surprised to see what little is left of those unfortunate enough to have moved too slowly crossing railroad tracks. He's come to expect, almost, that those who've crawled up under parked cars looking for a warm place to sleep on cold winter nights will sometimes be crushed beneath tires when unsuspecting drivers get in and start to drive away. In Gallup, New Mexico, local residents learn early to bang on their hoods and to peer underneath their cars before they climb in to start their engines in the wintertime. The banging on the hoods is meant to frighten away any stray cats that may have sought the warmth and shelter to be found up in the engine compartments; the look underneath is to see that someone has not sought a warm, dry place to sleep off the bad wine.

So there's just not a whole lot that can surprise Ed Pierce when it comes to the ways people find to die and to bleed and to injure themselves or others on and around the big Navajo Reservation.

• • •

When the Annex door opens this time, there is not the glare of bright sunlight as before. Instead, a very large, balding man with a shaggy walrus mustache is filling the doorway, blocking the sunlight from the outside.

The Navajo call him *Dághaałtsohí*—"Big Mustache." At six feet four inches tall, he is pushing 280 pounds. He wears faded cotton khaki trousers and dirty white running shoes. And although he sports a loosely knotted necktie and a blue oxford-cloth dress shirt, his overall appearance is rumpled and disarrayed. As he enters the small room, Pierce moves like some large animal—*lumbers,* really, like some awkward, clumsy bear so that those seated at the table are forced to shift and turn to follow his progress. He nods in greeting to all of those present.

Slowtalker's eyes are closed . . . they remain closed, and yet he nods his head.

"What are you doing here, Blair?" Pierce says this in his naturally gruff, but not-unfriendly tone of voice. "Don't tell me you got people sick over there at Keams, too?"

"Not yet, anyway, Ed," she says. "But I want to be ready just in case. Keams Canyon Indian Agency may be on the Hopi Reservation, but I have never known a disease to respect reservation boundaries."

"No, I suppose not."

"And you know Hopi is smack-dab in the middle of Navajoland," she continues. "And so what affects the *dine'é* affects the Hopi, as well. I've had no reports of incidents like what I understand you're seeing—at least not so far as I can determine at this time—but Sonny here *was* good enough to call and include me in this meeting."

"And I'm glad to see you here." Pierce directs an awkward smile at the woman. But he looks terribly worried as he turns to face Sonny Brokeshoulder.

"Sorry to be late, Brokeshoulder, but we had two women in acute respiratory distress come into the ER—one about midnight and the other right during the shift change at seven this morning."

"Respiratory distress? . . ." Sonny makes a face as he says it.

"Yeah. And I admitted both women to the hospital with a presumptive diagnosis of our thus-far-*un*diagnosed disease."

"Shit . . ."

LITTLE SPRINGS

At Little Springs Trading Post, Travis Austin sits at the kitchen table, talking with his wife.

"I don't think it could've been a fake, Lizbeth," he is telling her. "It just about had to be one of the lost Hopi tablets. I've heard stories about them all my life—I've talked to people who swear they've seen them and who've shown me drawings. I just *know* it was the real thing."

"But I don't see how it could have been. The old people have always said that even though those tablets were missing for a while, for a long time now they've been back at Hopi and are stashed away somewhere—two of them over at Hotevilla and the others at Oraibi. And they say that they'll be brought out at the proper time. Anyway, I don't see how some white archeologist could get hold of one, even in a trade—and especially not in a trade with no Navajo . . . I mean, how would a Navajo get their hands on somethin' like that?"

"I don't know. Maybe I'm crazy, but I feel like I need to let somebody over there know about this . . . tell somebody what it was I saw. Just in case.

"That fellow Lomaquaptewa—over at Mishongnovi—he's Bear Clan, isn't he?"

"I believe that's right."

"Well, I can be over to his place and back by suppertime—I just think somebody over there needs to know what's going on, and it seems to me like he's a pretty big chief." Travis stands and walks to the doorway. He stops and turns to wink at Lizbeth.

"Now don't you go and give away the store to any of those clan relatives of yours if they happen to drop by."

"Maybe I will." She smiles mischievously at her husband. "If some handsome young man drops by to call on me, I might let him have anything he wants. . . ."

Austin is smiling as he walks out the door and across the drive to his pickup. He climbs in.

The big blue dog that has been sleeping beside the porch gets to his feet, yawns, stretches, shakes his ears, sneezes, and ambles over to the truck. He sniffs at the left front tire, then lifts his leg and pees on it.

Austin grins now and speaks gently to the animal. "Hey, Punk—what're you doin'?" The dog cocks his head at the question. "You figure to send them mangy Hopi dogs over there some kind of a canine greeting, do you?"

Only on the third attempt does the pickup engine catch hold, turn over, and start. "If your old buddy Campbell shows up around here again, you're not to just growl at him, you hear? Next time, Punk, go on and take a big chunk out of that worthless bastard's ass!"

The blue dog stands watching Travis Austin bounce off toward the blacktop highway. Again the animal stretches and yawns—he sits down in the dust in the exact middle of the drive. He halfheartedly scratches his neck and ears, licks himself between his legs for a while, and then—as though he is finally overcome with exhaustion from the very effort involved in scratching and licking—falls over as though he has died.

And surely anyone who happens past might well think this dog *is* dead . . . except for the loud snoring sounds he is making, that is.

TSÉGHÁHOODZÁNI

Ed Pierce is relating the circumstances of the fatal case at Gallup on the previous Friday:

"Robert Greyeyes is—or should I say *was*—an eighteen-year-old Navajo man, in apparent good health, who was traveling by automobile with his family from Tídááchiid, about twenty-five miles this side of Shiprock, down to Gallup to attend a funeral. The family members report that when they left home at mid-morning everything seemed fine—as fine as could be expected, under the circumstances, that is. But then the young man began to complain of a severe headache and—in just a matter of a very few minutes, apparently—he started having difficulty breathing. His face was flushed and red, and according to his mother, he was 'just burning up with fever.' I've talked to everyone who was in the car that day, and they all agree that the progression of this guy's condition from apparent good health to being barely able to breathe occurred over a very short period of time. In fact, all of this happened in something like twenty or thirty minutes *at the most*. Anyway, the family—and the Greyeyes are a very traditional family—was extremely worried and pulled off the highway and into the gas station there at the Twin Lakes Thriftway to try and get help of some sort. They all agree that the boy was in dire distress at this point—that they were very frightened for his well-being.

"I understand that the clerk at the Thriftway also believed this to be an emergency situation and that she immediately telephoned Gallup—that the ambulance arrived at Twin Lakes within fifteen to twenty minutes of that call, and that the boy was close to death when the EMT boys arrived at the scene. These EMTs see a lot of sick folks, I should add, and their input is usually pretty savvy. They tell me they felt they were possibly seeing a severe asthma attack or maybe the final stages of a respiratory shutdown, like is sometimes seen with pneumonic plague."

"What *about* asthma?" Sonny asks.

"The family denies any history of it."

"Have you ruled out plague?"

"I've never seen a case of plague go down that fast, Blair," Ed Pierce says. "How about you, Foster?"

"No, but then I haven't actually seen that many cases of plague."

"Brokeshoulder?"

"Nope—sounds way too fast for plague, and I've seen several cases since I've been here. This is scary. . . ."

"Yeah, this is all just *real* scary," Pierce continues, "considering that the young man died of respiratory arrest en route to Gallup from Twin Lakes—a distance of about twelve miles. This means that if we can take what the family says as even fairly accurate, and I believe we can, Greyeyes went from an apparently healthy young man to a corpse in a matter of just over an hour."

Pierce looks around the room.

"So anyway," he continues, "it's just after noon and I'm looking at a case of sudden death from an unknown disease. When I talked with the Greyeyes family they told me that they were on their way to a funeral. . . ."

"Yvonne Tsosie's funeral?" Push interrupts.

''Right. Tsosie was Greyeyes's girlfriend. . . . Tsosie being the same girl who died at the clinic at Lukachukai a week ago.''

Push speaks now: ''How much ought we to make of the fact that the girl had been treated by a traditional Navajo medicine person just prior to coming to Lukachukai? I mean, I don't know the specifics, but they said she'd been involved in a ceremony of some sort.''

''She was seen by a hand-trembler . . .'' Sonny says.

''Get used to it, Push,'' Leslie says. ''Around here a good number of patients are referred to us by hand-tremblers.''

''. . . and it's not really a problem,'' Sonny continues. ''Traditional medicine people do a lot of good out here . . . and hand-tremblers don't treat people, rather their function is to diagnose and to recommend treatment. Same for stargazers and listeners, but you can go a long time and never hear anything about one of them—all the stargazers and listeners are just about gone, they say—hand-tremblers are still pretty common.''

''Yeah, so anyway,'' Pierce continues, ''it's evident that while Tsosie died not quite so suddenly as the boyfriend, her death seems to have been just as unexpected . . . for a young person in previous good health, that is.

''And I understand from your notes, Foster, that she died pretty much in the same kind of distress as Greyeyes?'' Push nods. ''And didn't the staff at Lukachukai tell you she'd complained of severe headaches and had spiked a fever before very rapidly going into complete respiratory failure?''

''That's right.''

Just then Silas Slowtalker stands up from his chair. The words he speaks now are even more measured than before:

''How come you all to think that people will get better when you put them in the white people's hospital? Those clinics and hospitals over there are where people go to *die,* not to get better. For a long time now the Navajo have understood that the *bilagáana* hospital, the white man's hospital, is a dead house. When some person is old and sick and about to leave the earth, his outfit will take him over there so that he won't have to die at his hogan and his family won't have to abandon it like is the Navajo

Way. It just don't make a lot of sense to take some young person there if you believe there's some kind of chance that she can be cured. You doctors think you know about everything—but a lot of the time you don't know shit. If there was a way for her to be cured, then it was the time to see about the proper ways—the traditional ceremonies.'' And the old singer looks sharply at Ed Pierce and at Sonny Brokeshoulder.

Each of the people in this room is aware—to a greater or lesser extent—that one of the most basic differences between Navajo and Western beliefs when it comes to healing has to do with the contrasts between the traditional Navajo healing ceremony and the Western idea of ''hospital.'' In the Navajo culture there is the Sing—the healing ceremony wherein the patient is attended by family and friends . . . talked to . . . touched . . . loved. There are essential human sounds associated with the Sing: the sounds of singing and the rhythmic pulse of water drums and the soft *shish* of rattles. And there are the earthy smells of burning sage and other herbs. In the white man's hospital, on the other hand, the patient is more often than not ignored—sometimes this is on account of a language barrier, with the Navajo patient, to be sure—but even when this is not the case, the person who is ill is often left *feeling* ignored. And then there are the prescribed times—the ''visiting hours''—for relatives and friends, times that often do not coincide with the times the visitor may be able to attend. And instead of being touched and loved, the patient is more apt to be poked and stuck with needles. What sounds there are are most likely the impersonal beeps of monitors and the foreign and mechanical voice of some invisible speaker coming over a paging system. The smells are not of the earth, rather they are strange and unpleasant smells, those of disinfectant and of death.

Silas Slowtalker has resumed his seat at the table now. With his eyes fixed on the window, his jaw is set and his face like stone.

''You know that's the way it is,'' he says, finally.

''Yes sir, but like Dr. Foster was saying, we were told by the family that Yvonne Tsosie had been diagnosed by a hand-trembler near her home,'' Sonny says. ''That it was the hand-trembler who told her to go to the Lukachukai station in the first place. . . .''

An awkward quiet has fallen over the room and Ed Pierce continues.

''With the two women I admitted this morning, we're looking at what appears now to be ten cases in a week of an unknown but serious illness that has resulted in at least four deaths in young, otherwise healthy-appearing individuals,'' he says.

''You say *at least*—does that mean you think there may be more deaths?'' Leslie asks. ''Deaths we don't know about?''

''It's a big reservation out there,'' Pierce says. ''And like Slowtalker has just reminded us, our hospitals are looked at as a last resort by a lot of the local population. . . . I for one won't be particularly surprised if additional victims turn up in some of the more-isolated areas before this thing is through.''

Sonny has been scribbling notes as Pierce talks. Now he says, ''That's occurred to me, too, Ed. But maybe we can just focus on what we know to be true—like, how it appears that in each case the patient's complaints begin with flu-like symptoms and rapidly degenerate into respiratory distress—and in about half the cases there is complete respiratory failure.''

''And because the fatality on Friday is clearly related to the Lukachukai case not only symptomatically, but also by the fact of close contact, can we deduce that we're looking at a contagious disease? One that's passed from person to person, perhaps casually?''

''If by casually you mean is the infection *airborne,* Leslie, I have to think that it's not necessarily,'' Push says. ''We don't yet know the incubation period, but the rule of thumb seems to be four or five days.''

''Oh, great!'' Leslie says. ''So if it *is* passed from person to person, and you came in direct contact with the young woman at Lukachukai . . . and Ed with the boyfriend in Gallup . . .''—and as she snaps to yet another contact, she turns to look at Wiley Bigboy—''and then Shorty here helped you with the autopsies, Ed . . . Oh, good grief! And now we're all gathered together here in this stuffy little room—breathing the same fucking air. . . .''

''Hold on now, you know that there are degrees of contagion, Leslie,'' Sonny says, more sternly than he'd meant to. ''So let's not get ahead of ourselves . . . there doesn't appear to be any connection between the Tídáácchiid couple and any of the other victims.''

''You mean there's no proximal connection, don't you?'' Push asks.

"Because there are just a whole number of factors that need to be considered here besides just whether or not the victims have coughed on each other—things like age and sex, previous health histories, social habits and occupations. . . ."

"Well, I can tell you that of the eight cases I've gotten reports on, all involve people who are relatively young—the Tídááchiid boy was the youngest at eighteen, I believe, and the oldest is a man in the hospital up at Farmington who's in his late twenties." Sonny is scanning the notes he has spread out before him on the table. "The breakdown by sex is that six of those stricken are male and two—now four—female—the one female fatality to this point has been Yvonne Tsosie and we know a little something about her health history since she'd been seen fairly regularly for pre- and postnatal care. But the other factors you're talking about are pretty much unknown to us."

"So as far as you can determine there's no single element of commonality among those people?"

"Just one, Leslie," and Sonny Brokeshoulder looks around the room. "They're every one of them Navajo Indians."

I'd like to try and keep our focus on communicability if we can,'' Push says. ''Let's remember that there was a whole roomful of family in close contact with Tsosie, *and* that she has a child—a child who's not ill, as far as we know. We certainly want to take every precaution, because it may well be that whatever bug we've got here *does* somehow jump from person to person—but I'm betting it takes more than just *casual* contact.''

''Well, let's hope so,'' Ed Pierce says darkly. ''Since by Blair's scientific count three of the six people in this room have recently come in contact with folks who started out with a headache and breathing difficulties and were soon deader than hammers.'' And with that both Pierce and Push look at one another and at a very frightened-looking Wiley Bigboy.

''What sort of lab work have we got on the fatalities, Sonny?'' Push asks.

Sonny puts his hands palm up and looks to Ed Pierce, who answers. ''When I realized the young man in Gallup was from the same household as a victim who'd presented much the same symptoms, I figured we didn't have much choice but to get postmortems on Greyeyes and on his girlfriend—if it wasn't already too late.'' Push can see from the way in which Ed Pierce glances toward Silas Slowtalker that he knows he's broaching a sensitive subject with talk of postmortems.

Pierce continues. ''We face strong culture-based resistance when it comes to obtaining permission to do an autopsy on Navajoland. But this was a very serious case, as far as I could determine, and because the remains of both victims were in Gallup at the time, and not actually on the reservation, I was prepared to impound the bodies of both individuals for the state of New Mexico. Fortunately, as it turned out, it wasn't necessary, since both families gave me the go-ahead. I can tell you that we were lucky in this case . . . very lucky."

Sonny knows that to understand why the families would have agreed to allow the *bilagáana* doctors to take charge of their dead children it is necessary to understand that Navajo people harbor an abhorrent fear of the dead that very nearly borders on necrophobia. To touch a dead body is to risk ghost contamination—never mind that the deceased was a loved one. The Greyeyes and the Tsosies would have been greatly relieved to have the white officials take care of what to them was the utterly gruesome task of disposing of the remains—even of the remains of their children.

And now Pierce is saying: "Even though the Greyeyes are a traditional family with the traditional Navajo worldview of what seems to me to be inevitable doom, these people were scared shitless."

Scared shitless, Sonny is thinking. But do Pierce and the others understand just what it is these people are scared *of*? It's likely they imagine the Greyeyes are afraid of an unknown disease—as *they* are—when in fact the Navajo are more likely afraid of what it was that *caused* the disease—a distinction a non-Navajo has a hard time understanding, if he or she can understand it at all. To the Navajo way of thinking, there are a limited number of means by which a disease may be contracted: through the *loss of the soul,* through *possession* by some dangerous spirit, by having some *foreign object* shot into the body by an evil person who practices wizardry, by breaking—intentionally or unintentionally—one or more of the many prohibited acts or *taboos* that inform the Navajo Way, by *lightning,* or by what is considered to be the most fearsome and evil of all means: *witchery*. For the Navajo, diseases are classified by their causes rather than by their symptoms. And any attempts at healing proceed from that central idea.

And while it hasn't been said out loud—not yet, anyway—there is little doubt that both the Greyeyes and the Tsosie outfits very probably believe that they have been witched.

''Have the autopsies been completed, Ed?'' It is Leslie's slow drawl.

''Yeah, Blair, we did both of them on Saturday.'' Pierce nods in acknowledgment toward Wiley Bigboy. ''Bigboy here was good enough to help me out on his day off.''

''And? . . .''

Pierce has a pained look on his face: ''I was afraid somebody was going to ask that . . . we're still waiting for some of the blood and tissue work to get back from Albuquerque, but the preliminary findings are pretty much inconclusive. Both Greyeyes and Tsosie died as a result of respiratory arrest brought on by a rapid and undiagnosed buildup of fluids.

''Hell, they *drowned* is what they did, Blair—both of them.''

MISHONGNOVI

There is a lone man working in the dusty gray soil of a small cornfield.

He is hoeing the earth around delicate green corn plants in a field that looks as though nothing should grow there, so blisteringly hot and dry is the earth at this place. No matter that the preceding winter and fall have been remarkably wet and that the landscapes to the north and east especially are unusually green—except for the young green corn plants, this land is barren and dead-looking.

And although he has not looked up from his work, this man has known for some time now that a vehicle has turned off the paved road some two miles distant and is making its way slowly across the dry, wash-rutted landscape—has known that the vehicle is headed directly for this small field where he is toiling.

When the pickup comes to a stop alongside the southernmost row of plants, the man whose field this is stops his work and leans on the handle of his hoe. Shading his eyes from the bright sun, which just now stands at its noonday highest in the sky, he watches as the driver of the truck switches off the engine. The door opens and a white man steps down out of the cab. The white man raises his hand in a half-wave.

"Haw!" Travis Austin uses the traditional Hopi word for announcing one's presence.

Clifford Lomaquaptewa balances the hoe across his shoulder—his right arm draped at the wrist over the wooden handle—and walks toward the man and the truck.

"This corn is growin' pretty good for it bein' so early on in the year," he says.

"Yes . . . yes, it is. Mr. Lomaquaptewa?"

"That's me."

"My name is Travis Austin, I have the trading post up there at Little Springs."

"I know," says Clifford. "I was at your store a time or two. There's an Indian woman who stays there at that place. She's Navajo, I believe—from up around *T'iis Náabas*," and although he is Hopi, Clifford Lomaquaptewa uses the Navajo name for the Teec Nos Pos community.

"Yes, that would be Lizbeth, she's my wife," Travis says.

"Oh, I see."

"Mr. Lomaquaptewa, there was a white man came into my place earlier this morning and he had with him something that I believe belongs to you—belongs to the Hopi people, I should say. I am of the opinion that it is something that is very old and very important. . . . I thought it best to tell someone over here. I understand that you are a *kikmongwi*—a leader for the village of Mishongnovi. . . ."

When Lomaquaptewa makes no response, Austin feels awkward. Still he goes on:

"Yes . . . and so, anyway, I came looking for you to tell you about it. I talked to an old man up there at the village who told me that I would find you down here."

"Practically ever'body knows that I work down here most days. These here corn plants take a lotta work, you know."

Because Lomaquaptewa appears indifferent, Austin wonders if he hasn't perhaps overreacted—if maybe the tablet was nothing, after all. But then the Hopi man says: "This thing that you saw . . ."

"It was maybe about the size of a playing card, only thicker, of course," Austin is indicating with his hands the stone's approximate dimensions. "It was a flat stone of some kind . . . kind of pinkish-colored, and there was writing on it. Not really *writing,* but more like pictures—*symbols,* I guess. Here, I'll show you," and the trader squats down beside the truck and with his finger begins to make lines in the dust. First he makes a drawing of the surface of the stone with the bear tracks and then, next to that, he sketches the opposite side.

"Of course it wasn't this big—it was more like the size of the palm of your hand without any fingers or the thumb. This side here seemed like it just had some lines scratched on it—almost like it was a map of some kind. I couldn't really see that the lines made much sense, though."

And in that brief moment it has taken the white man to sketch in the dust of the cornfield the crude likeness of what it is he has seen on the ancient stone tablet, the other man knows exactly what he is seeing. There are no words to express adequately the mixture of relief and alarm Clifford Lomaquaptewa feels as he recognizes—and this even before the trader has finished making his drawing—that the man who had visited the Little Springs Trading Post had somehow come to have in his possession one of the three sacred tablets that had been given to the People by the Bear Clan deity Söqömhonaw when the Hopi emerged into this, the Fourth World. This particular tablet—and it is the one that shows, on one side, the way the land is to be distributed around the main Hopi village, and on the other, the pawprints that indicate that it is the Bear Clan that is in charge of the land—this tablet had mysteriously disappeared from the priest's house at Hotevilla many years ago. For a long time after the disappearance, the talk among the people was that the tablet had been stolen by a woman who belonged to the Fire Clan and that the tablet was still in the village of Hotevilla—that it had never, in fact, even left that village.

"You were right to come here, Mr. Austin . . . this thing that you have seen is very important to the Hopi people. It is more important even than you can begin to know. You must tell me about this white man who showed you the tablet . . . tell me where I can find him.''

''His name is Campbell . . . Peter Campbell,'' Austin says. ''He and a woman who is an archeologist have been working some sites up north, around Piñon—I would have thought you knew about them.''

''So, it was the man who goes around with the yellow-haired woman digger who stays over there at Wepo Wash?''

''Yes, that's right. That's him.''

''For many years the Hopi have stood by and watched as outsiders have come onto our lands to dig up the floors of our houses. They tell us not to worry, that they come to study our ways. But for too long now we have stood by and watched as these white people—these people who call themselves anthropologists and archeologists—we have stood by and watched silently as they shook the dust from the garments of our ancestors.''

And with that Clifford Lomaquaptewa turns abruptly and walks away—away from Travis Austin and away from the cornfield. The man still balances his hoe across his shoulder as he walks deliberately toward the mesa that rises three-quarters of a mile distant out of the dry, gray landscape—toward a narrow, ancient path that winds up the mesa to the village of Mishongnovi.

Travis Austin calls out after him, ''I can give you a ride up, Mr. Lomaquaptewa. . . .''

But the Hopi man is already too far away to hear the offer.

TSÉGHÁHOODZÁNI

The meeting at the tribal complex annex had ended abruptly when Ed Pierce got a call from his assistant in Gallup telling him that the Sheep Springs woman he had admitted that morning had died, and that the lab in Albuquerque had faxed over the preliminary results of the blood and tissue samples from Greyeyes and Tsosie.

The early case-fatality rate now stood at five of ten cases—exactly 50 percent—and the prognosis for the four apparent survivors was poor. Added to that, the most unsettling thing about the lab analysis from Albuquerque was the fact that the normal white-cell counts observed in both those cases effectively ruled out bacterial infection—including the *Yersinia pestis bacillus* evident in plague—as the probable cause of death. If it wasn't bacterial infection, the presence of which is nearly always evidenced by a dramatic elevation in white blood cells, it was likely either environmental—that is, a food- or water- or possibly even *air*-borne poison of some kind—or else it was a viral infection that made these people sick. And viral infections include rabies, equine encephalitis, swine flu, yellow fever, and the like . . . every one of them deadly to a greater or lesser degree, and every one of them a species-jumper. Viral transmission relies on close contact, the infection often passed by means of a bite—either directly or through an intermediary such as a mosquito or a tick—or by sexual contact. Or, and this was possibly the worst-case scenario from the standpoint of health workers, viral infections are often airborne—one can become infected with a virus simply by breathing the same air as a carrier.

Pierce and Bigboy had left Window Rock for Gallup almost immediately. There were still blood and tissue specimens from Tsosie and Greyeyes on ice in the pathology lab at the hospital and Pierce was anxious to pack them up for overnight shipment to the Centers for Disease Control in Atlanta for further evaluation. He intended also to gather samples from the latest fatality as well as blood and other samples from the surviving patient.

''If that poor woman from Nazhoni is still alive when I get there, that is,'' he'd said.

Push had been nominated to make the first call to the CDC to request their assistance with this outbreak and to alert them to the arrival of what had to be considered ''hot'' specimens. As a result of the three years he'd spent in residency in Atlanta, Push has a number of friends at the Centers and the consensus is that of those gathered in the shabby little room in Window Rock on this day, he will be best able to predict the kind of information the research team in the Infectious Disease Unit is likely to want and need.

Either of you ever read one of those medical thrillers?''

Leslie Blair is poking at the remains of her taco salad. She is sitting at a table with Push and Sonny. The three have just finished having lunch at the Navajo Nation Inn and are about to go back to their respective stations.

''You know, those paperback novels they sell in airport gift shops? . . . The ones with stories about far-fetched medical catastrophes, like where rich people start dropping dead all over New York one day and then a handsome, silver-haired cardiovascular surgeon and a sexy, gorgeous blond virologist with huge breasts join forces to save the day by figuring out that some horrible disease from a Third World country has hitched a ride into New York Harbor on a cruise ship and is threatening to wipe out life as we know it?''

''Life as we know it just in New York? Or life as we know it everywhere else? I've never been to New York.'' Push Foster is thinking how distracting it is to hear Leslie Blair talk. Her voice—her soft southern drawl—seems so completely natural and easy and, at the same time, so out of place in the dining room of the Navajo Nation Inn. He really loves listening to her voice—and he's thinking how it would probably be just as distracting to him in Atlanta as it is here in Window Rock.

''You know, I saw a movie on television a while back that was sort of like that,'' Sonny Brokeshoulder is saying. ''Except that the deadly germs were being carried around in a couple of vials in some Russian spy's briefcase.'' As he speaks he is trying to attract the attention of the waitress so that he can get a refill on his coffee. ''I believe he was on a subway or someplace else that was real crowded when he opened up the briefcase and noticed that the vials were leaking. Talk about your suspense. It was great—the look on that guy's face when he saw that puddle . . ."

"You must be watching *old* movies, Sonny . . . nowadays it's mostly illegally imported research animals that spread horrible diseases to innocent suburban-American housewives and their pretty blond children," Push says. "Cute little monkeys are very popular in Hollywood, you know."

Leslie rolls her eyes. "Well, let me see now, laboratory monkeys or Communist spies or carefree love-boat passengers . . . I forget, exactly which of those categories is it that we get the most of out here on the big rez, Sonny?"

"You know, the more we talk about monkeys, the more I think maybe Sonny's notion to get a vet in on this is a good one."

"Oh, come on now . . . *monkeys*?" Leslie looks puzzled.

"Listen, if this thing is viral and is something new, we're going to have to be looking at animals," Push says. "And not just for flea control, either. It's a fact that new viruses emerge because people come into contact with animals that harbor them, usually monkeys or rodents . . ."

"There are not too many monkeys around here," Leslie says. "Lots of rodents, though."

". . . and people come into contact with these animals because there's usually been some change in their habitat—humans have moved into their space or vice versa, or else there's been a warming trend or some other climatic shift."

Just then their waitress appears to refill coffee cups and to take away the lunch dishes. There is the steady din of unintelligible conversation and the discordant clink and clatter of silverware and dishes reverberating through the dining room. As it happens, the tribal council is in session this week, and so the restaurant is busy with Navajo council members and lobbyists as well as with the usual lunch crowd of midlevel tribal employees and just-passing-through tourists.

"What's the story with your medicine man, anyway?" Push asks. "Except for grilling me about my tribal affiliation, he didn't seem to have all that much to say back there. And I had the impression he was maybe even a little put out with us for some reason.''

''Slowtalker? He's a council member and a *hataałii,* and he just happened to walk into my office yesterday at the same time I was making calls asking you guys to come over here this morning. I figured it wouldn't hurt to have a *hataałii* councilman in on this thing from the start. The *hataałii* part is important because I think it's crucial that we keep the traditional medicine people involved in tribal health matters—and the fact that he's also on the tribal council . . . well, you know how political Indian outfits tend to be. I thought it might be good to cover all our bases . . . with the traditionals *and* with the council. And Silas Slowtalker keeps a foot in both those camps.''

''I know I'm probably not being reasonable, but that old man gives me the creeps.'' Leslie shivers as though she's cold. ''He always has. I don't know exactly what it is about him . . . I think it's his eyes, maybe . . . the way he looks at me sometimes. He's spooky, is what he is.''

''It's not just you, Leslie,'' Sonny says. ''I think Silas Slowtalker looks that way at everyone.''

HASHKÉ

As soon as he's gotten back to his office, Push has taken the large Automobile Club Guide to Indian Country map from his desk drawer, unfolded it, and thumbtacked it to the bare wall behind the desk. There in the drawer, too, alongside the thumbtacks, is a clear plastic box containing various colored map pins. He takes the pins out, as well.

As he'd driven the fifty-some-odd miles of mostly bad road between Window Rock and Hashké, Push had struggled to make sense of the situation as he understood it to be. But while he'd been able to picture where Gallup is located in relation to, say, Window Rock easily enough, he'd realized he was not yet familiar enough with the lay of the land on the reservation to visualize clearly even the approximate locations—relative to one another, anyway—of the various smaller communities with their foreign-sounding names.

And so now Push is standing, studying the map of the Navajo

Nation . . . trying hard to focus his thoughts so that he might form a more precise mental image of this place he's come to.

As he traces with his eyes and with his index finger the broken black lines of unpaved roads and the broad purple band that marks the reservation boundaries on the map, Push goes over once again the facts as he understands them: Up to now there have been at least five deaths from an as-yet-undiagnosed cause. Two young people from a single household have died within a few days of one another—he locates the tiny community of Tídáächiid on the eastern edge of the Navajo Reservation and pushes two black-headed pins into the map. A similar death occurred during the same week at Chinle—a pin goes into the site of that medium-sized town at the mouth of Canyon de Chelly. A fourth person died at Shonto—it takes Push several minutes to locate that community to the north of the Hopi boundary. He then inserts a pin at Sheep Springs for Pierce's patient from this morning and backs away to gaze at the map with the five black pins marking each spot where a death has occurred—or, more precisely, marking those spots where the victims may be supposed to have contracted the illness or had first begun to notice the symptoms. Stepping back up to the map, Push takes a single white and four red pins from the box. He puts the red pins in those places where there have been reports of individuals suffering from serious illness marked by symptoms similar to those seen in the victims who've died. Besides the woman from Nazhoni admitted to the hospital at Gallup this morning, there's been one at Wide Ruin, south of Ganado, one from up around Many Farms, and another one way over on the western edge, near Grey Mountain. Both the Wide Ruin and Grey Mountain cases involve Navajo men in their late twenties. The white pin he places in the map at Fort Defiance, just north of Window Rock, to mark the site of the single known recovery.

So, except for Tsosie and Greyeyes, the cases are relatively widespread, geographically. What then is the common factor? *We need to be looking for a* key, Push is thinking—*something that connects these people—something* other *than the fact that they're all Navajo*. Sonny Brokeshoulder had said that neither the Chinle nor the Shonto fatality had undergone an autopsy, but that according to the docs who'd attended them, both had fit the pattern seen in Greyeyes and Tsosie—acute respiratory distress that struck without warning and very rapidly deteriorated into complete respiratory failure. The same could now be said of the Sheep Springs case.

The Grey Mountain patient had been transported to the border town of Flagstaff for treatment and Push is confident that they'd have done X rays and lab work there. At lunch, Sonny had promised to get on the phone as soon as he got back to his office and to have copies sent over of any X rays and the results of whatever other tests they might have run at Flag.

Push sits down at the desk. He arranges his notes and turns to look up once more at the map with its colored pins. He sighs, and then he reaches for the telephone.

It's five o'clock and Push Foster is sprawled awkwardly across the heavy wood-framed chair which, along with the small writing table and the narrow single bed and chest of drawers fashioned from the same wood in the same heavy pattern, makes up the furnishings of the tiny bachelor-quarters room at the Hashké Indian Hospital.

He's been on the telephone for nearly three hours straight—first in his office and now in his room. During that time he's spoken with various officials at the Departments of Public Health in Albuquerque and in Phoenix; with the Office of Public Information of the U.S. Army Medical Research Institute of Infectious Diseases at Fort Detrick, Maryland; with authorities at the Centers for Disease Control in Atlanta; and twice with Sonny Brokeshoulder at his office in Window Rock. The conversations with Sonny have been to keep his friend up to date on all that's transpired during the other calls.

More than just connections, Push has friends at the Centers for Disease Control. He knows exactly with whom to speak, and how to get through to them. His concerns very quickly become their concerns.

The onset of this disease is remarkably rapid, Push explains, with little or no warning . . . and respiratory symptoms predominate all others. That's scary enough, but add to that the CDC's and the World Health Organization's own estimates that in the United States deaths from unexplained respiratory disease number anywhere from 50,000 to 150,000 people each year, and a real sense of urgency builds. The mere suggestion that some unknown infection may be emerging to boost significantly an already sizable number of fatalities is just the sort of thing that gets the attention of the docs in Atlanta. They will be anxiously awaiting blood and tissue samples and anything else Push can gather up and overnight to the labs. They'll get right on it. They're taking this very seriously.

The CDC not only wants to be kept informed of any and all developments—they're also prepared to send a team out as soon as Push and the others are ready to make an official request for on-site assistance.

Officials in Albuquerque have indicated that they are prepared to offer whatever assistance they can—it is clear to Push that the lab results, which revealed no evidence of bacterial infection, have surprised the New Mexico authorities as much as they have surprised Ed Pierce and the others. Albuquerque listens as Push speculates on the possibility that if what they're seeing isn't bacterial—isn't plague—then it might well be viral or, worse still in some respects, it might be something environmental: some toxic chemical . . . perhaps an accidental spill or release involving biohazardous material. Albuquerque listens, but they're not pleased with the direction of the conversation. The mere mention of biohazardous materials is enough to cause great concern in local and state government offices over the possibility of stirring up alarm in the general public. As much as anything, Push thinks, Albuquerque is worried about the very real prospect of any such speculation getting out to the media and the effect it would have, particularly on the state's tourist economy.

The reaction from Phoenix is one of considerably less concern. As much as anything, the response seems to be: *Ten people getting sick can't be all* that *serious. . . . And you say the outbreak is confined strictly to the Navajo Reservation? Well then, you all just be sure and let us know if it seems to be spreading among the rest of the population. Thank you very much.*

Push has long heard rumors about the research conducted at the Army's Medical Research Institute of Infectious Diseases in Maryland. And in spite of a public-information officer whose sole function it is to persuade the public otherwise, Push is aware that the military has for decades been involved with biological and chemical warfare investigations and that the people at Fort Detrick are probably as up-to-date as anyone in the country when it comes to germ research.

"Any chance your people at USAMRIID have been conducting tests upwind of Four Corners?" He knows enough to pronounce the institute's acronym "You-Sam-Rid."

"Certainly not!" he's told. "The Army isn't involved with that sort of thing any longer—that research officially ended forty years ago!"

"Well, sure, *officially*—but there *have* been incidents . . . let's not forget about Skull Valley." Push is referring to secret nerve-gas tests in Utah in the late sixties that went terribly wrong and killed something like six thousand sheep. "And aren't there some old Cold War–era weapons-storage facilities located out east of Gallup, New Mexico? At the Fort Wingate Depot?"

"Well, yes and no . . . there are a number of underground storage bunkers at that location—that information is not classified. . . ."

"Couldn't there be some hazardous gases out there? Something leaking, maybe?"

"Those bunkers are for the storage of inert chemical materials only, the government's *official* position has always been that no lethal or, for that matter, even dangerous, biological agents have ever been stored or tested at that site." It sounds to Push as if the voice on the other end of the line has made a point to stress the word *official*.

"I see. So then am I hearing that it is *possible* that what we're seeing is the result of an accidental spill or release . . . of some volatile chemical agent?"

"No, absolutely not . . . it's unthinkable even to consider such a thing," the voice says. "And besides, any weapons-grade material of that kind—if there ever *were* any weapons of that kind, and I'm not saying there were—would most certainly be contained and stored safely inert and under constant monitoring."

Still, authorities at USAMRIID are concerned enough with what Push is saying to agree to check into the matter and get back to him.

• • •

When Priscilla Yazzie answers the phone at Window Rock, her voice sounds strained. ''This is the third time you've called since lunch, Dr. Foster. And besides that, every one of you guys looked very nervous when you left out of here today,'' she says. ''I don't mind telling you that I didn't like seein' that one little bit. Now I know for sure that this thing's real bad news. Why, Sonny even had me stick a big map of the reservation up on the wall in his office . . . and then he spent twenty minutes in there starin' at that map and puttin' big dots at all the places where there has been cases of the sickness.''

''Now, Priscilla, don't you go reading too much into all this . . . it may not be nearly as bad as it seems. I've got a map up in my office, too—it makes it easier for us to talk about it when we can both be looking at the big picture at the same time, you know.''

''Yeah? Well, I *hope* it's not as bad as it seems. Anyway, Sonny's been askin' about every two minutes if you've called again,'' she says. ''I don't see why you two would be talking so much about it if it wasn't as bad as it seems, but I better go on and buzz him for you now.''

Push fills his friend in on his conversations with the people at USAMRIID and the CDC.

''And you know, I don't mean to sound cynical, but it seemed to me like Phoenix was saying that as long as this thing stays up here on the reservation then it isn't all that big a deal, Sonny. It's clear that they don't appreciate the gravity of this situation. And I hate to be the one to come right out and say it, but the way these things usually go, it's likely to take one or two white people getting sick and dying to get the state government's full attention.

''So far I've had the most helpful response from the CDC,'' he continues. ''That's no surprise, of course—since this is right up their alley. On the other hand, I *did* have to remind them that this is not Atlanta—point out that there just aren't a whole lot of toxicology labs in Window Rock.

''And then the Fort Wingate angle is nagging at me, Sonny. USAMRIID doesn't even want to hear talk about a possible connection, of course—but, man, if there's even a remote chance that there's been some kind of an accident out there at the Army depot, or that some top-secret biological experiment has gone wrong . . .'' and his voice trails off.

Sonny says that he's spoken directly with the president of the Navajo Nation about the situation and tells Push that it looks like they can expect good cooperation from that office.

"You know the way these gossipy Indians are," Sonny says. "Now the word's all over the place that the Greyeyes and Tsosie families believe this is ghost sickness. We're going to have to get some medicine people to work on this as soon as we can—to help keep calm out there among the traditional people—and I'm talking about more than just Silas Slowtalker, too."

"Do you think the president will go along with that, Sonny? I mean, getting traditional people to work with us?"

"I feel pretty sure I can get him to go along with it. Hell, I just need to make him think it was his idea, is all." He laughs. "Did you know that he has a singer on his staff? A medicine man whose full-time job it is just to guard his office against witches? This is not Washington, D.C., you know—but this is how things work up here . . . we Navajo Indians are just real serious when it comes to witches."

Sonny tells Push that there's been a report of yet another presumptive case, this one at Tuba City. "They're watching it closely and will keep me posted." He then says that he's planning to drive up to the Second Mesa village of Mishongnovi. Even though there have been no reports of illness on the Hopi Reservation, Sonny wants to talk with a village elder there.

"Why don't you be waiting there at the Cross Canyon turnoff tomorrow at nine-thirty," he says. "Then you can follow me down to the Kinlichee Chapter House at Ganado and we can leave your vehicle and drive up to Hopi together. I'm thinking that Clifford Lomaquaptewa may have some notions about all this stuff. He's surprised me before and I have a hunch he might just do so again.

"Besides, it's about time you had a look around Hopi—I figure you're about due for some of the strong power that place puts off . . . or at least you could maybe get you some piki bread." He tries to make his voice sound light. "Anyway, you should try to get yourself a good night's sleep—we'll probably have to traipse all over those Hopi mesas to locate my old friend."

After he hangs up, Push washes his face and then sits on the edge of the bed. He reaches for the telephone and dials one more number. The voice he had hoped to hear answers on the third ring:

"Leslie? Hi, this is Push Foster."

"Well, hey, Push . . . I was hoping you'd call."

Push feels an odd tightening in his stomach. "Why? Don't tell me you've got people getting sick in your area now?"

"No, no, nothing's happening here yet. . . . I was just eager to hear what the people in Atlanta had to say, is all."

Push fills Leslie in on what's transpired in his conversations with state Public Health officials and with USAMRIID and the CDC. And he tells her about the new case at Tuba City and that he and Sonny are driving up to Second Mesa tomorrow morning to talk with a Hopi headman that Sonny knows.

"That would be Clifford Lomaquaptewa," Leslie says. "He's an important person up here . . . and a very nice man, too. On top of which, his wife is a real hoot—I hope you get to meet Mary Esther."

"Oh yeah? Well say, maybe you'd like to come along with us," Push says. "We could stop by Keams Canyon and pick you up. . . ."

"Afraid I couldn't get away, Push. I've got the place pretty much to myself tomorrow—this is the time of year when several of the clans around here go out to gather eaglets to raise ceremonially for use in the Home Dances that are held later on in the summer. It's a very important religious event and the people are expected to participate. Anyway, once you've been out here awhile, you'll understand that there are certain times when your nursing help simply doesn't show up. It's a strict cultural and religious thing with the Hopi. I don't think the Navajo are quite so strict.

"But you guys could still stop by here tomorrow. You'll be going right past on your way up to Mishongnovi, and I'd like to show you where I work . . . if you have time, that is. . . ."

"Sounds like a plan to me. I'm supposed to meet Sonny at the Cross Canyon turnoff at nine-thirty—and I guess that's what, maybe an hour from Keams?"

"About that."

"Good . . . then I guess I'll see you in the morning."

When he hangs up the phone, Push goes into the bathroom and looks at his face in the mirror over the sink. The smile he sees there looks almost silly.

So here he is, smack-dab in the middle of what's looking more and more like a bona fide medical crisis, and still he can't help feeling for all the world like a schoolboy with a crush.

He makes a somber face: "Get it on your mind, Foster," he says. And he says it out loud.

LÓKÁAHNTEEL

"I kind of figured that was your beat-up old truck the minute I saw it parked out front when I drove in to work yesterday morning." Sonny is looking at Push Foster's 1972 Chevy pickup with exaggerated distaste.

"I don't know, man, but it seems to me like you rich Oklahoma Indians ought to be raking in enough of those oil-and-gas-lease royalties the Great White Father sends you every month that you could at least afford to get yourselves a new vehicle once in a while. Important tribal big-bellies like me shouldn't have to take a chance on being spotted hanging around with someone who drives a smoke-belching old reservation heap like that, you know."

Rolling his eyes in exasperation, Push looks over at his friend. Sonny had waited while Push locked his truck and climbed in the front passenger-side door of the shiny white Dodge Crew-Cab with the Great Seal of the Navajo Nation decals on the doors.

"Hold on there," Push says. "Seems to me it was you who

advised in the first place that I not show up out here driving some kind of fancy big-city car. I'd have thought you'd be proud to see I had enough sense to get something that generally starts in the morning and which I wouldn't miss too much if it got swallowed up in one of these potholes. . . .''

''Well sure, I said you shouldn't ought to show up the local populace by cruising around in some little red sports car, but I didn't mean for you to add to the 'Indian clunker' stereotype with that rusted-out twenty-year-old piece of junk, either.'' Sonny is smiling broadly.

''That is a perfectly good vehicle—especially for driving on these washboards you call roads. Besides, it's paid for. And while we're on the subject, I can't figure where you get off lecturing me about *stereotypes*.'' Push reaches out to tug playfully on one of Sonny's braids. ''The way I see it, all you need now is a couple of turkey feathers sticking up out of your head, maybe a dab or two of war paint, and to let out one of those bloodcurdling redskin hollers you were so famous for back at school and you'd be scaring all the tourists away.

''Seriously now, the last time I saw you, Brokeshoulder, you were as clean-cut as any college-educated BIA drone could be . . . what's the story behind the braids, anyhow?''

Sonny grins. ''Traditional hairdo . . . what can I tell you?''

''*Traditional?* I don't generally associate braids with the Navajo.''

''Yeah? Well, I just can't see myself giving in to the scab-headed buzz-cut look that so many of the men our age around here seem to favor. Not that they approve of me all that much, mind you. Didn't you hear Silas Slowtalker yesterday? When he was calling me *Tsii'yishbizhii*? He was referring to the fact that I wear braids. Handing out nicknames is almost a passion with Navajo people, you know. Like at lunch the other day? When Josephine Manygoats, the chubby woman who showed us to our table, called you *Tółí*? That was her way of admiring your fair-skinned complexion. In fact, I got the feeling Josephine thought you were about as pretty as anything she's seen around here for a while and was flirting with you about as hard as she dared.''

''Not hardly.'' Push laughs.

''And speaking of flirting,'' Sonny presses on, ''I'd say it's fairly clear that our Doc Leslie considers you to be kind of a pretty-boy, too,'' and Sonny is grinning even more now at Push, who can feel himself blushing.

Sonny reaches across the cab of the truck to point toward Push's head. ''But since you brought up the subject of hair, I expect you may also have noticed that mine's still got most of its naturally handsome dark color while yours seems to be turning white—why, it's almost as though you're becoming some kind of elder or something.''

''I'll have you know that my hair is a distinguished-looking salt-and-pepper gray—I am not, after all, one of those hang-around-the-powwow types who dye their hair that ungodly-looking shoe-polish black. To be perfectly honest, I have never cared all that much what my hair turns, just as long as it doesn't turn *loose*.

''I don't know, but it looks to me like you've been out here maybe just a little too long and that you're starting to go back to the blanket, Sonny. Or maybe you've been watching too much TV. . . . I'll bet you've been watching that *Dances with Wolves* movie over and over on your video machine.'' Push slaps his thigh with a loud smack. ''Damn, that's it, isn't it? You're pulling a Wind-in-His-Hair, aren't you? Why, I wouldn't be surprised to hear you start grunting *'How!'* and *'Ugh!'* and talking pidgin English. . . .''

''Doggone it, Foster, you know good and well I am not allowed to discuss my traditional hairstyle or my stoic mannerisms.'' Sonny's face takes on a hurt look. ''And you know I can't reveal secret Navajo religious rituals—especially not to some Oklahoma half-breed like you.''

And now as they drive west out of Ganado—past the turnoff to Hubbell Trading Post and through landscape that changes from desolate sandhills to high desert plains within a half-dozen miles—both men are quiet. The good-natured banter has been edged with an unspoken nervousness, and both are conscious of a pall that hangs over them.

''So what do we do now, Pushmataha?'' Sonny asks, his voice more sober than Push recalls ever having heard it. ''I mean, where do we start? How do we even begin to look for the needle in such an enormous haystack?'' And he makes a sweeping motion with his hand across the vast landscape through which they are passing.

''There's just not a whole lot we *can* do at this point, Sonny . . .

the blood and tissue samples are on their way to Atlanta, but it's going to take some time now. Besides, you're the one who's insisting that we talk to traditional healers. . . . I'm not sure that this Hopi medicine man we're going to see can add all that much, but I'm trying to keep an open mind."

"We have to take into account these people's views on what's happening. I mean, I've seen things since I've been out here that I can't even begin to explain, Push. . . . If I've learned anything, it's that there's just a whole lot of stuff these folks know that we didn't hear about back in medical school."

"I know you're right," Push says. "And while the guys with the microscopes are doing their thing in the labs, we have to keep looking for anything that's common to the people who've come down with this sickness. There's got to be a thread, you know. The first consideration in infectious-disease research is, Is it something new? Does a problem actually exist? So far, we've seen fewer than a dozen cases. What we have to do is get together a detailed profile of the victims *and* the survivors that takes into account the obvious factors—age, sex, previous health, lifestyles, eating habits, occupations . . ."

"We already have a lot of that basic information, but to be thorough we'll have to talk to family members and friends of the victims, and that's going to be a real problem," Sonny says. "At least when it comes to those who've died, it is—a Navajo does not speak about the dead, period. And it's a terrible thing to ask him to do so."

"Well, we're going to have to try and find a way around that particular taboo, Sonny. Because the next thing we'll need to do is to determine where and when and the circumstances under which those stricken first displayed symptoms. It's the only way we'll even begin to establish what elements of commonality exist.

"And I don't think we should rule out some kind of government screw-up," Push says. "A leak from some biological-weapon-storage facility or some kind of test gone haywire . . . just because the public-information officer at USAMRIID denies it doesn't mean it hasn't happened. Hell, the very fact there is a denial is pretty good evidence that they're concerned it *might* have happened!"

''But doesn't the fact that what we're seeing is so widespread across the reservation make the possibility of that less likely?'' Sonny says.

''You're probably right . . . but we have to keep every possibility in mind,'' Push says.

''Jesus . . . it's depressing to think of all the possibilities, Push.''

''And there are some that haven't even occurred to us yet. And if this turns into an epidemic we'll need all the help we can get. And from whatever source we can get it, too,'' and Push sighs.

''So, I guess we may as well talk to a Hopi medicine man while we wait to hear something back from Atlanta . . . otherwise we'll just end up sitting around and talking ourselves into thinking this one could be the big one—the Doomsday Bug.''

''Oh, man, don't even talk like that, Push.''

''There are people a whole lot smarter than either one of us who're predicting that it's going to come along one day, Sonny. There are already some real gruesome bugs out there—AIDS, Ebola, Marburg and Lassa fevers. . . . And the doomsayers will be quick to tell you it's just a matter of time before some new one shows up that'll make all the others look like a walk in the park. . . .''

And again, both men are quiet for the next several miles—each deep in his own thoughts.

The radio in Sonny's truck is tuned to the AM superstation that broadcasts out of Window Rock and reaches clear across the reservation. In the Navajo language, radio is called ''Wind That Speaks,'' and this particular station plays an odd mix of traditional Navajo songs and ''Hit-Kickin' Country Music'' punctuated by public-service announcements of Chapter House meetings and rodeo results and news of local interest reported on the half hour in both Navajo and English. Just now there is an announcement for a Memorial Day Weekend concert scheduled to be held at Red Rock State Park just east of Gallup. Typically, the announcement ends with a caution not to drink and drive.

And soon Sonny is bobbing his head and tapping his hand on the steering wheel in time to the sound of the song that is playing.

''You know, I still prefer the real country music . . . these new kid singers that are so popular nowadays, about all they know how to do are those silly line dances and cowboy rap songs.'' Sonny spits out the window in feigned disgust. ''Real cowboys don't line dance, you know.''

''How is it you're talking cowboy this and cowboy that so much when all along I've been thinking that you were an Indian? . . .''

''What? You don't think Indians make good cowboys? And I suppose you think only white people can dance? Why, I saw a mimeographed notice taped to the door at the FedMart store just the other day announcing that somebody's going to be giving country-and-western dance lessons at the Senior Citizens Center over at Many Farms. I mean, honestly, can't you just picture that, Push? Two rows of wrinkledy little Navajo grandmothers lined up facing each other across the room, tapping their tennis-shoed toes to tape-recorded guitar music and trying to learn how to do some kind of silly line dance steps, for godsake?''

Sonny has just steered around a curve and is heading down a long grade. He begins to slow the truck.

''This is the Keams Canyon turnoff—at the bottom of this hill,'' he says. ''I understand you made a date to stop at the hospital to check in with Dr. Leslie Blair.'' He looks across at Push and winks. ''Oh, don't act all embarrassed, I talked to her last evening and she bragged that you'd called. I was hoping to get her to get in touch with as many of her sources as she could manage this morning—see if maybe anybody's heard anything new about our illness or if there have been any unusual incidents that haven't been reported yet . . . you know, medical business.''

KEAMS CANYON

Push and Sonny find Leslie Blair in her office in the yellow-block building across the street from the hospital.

''I've gone over files until I don't think I can look at another one.'' She smiles, but she is clearly exasperated. ''There's nothing I can find to make me think we've had anything here over the past few months like what you've been seeing. I did come across a couple of cases of respiratory failure, but there's no apparent connection between the two and both had histories of lung disorders. Nothing abrupt about the onset—nothing remarkable, at all.''

''Well, thanks for checking, anyway. We're on our way up to Second Mesa,'' Sonny says.

''That's what Push said. What makes you think Clifford even has a notion that anything's happening, Sonny?'' Leslie asks. ''And that if he does, he'll talk about it?''

''I'd be surprised if Clifford *didn't* know what's happening. And you have to remember that Clifford is Hopi. And a Hopi can't hardly contain himself if he thinks there's a chance he can show up a Navajo if he thinks he maybe knows something more about a subject.

"Besides, that's why I'm taking Push along. Clifford will be especially eager to show off in front of a civilized Indian . . . especially one who's new to the area."

Leslie smiles up at Push. "And you mean to say you've been friends with this guy for several years?"

"What can I tell you?" Push is grinning. And then he says: "You won't change your mind? Take the afternoon off and ride along with us?"

"No, it's just me today. The minute I'd leave, there'd sure enough be some emergency. Yesterday this place was deserted. We had one drop-in at the clinic. Maybe you know her, Sonny—an archeologist who's excavating up north of here? Vogel's her name, Sabine Vogel? . . ."

"I know *of* her—at least I've heard talk of a yellow-haired digger up around Piñon."

"That's her. Nice woman. Came by to see if I could prescribe something for allergies—complaining of eye irritation and headaches and said she felt she was developing a sensitivity to juniper pollen."

"Not the best malady to have in this part of the country . . . lots of juniper."

"No . . . no, it isn't. We had quite a long visit. I've always been interested in the kind of work she's doing out there. She invited me to come out and see the dig on Sunday—drew me a map to the site. Said her partner would be away for a few days and that she'd love an opportunity to have another woman to talk to and to show around.

"I was telling her how last year there was that crew working down near Tolani Lake—you remember, Sonny? And that three of them contracted bubonic plague. I told her to be careful and to stay away from any dead animals that might have fleas—rabbits or prairie dogs."

"Plague is practically endemic to this part of the country, Push," Sonny explains. "It's almost a permanent disease."

"I can't help thinking that if viral diseases can be species-specific, why not race-specific?" Leslie is tapping the end of her pencil on her desk. "We know that there are illnesses that are much more prevalent among certain races or ethnic groups, and between genders—why not a virus that only affects, say, Indian people? Or more specifically yet, *Navajo* people?''

''I think there's way too much genetic mixing for that, Leslie,'' Push says. ''At least in this country. Let's face it, no matter how proud we all might be of whatever ethnic gene pool we've sprung from, it's not likely that there are many full-blood anything's left. So whatever gene it is that might be affected by a specific virus in one person could just as well be that one gene that's been passed down by crazy old Uncle Willard . . . . the one that everyone in the family tries to keep hidden away in the broom closet.

''No, I think it's much more likely that we can expect to see connections having to do with lifestyle than we are to purely genetic factors.''

''Either way,'' Leslie says. ''I'm betting we're in for a period of isolation around here—a fear of native people, anyway. At least as long as the only people getting sick are Indians.''

And with that, Leslie Blair leaps to her feet, nearly upsetting her chair.

''Oedipus! Goddamn it . . . You big shit!'' she cries out as she rushes around her desk and toward the open window in the wall directly behind her visitors. ''Get that nasty thing out of here!''

''Jesus, Leslie!'' It's Sonny Brokeshoulder who cries out this time. ''You nearly caused me to stroke out!'' And so saying, he makes a dramatic gesture of clutching his chest as he turns to see that the woman is shooing a large gray cat off the windowsill. There is a mouse dangling from its jaws and it is plain that the mouse is still alive.

''Sorry, guys. I'm not some helpless female who faints at the sight of a mouse, for godsake, but the sound of Oedipus crunching on bones . . . I mean, *ugh*! That goddamned cat knows better than to be bringing his victims in here. . . .'' And she closes the window sharply.

''You know, Leslie''—Sonny is grinning widely at her obvious embarrassment—''seeing your cat chomping down on that mouse reminds me of just how hungry I am. Do they still pass out those good free lunches over at the cafeteria?''

''Oh, *Sonny*!'' She makes a face. ''I suppose as long as I'll claim you as my guest, they do.'' Leslie checks her watch. ''It's almost eleven-thirty and they normally serve lunch from eleven to one or so.''

"Oh man, Push, you have *got* to try the meat loaf they fix over there. . . ." Sonny Brokeshoulder is rubbing his hands together briskly as the three walk down the hall toward the central stairway.

"Meat loaf?" Push makes a face at Leslie Blair, who has by now recovered her composure and is smiling at Sonny's antics. "And *institutional* meat loaf, at that? Oh well, I suppose this is about as good a day as any other to die."

And Push winks at Leslie: "That's an old Indian saying, you know—the one about it being a good day to die . . ."

MISHONGNOVI

The smell is acrid and strong—overpowering, nearly—in the midafternoon heat.

"*Whew* . . . Man, it's like there's a sewer backed up or something." Push Foster is following Sonny Brokeshoulder up a steep, narrow path that winds its way toward the village of Mishongnovi, an ancient community perched—precariously, Push thinks—on the southernmost tip of Second Mesa, the middle of the three Hopi mesas that point, fingerlike, south from the southern edge of Black Mesa. Little more than a goat track, really, the entire path is strewn with trash—aluminum cans and plastic two-liter bottles, and tattered plastic sacks and candy wrappers, and corncobs and the dried and shriveled rinds of rotting fruit.

"No sewers *to* back up around here. I'd say it's more likely we're walking where the women dump their chamber pots every morning." Sonny stops and turns to look out over the road below the mesa, far down to where the truck is parked. He is breathing rapidly from the exertion of the climb and, taking a white handkerchief from his hip pocket, wipes a trickle of sweat from his temple.

"Of course, they wouldn't call them chamber pots—heck, I don't even know where *I* heard of that term—more than likely they use old coffee cans. Probably they use the big three-pounder-sized cans . . . Hills Brothers, I'd guess, it being the most popular brand around here."

Sonny Brokeshoulder likes to conjecture. When he gets an image in his head, it seems he often can't let it go until he's made up a story to go along with it.

"You know, when the white guys first started coming around here they wrote down in their journals how these Hopis were so uncivilized that when nature called they'd just stop whatever they were doing at the time and do their business right then and there. Of course, they couldn't say that about the Navajo. . . . Navajo people know good and well that witches will use such stuff against you if they get the chance. That's how come we Navajo go way off to hide whenever we feel the urge. I guess you civilized Indians just nearly have to have a flush toilet right inside your house, huh?" And Sonny laughs. "Keeps the witches away, does it?

"Anyway, there's probably some real long Hopi word for those cans they pee in." His breathing comes slower now—normal, almost. "I mean, they wouldn't just come right out and call them coffee cans.

"A Navajo would say *bii' da'jilizhí* . . . which means 'night jar.' Funny I should know that, don't you think? When there's so much of the language that would be a lot more useful to me that I don't know." He shakes his head. "But anyway, I haven't got a clue what the Hopi call them. I'll have to look into it," he says, and starts back up the path.

"Look into the *word,* that is . . ." Sonny stops and turns to grin broadly at his friend. "I'm not about to look into one of those coffee cans."

Stepping onto the rocky escarpment that rises six hundred feet above the surrounding plateau, the two men stand close up beside the edge, catching their breath for a long moment and gazing out across the way they have come, across the tortuous, dry, inhospitable landscape that stretches now far beneath them—stretches south and west to the dark purple outline of the mysterious San Francisco peaks that rise up north of

Flagstaff. The mountains that the Hopi call *Nuvatukyaovi*—and that the Hopi gods call home. Push is thinking how, from the highway in the valley below, it is an easy thing to look up at this spot where they are now standing and to see only rock—how even if one is consciously looking for signs of this village, it is easy to miss seeing, so indistinguishable are the broken-stone-and-mud dwellings at this place from the rugged mesa upon which they sit perched.

A single raven scolds the two men as it hovers beside them—gracefully, lazily riding the thermal wave high above the ground below yet precisely on a level with their heads where they now stand looking out. Push can see clearly the stark glint of yellow eyes as the large black bird cocks its head to gaze directly at him. He nods as though in greeting and is surprised by the immediate flush of awkward embarrassment that he feels at having done so.

Push is remembering a fall day many years ago. Remembering walking with his friend in wooded country through scrub oak with leaves of burning red and yellow. Remembering that the air that day was sharp and cold . . . that he and Sonny were carrying single-shot .22-caliber rifles.

"Sonny, do you remember back when we used to go squirrel and rabbit hunting down at Newcastle?"

"Sure . . . down along the South Canadian river bottom on your family's allotment," Sonny says. "In the fall of the year . . . September and October . . . what was it that they called them? Those Choctaw months, I mean?"

"September is *Hvsh Hopóni*—'Cooking month.' " Push realizes that he hasn't thought of these things for a long time now. "And October, I think, is Little Hunger month—yeah, that's it, *Chvfiskóno*—'Little Hunger.' "

"I used to wonder how come you never learned to talk Choctaw, Push. I mean, all I ever remember hearing you or any of your people say were a couple of greetings and maybe a word or two."

"Not many people left in Oklahoma who remember the language, I don't think—anyway, nobody in my family could speak more than a phrase or two. The only reason I know the names of those months is because the words were written on the calendars that the chief sent to tribal members every year and that my grandmother used to have hanging in the kitchen. Hell, it ought to tell you something when the Principal Chief of the Choctaw Nation of Oklahoma doesn't even speak Choctaw."

"Is that a fact?"

"Bingo parlors and tax-free cigarette sales . . . that's pretty much taken the place of traditional dances and the stickball games and language in Oklahoma. I was in Mississippi once. Went there to see the original homeland—the cave mound at *Nanih Waiya* where the Choctaw people and their little brothers, the Chickasaw, are said to have emerged into this world. I wanted to see Dancing Rabbit Creek, where the famous treaty was signed by the chiefs and headmen—including, by the way, some of my own blood relatives. That was the treaty that gave the good land to the white folks in exchange for some wasteland that nobody else was interested in. But of course that was before they found oil, you understand.

"Anyway, the Mississippi Band of Choctaw are descendants of the ones who hid out and wouldn't remove to Oklahoma in the 1830s. It was something to see—those Mississippi Chocs, I mean—like how they still play the old stickball game . . . *Ishtaboli*, it's called . . . and I'm talking a rough-assed game, too. They play barefoot and wear no pads or protective gear of any sort, and on top of which they're running up and down the field swinging these three-foot-long hickory sticks in each hand! I understand that in the old days it wasn't all that unusual for a player to sometimes get badly injured or killed even. I'm serious when I tell you they had girls' teams there that would make the NFL look like a bunch of pantywaists."

Push is rubbing his hand across his chin and staring out across the barren landscape as he recalls the green and swampy forests that grew along the Pearl River valley near Philadelphia, Mississippi.

"But you know, as much as anything else, I can still remember how wonderful it seemed to me that the Mississippi Band all seemed to speak the old Choctaw language, Sonny. Even the little kids . . ."

Both men are quiet for a long while. Then Sonny says: "Of course, mostly I remember how the squirrels and rabbits we were hunting somehow always seemed to know when we were coming, and how your relatives would laugh whenever we complained about how frustrating it was that we never could manage to hit anything.''

''My Aunt Boolah said it was one of the Little People who kept on messing with us. Remember? She said it was the one they call Thrower.''

''Yeah, that's right, isn't it? You know, I'd completely forgotten that's what she said . . . that it was one of the Little People that kept scaring off the critters. The Little People that the old-time Choctaws say live in the woods and pester people.'' Sonny hasn't thought about such things in many years, and now the memories come flooding back quickly, triggering connections that haven't occurred to him until now.

''You know, the Hopis have a Kachina that they call Thrower—*Ñüi'tiwa* is the Hopi name for him, I believe. And he's kind of a scamp, too—seems like the main thing he does, he goes running around the crowd of onlookers at the dances handing out cooking pots to the village women in exchange for 'favors' . . . you know, he pretends to copulate with them, dog-style, right on the spot.'' He laughs. ''Seems like the women don't mind much all this foolishness going on, either, and the people watching sure enough get a big kick out of it—hollering and laughing.

''And we Navajo have something kind of like it, too—except we don't call it Thrower. We say *Be'gochidi* . . . and we say he usually goes around invisible, but if he wants to he can shape-shift into just about anything he takes a notion to be. You know, like some animal or a tree or a bush or something. And if *Be'gochidi* decides to take a human form, he usually appears with blond hair and blue eyes—dressed up like a woman. He's a real pest, too. Like, he'll sometimes sneak up on a guy when he's out hunting? And right when the guy's getting ready to shoot a deer or whatever it is he's after, old *Be'gochidi* will reach around from behind and grab the hunter by his testicles and holler out some kind of nonsense real loud. . . . Of course, it's not all that surprising that this tactic would scare the guy half to death—just naturally cause him to miss whatever it is he's aiming to shoot.''

Sonny smiles and shakes his head. ''And they say he'll sometimes pull the same sort of stunt on couples when they're in the middle of having sex—you know, grab the guy by his testicles and make this real loud noise.'' Sonny laughs. ''That'd be pretty distracting, don't you think?''

''I don't know about either one of those characters,'' Push says. ''But I figure you'd need to be a full-blood Navajo or at least about half Hopi to appreciate the humor in having something like that happen to you, huh? Kind of makes Aunt Boolah's Little People seem pretty tame, just tossing pebbles and twigs at folks.'' Push is laughing.

''You know, you're pretty lucky, now that I think about it. . . . I mean, it's a whole lot harder to keep up with Navajo and Hopi ways than it is with the ways of you city Indians—wouldn't you agree, Pushmataha?''

Push is smiling.

''Did I ever tell you that Aunt Boolah died a few years ago, Sonny? I guess she went sort of batty there toward the end of her life. Folks at home say she got to where she was telling everyone that there was somebody living up in her attic . . . pounding on the ceiling at night and kicking the walls so that she never could get any sleep. They say she made her boys go up there with flashlights several times even and check it out. They never did find anything. . . .''

''Maybe it was her Little People trying to tell her something.'' Sonny says this with respect. ''Maybe it was old Thrower.''

''Maybe so . . .''

A quarter-mile to the south a small white airplane drones past—clearly flying below the height where the two men stand and the raven hangs suspended, the single-engine plane sounding sputtery and looking for all the world to Push as though it is moving far too slowly to stay aloft—he thinks even that it may, at any moment, fall from the sky.

And Push tries hard not to think about the plane falling to the earth—from the time that he was a small boy he has always felt that to anticipate problems is to cause them . . . believed that thoughts—like words—are extremely powerful. Believed that, just as words are powerful enough to bring whatever it is you voice, negative thoughts can also cause dreadful things to happen. This in spite of his education in the sciences, where such ideas might seem primitive at best, foolish at worst.

In fact the plane does not fall from the sky. Not this time, anyway, and Push is relieved that he has not caused it to fall by imagining it so—that he has kept the flying machine aloft . . . kept the world spinning with the power of his mind.

Still, it seems awkward and out of place, the small white airplane does—in stark contrast to the natural grace of the shining black bird as it drifts and turns noiselessly—now around and down . . . now climbing high above the ancient, timeless Hopi landscape. The raven pursuing in silence its way according to some ancient blood sense . . . the sputtering flying machine following doggedly the narrow black ribbon of asphalt highway, east toward Keams Canyon and, pursued far enough he thinks, on toward Window Rock and Gallup and beyond.

And just then the raven strokes its wings powerfully and gracefully against the still, hot air to climb toward the next invisible thermal plateau and then to drift lazily down again—and to Push's ear the sound of the bird's feathers on air seems remarkably loud against the silent, empty backdrop of the startlingly bright, cloud-empty sky.

Push's gaze cannot help but follow the slow-motion movement of the shining black creature and at first he believes it is his imagination when he hears a voice. And then he is startled—he's astonished, actually—to hear the words he has thought himself only imagining being spoken aloud, and he realizes that the voice is that of Sonny Brokeshoulder, and that he is speaking to the raven:

"Hey, *Be'gochidi,*" Sonny is saying. "Listen to me: I bring you greetings, you clever old trickster . . . you coyote. I was wondering why you would come right out and show yourself to us like this."

Push is grinning at Sonny's demeanor. His old friend is really getting into talking to the bird, he thinks—and getting into it in a voice that is uncharacteristically loud and overly dramatic. And it is even more uncharacteristic of him that he is making exaggeratedly broad and swooping gestures with his arms in the manner of some grand orator.

"We see that you've chosen to take the shape of a handsome black bird on this particular day. And we're wondering, have you come here to pester us? Because if you have, I want you to remember this: We are not hunters. So if it's in your mind to sneak up and grab somebody by their private parts, I'd just like to ask that you make sure it's that other fellow over there," and Sonny motions toward Push. "He may not look like it, but he used to be about halfway famous as a hunter of small game animals back in Oklahoma when he was a much younger man. Back before he got so fat and lazy, that is. But then I imagine you probably already know all about that."

And stepping back, away from the edge of the precipice, Sonny looks over at Push. "Well, son-of-a-gun, did I really say all that?" he asks, a sheepish grin spreading across his face. And both men are chuckling as they turn from the mesa's ragged edge and move on toward the cluster of small one- and two-storied mud-and-stone dwellings that make up the Hopi village.

Push is surprised to see that there are televisions in this village. He's surprised, that is, to see that there are bent and awkward-looking television antennas stabbing up into the clear sky from the roofs of several of the mud houses when, at the same time, there don't seem to be any electric power lines. It's hot and dusty here and there's not a breath of moving air and little immediate life to be seen. Doors stand open and there is the low drone of sporadic, unintelligible conversation and a steady, far-off, and so muffled chatter of children playing. Leaning against a wall beside one of the doors there is a weathered board upon which a sun-faded, crudely hand-painted sign announces that, inside this place, there is—or perhaps, are—Potterys for Sale.

Two scruffy-looking, rib-skinny dogs are passing time by snapping halfheartedly at buzzing flies and, with only slightly more enthusiasm, at one another in the tiny quadrangular plaza around which the houses of this village are situated. Two small, half-naked boys of three or four years who have been playing in the dust alongside a sunburned wall near to where the dogs are stop their game to stare with black, limpid eyes as Sonny and Push step onto the plaza. Recognizing immediately that they are not of this village, these two tall men, the boys dart skittish and frightened into a darkened doorway where they stand huddled, clasping one another and peering, wide-eyed, out from behind a torn screen. And in that brief moment the village has become suddenly silent and empty. Even the dogs have disappeared as though into thin air. It is, at once, as if this place has been completely deserted for a long, long time.

Push thinks it curious that Sonny Brokeshoulder has begun to sing softly as he makes his way directly toward the east-facing doorway of one in a series of conjoined small houses, some of which are two-storied and others not. These houses are more like apartments, really—sharing common walls as they do—set back to one side of the little plaza. As he follows him toward the door, Push wonders what it is that has caused his friend to choose to approach this particular place rather than any other one—so indistinguishably alike are all the dwellings here.

And then, standing beside the door, Push can see that the opening is not so high as one would ordinarily expect a doorway to be. The entrance to this house is barely six feet in height, if it is that. And there is a lizard with a body as long and as thick as a large man's hand perched head-down and motionless on the sun-baked mud wall beside the door. Apparently unimpressed by the presence of the two men, the lizard does not abandon its place on the wall, but rather goes on sunning itself—staring at nothing with bulging and lidless yellow eyes.

Sonny does not call out or knock at the door. Rather he moves a few paces away and, as though his business is with someplace other than this place even, continues to sing softly—so softly as to be almost soundless. It is clear to Push that this particular doorway is their destination—has been their destination from the very start—and yet Sonny makes no obvious move to announce his presence or to intrude in any way.

What Push is seeing is how completely and seemingly effortlessly his old college friend has gone over to the Navajo way of doing things. Like this, for example: While a white person will most likely rap sharply at a door and perhaps even shout out a greeting of some kind, it is the Navajo way to approach another person's home slowly, all the while making some relatively low and therefore unobtrusive sound, and to wait patiently for some occupant of the dwelling to appear . . . for it is the Navajo way to understand and appreciate the fact that there are those who might not always be prepared to greet visitors, and that the gracious thing to do—indeed, the only proper thing to the Navajo way of thinking—is to afford those inside whatever time they require to make ready for a visit.

And sure enough, after a few moments have passed, the door to the small house slowly opens . . . opens with a creaking sound, even. And at that sound, the lizard darts—incredibly swiftly, Push thinks—across and up the dust-darkened mud wall, to disappear over and onto the roof of the house. Push blinks his eyes. He is unable to see who it is that has opened the door—so dark is it inside, and so blinding-bright out here in the sunlight.

And then a voice comes from out of the darkness that is the room that lies behind the door: ''Oh . . . is that you, Sonny?''

The voice belongs to a woman.

''Why, look here, girls . . . it's our Navajo friend Sonny Brokeshoulder come to visit us from over at Window Rock. It's good to see you, Sonny. Come inside outta the sun and have something cool to drink—isn't it a warm day?'' A very brown hand pushes the screen door open wide. ''Come in . . . come in,'' the voice says. ''Come on in and I'll fix you both something to eat.''

The two men must duck their heads slightly to avoid bumping them as they pass through the low doorway.

''Oh, no, Mary Esther. No food for us, thank you. I'd like you to meet my friend Push Foster—he's a doctor at the Hashké Indian Hospital. It was a long time ago that we used to be in school together back in Oklahoma—at college, you know.''

Push smiles at the woman. ''This is Mary Esther Lomaquaptewa, Push,'' Sonny says. ''Mary Esther is Clifford's wife . . . Clifford Lomaquaptewa . . . the gentleman we've come over here to see.''

The woman takes Push's hand and holds it gently for a long moment.

''How do you do?'' she says. ''I'm happy to meet you.''

She is, he guesses, in her mid-to-late forties. She is very short and she is very fat—so much so, in fact, that she seems to be nearly as wide as she is tall. She is wearing shocking-pink bicycle pants that come to just above her knees. The tight stretch Lycra material accentuates the woman's largeness in a way that is, to Push, nothing short of remarkable. She wears a bright purple T-shirt with a sunburst logo that proclaims her to be a fan of the Phoenix Suns basketball team. The shirt—despite being of a size that is very probably as large as there is available—looks to be uncomfortably tight across Mary Esther's very broad chest and back.

"And I'm pleased to meet you, Mrs. Lomaquaptewa," Push says as the smiling woman motions for him to sit on a scratched gray metal folding chair near the small refrigerator, from which there comes a constant hissing noise—it is this hissing noise that tells Push the appliance operates not on electricity, but rather on gas. There are on the refrigerator door a half-dozen color photographs of people—family snapshots and school pictures, Push imagines—held in place by magnets of varying shapes. Above the photos there is attached to the freezer-compartment door a red, white, and blue bumper sticker that reads: Let's Rodeo. A small battery-powered black-and-white television set with awkwardly bent rabbit-ear antennas that sport small tinfoil flags is balanced atop the refrigerator. The television set is clearly the centerpiece of this room—of this house, really, since it looks very much to Push as if this entire dwelling is made up simply of this one medium-sized room.

A sagging double bed is situated against the wall farthest from the door. The bed is covered with a brightly colored Pendleton blanket, and scattered on it too are several embroidered throw pillows.

Just now the television on the refrigerator is tuned to a daytime game show. The picture is out-of-focus fuzzy and snowy—it rolls periodically in that maddening way that Push remembers television sets *used* to roll, and the sound, while loud, is mostly unintelligible due to the steady—and so annoying—hum of static. At a medium-sized chrome-legged and Formica-topped table there are seated two very round women—both of whom appear to be some years younger than Mary Esther, though not of an age young enough to be her daughters. Laid out on this table are a stack of thick-sliced pink bologna sandwich meat that has been wrapped in white butcher paper, a plastic-bagged, store-bought loaf of machine-sliced white bread, and a very large jar of mustard. The mustard is bright yellow except for the dried black residue around the mouth of the open jar. The two women at this table are busily preparing sandwiches. A very small boy holding a half-eaten sandwich is peering out from behind one of the women at the table—there is mustard on his face and on the Batman T-shirt that he is wearing. A small dog is peeking around from behind the other woman. Although the animal isn't trimmed neatly in the manner in which the breed is most often seen, the dog appears to be a poodle—a somewhat dingy white poodle. And like the little boy, the dog has mustard on its face.

"Well, say—is that my old pal Harley I see hiding out back there?" And as he bends over and pats his thighs, Sonny is indicating the dog, and not the child. "Come over here and see me, Harley-boy."

"No, that's not him. I'm sorry to have to break the news to you, Sonny, but our good friend Harley-Davidson got ran over a couple'a months ago by one of those big trucks that comes up here from Flagstaff to deliver the butane gas." Mary Esther is shaking her head sadly. "Thank goodness, he never knew what hit him. You know, it just about broke my heart in two to see him ran over like that. I mean, that darned big old truck just about mashed the poor little thing flat as a pancake."

Mary Esther wipes something from her eye—a tear, perhaps?—and then she makes a loud smooching noise. The dingy little dog with the mustard on its face makes a high-pitched yipping sound and scurries toenail-clicking-sliding from its hiding place behind the seated woman over to cower behind Mary Esther's legs. It peers around her ankles to look bug-eyed-frightened at the two strange men. Mary Esther reaches down to scratch the dog's ears.

"This guy here is Harley's replacement," she says. "He's a little bit shy. We got him over at Flag at the flea market where we sometimes go to sell some of the jewelrys that Clifford makes in the wintertime. There's a guy over there who raises poodle-dogs. He gave us a pretty good bargain. His name is Barkley—actually his whole name is Charles Barkley. I mean the dog's name is Charles Barkley—not the guy at the flea market who raises the poodles and who gave us the good bargain." Mary Esther chuckles. "We usually just call him Barkley for short most of the time, though . . . you know, on account of he's always barkin' at ever'body."

"Well say, I'm awful sorry to hear about Harley-Davidson," Sonny says. "He was a very nice dog. I hope this Barkley guy will turn out to be a good one, too. . . . Is Clifford at home, Mary Esther? We'd like to visit with him awhile about some things."

"He's not here right now . . . he's doin' some business down below at his cornfield. He ought to be back, though, now that you're here. I guess you'd be wantin' to visit with him about all of the sickness that's goin' on over there, huh?''

''You know about that?'' Sonny glances quickly at Push. ''Is there sickness going around here at Hopi, too?''

''No, we're all in pretty good health as far as I know about, Sonny. Clifford just told me that there's somethin' bad goin' around among you Navajo peoples, though.''

''Well, it's true, Mary Esther, there's something strange going on over there . . . but I wonder where Clifford heard about it?''

''Oh, I think that he dreamed it.''

And just then, silhouetted in the still-open doorway leading out into the dusty plaza, there appears the shadowy figure of a man.

There is no sense that this shadow of a man has just now stepped up to the doorway. It is, rather, almost as though he's been standing there all along.

"Sonny Brokeshoulder." The silhouette speaks. "I was thinking that it was you who was here and so I stopped working down below to come up to see you."

As Clifford Lomaquaptewa steps into the relatively cool darkness of the room, Push can see that he is wearing a long-sleeved blue-plaid cotton shirt, faded khaki trousers, and dusty black tennis shoes. His hair is cut in the traditional Hopi style with straight bangs across his forehead and he wears a yellow head scarf knotted above his left ear. He is carrying a wooden-handled hoe and a pointed digging stick. From the heavy dust on his clothes and on his hair and on his hands, it is obvious that the man has been toiling in the fields. He is very dark-skinned and, because he is smiling pleasantly, Push can readily see that there is a gold crown where an eyetooth would normally be and that there is a dark gap where the man's two bottom front teeth are missing altogether.

"Hello, Clifford . . . *Yá'át'ééh*." Sonny repeats his greeting in Navajo. "We were just about to come down to look for you. This man here beside me is Dr. Push Foster." Push extends his hand. "He's the new doctor down there at Hashké," Sonny adds by way of introduction. "And he's an old friend of mine of many years.

''Push, this is Clifford Lomaquaptewa, the man I told you about. He's an important headman here in this village.''

''How do you do,'' Push says. And as Clifford Lomaquaptewa takes the hand he offers, Push notices the man's grip, like that of his wife, is light but not brief—not at all the too-firm, pumping display of the white man, but rather a lingering warm touch that is as gentle as it is pleasant.

''Welcome to my home, Push Foster,'' he says. ''I hope that Mary Esther here has given you a cool drink or some good hot coffee and sugar.'' The Hopi man looks around the room—disapprovingly, Push thinks. ''I see that these women here are preparing lunch-meat sandwiches when they oughta be seein' to the *knukwivi*—that's what we called the tasty stew that was always cookin' in my own mother's house over there. A person could always know that there was gonna be coffee and cooked food anytime he came to visit in those days. I don't know what to say about the way the young people nowadays have forgotten a lot of their manners,'' he gives an irritated shake of his head. His wife and the two other women are smiling at Push and Sonny, apparently not in the least concerned with the mild scolding they have just received.

''It's awful warm out there today,'' Clifford says. ''But we will have winds tomorrow, and some rain will come soon.'' This last comment is offered up simply as a fact and not as a prediction: *Some rain will come . . . soon.*

Because the air is almost painfully clear and bright and dry, Push wonders at the man's statement. Curiously, however, he feels no doubt whatsoever that it will rain soon.

It is not like Sonny Brokeshoulder to speak so directly to the reason for their visit, yet he begins almost immediately: ''Clifford, you are Hopi and I'm Navajo,'' he says. ''Our people have not always gotten along so good, but we've known each other for a long time now, you and I. We understand and respect one another and I like to think we're sensitive to each other's cultures. We both know that when there's harmony in the world, things go right.''

Clifford Lomaquaptewa nods in agreement.

''But now it looks like there's something bad going on,'' Sonny continues. ''And I came to see what you think about it. Right off the bat, I will say I understand that just coming out and asking questions is not the proper way of getting information—that's pretty much the white man's way and it just doesn't set well with most Indian people. But Clifford, we believe that something is terribly wrong over there—there's a sickness going around very quickly on Navajoland and we maybe don't have much time and so I hope you'll understand if we're not as proper as we ought to be.''

Clifford Lomaquaptewa has listened quietly, and again he nods.

''It's true that from time to time we maybe can't do something in the same way that our elders would have done it, Sonny—things nowadays just seem to go too fast for our own good. But I think that as long as our hearts are in the right place, it's probably the best we can do.'' The Hopi man gazes directly into Sonny Brokeshoulder's eyes.

''What is it that you want to ask me?''

''My friend Push and I were thinking maybe you could tell us if you know anything about the sickness that's goin' around back over there.''

Clifford Lomaquaptewa rubs his hand across his chin.

''Maybe it would be better if we was to go outside of this house to talk about these things,'' he says. Before he can reach the door, however, he hesitates. ''But then it's awful warm out there in the sun.'' He turns back into the room and sits down on a wooden ladder-back kitchen chair and motions his visitors toward two similar chairs. ''Take a load off your feet and sit down here by me—I'll see if maybe Mary Esther will turn the sound off on that there TV set so we maybe can talk right here . . . where it's shady and cool and the flies aren't quite so numerous and pesky.''

As Push and Sonny settle into the chairs, the two younger women quietly leave the house, taking the young boy and the dog along with them. Mary Esther Lomaquaptewa places cups of steaming-hot coffee in front of each of the three men and turns the television set off . . . then she busies herself at the far side of the room.

''This is some kinda bad thing you got goin' around over there, you know,'' Clifford says, blowing on the coffee. ''I been thinking about it for quite a few days now, and I can't see that it's gettin' any better . . . only that it's gettin' worse.''

''We're trying to rule out certain things, Clifford,'' Sonny says. ''We have laboratories in Albuquerque conducting tests on blood and tissue samples of all of the sick people, but so far about the only thing they can tell is that it doesn't seem to be any of the kinds of things they've ever seen before. So now we're sending samples to the top doctors in the country—hoping that they will know what to make of all this. . . .''

''The Earth is gettin' sick, Sonny. The air is dirty from all them cars that the young people are drivin' around nowadays and from those airplanes that I see every day flying around up there in the sky and making all of that white smoke. They tell on Mary Esther's TV about how in some places whole rivers are plugged up from the government's dams and how whole mountains are catchin' on fire and how some of those white men from Florida are flyin' around up there in big rocket ships—goin' all the way up to the stars and to the moon, even. It just isn't right, don't you know? That's not the way things are supposed to be happening.

''People goin' to the *moon* . . . Do you remember that time a few years back when those white men came over there to Grey Mountain to practice for going up there?'' Clifford points to the west. ''They said that Grey Mountain was about as close to how the moon is as any place they could think of and so they went around pretending like that *was* the moon.'' Clifford sips the strong black coffee out of a spoon.

''They tell about how there was an old Navajo man who lived over there who was takin' his sheep around like always and how he happened to see those fellows pretendin' they were walkin' around on the moon and he asked somebody who could talk his language to tell him what those guys was up to. At first he didn't believe them when they told him they were gonna fly up there in a rocket ship, but then I guess they convinced the old guy that what they were tellin' him was the truth, 'cause then he started to believe their story. And then he told them the story about how the First Navajo People was said to have stopped at the moon one time when they was on their way to visit the sun, and he figured that maybe some of them early visitors mighta liked it there or else got left behind by mistake or something. . . .'' And again he pauses in the telling of his story to sip coffee from his spoon.

''Anyway,'' he continues. ''The old man said he wanted to give these white men a message for in case they saw any Navajos who might still be livin' up there. So I guess they allowed him to talk into one of their machines to make a record of the sound of his voice to take up there with them.''

And Push realizes that Clifford Lomaquaptewa has, with this story, worked around the indirectness that the tradition of his culture requires—has spent the required time in getting ready to get to the point.

''And do you know what the message he sent was?'' Push asks.

''They say that it was a very short message.'' And from the trace of a smile on Clifford Lomaquaptewa's face, it is clear that Push has done exactly the right thing in asking.

''They say that what the old man said into their machine was this: 'Watch out for these white people. They will try to make a treaty with you—and claim the moon for their own use.' ''

And at this, all three of the men laugh.

''That's a very fine story,'' Push says.

''Yes, it is a fine story,'' Clifford says. ''But of course it ain't true.'' And he sips noisily from his coffee.

''Navajos ain't never been up to the moon—that's just one of their stories. Hopis have been up there, though. I'm pretty sure those spacemen must have seen some Hopi rock writing whenever they looked around. I figure they maybe even brought some back down to put in their museums in Washington, D.C.'' He shakes his head and gazes out the door. ''I wouldn't put it past them . . . white people have a real thing about displayin' Indian stuff, you know, feathers and pots—even Indian bones.''

And after he's taken yet another drink of coffee, Clifford continues in all seriousness: ''Everything's all messed up, it seems like. And now the young people are forgetting all about the old ways. They go around talkin' on their telephones that don't have no wires and listenin' to music from those little boxes that do have wires—wires that go right into their ears and heads. And all the while they are talkin' and listenin' they are forgetting how to speak the old languages . . . never even bothering to learn how to do the dances or the ceremonies.'' He is shaking his head sadly now. ''It's a shame, you know? . . . It's just a pitiful shame. It's no wonder that there are all these bad things happening.

''Everything's all mixed up and crazy. Like how it started with the weather awhile back. There was just way too much rain and snow the past two winters, and still it wasn't nearly as cold as it usually gets. So now I got corn starting to get tall down there in my field and it's not time for it to be hardly even sprouting yet. At first it makes you think that maybe it's gonna be a pretty good growin' time, but then you start to noticing some of the other things—things like how there's so many little wild animals. How there's way more rabbits than usual, and how the mice are so numerous, and at the same time there don't seem to be as many of those red-tailed hawks and burrowin' owls and coyotes as there usually would be to catch and eat all those extra rabbits.'' Clifford stares out the door for a long time before he continues.

''And the Snake Society people over there at Walpi been sayin' how they ain't seein' very many snakes—and of course it's the snakes that eat the mice. So it turns out that the mice and the rabbits are having a contest with each other to see who can eat up all the green corn plants almost as quick as they start stickin' up outta the earth.''

''And you think that these things are connected with the sickness among the Navajo?'' Push asks.

''*Every*thing's connected, Dr. Foster. . . . The Earth and everything that lives on it has just nearly got to be working together or else something is bound to start to die off. And it seems like this time it's people,'' and Clifford looks directly at Sonny Brokeshoulder. ''And it appears, my friend, that maybe this time it's Navajo people that is startin' to die off.''

''How is it that you know about what's happening over there, Mr. Lomaquaptewa?'' Push asks. ''I mean, how is it that you've learned that people are getting sick and dying on the Navajo Reservation . . . and that so far whatever it is seems to have affected only Navajo people?''

Clifford Lomaquaptewa sits for a very long time before answering. Sits staring out the open doorway toward the blue mountains in the distance.

''I don't rightly know how it is that I know these things, Dr. Foster . . . I just seem to know.''

''Your wife told us that she thought maybe you'd dreamed it,'' Push says.

And still, the Hopi man's eyes are fixed on the clear blue sky beyond the edge of the mesa—fixed on the purple that is the faint outline of the San Francisco peaks—*Nuvatukyaovi*—some eighty miles distant.

''Maybe that's so,'' he says. ''Maybeso. . . .''

It is night now and Clifford Lomaquaptewa is sitting alone smoking a cigarette on a low bench outside the open door of his Second Mesa home. He is watching the stars when Mary Esther pushes open the screen and steps out into the darkness.

"*Baywatch* was pretty entertaining tonight," she says. "You really should look at it sometime."

Clifford says nothing.

"It was good to see Sonny Brokeshoulder today, wasn't it?" she continues. "Did you tell him about what that trader said?"

Clifford turns his head and looks up at his wife. Still, he says nothing.

"Did you tell Sonny about the tablet? About the white man havin' it, I mean?"

Clifford stubs his cigarette on the wall. "The stars are very bright," he says. "There aren't any clouds out tonight, but we're still gonna see some rain before too long."

Then he stands and walks away from the house and out to the very edge of the mesa.

And Mary Esther goes back inside.

On Friday morning this story appears on page one of the *Albuquerque Journal:*

SILENT KILLER STALKS NAVAJO RESERVATION

A mysterious, flu-like illness has left at least seven dead and an as yet undetermined number hospitalized over the past three weeks.

The victims—all Navajo Indians—reside in the Four Corners area of New Mexico and Arizona.

Health officials are baffled and have expressed fear that the death toll will rise in the days to come as officials search secluded areas of the reservation for more victims.

According to one source inside the Indian Health Services hospital in Gallup, symptoms are reportedly much like those of the common cold and flu—coughs, fevers, red eyes, and muscle aches—which accounts for the uncertainty as to whether people actually have the deadly illness or simply a case of common flu in the early stages.

The symptoms of the mysterious disease—which has come to be called Navajo Flu—rapidly worsen and can result in death from total respiratory shutdown, or suffocation, within a matter of hours.

TSÉGHÁHOODZÁNI

Late Friday morning Sonny Brokeshoulder receives a call from Ed Pierce. Wiley Bigboy has come down with what appears to be flu, and Pierce has arranged for him to be admitted to the isolation ward at the IHS hospital at Gallup.

"This is definitely not something we want to have to contend with, Brokeshoulder." The big man's voice is almost a whisper. "Greyeyes and Tsosie lived together and they're both dead. Now, I don't know about you, but this suggests to me that we're looking at person-to-person contagion—that this is airborne and it's being passed around by casual contact. And if that's the case, my friend, we're just in a whole shitload of trouble." It is as though Pierce is trying to keep his voice under control—trying to keep a secret. "You remember the old medical-school adage, don't you—that in virology and bacteriology it's the doctors that are always the first to die? Goddamnit, we are the point men in this skirmish—people like you and me—and if anybody's subject to catch whatever's going around killing folks, it's us stethoscope-carrying freedom fighters who think we're going to ease the suffering by begging the sick guys to cough in our faces while we make intelligent pronouncements like, 'Where does it hurt?' and 'Say ahhh.' "

"Now listen, Ed . . ."

"No, you listen to me—I've spent this entire morning trying to put together a list of all the people who even might have come in contact with just the patients I've seen here . . . do you have any idea how quickly those numbers add up?"

"Easy now . . ." Sonny says. "We've got to keep this in perspective. We know that contagion is never absolute—I mean hell, if it were, life-forms wouldn't have ever made it this far. It wouldn't have taken but one or two nasty viral infections getting started somewhere back down the road and there would have been a catastrophic mathematical progression to the point where no species could have survived."

"Let's just say we know that contagion has never been absolute *yet,* Brokeshoulder—you know as well as I do that the fucking microbes are getting better at their jobs all the time . . . and who are we to say this one isn't the *big* one—maybe even the Doomsday Bug?"

"*Damn!* . . . There's that word again," Sonny says. "What's with you guys, anyway? Let's don't use that word *doom,* okay? How are *you* feeling, Ed? Are you all right?"

"Well hell, Brokeshoulder, I was feeling just fine and dandy up until Shorty Bigboy waltzed in here coughing and sneezing his way through the goddamned building just as proud as he could be that he might get to take the rest of the day off. I mean, shit, I don't know what that burr-headed little peckerwood was thinking about . . ."

"Try to calm down, Ed," Sonny says. "It's not Wiley's fault that he doesn't make all the right connections. Why, I'm not sure I would've if you hadn't called."

"Of course, I know that," Pierce says, his voice beginning to regain control now. "I don't mean to sound paranoid or to start you worrying any more than you already are. But goddamnit, Brokeshoulder . . . We're out here facing what may turn out to be something more terrible than anything any of us can begin to imagine and we're supposed to make do with the scientific equivalent of baling wire and chewing gum. About the best medical advice we can offer these poor devils at this point is, 'Now you folks be sure and wash your hands real good, you hear?' "

"I know, Ed . . ."

"And Jesus, but that piece in this morning's *Journal* has caused this place to go absolutely bonkers. Just who the hell is this 'source' they're talking about here at the hospital, I'd like to know? On an unusually busy day this time of year we might expect to see maybe seventy or eighty people through here. So far today we've had more than three hundred. Hell, they're still lining up out there and it's not even noon.

"And now the administration people are telling me that half the goddamned nursing staff has started calling in sick—shit, they ain't sick . . . they just don't want to be around anybody who *is* sick, is what it is, Brokeshoulder. And it's hard to blame them since the truth is, anybody who falls in here complaining about a case of the fuckin' sniffles could very well have contracted this killer virus, for all we know. I mean, shit, we really can't tell. . . . And it's looking more and more to me like if we misdiagnose this thing on the first try, the next call is most likely going to be for the undertaker. . . ."

"Yeah, this morning's newspaper story has got a lot of people upset. I figure we need to get out a news release of our own—preferably one that makes what's going down here sound at least halfway routine."

"*Routine?* With most of the people who are in on this already just about paralyzed with fear? Look, I know we can't afford to start a panic, but it's hard for me to think of a way to call this routine." Pierce sounds exasperated. "Well, at least we've got Shorty where we can keep a close eye on him, Brokeshoulder. I've got them watching for any signs of acute respiratory activity and I'll keep you posted."

"Okay, Ed. And be sure and get a series of blood cultures from him, will you? The people at the CDC are asking that we overnight them specimens from even the suspect cases."

"Right . . . I've already got the samples together." And for a moment, Ed Pierce's voice takes on a calm and even tone: "Did I ever tell you that my mama was a Jesus freak, Brokeshoulder? You know, one of those who wander around reciting Bible scriptures and singing snatches of hymns all day?"

"Yeah, I was brought up in a house like that myself, Ed."

"Is that right? I was wondering if maybe we shouldn't think about . . ." His voice trails off.

"What's that, Ed?"

"Oh, nothing, really . . . Listen, I'll get back to you if anything new turns up on this end." And Ed Pierce hangs up.

As he hangs up the telephone, Sonny sees Priscilla Yazzie standing in the doorway to his office.

There is a strange and frightened look on her face—it is evident to Sonny that the woman has overheard his end of the conversation with Ed Pierce.

"Shorty helped Dr. Pierce to do the autopsies on those young people last weekend, didn't he?" Priscilla asks. Sonny nods his head. "Do you think maybe he might've caught whatever it was that killed those two, Sonny?"

"You were listening in on my conversation, weren't you? Now you listen to me, Priscilla, and you listen good. I think that Shorty Bigboy has a case of the flu, is what I think." Sonny's voice is hard and on edge; he is very worried—more worried than he has allowed himself to realize before this moment—but doesn't want the worry to show.

"Not a word about any of this is to leave this office, okay? Will you promise me that?" There is a moment when Sonny is uncertain as to whether Priscilla is even hearing his voice, so vacant is the look in her eyes. "*Priscilla?* Do you understand me, Priscilla?" The woman nods her head and turns to leave.

"Wait a minute, Priscilla." Sonny begins making hurried notes on a yellow legal pad. "How about you help me make up some notices that we can Xerox and get somebody to start posting around town and maybe distribute to the Chapter Houses and the Thriftways. . . . Let's see, we need to remind people to wash their hands regularly and not to touch any dead animals. . . ." Sonny is making a list, but he is distracted. His mind is someplace else entirely.

"And to use flea powder on their pets—on their dogs and cats . . .

and if anybody in the outfit shows any of the flu symptoms they're to take them to the clinic right away for a checkup. . . .''

Priscilla looks hard at her boss. ''And what do you think the people at the clinic are gonna tell you if you come in there with the flu symptoms, Sonny? I figure they'll just tell you that you have the flu and to go back home and take some aspirin. Besides, that Greyeyes boy didn't even get a chance to start feelin' all that bad before he was dead, as I heard it.''

''Come on now . . . you have to help me out here, Priscilla.'' Sonny feels a knot tightening in his stomach.

By midafternoon, reports of eight additional suspect cases of the mysterious sickness have reached Sonny's desk at Window Rock.

When Priscilla Yazzie comes into Sonny's office to bring the mail after lunch, she counts twelve of the red pushpins in the big wall map behind the desk. Of the twenty-eight suspected cases so far, there have been a dozen fatalities reported. And in every instance, the victims have been living on the Navajo Nation.

Why is it that telephones always ring louder in the middle of the night than they do in daylight?

Sonny Brokeshoulder bangs his knee hard against the heavy wooden blanket chest as he stumbles from his bed to reach the jangling instrument that has startled him from his sleep.

"Hullo?"

"Sonny, it's Push. I'm sorry to call you at this hour, old buddy, but Leslie just telephoned from over at Keams Canyon—she thinks she's got a hot patient in her clinic and thought we ought to know. . . ."

"Yeah . . . okay . . ." Sonny is struggling to clear his head of the fog of sleep. "Uh, what time is it, Push? I can't see my watch."

"It's just past two-thirty, Sonny. Listen, I think we should get over there. This looks like it may be a chance to see this thing at work, you know."

"Yeah . . . Let me think a second. . . . How long will it take us to get over there to Keams this time of night? . . ."

"The way you drive? I figure an hour and a half from Window Rock if you don't run into any sheep on the road."

"Did Leslie give you any details on her patient, Push?" Sonny's brain is beginning to function normally now. "Is she fairly confident it's what we're looking for?"

"Just that it's a middle-aged Navajo woman in life-threatening respiratory distress. Apparently the woman was brought into Keams by her husband, who is not himself sick."

"Uh-huh . . ."

''And Leslie says I should tell you that she feels sure that everything points to the woman having the same thing that took out Greyeyes and Tsosie and the others, and that she really would like for us to see this.''

''Well, I guess we'd better get on over there, then.''

''Sonny? . . .''

''Yeah, Push?''

''Sonny, Leslie says we'd better haul ass—those were her exact words: *haul ass*. She says she doesn't think this woman will live to see the morning sun.''

''Okay. Sounds like you'd better meet me there in the parking lot at Ganado again—where we left your truck last week. It'll save us a little time, anyway. I'll be there in thirty minutes, tops.''

''Well now, I guess that's pretty much what I'd call haulin' ass,'' Push says. But Sonny Brokeshoulder has already hung up the receiver.

KEAMS CANYON

It's after four in the morning when Sonny steers the Dodge up the steep drive of the Keams Canyon hospital. The clear sky to the east is just beginning to glow with the pale light of dawn. It's Sunday and there are only a half-dozen or so vehicles parked in front of the red-brick building at this hour. In the cab of the weathered pickup beside which Sonny parks, there is a large-sized, dark-colored dog sitting patiently on the driver's-side seat. The dog looks briefly at Push and Sonny and then goes back to watching intently the entrance to the hospital building.

As Push and Sonny hurry up the sidewalk toward the main entrance, the door opens and Dr. Leslie Blair steps out and into the blue-white glow of the mercury-vapor light.

"I'm sorry, guys," she says, and her voice sounds tired—exhausted, really. "My woman died about forty-five minutes ago—right at three-fifteen. There was just no way I could let you know. I'm really sorry to have dragged you all the way over here. . . ."

''Hey, that's okay, Leslie,'' Push says. ''We'd like to take a look at her anyway, and help you take samples so that we can get them sent off to Atlanta first thing in the morning.'' The two men follow Leslie back into the building.

''Do you still feel confident that this is our disease?''

''It just has to be, Push. An acute episode of severe respiratory distress and then total shutdown. I had her on a ventilator and was pumping her full of every kind of bronchial-dilating medication I could lay my hands on—nothing was doing any good at all that I could see. It's a helpless feeling, let me tell you.''

''Well, let's get a look at her.''

Before the three enter the small examination room where the body of the dead woman lies stretched on the gurney, they each don surgical gloves, masks, and gowns. On the door of the small room there is a bright orange sign: Restricted—Contaminated Area.

Push begins his examination of the dead woman. ''So, tell me—what do we know, Leslie?''

''The patient's name is Lizbeth Austin,'' she begins to recite the history as she knows it.

''Aw, shit . . .''—and it is Sonny Brokeshoulder who speaks—''Not Lizbeth . . .''

Push and Leslie look up. ''What is it, Sonny—you know this woman?'' Push asks.

''Yeah, I know her. . . . I didn't recognize her at first—just seeing her laid out there like that. Lizbeth is from up there at Little Springs. A really nice woman . . . she's a well-known weaver, too. I've got one of her rugs hanging in my office . . . the small one by the window . . . it was the only one I could afford. . . .''

Leslie goes on with her clinical history: ''Thirty-seven years of age, she's Navajo, married to a white trader—like Sonny said, they run the post at Little Springs, been there for almost twenty years, I understand. Husband's name is Travis Austin, he brought her in just after midnight . . . says she woke up this morning—yesterday morning, I guess it'd be now—with what he and she both took to be a bad cold or maybe the start of the flu. According to him it got progressively worse throughout the day, but she apparently refused his offers to take her up to the clinic at Tuba City.''

''Well, that's too bad,'' Push says. ''Maybe getting her in to see someone quicker might have made a difference.''

''The husband says that someone or other in her family had a bad experience there at Tuba and that she insisted that she'd be better off at home.''

''You got X rays, I hope?'' Push says.

''Yes, they're on the light box there behind you. The chest views clearly indicate the same near-total white-out of the lungs that you saw in the Tsosie girl—Lizbeth Austin was filled up with fluid. . . .''

''*Damn*. Would Tuba City have been closer to their place?'' Push asks. ''Shouldn't they have gone there?''

''It's about the same distance from Little Springs to here as it is to Tuba City, really,'' Sonny says. ''Tuba's kind of depressing, though—can't say that I blame Lizbeth much . . . not wanting to go up there, I mean.'' Sonny's voice sounds defensive.

''I don't mean to suggest it might have been a *better* place for her, I was just wondering if it was closer, is all.'' Push is taking swab smears from the dead woman's throat and nose. ''And you say that the husband shows no symptoms?''

''None at all. In fact, he claims to feel exceptionally well under the circumstances, and he denies having any of the symptoms that his wife exhibited,'' Leslie says. ''No coughing . . . no sign of eye inflammation . . . and his temperature is normal.

''Listen, I know that I brought this up when you all were over here the other day, and I don't want to beat a dead horse, but are you still ruling out a race-specific virus? I mean, Lizbeth Austin is Navajo and she's dead. Her husband lives and works and sleeps beside the woman twenty-four hours a day and he's evidently well. The one and only obvious difference being that Travis Austin is not Navajo—he's white.''

''I don't say that we can rule anything out, Leslie,'' Push says. ''I'm not persuaded that this sort of thing *could* be race-related, but on the other hand everyone we've seen dead or dying so far has been Navajo, and I'll admit it's getting harder and harder to chalk it all up to coincidence.

''Like I said, we'll help you gather blood and tissue samples,'' Push says. ''And can we maybe get our hands on a little dry ice to pack the specimens in so that we can get them off to the CDC lab as soon as possible?''

''I'm one step ahead of you,'' Leslie says, and she is smiling now. ''I have your dry ice all ready for you in the cooler in the kitchen.''

''You're more than just one step, you're *way* ahead of me, Leslie.'' Push is smiling, too. And he pulls off his gloves and tosses them into the red trash bag marked CONTAMINATED.

''Now then, I think we should talk to Mr. Austin. We've got to get the most precise and complete histories we can on these cases. I assume he's around here somewhere?''

''He's across the way in my office,'' Leslie says. ''He's pretty upset, as you can imagine.''

''Yeah, well, maybe we all ought to go on over and see him,'' and Push rubs his eyes. ''Man, but I hate this part of the job,'' he says as he strips off the surgical gown and mask.

On impulse, Leslie Blair reaches up and straightens the open collar of Push's shirt—her fingers linger for the briefest moment on the cool skin of his neck and she feels the blush of heat in her face. Surprised that she's embarrassed herself by the gesture, she feels uncharacteristically awkward as she turns abruptly and goes out the door.

Dawn has broken over Keams Canyon when Push and Sonny follow Leslie out the hospital door and into the parking lot. The air is clean and sharp. They are walking toward the yellow-block structure that is across and below the paved lot. Beside the yellow building is a large grassy area with trees. There is a lone man standing near a large elm tree, smoking a cigarette. The man is tall and dark-tanned. He wears a full beard and faded Levi pants and jacket.

"That's Travis Austin," Leslie says, and the three turn to walk toward where the man is standing.

As they approach, the stocky, big-headed blue dog that Push had noticed earlier sitting in the cab of the pickup trots over from where he's been sniffing about the shrubbery. The animal's stub of a tail is raised and the hair across his shoulders stands on end as he positions himself menacingly between the bearded man and the three approaching strangers. The low-pitched growl and the firm manner in which the dog has set himself squarely in their path causes the three to stop dead in their tracks.

"Travis?" Sonny says. "It's me, Sonny Brokeshoulder. I'm so terribly sorry about Lizbeth, Travis. . . ."

"Oh, hey, Sonny." Austin looks up and flicks his cigarette down the hill. *"Punky,"* he speaks to the dog. "It's okay, Punk, these are friends . . . they were trying to help out Mama. Go get in the truck."

The animal turns and looks up at Travis Austin. The bristles across his shoulders relax, and the stub of a tail wags tentatively.

"Go on, now," Austin says. "Get in the truck . . . we'll be goin' on home in a bit." And the dog trots to the pickup and jumps up easily into the bed and then on through the open pass-through window where he takes up his post on the driver's-side seat, watching the hospital entrance.

''He saw her go in there,'' Austin says. ''He's gonna have a hard time understanding why she doesn't come out. Hell, I always talk about Punk being *my* dog, but he was just real crazy about Lizbeth, you know. . . .''

''Everybody was crazy about Lizbeth,'' Sonny says. ''Travis, I want you to meet Dr. Push Foster.''

The two men shake hands. ''I'm sorry for your loss, Mr. Austin. I know it's not a good time, but I wonder if you feel up to talking with us about your wife's illness? I don't know if Dr. Blair had a chance to tell you, but we think that Mrs. Austin may have contracted an illness that we don't have much experience with, and we think that you may be able to give us some important information. Maybe we could get some coffee in Leslie's office and visit awhile?''

''That'd be fine, Dr. Foster. I'll help you out in whatever way I can. But then you understand I'll be needing to collect Lizbeth and take her on home to Little Springs.''

''Now, I'm not sure that would be such a good idea,'' Push says. ''Taking her out of the hospital, that is. You see, chances are what she had is contagious and I'm sure you wouldn't want to expose yourself or other people unnecessarily. . . .''

''I know you mean well, Foster, and that you have a job to do, but I figure I've already been about as exposed as I'm likely to be, and I certainly don't intend to put anyone else at risk.'' Austin looks hard at Push. ''On the other hand, I do intend to take my Lizbeth home.''

Push stands looking into the trader's eyes for a long moment. ''All right, Mr. Austin,'' he says. ''If maybe we could just visit for a little while, then Sonny here and I could give you a hand with the arrangements so that you can be on your way home.''

Travis Austin's eyes soften. ''I'd appreciate that,'' he says. ''Thank you.''

It's midmorning now as Push and Sonny stand watching Travis Austin's weathered pickup maneuver down the hill and away from the hospital, past the cut-stone agency-employee housing units, and on out toward the highway. In the bed of the truck is the simple white pine coffin that holds the remains of Lizbeth Austin wrapped neatly in the new, brightly colored Pendleton blanket that her husband has picked out at the Keams Canyon Trading Post.

"I think Lizbeth would have admired this one very much," Julian Blanchard, the trader, had said.

Julian had refused Travis's offer to pay for the blanket. "I've got two of her fine weavings back there in the rug room," he'd said. "One is from about 1970, when she was just a girl and was still learning to weave, but the other one I got from her just last year . . . wouldn't you rather have one of those?"

"No, but thanks anyway," Travis had answered. "Lizbeth was always proud to have people see her rugs, I guess they ought to be out where they're more likely to be admired, Julian. I think this Pendleton will do us just fine."

Also in the bed of the truck, sitting ramrod straight beside the head end of the pine box and directly behind the driver's seat, is the blue dog.

As the three men had lifted the coffin into the truck, Travis had talked easily to Push and Sonny about his wife and about his plans.

"I aim to burn her loom, Sonny," he'd said. "I don't think I could bear the thought of anybody else weaving on it." And he'd motioned the dog up into the truck before latching the tailgate.

"You know, I keep trying to remember the way things were back before I knew Lizbeth, trying to imagine how it's going to be now, I suppose . . . it's funny, but I can't seem to recall the world without her in it."

And he'd allowed himself a smile when a little later he'd said to Push: "It's a good thing for him that this dog here wasn't officially Lizbeth's, you know. According to Indian ways, a person is always to remember to treat their animals well on account of when that person dies their best dog is supposed to be buried alongside of them. The way the story goes, there's a deep and dark chasm that you've got to cross over on your journey and there's a log across that chasm that's just barely long enough to reach across. They say if you've been good to him, your dog'll help you out by holding the end of that log steady in his teeth while you make your way across."

Travis Austin had rolled a cigarette and looked out at the clear morning light on the red canyon wall. His eyes were bright, and for a brief moment Push wondered if it could possibly be the beginning of the inflammation that he was concerned about. But then he'd thought better of it when he heard the trader say, "The older, traditional people are all the time cautioning you that that's how come you better be sure you've always treated your dogs with kindness and respect—you know, so that you can count on them at that crucial time."

Travis had cleared his throat and turned away from Push and Sonny to scratch the head of the dog reassuringly. The animal was sitting beside the coffin . . . he was panting nervously and his hackles were raised slightly as he sniffed the fresh white pine box.

"Yeah, we're takin' her home now, son," he'd said to the dog. "Don't you fret." And then: "Lizbeth treated everyone with kindness and respect. Hell, I figure she's already across that old crevice and safely on the other side—all her troubles are behind her now. But me, I'm pretty much apt to need some help with the log when my time comes. So I guess old Punk here is in for a pretty smooth ride from here on out."

What do you make of it, Push? I mean, other than Lizbeth Austin being Navajo, do you see anything that connects her to Greyeyes or to any of the other cases we know about?''

''All the victims that we know about so far live on the reservation. Most are from small communities—Tídááchiid can't have more than a half-dozen families, can it? And Shonto?''

''Shonto's not even that big,'' Sonny says.

''And now half the population of Little Springs has been wiped out, since the Austins are the only two people who live up there.''

''I don't know if Travis will be able to stand it there alone. . . .''

''And what else do we have that might be common to them all?'' Push is saying. And he answers his own question: ''Well, there's livestock of one kind or another at all the places . . . and house pets. . . .''

''You're describing ninety-eight percent of the outfits on the Navajo Nation, you know,'' Sonny says.

''Don't I know it . . . and that's exactly what has me so stumped.'' Push rubs his hand across his face. ''Let's go back in and make certain that Leslie didn't have any problems getting those samples sent off to Atlanta on account of it being Sunday. Then I think we're going to have to make some calls. It's time we lean on them at the CDC, Sonny . . . and not just to let them know that new specimens are on the way, either. We've reached the point where we've got to go on and make the official call—the Epidemic Aid Request that the government bureaucrats require. We need to tell them it's time they get some of their top virology people to work on this . . . and I mean more than just the field team that gathers specimens. That crew should already be out here, in fact.''

''Whew, I can't tell you how glad I am to hear you say that. . . . I've been trying my best to keep up my stoic appearance, but frankly, I'm one scared Injun,'' and Sonny smiles weakly at his friend. ''Let's go call in the cavalry, Dr. Foster.''

WEPO WASH

It is early on Sunday morning—the morning of the day that Sabine Vogel is to die, and she has really only now begun to appreciate the fact that she is ill. In truth she is much worse even than she can imagine . . . she is sicker than she's ever been in her life.

The sun is fully risen at the Wepo Wash campsite and, after considering the various possibilities that seem reasonable to her, she concludes it likely that she's simply coming down with a bad cold. Certainly she hopes it's a cold and not a case of the flu. She's just come through a fitful, restless night and, although it is her habit to be up well before first light, has only just now forced herself to get up off the cot and set about preparing tea. She's awakened with a violent headache and her back muscles are sore . . . tender to the touch. Even in the distortion of the small, shiny metal camp mirror she can see that the skin on her pale face is slack and her eyes are sunken. As hard as she tries, she cannot keep her eyes more than halfway open—they're angry-looking and inflamed—and while her lack of sleep and the near-constant blowing of sand and dust would tend to irritate her eyes, certainly, this is more pronounced even than she would expect. She believes she may have a temperature, but she can't muster the energy to go and search for the thermometer that she's confident is there . . . somewhere. It is as though she is moving in slow motion—when she can muster the will to move at all, that is—and she is unsteady and weak. A persistent dry cough has come upon her suddenly. She takes three aspirin tablets and lies back down on her cot as she waits for the water to boil.

It is nine o'clock.

A little more than eighteen hours ago Peter Campbell had left in the Land Cruiser. She expects he'll be away for a week, possibly ten days at the most. The original plan had been for them to travel together to Santa Fe—for the both of them to report their progress to the board of trustees and to scrape and bow and try to squeeze the rich old biddies for a little more time and money—and for Peter to quietly show the stone tablet around Santa Fe and try and get a feel for what sort of interest there might be in the Indian antiquities collectors' community. Raising funds for archeological excavation is as time-consuming—indeed, as tedious—as the actual fieldwork. More so, in fact. She had wanted to go with him, but he'd argued, perhaps a little too persuasively, that because the board consists mostly of moneyed widows who look upon him as a dashing soldier of fortune, they'd be much more apt to take out their checkbooks if he were there alone.

She has some trepidation about Peter showing the tablet around without her being there to keep an eye on him. Certainly there are wealthy private collectors who could and would offer up more money than most museum budgets could afford, but she'd been adamant in her insistence that this piece not fall into private hands and feels fairly confident that Peter will honor her wishes. Besides, the dig had been going remarkably well, the weather was being cooperative—it was hot, to be sure, but manageable nonetheless—and the site perfectly safe and secure. She insisted that she would be just fine—the supplies were laid in and she had everything she could possibly need, even if he should be gone more than a week, which he wouldn't.

And so Peter had gone off alone. It was just after lunch when she'd watched as he drove the Land Cruiser up and out of the sandy wash and north toward the road to Piñon. She'd felt the first real twinge of tenderness in her back and shoulder muscles as she'd raised her hand in a wave of good-bye. He hadn't waved back.

And so it is that Sabine Vogel has arrived at this place—at this moment—on the morning of the day that she is to die. And only now has it begun to dawn on her that she is worse off than she'd thought. She feels like hell, in fact. She believes herself to be completely alone and she is frightened . . . she is terribly frightened.

But today is Sunday, she thinks, and she remembers that the woman doctor from the Keams Canyon hospital had promised that she would come out to see the site. . . .

Expect me about noontime, she'd said.

What a stroke of luck . . .

LITTLE SPRINGS

Less than a quarter of a mile before he reaches Little Springs, Travis Austin passes a woman who is walking toward him alongside the highway. Coming from the direction of the trading post, she walks with her head and eyes cast down and her shoulders slumped. Her clothes look ragged and her dark hair is dusty and matted. Travis doesn't get a good look at the woman's face, but he feels certain she's not someone he's seen around there before. But then it's not all that unusual to see Indians walking on reservation roads—miles from any apparent destination.

Turning into his drive, Travis brings the vehicle to a stop beside the small stone outbuilding behind the house. As he steps out of the truck he looks back up the road to where he'd seen the woman. The landscape here is flat and barren, but he can see no sign now of the walker.

He reaches out his hand to touch lightly the white pine box there in the bed of the truck, and then he rubs the blue dog's head. "Wait here a minute, Punk," he says.

And he turns and goes inside the shed. He intends to fetch the shovel and the pickax that are kept there . . . it's past noon and the sun is high and hot. He knows that the digging will be hard in the dry, rocky soil, but he knows, too, that the Navajo Way requires that he bury his wife's body before the sun has set.

As his eyes grow accustomed to the darkness inside the small storage space, Austin sees two dark forms in the middle of the room. Leaning closer, he recognizes that the forms are those of Lizbeth's cats and that both are lying as though they are sleeping—motionless on the cool, hard-packed dirt floor. He kneels down and touches first one and then the other. Neither animal appears to have been injured in any way, and yet both are dead.

And now, for the first time that he can recall, Travis Austin feels tears begin to well up in his eyes.

TÍDÁÁCHIID

There is a very old woman straightening the red and gray and black rough-woven wool blanket and adjusting the frayed string cinch on the scuffed and badly worn saddle that sits perched high on the bony withers of the skinny piebald mare standing bored and sleepy-eyed beside the brush arbor corral.

Even before this old woman has heard the sound of approaching trucks, she has been aware that the three dogs who wait patiently for her to finish her preparations to begin the day's work have pricked their ears alertly and raised their heads, sniffing at the fresh morning air.

Two identically outfitted green Suburban utility vehicles are slowly maneuvering in four-wheel drive the tortuously steep incline that leads up and out of the deep, sandy wash and right up to the door of the dilapidated house trailer that has been the Tídááchiid home of Robert Greyeyes and Yvonne Tsosie and their infant son.

Has been the home of Greyeyes and Tsosie . . . both are dead now. The baby boy lives with the Tsosie girl's mother's outfit, a quarter-mile away.

And a quarter-mile away Juanita Tsosie, too, had first heard and then seen the approaching trucks . . . just moments before.

She had been arranging freshly washed diapers on the low mesquite bushes that grow beside her home . . . and she had waited, face averted, for the thick, choking dust to subside as the two big trucks rumbled past her place.

And now the old woman speaks softly to her dogs—and the dogs crouch low to the ground and whine at the first sound of her voice.

She cups her hands over her yellowed, rheumy eyes to shade them from the bright morning sunlight and watches as the two dust-caked green vehicles come to a stop, one in front of the other, on the bare dirt half-circle that has been the driveway in front of the now-empty trailer. The windows of both Suburbans are tinted nearly black to block out the glaring sun and they are covered over with thick red dust and road grime. Try as she may, the old woman cannot make out who or what is inside the two vehicles. The early-morning air is quiet now except for the popping sound of the expanding and contracting metal of the overheated engines—the engines that have now been turned off—and the trucks sit quietly for what seems to the old woman far too long a time without anyone coming out from them.

Less than a hundred yards from where the woman is standing with her hand resting now on the horse's flank—from the dark-shadowed doorway of a decrepit forked-stick hogan situated close up beside the edge but on the opposite bank of the wash—Sampson Billy is also watching the two Suburbans.

Tídááchiid, New Mexico, is a tiny community located on the Navajo Reservation in the northwestern corner of the state near the place where it shares a point in common with the neighboring states of Arizona and Utah and Colorado: near the Four Corners.

Within a very few moments every resident of the Tídááchiid Chapter knows very well that there are outsiders present. Understand, it is not because some message has been passed announcing the arrival of the two strange trucks. There are no telephones in Tídááchiid, and not a single word has been spoken aloud among any of the people here in those brief few moments since the sound of the approaching trucks could first be heard. And still, every person who is on this day alive in Tídááchiid is very much aware that two *bilagáana* government vehicles have driven up from the south . . . everyone is aware that the two trucks are parked directly in front of the Greyeyes place . . . and each is aware of these things even before the two trucks' engines have been shut down.

And so when the doors of the two vehicles have begun finally and slowly to open, when all eight side doors have begun to open precisely at the same moment, as if by some inaudible signal, it is not only the old sheepherder who watches—watches with no real comprehension the scene unfolding before her—rather there are at least a half-dozen other individuals who are, at that very moment, watching the first movement of the foot as it stretches from the dark-shadowed interior of the lead vehicle, as it stretches tentatively down and toward the bare dirt beneath the now-open door as though it is not at all certain of finding firm ground upon which to step. It is not only the woman and her dogs who watch that first foot—wrapped as it is in an odd protective layering of paper—who see that first foot attached by a duct-tape-wrapped ankle to a blue-plastic-shrouded leg. There are, in fact, many eyes that watch as the bright blue, puffy plastic suit emerges ungracefully from the Suburban—the bright-colored suit that encases entirely the large, manlike figure: A tall figure it is, with a hood covering what might be a head, a head with an opaque hard-plastic face mask where a normal man's eyes might be, and a pair of thick, black cylindrical cans attached to each side of the thing's face—attached to those places where a normal man's cheeks might be. And then—and it is this that, to these Navajo watchers, is most appalling—once the first large figure is finally out and standing upright beside the truck, it is followed straightaway by seven more, slightly smaller still-blue figures, each one emerging from a separate door, each one wrapped mummylike in exactly the same attire, each one as horrible-appearing as was the first to the confused and frightened eyes of these gentle people who have watched this scene unfold.

And the first to react to what is happening is the old woman sheepherder.

So horrified is she by what she is witnessing that she suddenly scrambles up and onto her horse . . . so charged is she with fear at the sight of these ghastly apparitions that the old woman mounts the animal with a near-astonishing and wholly unexpected grace. She roughly jerks the reins to pull the still-dozing animal's head abruptly about . . . jerks the headstall away from the direction where the awful blue figures are emerging—stiff and robotlike—from the two green trucks. Her mouth has gone dry with fear, yet she manages to cluck her tongue and, grasping at coarse black mane, digs her tennis-shoed heels into the nag's bony ribs. And with a startled burst of energy more appropriate to a younger animal, the aged mare gathers herself quivering for one brief moment before—dumbfounded, really, to have been so roughly and unexpectedly asked to move quickly—she leaps straight up and, turning round in midair, lands splay-footed-awkward, grunting and farting, her ghost-frightened rider clinging, precariously off-balance. The old mare scrambles frantically to gain footing on the deep-dusty ground before bolting, wide-eyed and snorting, headlong through sparse greasewood and sage, past the small milling flock of shaggy-haired goats and pitifully bleating ewes that appear stunned to see the horse react so. And the three dogs, who've been crouching low—alert and watching in a nearby patch of shade—now themselves scramble, yipping, in the roiling billows of dust raised up by the horse's churning feet. And within a heartbeat the old Navajo woman and her horse and her dogs have disappeared . . . exploded, really, back down the wash and up out the opposite side—back down the very road from which the trucks and their frightening cargo have only just arrived.

And when Juanita Tsosie sees the old sheepherder and the mad confusion of animals that accompany her—sees the look of wide-eyed terror on that poor woman's face and how she clings so desperately to the scuffed saddle horn and to the mare's tangled, coarse mane, as it tears wildly, striking out blindly at the shrill-yipping dogs that nip and tumble at its heels, down the hard-packed dirt road that passes in front of her home—Juanita Tsosie gathers her orphaned grandchild close up to her breast and dashes inside her hogan to cower behind the rough plank door.

Say what?''

And so saying, the blue-clad figure leans in closer to the larger form and speaks more loudly still. Its voice, while gratingly loud, sounds mechanical and garbled, encased as it is in the heavy plastic suit.

''You gotta speak up,'' it says. *''Everything sounds muffled . . . it's these filters and the hoods and all.''*

The larger one is having difficulty establishing a seal between the hard-rubber mask of the respirator and its face. *''I said, let's get this crap done as quickly as possible—I don't know how long I can take wearing this hot goddamned contraption!''*

''Yeah . . . Don't I know it. . . .''

And now all of the blue figures are standing beside the trucks, in a crooked line, facing the Greyeyes house trailer. It's early still, but already the morning is heating up. And it is stiflingly hot for anything wrapped, as these eight are, in cumbersome bioprotective oversuits, wearing ill-fitting microbe-particle respirators.

There are only twelve viruses in the world known to require the use of Biohazard Level 4 protective measures. Those twelve viruses are what are known in medical circles as *species-threatening . . . slate-wipers . . .* viruses that are fast-moving and deadly.

They say that anyone who's ever seen what these viruses do to the human body—those individuals who have survived the experience, that is—will never forget what he or she has seen.

The blue suits that are worn by the team at Tídááchiid on this day are the same as those worn by Level 4 Biohazard research scientists. Clearly *someone* believes that this is a deadly serious event.

WEPO WASH

Sabine Vogel has awakened with a start. Her shirt and trousers are sweat-drenched and every muscle of her body is in agonizing pain. Her eyes flutter as she strains to read the numbers on the face of her watch. She thinks that she's maybe dozed off for only a few minutes, but in fact for hours now she's been slipping in and out of a fevered consciousness brought on by the overwhelming infection that ravages her weak and dehydrated body. It's after two o'clock—midafternoon—and she is suffocating in the still, heavy heat of the closed tent. The only sound she can hear is that of her own gasping, shallow breathing.

But just now she is aware that there is a slight movement in the tent—there is something beside the cot, and Sabine struggles with all her might to open her eyes. . . . She is trying to make out the shadowy, dark form that she senses there beside her. It is the form of a woman . . . a tall woman who is standing over her, peering down into her face.

Oh, thank god . . . she's come . . .

And Sabine stretches her hand out toward the dark shadow of the woman there beside her . . . reaches to touch the other . . .

"Dr. Blair," she says weakly. She is only barely able to form the words between frantic gasps for air. "Oh my god, Leslie, thank you for coming . . . you have to help me . . . please . . . I'm so very sick . . ."

But her outstretched hand touches nothing. And there is no answer to her words . . . no sound at all comes from the woman. And Sabine fights desperately now to raise her head up off the cot—wills herself to focus on the blurred image of the face that she knows to be there above her.

She's watching me, but she won't answer when I speak to her. If only I could see her clearly . . . There, I can see her face now . . . Oh god . . . it's not the woman from Keams . . . it's someone I've never seen before . . . an Indian woman . . . she's just standing there . . . watching me. . . . Wait, she's trying to say something to me, but I can't make out her words . . . I can't understand her. I don't know which it is . . . I don't know if I can't hear her or if I can't understand her . . .

"Oh, yes . . . please . . ."

She's trying to give me a drink of water . . . And she's trying again to speak to me, but I can't make out what she's saying and I don't think she can understand me. My god, her face . . . Her face is bleeding . . . She's been very badly hurt. . . .

And Sabine Vogel slips back into the blackness of unconsciousness for what may be a moment or what may be an eternity. But when she manages to open her eyes again briefly, she believes at first that the Indian woman has gone: Did I only imagine her? . . . Was I dreaming? No . . . there she is again . . . now she's motioning for me to sit up . . . I want to, but I can't . . . Oh, Jesus God . . . I hurt so badly . . .

"I am so afraid!"

But mercifully, Sabine Vogel won't be afraid for much longer. For she is very close now to death.

TÍDÁÁCHIID

Jesus Fucking Christ . . . I thought they said that by doing this stuff early, it wouldn't be quite so goddamned hot!'' Another of the figures has leaned in to speak to the larger one. *''I feel like I'm in a friggin' Ziploc bag!''* It, too, is talking loudly, yet its voice still sounds oddly muffled and is very nearly unintelligible.

''It's never gonna be what you'd call comfortable in these get-ups, gentlemen—but the alternative to wearing them is something I doubt seriously any of us would want to consider. So what do you say we stop all the bellyaching and get this show on the road.''

''What about them?'' Still another of the figures is indicating the small group of men who are standing beside an old and battered pickup truck some distance away, watching the Biohazard Team members as they take their gear from the cargo compartments of the vehicles.

''What about them Indians over there? Aren't they at risk? You know, just by the very fact that they're out here?''

''They'd better hope whatever we're dealing with isn't highly

communicable—isn't airborne, anyway. Until we can get a lock on the reservoir and the transmission—on what the host for the bug is and how it's passed around—we just have to try and keep those people back out of the way."

This team of medical-hazard specialists may not know it, but that won't be much of a problem—keeping these people back out of the way. For while some cultures make almost intimate preparations over their dead—friends and relatives getting together to wash the body, loved ones filing by an open casket to touch or sometimes even to kiss the corpse—that's not something these outsiders can expect to see here . . . not with these Indians. The traditional Navajo won't even speak the name of the deceased for several days after he's died, and later will avoid speaking the name aloud owing to his culture's firmly held belief that the ghost or spirit of the dead will hear its name and believe that it is being summoned. The traditional Navajo is loath to set foot in a place where some person has died—preferring instead to abandon even the family home altogether rather than to do so.

Such traditionally held beliefs will no doubt work to the advantage of the village of Tídááchiid in this case.

"Besides, I'd say from the way that old lady lit out of here on horseback a minute ago, with that scroungy pack of dogs chasin' after her, we're as scary a sight as these folks have seen around these parts."

"Yeah, that woman looked like she'd seen a ghost," the larger one says, turning to look down the wash in the direction the sheepherder has fled.

"If she only knew the half of it . . ."

For nearly three hours the main six-man team of blue-clad investigators has scoured every inch of the house trailer and the area immediately surrounding it.

The other two, it turns out, are along to act as guards. Armed with 9mm sidearms, these individuals have cordoned off—with a long yellow plastic ribbon—the entire area within twenty yards in all directions of the trailer and have spent the remainder of the morning standing by and watching for . . . watching for *what,* exactly?

The main team has worked mostly inside the trailer, gathering samples of every imaginable sort: samples of tap water, of foodstuffs, and of dust and mold from various sites. Samples of dirt and traces of dust have been swept up and saved, including rodent droppings from both inside the living space and out. Soiled linens and various articles of clothing have been gathered up and stuffed into green plastic garbage sacks. Hair samples have been plucked from hairbrushes, and bristles cut from toothbrushes . . . soiled and dried-out disposable diapers have been retrieved from the two fifty-gallon trash drums that stand behind the house trailer. Even old tissues, tissues into which someone has obviously blown his or her nose, have been gathered together in a brown paper sack. No slightly moist area has been left unswabbed, nor has the unlikeliest sample escaped detection . . . escaped being picked up and placed into a plastic bag to be marked and then carried out and set on the ground beside one or the other of the waiting Suburbans.

• • •

Had there been even a single Navajo attached to the Biohazard Team gathering the samples—and there had not been—he or she might have understood that all of this was necessary to the investigation. Might have understood it intellectually, that is—but cultural instinct would no doubt have found it abhorrent. For a Navajo would have known that witches—and there are few among the Navajo even today who doubt the existence of witches—use many of those items being collected by the team to work their evil. To purposefully gather these things would be, to a Navajo at least, clear evidence of the gatherer's intent to do harm.

Witchcraft is the most heinous of all Navajo crimes.

And then, at the end of the three-hour ordeal, the guards—by then bored and sweltering in their Biohazard protective suits—are eager to finally use the heavy metal lag screws they've brought along to attach padlock hasps to the flimsy aluminum doorframes of the trailer. And duct tape to affix bright-orange-lettered KEEP OUT signs to the house's exterior and to several nearby fence posts. And they leave the yellow-ribboned barrier in the place where they have earlier attached it.

One of the guards then retrieves a large yellow cylinder from the pile of gear lying beside the trucks. The cylinder is pressurized and has been fitted with a misting nozzle. One at a time, each of the Biohazard Team members steps up to the guard, raises his arms above his head, and turns slowly while he is sprayed thoroughly with a strong disinfectant solution. And then—still swathed in the heavy blue garb—each climbs clumsily back into the truck by which he arrived. Once the two guards have doused one another and all the remaining exposed surfaces of the sample packages that stand piled beside the trucks, they load the packages into the cargo areas and then spray down the exterior of the trucks themselves. Only then do the guards climb inside.

Five minutes later the truck engines rumble to life and, turning toward the wash, lumber slowly back down the way they have come.

Eeh Tee . . .''

Sampson Billy is the first to speak after the trucks have left Tídááchiid. He has not once moved from his open doorway in all the time the outsiders have been in the village.

All morning long he has watched the goings-on across the wash with quiet interest and a dignified curiosity. At the same time, Sampson Billy's wife has remained inside the dark and relative cool of the hogan. Once or perhaps twice she has come up beside her husband to stand quietly and look past him and out toward the blue figures moving in and around the trailer. Mostly, though, she has gone about her everyday business.

And finally Sampson Billy has spoken.

''Eeh Tee,'' he says again.

The man's wife looks up from where she is sitting—looks up from the cup of scalding-hot coffee into which she is spooning heaps of white sugar from a brown paper bag.

''What are you tryin' to say, old man?'' she says. ''What does that nonsense mean, *Eeh Tee*?''

Sampson Billy looks disgusted. Mary Billy has been a good wife, there is no doubt about that—it's just that sometimes she seems a little . . . well, a little *dense,* is what she seems.

''That's the name of that picture show,'' he says gruffly. ''I'm sayin' to you that all this business reminds me of the picture show—the one that is named *Eeh Tee* . . . the one about that creature who comes down from the stars. I'm reminded of that part there at the end of the show when those government men come chargin' in all dressed up like space commandos . . . how they wind up scarin' ever'body half to death.

"That's what those guys over there reminded me of just now . . . *Eeh Tee*."

Mary Billy blows on and then sips noisily from the steaming cup of coffee. She adds another heaping spoonful of sugar before she speaks. "I think you been watchin' too many of them shows on the TV, old man. You come on and eat some of this here mutton stew I cooked up while you was wastin' the whole mornin' bein' nosy . . . and have some of this coffee, too.

"It's very tasty with some sugar in it, you know . . . it's that good kind that comes in the red can with the picture of the Mexican guy and his donkey that the chubby grocer brings all the way from out there in California or somewhere."

TSÉGHÁHOODZÁNI

It is seven-thirty in the morning and the dining room of the Navajo Nation Inn is completely deserted.

Sonny turns and walks back out to the front desk. The night clerk, Eugene Etcitty, is reading the morning newspaper and yawning.

''Hey Eugene, has the restaurant finally shut down altogether?'' Sonny asks. ''Can't I at least maybe get some coffee?''

''Oh, hello, Dr. Brokeshoulder. No, they're open—there's some people in the kitchen, I was just back there to get me some sugar for my coffee. Go on in and pick yourself out a table, I'll go wake up a waitress.''

''Thanks, Eugene.''

''Of course, I don't know how long we'll be able to keep being open, though—especially if it means payin' the staff. Did you ever see this place so empty as it's been this past couple of days?''

"I was in here at lunchtime just last week and had to wait for a table. . . ."

"That was before the stories in the papers. Now even the Indian Country bus tours out from Amarillo and Albuquerque that have standing reservations for all the rooms in the new wing have been callin' to cancel. I guess the Texas newspapers have heard about our problem, too."

Sonny has helped himself to coffee and is sitting at the table nearest the cash register when Josephine Manygoats comes back out from behind the swinging doors that lead to the kitchen.

"It looks like I'm gonna have to be your waitress this morning, Sonny," she says. "The bosses are layin' off people right and left since there hasn't been much business. I may be the dining-room manager, but if I don't look busy I'll probably be out of a job myself. . . . The next thing you know, they'll be tellin' me to make up the rooms, too," and she hands him a menu.

"I'm glad to see you haven't decided to skip outta town like everybody else. What's the matter, aren't you scared you'll catch somethin' by comin' in here?" Josephine is carrying her own full cup of coffee. She sits down in the chair directly across from Sonny and smiles at him pleasantly.

"Eugene says the hotel rooms are mostly vacant."

"Yeah, as far as I know they're down to one couple who are stranded here because their motor home's in the transmission shop and they either haven't got the sense or the money to catch a bus to Albuquerque. And then they said there's some of those foreign sight-seers who probably can't understand English and so don't know how dangerous the rest of the world figures it is here on the rez."

Josephine Manygoats looks up at Sonny and grimaces nervously, to show that she's trying to make light of what she knows to be a dark situation.

"I kind of appreciate it that it's so quiet around here," Sonny says. "Don't have to wait so long for service that way."

"And I guess that's a hint, huh? Well, of course you would like gettin' all the attention showered directly on you—bein' the only customer, and all. But I can tell you, an empty dining room isn't exactly the most cheerful place when you're counting on tips to pay the bills.''

Josephine drains the last of her coffee: ''Now then, what would you like for breakfast? And don't even *think* about ordering biscuits—Gilbert is poutin' over the fact that even the senior citizens who get their food for half price are stayin' away and so he's refusing to make a lot of the stuff that's listed on the menu.''

''Okay, how about if I just have some white toast, then, and a large glass of orange juice?''

''That should be easy enough,'' she says. ''Gilbert will earn his paycheck and all he'll have to do is push down the lever on the big toaster machine. I could probably even do that myself . . . maybe I should become a cook. I'll be right back.''

When she brings the toast and juice, Josephine sits again and says: ''Did you hear that there was only about a couple of hundred people showed up last night at the big concert out there at the park? They had been predicting there would be something like eight hundred in attendance. But that was back before people started getting sick.''

''I wouldn't have thought there'd have been so much concern over an open-air event . . . mostly we've been advising people to stay out of closed-in situations,'' Sonny says.

''Well, they sure stayed away from that concert,'' she says. ''My sister Shirley went out there last night. She says that about all anybody was talkin' about was the big Navajo Flu epidemic.'' Josephine gets up and refills Sonny's coffee cup and then her own.

''Wasn't this the concert where it was supposed to be the White Trash Band with Rounder Stubbs who was putting on the show?'' Sonny asks.

''Uh-huh . . . Shirley said that Stubbs was almost an hour late getting started and that she heard they couldn't hardly persuade him to come out from his private bus. Can you believe that? She said that he was too chickenshit to come out from his air-conditioned bus and take a chance on breathin' reservation air. It was like he was afraid of catchin' the mystery disease! Can you *believe* that? And him not even an Indian, either?''

''Some people have pretty strong fears, Josephine,'' Sonny says.

''Well, I'm beginnin' to get a pretty strong fear myself that if this thing doesn't blow over pretty soon, all this country around here is gonna end up bein' a ghost town.''

''Well, I don't know that it'll make much of a dent in the restaurant business, Josephine, but you're about to see ten or twelve new customers checking in here to the hotel—if they haven't already.''

''More doctors?'' she asks.

''I guess most of them are doctors,'' Sonny says. ''They're a team of government people who've come in from Atlanta, Georgia, and I suggested that they should headquarter here.''

''Well, thank goodness,'' she says. ''I hope Eugene can find them some vacant rooms,'' and she smiles at Sonny.

''I should warn you, though,'' Sonny says as she refills his coffee cup yet again. ''These white government doctors are notoriously poor tippers.''

''You're tellin' me? I can spot those cheapskate BIA employees from clear across the room—and those skinny ties they wear and those pocket-protectors are just the first signs.'' Josephine lays Sonny's check on the table. ''Thanks for being brave enough to come in here, Sonny. Since I've been demoted to waitress and dishwasher, we don't have a regular cashier, so you can just pay Eugene out at the front desk.''

Sonny leaves two one-dollar bills on the table for a tip and walks back out to the lobby. He hands the night clerk his breakfast bill and five dollars.

As Eugene counts out change, he says: ''You know Ernie Watson, don't you, Dr. Brokeshoulder? The EMT ambulance driver from Gallup? Well, he was in here late last night. Said that him and his partner picked up a Indian girl out at the park who had passed out during the concert—said that she couldn't hardly breathe and that they had to rush her to the Gallup hospital with their sirens on and everything.''

''Is that right?'' Sonny says. ''Maybe she just got worn out from dancing.''

"I don't know about that . . . Ernie Watson said it looked to him like she had *it*."

"It?" Sonny says.

"You know . . . the Navajo Flu." And Eugene Etcitty furrows his brow seriously. "The *silent killer*."

Back in his office, Sonny is on the phone to Ed Pierce.

''Listen, Ed, your EMT boys need to put a clamp on it—the first thing I heard this morning from the desk clerk at the Inn was that Ernie Watson is running around over here announcing to whoever'll listen that some girl fell out at the concert at Red Rock Park last night. Somebody needs to get him aside and give him a good talking-to.''

''Right, I'll take care of it, Brokeshoulder,'' Ed says. ''But I've got to tell you, that was going to be just about my first order of business this morning . . . notifying you that a sixteen-year-old Navajo girl was brought in here last night in acute respiratory failure, and that she died before dawn.''

''Same girl Watson was spouting off about?''

''Yeah. Seems she went out to the concert with some friends and they apparently were all of them dancing and carrying on in a festive mood. Her friends said that after a couple of hours the girl started complaining of a bad headache and then passed out . . . *fainted,* they said. The security people out at the park called the EMT guys right away and . . . well, from there on it was pretty much the same story as we've seen with the others.''

''So that makes thirteen dead that we know of?''

''Yeah . . . that we *know* of. But on a little bit brighter note, the second order of business for me this morning was to let you know that Shorty Bigboy is off the ventilator and asking for his pants.''

''You mean he's better? Breathing on his own?''

''Hell, Brokeshoulder, he's more than just better—he appears to me to be almost fully recovered. If he ever even had our disease, I'd say he's over the hump. His temperature's normal and he has a voracious appetite. . . . I got a fresh chest X ray on him this morning and it's remarkably clear—looks normal, in fact."

"I don't know, Ed. It sounds to me like maybe Shorty had some other bug. The girl at the concert, now she fits more the pattern, I'd say."

"The pattern being that she died . . ."

Sonny hangs up the phone and immediately dials Push Foster at Hashké.

He tells Push about Bigboy's apparent recovery and about the latest fatality at Red Rock. Push has already heard about the girl's death.

"I must have been the last to get the word on that one," Sonny says. "The minute I walked in the door here Priscilla started in on me. She says that Window Rock is all abuzz. The dead girl was a popular student at the high school here—first string on the girls' basketball team.

"It's building up a head of steam, Push. Before I called Ed I'd just gotten off the phone with the president. He's ready to go on the warpath . . . he's got the radio stations issuing alerts in Navajo and in English every half hour and has told the tribal newspaper to hit this story hard. And he's even put out a call for a Nation-wide gathering of medicine people."

Push is quiet for a few moments before he responds: "*Clinton?* You mean to tell me that Bill Clinton's in on all this now?"

There is a long silence on the other end of the line. Finally Push says, "Sonny? Hey, *Sonny* . . . you know I'm just joking, don't you? Just trying to inject a little jocularity to offset the stress."

"Well *shit,* Push . . . you know you had me goin' there for a minute?"

WEPO WASH

The day is at its hottest as the blistering bright sun begins to settle in the late-afternoon sky.

The shadow cast by the jagged western ridgeline has only just begun its slow creep up the opposite slope of Wepo Wash. The matched pair of blue nylon dome tents—positioned as they are so as to catch the first morning rays of sunlight—are already completely in shade. The air here is suffocatingly still and there is a strange noise coming from one of the tents. It is an oddly low-pitched and monotonous buzzing noise that has been increasing in volume, subtly but steadily, over the past several hours.

And now the something that has been watching with black eyes from high on the side of the wash begins to stir from its place. The thing has begun to move slowly down the steep incline . . . begun to move toward the campsite. It moves cautiously at first, creeping from place to place, stopping now to crouch behind a rock or scraggly brush—to watch and to listen. But the only sound to be heard is the monotonously steady, buzzing drone that comes from the sleeping tent.

And then, this thing that has for so many days watched the comings and goings in this place—having worked its way down to the point that it is standing, finally, in this place—moves in a crouch, directly and deliberately, to the sleeping tent and, reaching it, peers inside. The nylon door flap to the tent is not zipped closed and so hangs halfway open. Inside the shade-darkened tent are two low, aluminum-framed sleeping cots, and positioned between the cots is a small folding camp table. There on the small table is a tape player/radio—the switch is in the *play* position, but the batteries are long dead—and alongside that a small clay dish holds two silver and turquoise rings and a single silver earring. There is a half-empty cup of tea and another cup—which is tipped over and is lying on its side—from which have spilled the pens and pencils that it held, several of which have rolled off the table and onto the nylon floor of the tent. And there beside the cot, also on the floor, is an open spiral-bound notebook, with a black-inked script that has begun precisely and neatly but has deteriorated with the writing until ultimately it is little more than illegible scrawls and scribbles.

And finally, stretched out on the cot nearest the doorway, there is the body of a woman. Dressed in stained and rumpled khaki trousers and shirt, the woman is lying on her back, her head pointing toward the doorway, her left leg hangs off the cot and her bare left foot rests on the floor of the tent as though she is trying somehow to steady herself. Her red-tipped fingers are clutching at the material that is the front of her shirt. The bedsheets of the cot are wadded and twisted beneath her. Two pillows have been positioned not beneath the woman's head, but beneath her shoulders—they prop her torso up off the low bed with the result that her head is thrown back at an odd and awkward angle, her neck extended and her throat exposed. Her face is swollen dark—a black-purple, almost—and her mouth is stretched wide in a ghastly rictus of death. Her eyes are open and staring. It is as though this woman has died while in the very act of emitting some horrible and, indeed, horrifying scream of fear. Or perhaps it was a cry of rage.

And the sound—the near-maddening buzzing sound that practically fills the tent—is coming from the flies. For there are neon-green blowflies and common black houseflies swarming and crawling over and around the dead woman's eyes and lips—covering, almost, her entire face. And flies are buzzing, too, around the cot beneath and between her legs where, at the moment of her death or perhaps in the last hour of her life—and what matter does it make, really?—the woman has apparently lost all control of her bodily functions. Oh, but the foul smell of shit and urine—the putrid stench of death—is overwhelmingly heavy in the enclosed, stifling heat of this tent.

And now this thing that has come down off the side of the wash backs cowering away from the sleeping tent and the stinking dead woman and moves deliberately toward the working tent where the spoils and artifacts from this excavation have been so carefully stored.

And so, added to the maddening drone of the flies, there is now in the dry desert air of this place yet another sound: The hollow sound of breaking clay . . . of pottery being smashed.

TÍDÁÁCHIID

Only a couple of days have passed since the two green trucks carrying the blue-shrouded CDC investigators first drove into Tídááchiid, but things have not been the same since.

For one thing, the strange beings in the blue suits have returned on at least two occasions to comb the areas around woodpiles and trash barrels and corn- and grain-storage bins. From the doorway of his hogan, Sampson Billy has watched until the trucks have driven away and then he's crossed the wash to inspect those places where the blue suits have been walking.

''Those fellows are crazy,'' he later tells his wife. ''They put out a whole bunch of small cages with food inside of 'em. It looks like they're tryin' to catch themselves some little animals . . . but I don't know why.''

And the following day Sampson Billy has again watched as the trucks have returned and the blue suits have carefully emptied the cages of the animals trapped inside and then reset them and once more driven away in the green trucks.

And for another thing, several more vehicles have begun arriving in Tídáachiid. And while perhaps not so frightening in their appearance as the green trucks with the black windows, these vehicles have carried with them passengers at least as foreign and at least as invasive. At first they have come quietly enough—driving slowly into the village in rental cars and RV mobile news vans with otherworldly satellite dishes mounted on the roofs. At first, too, these outsiders have been shy and tentative—wary, even—about venturing outside the safety of their vehicles. Rather they have driven slowly into the center of the village, stopped and looked around awhile, and then driven cautiously away again. Only rarely have they turned off their engines. It is as though they feel they need to be ready for a quick getaway in case . . . in case *what?* Once, a side window in one of the vans has opened briefly and a handheld video camera has appeared to slowly pan the Greyeyes mobile home and then across the wash toward Sampson Billy's place. Then, after a couple of days of this, the intruders have grown bored with merely reporting and recording their own impressions of this odd little community where the first cases of the mysterious disease have occurred. And so they have set out to try and talk to the residents and to ask them questions concerning those who have died: Impertinent questions, to the Navajo way of thinking. And it is only a matter of time before they've begun to more aggressively snoop and to pry and to actually physically invade the homes and lives of the simple people of Tídáachiid.

Queenie Chee—the old woman sheepherder who'd bolted that first morning at the sight of the advance team of CDC investigators in their space-age Biohazard suits—has steadfastly refused even to respond to the knocks and honks when the first wave of reporters try to visit her. Then when they persist and return a second time, she opens the door to her hogan just wide enough to allow her motley pack of dogs to charge, teeth-bared and snarling, at the startled and frightened pair of young men—one of whom has frantically hurled his newsroom-issued tape recorder at the attacking mob and scrambled headlong back into his car, skinning his knuckles and ripping his brand-new khaki Dockers on the metal doorpost in his mad rush to escape the shrieking animals. His companion, meanwhile, has frantically clambered up to the roof of their vehicle and danced there precariously, all the while swinging his camera by its strap and calling out mournfully for someone to help him.

Subsequent teams of would-be interviewers who have dared to approach the home of Queenie Chee have been greeted by a crude sign—hand-lettered on a broken piece of plywood and nailed to a post—that reads:

GO AWAY—I DON'T NO NOTHING
MY DOGS WILL BIT YOU!

And there beside the sign stands a very old and very small Navajo woman, chunking stones and bottles with fearsome accuracy at the strangers and their vehicles.

At his place near the wash, Sampson Billy has set up a metal folding chair in the shade of a brush arbor beside the dirt road where it passes closest to his hogan. For the past three days he has spent the daylight hours sitting in the chair and waving at those who pass by. Of the Navajo people who travel this road—and they are few, really—most go on foot, some are astride horses. The outsiders are obvious by their vehicles.

A Styrofoam ice chest with a pink terry-cloth bath towel spread over it is placed beside the chair. Arranged in an orderly fashion on the towel are several pairs of hammered silver earrings and a half-dozen finely sand-cast bracelets and two strings of necklace—one red coral and the other green turquoise and liquid silver. There are several small brown paper sacks—their tops twisted closed and tied up with string.

Like Queenie Chee and several of the other residents of Tídááchiid, Sampson Billy has painstakingly printed up a sign for the newspaper and television reporters and the state medical investigators to see. Unlike the others, however, Sampson Billy's sign does not warn visitors away from his property. Rather he hopes it will attract them.

Sampson Billy's sign reads:

REAL INDIAN JEWRY 4 SALE

COLD POP—50¢

BOWEL CHILI—$1

FRY BREAD WITH SUGAR—$1

HOT COFFEE—50¢

BAG OF ROASTED PINYONS—$2

For a long time now, Sampson Billy has held to the notion that if white people come to him begging to be scalped, it is perfectly reasonable—it's his *duty,* he might even say—to get out his knife and commence to scalping.

TSÉGHÁHOODZÁNI

Late Thursday afternoon, Sonny Brokeshoulder receives a faxed letter from Atlanta. The CDC lab working on the Four Corners virus has come up with an answer based on the findings of the field investigations.

"They say they're pulling everything together and expect to have preliminary findings and recommendations to us within a matter of hours," he tells Push. "I don't think there's much point in you coming over here to wait up all night, but I'll call you as soon as I hear something. I want to see if I can't get Ed and Leslie to come over first thing in the morning, too . . . and my veterinarian friend in Tuba City that I mentioned to you, Joe-Willie Begay, I think I'll try and get hold of him, as well."

Already huddled together at the conference table when Push and Sonny enter the trailer-annex meeting room the next morning are doctors Ed Pierce, Leslie Blair, and Joe-Willie Begay. Leslie is reading aloud to the others from an article in the *Albuquerque Journal*.

"Morning, everyone," Sonny says.

"Have you two seen this morning's paper yet?" Leslie looks up as they walk in. "Is there anything at all these idiot reporters won't latch on to? I mean, for Christ's sake—will you *look* at this: Now they're actually reporting as though it's newsworthy that some blind self-proclaimed shaman from Japan has traveled all the way to Los Angeles, and then hired a limousine to drive him here to Window Rock so that he can put himself into some sort of a New Age trance that will supposedly enable him to let us nonbelievers in on what exactly it is that's killing all these Indians—*Jesus H. MacCarthy*!"

"Yeah, I saw that . . . incredible, isn't it?" Push is anxious to get on to the business at hand. "What we've got for you is definitely not New Age, and it's not even been reported in the papers yet, as far as we know, anyway."

Priscilla Yazzie comes hurrying into the room carrying several stapled sets of the CDC report.

"I wanted you to know as soon as possible that we've gotten the preliminary report and some recommendations from Push's contacts at the CDC," Sonny says. "They got in touch late yesterday to say they were onto something and then I guess worked through the night getting a report prepared for us. Push has been on the phone pretty much steady since five this morning, and what Priscilla's passing around now has just come over the fax in the last hour. We want to get you briefed as quickly as possible so that we can start getting the word out there.''

Priscilla is handing out the CDC report and recommendations. ''These are still warm from the copy machine,'' she says. ''Hot off the press, so don't burn your fingers.''

''Okay . . .'' Push looks around the room. ''In a nutshell, the CDC is saying that our disease is caused by a virus . . .''

''No big surprise there,'' Pierce says. ''That's what we've been thinking since the plague was ruled out, isn't it?''

''. . . a virus associated with rodents,'' Push continues. ''It's not something they've seen before, but everything points to it being a Hantaan-like virus . . . and they're saying that the Hantaan virus is typically rodent-vectored.''

''This is a virus that's spread by rats?''

''More likely by mice, Leslie. Common mice, which are not themselves affected by this specific strain of the infection, but which shed the virus into the environment where it can be contracted by humans . . . and as we're seeing, this is a virus that is, as often as not, fatal to humans.''

''Any indication yet of why it's only affected Navajo Indians, Sonny?''

''It must just be a matter of numbers and opportunity, Leslie. Maybe there are more Navajo coming into contact with more mice . . . we don't really know.''

Ed Pierce has been scanning the report. ''No Hantaan virus has ever been reported in this country, has it? I recall it was first identified in Korea in the early nineteen fifties. And besides, Hantaan's a virus that affects the *kidneys,* isn't it, Foster? It even says so here in the report. . . .''

''That's true. But what they're saying is that it's Hantaan-*like,* Ed. Our patients have succumbed to what they're now calling Hantavirus Pulmonary Syndrome—which just means that from here on we can put a name to it—we can say we're dealing with a *hantavirus*. CDC's been working closely with the World Health Organization on this, and both think that what we have here is a previously unrecognized strain of the virus . . .

they're actually excited—they say we're lucky to be seeing a textbook example of an emerging virus."

"Lucky, huh? Well, that's just great," Pierce says. "A new virus—a previously unrecognized hantavirus—that's often deadly and its reservoir is the common mouse. That's not exactly good news is it, Brokeshoulder? How is this going to set with the local community?"

"A lot of people are skeptical about what they've been seeing reported on the television and in the press, Ed—and not just Navajo people, either. The medicine people say that there's a hole in the sky . . . that bad things are spilling down on our heads. I've heard everything from theories that this is being caused by jet airplane exhaust and young people eating too many Big Macs to rumors that it's something Saddam Hussein snuck over here and secretly sprayed the Chapter Houses with during the Gulf War."

"And we always have the activists—who attribute practically anything that goes wrong to some plot by the federal government to take back reservation lands by killing off all the Indians," Leslie adds.

"We need to all of us study these recommendations and the report very carefully," Sonny says. He adds that Priscilla is getting together press packets to distribute to the newspaper and TV and radio stations: "I'm hoping that if we give them enough information, they may get it halfway right for a change."

"I noticed when I came in a while ago that there are reporters already beginning to gather out in front of the Council Chambers," Leslie says. "Did you see all those trucks, Sonny?"

"Yeah, and the phone's been ringing off the wall in the office all morning," Priscilla Yazzie says. "How in the world do those people find out we're getting news before we even get it, is what I'd like to know?"

"That's why we're over here instead of meeting in my comfortable office," Sonny says. "I guess there's some advantage to having an ugly pink run-down trailer house without a telephone line to hold our secret rendezvous in," and he smiles weakly. "Nobody figures anything important would go on in here."

"Having determined that the disease is viral and identifying the host is an enormous part of the battle," Push says. "The guys in Atlanta admit that they're amazed they've been able to so quickly determine that the bug is carried by mice . . . you know this very well could have taken weeks, if not months.''

''According to this report, they're not just saying it's mice in general, but that it's specifically the deer mouse, Dr. Foster,'' Joe-Willie Begay says. ''And while I'm as impressed as anyone to see that the scientists back there can be so precise, I've got to tell you we couldn't have asked for a worse carrier if we'd tried. . . .''

''How's that, Joe-Willie?''

''In the first place, deer mice are exceptionally common out here—they're just about everywhere, Dr. Blair. I mean, there's probably a half-dozen in this very trailer right now.''

''*Jesus,* did you have to tell me that?'' and Leslie glances wide-eyed around the small room.

''And to be honest, I'm surprised we didn't pick up on the mouse angle ourselves. What I'm saying is, we really should have figured they were involved without having to wait for the CDC team to tell us. I don't know if it's as bad here, but we're seeing easily an eight- or tenfold increase in the rodent population over what we'd normally see this time of year up at Tuba.''

''They're overrunning us all around here, too,'' Sonny says.

''And deer mice are especially easy keepers, if you know what I'm saying. They'll eat anything, they don't hibernate . . . Like I said, we couldn't have asked for a worse carrier.''

''And to add to that,'' Push says, ''this is an extremely fast-moving virus. Once the disease is contracted by a human, it appears to multiply in the body like wildfire. And if it multiplies anywhere near that fast in the host population—in the mice—well . . .'' His voice trails off, and then he adds: ''I don't even want to think about the numbers, then.''

''Do the people in Atlanta have any estimates on when we might be seeing a vaccine?''

''*If* we might be seeing a vaccine is more like the question, Sonny. It's going to take some time for them to get to a point where they can make even an educated guess as to how stable this particular virus is . . . and that's what it takes to determine the likelihood of a vaccine.''

''The polio virus is extremely stable,'' Ed says. ''So we've just about wiped that one out. On the other hand, the influenza bug mutates and changes so rapidly that every flu season our vaccines are, at best, a matter of guesswork.''

''So what's the plan?'' Leslie asks.

''Our most pressing task right now is to get the word out to people to avoid rodents *and* any place they might nest or have been hanging out,'' Push says. ''This report indicates that the virus is shed in the saliva and excreta of the infected mice—the CDC identifies the bug and its reservoir but then leaves it to those of us on-site to determine the way in which the bug is passed to humans. This is a respiratory illness and so we can assume that transmission is airborne or aerosol—on tiny droplets of water. But since mice are not likely to breathe on us or to cough or sneeze in our faces, we have to consider methods of transmission. If the virus they shed can lie dormant in dried droppings and in materials on which they've urinated and slobbered, then it stands to reason that if those droppings are disturbed—by sweeping, say, or shaking hay, or scooping feed for livestock—dust particles carrying the virus become airborne and humans are subject to inhale the virus along with the dust and thus become infected.''

''I can just see it coming.'' Ed Pierce is shaking his head. ''Our best medical advice is now going to be: 'Don't sweep the mouse turds out of your hogans, ladies, or else you and your family are apt to get sick and die.' ''

''Actually, that's probably closer to the truth than you think,'' Push says with a pained smile. ''The Center recommends instructing those most at risk to use spring-loaded traps with bait and not to put out poison, since rodents that eat the poison tend to go off and hide someplace to die—the feeling being that's it's better to know where the bodies are, I guess.''

''I take it then that we should be asking people who come into the clinics with suspicious symptoms about any recent exposure they might have had to rodents?''

''I think it would be a good idea, Leslie—but with this sort of thing patients are generally unaware that they've *been* in close contact with mice or rats or their droppings, so I wouldn't want to get too complacent if someone denies exposure.''

''We all probably ought to quit feeding our house cats, too, so that they'll get to work on the mice, huh?'' Ed says.

''Uh . . . what *about* cats?''

Push looks at Leslie: ''I'm sorry? What're you getting at?''

''Cats,'' she says. ''Has there been any indication that house cats may contract the virus from the infected mice and then pass it on to humans?''

''There's a good question,'' Push says. ''And it makes a lot of sense, but it hasn't come up for consideration as far as I know.''

''Didn't Travis Austin over at Little Springs find his cats dead . . . right after Lizbeth died? . . .'' Sonny asks.

''That's right,'' Leslie says. ''And there have been at least two or three cats that have turned up dead that I've heard about recently in the housing units back at Keams.''

''What about what's his name?''

''Oedipus? He was just fine when I left him this morning, Push.''

Sonny is tapping his pencil on the table. ''Joe-Willie?'' he says. ''You have something to add?''

''I was just thinking that the boom in the rodent population may well have inspired a lot of people to put out poison. And I'm thinking that the dead cats you're seeing could possibly have been themselves poisoned by eating poisoned mice—I know it's happened before.''

''Another good point,'' Push says. ''But if it's either a case of the cats getting the poison secondhand from dead rodents or getting sick and dying from the virus, I don't think we have too much to worry about . . . as far as cats being *carriers,* that is. The rule of thumb in this sort of thing is that if a species is highly susceptible to the pathogen, it's most probably *not* the host.

''Most bad germs get along and live happily enough in their hosts without causing disease—they're only deadly when they leave their primary reservoir and jump onto something new. But all of this is conjecture—there's really no way to accurately predict when something like this may take a notion to mutate. . . .''

"Well now, I know that makes *me* feel a lot better," Leslie says, and she makes a face at Push.

"Uh, Dr. Foster?"

"Joe-Willie, I sure wish you'd call me Push, like everyone else does."

"Yessir," he says. "Uh, I think there's another thing we ought to consider. . . ."

"What's that?"

"I think we'll want to recommend to people that they not let up with flea-control measures at the same time that they're waging war on mice . . . you know, on account of plague."

"I'm not sure I see what you mean," Push says.

"Well, we go to exterminating all the mice—and you know of course I'm being facetious when I say *all* the mice, since we aren't likely to even come close to that—and the flea population will be forced to seek out a new food source, which will have the possible effect of setting off a whole new epidemic of plague."

Sonny Brokeshoulder is staring at the veterinarian. "Joe-Willie Begay," he says. "When did you go and get so smart?"

"Why heck, Sonny." Joe-Willie grins. "Most of the people-doctors I know only ended up going to medical school because they didn't have good enough grades to make it into veterinary college."

And then, looking around the table, Joe-Willie blushes and adds: "Present company excepted, I'm sure."

"Oh, and one more thing," Sonny says. He is standing now as they prepare to leave the room. "And Ed, I think this will be of interest to you particularly. Among the many blood samples we'd sent to Atlanta were some taken from Wiley Bigboy. . . ."

"Don't tell me . . ." Ed Pierce says.

"You guessed it. They say Shorty's blood samples reacted to Hantavirus antigens. He was lucky, I'd say."

"I guess he *was* lucky . . . he survived our disease."

LITTLE SPRINGS

Push shuts off the motor of the pickup and watches the big blue dog that is watching him.

"Hey there, boy," he says. "How you hanging?"

Travis Austin has just finished painting the wall on the west side of the trading post when Push arrives.

"The dog won't bother you, Foster," he calls out. "Get on down and come sit in the shade."

"I'm partial to dogs as a rule, Mr. Austin," Push says, as he climbs down out of his truck and walks toward where the trader is working. "But this guy here just doesn't seem like he'd be one to mess around with."

"Punk's a good boy . . . looks a lot fiercer than he really is." The two men shake hands.

"I had some business to attend to over at Tuba City and thought I'd swing past to see how you're doing," Push says.

"Thought you'd come out to see if I'd succumbed to the dreaded Navajo Flu, did you?" His smile is warm.

"I admit I couldn't help but be a little concerned—but mainly I just wanted to say hello." Push returns the smile. He likes Travis Austin.

"I appreciate that," Austin says.

"I was just painting over the sign," he adds, pointing at the wall. "For more than fifteen years there was writing there that said Stop and See a Real Navajo Indian Weave a Real Navajo Rug . . . Lizbeth insisted that it say that, you understand. She would sit out there at her loom for hours at a stretch . . . anytime there were tourists here. Let them take her photograph, too. And she wouldn't accept money for letting them do it, either." He is smiling at the memory. "I think some people might even have bought goods here on account of that—on account of they appreciated not being ripped off."

"I wish I'd known her," Push says.

The blue dog has come over and sniffed a long time at Push's trouser legs. Then, apparently satisfied, he's plopped down in the dust at the feet of where the two men stand talking.

"You'd have liked her," Austin says matter-of-factly.

"She's out there," he adds softly, and he points vaguely toward a low mesa that rises in the east.

Push feels slightly embarrassed at the big man's sorrow as he tries to think of something to say.

Austin senses his visitor's discomfort.

"Say, did you see my new satellite dish?" he asks. "We never had a television out here before, but it's just so quiet in the evenings now . . . I would never have imagined it would be this way.

"Actually, Punk here has decided it's his own personal television set . . . ever since he discovered that there's R-O-D-E-O broadcast from Mesquite, Texas, on the Nashville Network a couple of nights a week." Austin has spelled out the word *rodeo*. "Did you ever know a dog to get hooked on watching TV, Foster?"

"No sir, I don't think I've ever heard of such a thing."

"I mean, he doesn't just favor the rough stock events like bull riding and saddle broncs, either—he gets real excited over the barrel racing, if you can believe that," and Austin is smiling at the big dog sleeping in the dust.

"Here . . . watch this: *Hey, Punk,*" he says. And the animal lifts one ear tentatively.

"Rodeo!" And this time he speaks the word rather than spelling it, and the dog jumps up as if he's been shot and runs to the back door of the trading post and stands prancing and whining . . . looking back furtively at Austin, who stands gazing at the animal for a long time.

"I don't know," he says, rubbing his hand across his eyes. "I just don't know how long I can stay out here alone."

Later, as Push prepares to drive away from Little Springs, Travis Austin is standing beside the truck—his blue dog is sitting at his feet.

"I just don't understand it," Austin says. "You say it's a virus that's spread to people by mice? I don't see how that can be—I mean, we've always had mice around here. Why would they turn on us all of a sudden like that?"

"I doubt that it's all of a sudden, actually. The mice have probably carried the virus for years. But viruses are unstable—they can suddenly mutate . . . shape-shift. It's what makes them so difficult to deal with."

"Lizbeth had told me how the old people always said you should stay away from mice. . . . *Burn your clothes if they get on them,* they said. . . ."

"You can't feel responsible, Mr. Austin . . . both you and your wife lived and worked side by side. There's no telling why she should have contracted the disease while you didn't."

Austin stands looking off toward the mesa for what seems to Push a very long time.

"You know, most evenings I stand out here looking up there, just around the time when it's beginning to get dark. More than once I'd almost swear I could make out someone standing near to the spot where I buried her. I don't know, it looked like a woman, maybe . . . just standing up there. But then by the time I got up there, there wasn't anyone around . . . no sign anyone had been there, not even tracks in the dust." Travis Austin reaches down and rubs the big dog's head. "I'm probably just *wishing* I'd see someone up there, you think?

''Hell, me and old Punk here, we just can't help but wish our Lizbeth would come walking down off that hill.''

Again there is an awkward silence before the man speaks: ''I should probably tell you that I opened her casket, Dr. Foster. I know I told you I wouldn't, and I really hadn't meant to. It's just that I'd forgotten about her moccasins . . . had forgotten to switch them, back there at Keams.''

''I'm afraid I don't understand. . . .''

''No, I don't suppose you would. . . . It's a Navajo thing. You're supposed to switch them—put the right moccasin on the left foot and the left one on the right foot before you bury someone. I'm glad I remembered . . . Lizbeth would've been real put out with me if I hadn't.''

''Then I'm glad you remembered, too.''

''Did you like it there? Living in Atlanta, Georgia, I mean?''

''It's an awfully big city . . . with all that implies.''

''You think me and Punk might like living in a place like that?''

''I doubt it,'' Push says.

''Yeah, so do I . . .'' And he turns back toward the house.

TSÉGHÁHOODZÁNI

For three days running the word has been passed among the Chapter Houses and twice an hour over the Navajo-language radio broadcasts that the president has called for there to be an unprecedented gathering of traditional medicine people at the Navajo Nation Fairgrounds at Window Rock on Saturday.

"Man, I don't ever remember hearing of anything on this scale," Sonny tells Push. "You know these singers can sometimes be just real jealous of one another—a lot of times you'll hear that one of them thinks that old so-and-so over there isn't a good person, or that he's a witch, even. Getting a whole bunch of them together in one place at the same time is going to be something, all right."

"How many do you suppose we're talking about?" Push asks. "I mean, are there really all that many medicine men practicing nowadays?"

"Oh, hell yes. They've even got an official association that manages to sometimes get itself organized enough to hold meetings to discuss medicine stuff. And I've heard that there's been something like a thousand members or more at any given time—of course, some of that number are herbalists, though. And that still doesn't include the *ndilniihii*—the hand-tremblers—or the stargazers. They're considered medicine people, too.''

''So you're telling me you think there might be maybe a thousand medicine men at this gathering tomorrow?''

''Maybe so,'' Sonny says. ''And not just medicine *men,* but medicine *people*—men and women both. How many actually show up probably depends on how much free food they're going to put out, of course,'' and he grins.

''New Mexico state health officials don't think we should be doing this at all, you know,'' he says. ''And certainly not at the fairgrounds, where there's livestock and where livestock feed is stored. They're saying that the medicine people are running a risk of stirring up dust by dancing—dust that could carry the virus. And they're saying that the plants and herbs that are used in the different ceremonies could very well have been infected by field mice . . . they're *demanding* that this whole affair be called off.''

''What do you think, Sonny?''

''I don't think there's any way that these traditional medicine people are going to listen to a bunch of *bilagáana* government employees telling them that their sacred ceremonies might end up making them sick. Those agency types don't have a clue as to what goes on in these ceremonies, Push. But I felt like I had an obligation to tell the president about the concerns.''

''What did he say?''

Sonny smiles at his friend: ''He said I should tell them they could go to hell.''

''Okay then, since it's going on as planned, it sounds like a gathering I'd very much like to see. Think there's any chance? . . .''

''I'm way ahead of you, Push. The president's people have put out the word that this is strictly a gathering of medicine people and that outsiders will not be permitted onto the fairgrounds during the ceremonies. You and I aren't exactly the kind of medicine men they have in mind, but we're not outsiders, either. So I've already spoken to the president and several of the Council members and they've given the okay for us to be present,'' he says.

''You understand, of course, that I did have to guarantee them that I wouldn't let you pull any of your Choctaw voodoo stuff. . . .''

Only the livestock entrance gate leading to the east side of the rodeo grounds is open on Saturday morning. There are at least a dozen uniformed Navajo Tribal Police officers checking anyone who attempts to enter the fairgrounds when Push and Sonny drive up.

A very large policeman in mirrored sunglasses leans down to peer into the cab of Push's Chevy.

''Oh, it's you, Brokeshoulder,'' he says.

His large, meaty hand rests on the butt of the big black .45 automatic weapon that hangs from his shiny black tooled-leather belt. Push can't help but notice that the highly polished holster holding the sidearm is decorated with an intricate red, white, and blue beadwork design.

''*Yá'át'ééh,* Earl,'' Sonny says.

Still leaning down, the big man studies Push for a long moment. ''I don't believe I've met you, sir,'' he says.

''This is Push Foster,'' Sonny says. ''Push, meet Tribal Lieutenant Earl Tso.'' The two men shake hands. ''Dr. Foster is our new doctor at the Hashké hospital, Earl. Heading it up, actually—he's here this morning at the invitation of the president and the Tribal Council . . . you're supposed to have his name, I think.''

''Yes, I'd heard there was a new doctor at Hashké—and I remember seein' the name Foster on my list.''

The officer points across a dirt lot toward where two young cops are directing vehicles into parking spaces. ''You men can leave your truck over there and walk on up to the grass arena—that's where everybody's getting together.'' He eyes the interior of the truck's cab suspiciously. ''No cameras allowed,'' he adds.

''How's the turnout, Earl—lots of singers show up?'' Sonny asks.

''I'd estimate we're looking at a hundred and fifty, maybe even two hundred *hataałii,* so far, Brokeshoulder. A lot of the older guys especially are bringing along young assistants and sometimes their whole outfits, even. We've been advised not to turn them away if a singer insists on having his helpers—and nearly all of them do. Quite a few herbalists and *ndilniihii,* too.''

''Any newspaper or television people slipping past you?''

''Not a chance,'' he says, his back stiffening. ''Carload of crystal huggers wandered up a little while ago and asked could they maybe sit in and beat their drums and soak up some of the 'power' . . . said they were brothers to all 'Native Americans' . . . I guess you know what I told them dick-heads.''

Tso lifts his sunglasses from his eyes and looks closely into Push's face, squinting. ''What tribe you say you're from, Foster?''

''I'm Choctaw . . . Oklahoma Choctaw.''

''Oh . . . you're Choctaw, huh? Lucky for you. This sickness that's goin' around appears to be zeroing in on just us Navajo people, from what I understand. . . . Anyway, all the cases I've heard about have been Navajo.''

''That's true,'' Push says. ''But I think we have to take into account that this is an area where most everyone is Navajo. It's like, if somebody was to drop a bomb on Window Rock, very few of us would be surprised when most of the casualties turned out to be Navajo people.''

''Be kind of hard to miss us, huh?'' Tso says. ''I see what you mean. So I guess if that same bomb was to fall on, say, New York City, then there'd probably apt not to be even one Navajo Indian on the coroner's list of the dead and maimed—more'n likely there'd be nothin' but muggers and pretty-boys who like to dress up like girls on that list.''

''Well, I'm not sure that's the way I'd like to put it, but you do get my point, I think.''

''Well, thank you, Dr. Foster,'' Tso says. ''I believe I'm beginning to breathe a little easier, already.'' And as he motions them on toward the parking area, he says cheerfully: ''Now Brokeshoulder, you have yourself a good time watchin' the doin's in there . . . try to learn somethin' and don't let any of those medicine people give you any shit about your pigtails,'' and he grins broadly.

''Oh, and Foster?'' he adds.

''Yes, Lieutenant?''

''Don't you worry none—any more Choctaws show up, I'll tell 'em you went on ahead.''

''Odd sort of fellow, that Tso,'' Push says, as he maneuvers the truck into the tight space indicated by a young police officer.

''Yeah, but Joe can be a good guy—most of the time, anyway.''

''*Joe*? I thought you said his name was Earl . . . and how come you say he's a good guy just *most* of the time?''

''Officially his name is Earl, but then there are those times when he gets to thinking he's maybe a little too important—like when being a Navajo Police officer goes to his head, you know—then lots of folks around here take to calling him *Joe* . . . you know, as in *Joe Leaphorn*.''

It takes him a moment, but then Push smiles. ''Oh yeah . . . I get it,'' he says. ''And I imagine he likes the comparison, too.''

''Oh, you bet he does,'' Sonny says.

As the two men walk toward the grassy arena where powwows and song-and-dance social events are commonly held, there come the smells of strong coffee and of the boiling-hot lard used for cooking frybread. A steady stream of people—men, mostly—are also walking into the arena. Several are carrying suitcases or duffel bags, blanket-rolls and, in one case, a footlocker: the *jish,* or medicine bundles of the *hataałii.*

Push is surprised at the number of people who are gathered in the dance arena. There are groups both large and small, and there are lone individuals scattered here and there. And above it all, there is the low and constant murmur of conversation mixed with the high-pitched resonance of men's voices singing and chanting . . . human sounds accompanied by the rhythmic beat of handheld water drums and the muffled *shish* of gourd rattles. The smell of burning sage and other herbal incense hangs heavy in the warm morning air. And that air is still.

As they make their way through the crowd, Push and Sonny stop now and again to watch the medicine men and to listen to the singers and to eavesdrop on the low conversations. Because all of the ceremonial prayers and most of the conversations are carried on in the Navajo language, Sonny does his best to translate for Push.

At one place a very old man is sitting on a finely woven rug. He is completely surrounded by a group of younger men and women—some of whom hold burning smudge sticks and shallow baskets filled with cornmeal and dried herbs and ceremonial rattles and whistles. The old man is speaking rapidly in the barely audible, singsong cadence of his language. From the rapt attention of the people gathered around the man, Push is unsure if this is a set ceremony he's hearing or perhaps some story that the older man is telling.

Sonny listens intently and in a low voice relates to Push all that he is able to understand of the words that he is able to hear: ''This singer's saying this is not a new thing . . . he's telling these people how this same bad sickness has been visited on the Navajo people two times before . . . two times in his lifetime . . .'' Sonny is studying the words.

''Now he's saying that the first time it came he was just a small boy—and he's counting up the years that have passed since it happened . . . he's saying it was sixty-five . . . no, *seventy*-five years ago. . . .''

''That would be what, 1918?'' Push says. ''Remember, there was the terrible influenza in 1918 . . . a worldwide pandemic that killed millions of people. . . .''

''He's telling how the sickness came again when he was a young man . . . says it was the year before his first child was born—in 1934, I think he's saying . . . I'm sorry, the numbers are hard for me, Push.''

''That's okay . . . what else?''

''He's saying both those other times were much like this one . . . that the winters before were short and warm and that there were abundant piñons all year long . . . that the small animals were very numerous . . . and that they ate the grain where it was stored and that many people got sick and many of them died. . . .''

Sonny is listening and frowning.

''What is it?'' Push asks. ''What's he saying now?''

''Nothing . . . He's changed the subject. He's finished with his story now, I guess,'' Sonny says. ''He's started reciting a traditional prayer, is all.''

A short time later, Sonny directs Push's attention to where an old woman wearing a faded purple blouse is sitting in the bleachers drinking coffee from a Styrofoam cup. He tells him that the woman's name is Birdy Tooclanny, and that she's a well-known hand-trembler.

''She's from up there around Tídááchiid,'' he says. ''I'll bet you she's the one who did the ceremony over that young woman up there . . . over Yvonne Tsosie before she died.''

''Do you think we can talk with her?''

"Let's go see. I don't know if she'll talk, or even if she will, whether she'll talk in English—although I suspect she'll be able to understand you, so watch out what you say."

"*Yá'át'ééh,* grandmother," Sonny says to the woman when they've climbed into the bleachers. "Do you remember me? I'm Sonny Brokeshoulder, I stay down here at Window Rock. This man here beside me is my friend Push Foster—he's the doctor over there at Hashké."

The old woman cups her left hand over her eyes to shade them from the bright sun. She peers up into Push's face. Her eyes are milky-white with age. She sets her coffee cup on the bench beside her and offers her hand to Push. She smiles, but says nothing.

Sonny begins to speak to the woman in Navajo. She listens for what seems a long while, and then begins to speak excitedly. Her eyes dart from Sonny to Push, and her hands flutter about in front of her mouth as she speaks.

Sonny translates his own and the woman's words in bits and starts: "I asked her if she would talk about the Tsosie girl to us . . . asked how the girl had been acting when she saw her."

"What's she say?"

"That she believes this girl may have been going around the ruins over at Canyon de Chelly—the Anasazi ruins—and that she was probably gathering broken pottery off the trash heaps."

"Why would she do that?"

"Some of the potters nowadays believe in grinding up the bits of pottery that they find and adding it to their fresh clay—they say it makes the vessel stronger and that that way the old potter has a hand in it, too."

"You don't usually think of the Navajo as being pottery makers," Push says.

"Oh, there's a couple of Navajo families that are doing it—trying to bring it back, anyway. One outfit from up there around Shonto is even getting fairly popular with some of the collectors, I think."

"Is she saying that picking up the pottery pieces had something to do with the girl's illness?"

Sonny speaks some more with the old woman.

"She says that messing with the belongings of dead people causes grave sickness in the living . . . *ghost* sickness, she says."

Now the woman begins to grow agitated . . . her words come rapidly and her voice rises in pitch.

"What is it that's getting her so worked up?"

"It doesn't make a lot of sense to me . . . I think she's saying that there was a strange woman in the hogan on that day when the Tsosie girl was so sick . . . and she's insisting that she wants you to tell her who that sad woman was."

"Why does she think I would know? Do you have any idea what she's talking about?" Push asks.

"Like I said, it's not making much sense to me . . . but then I might not be understanding her, is all," Sonny says. And he again tries talking to the woman in Navajo.

"She keeps saying over and over that there was a dark woman with marks of some kind on her face who came into the hogan that day . . . and that some of the people who were there didn't see the woman and that those who did didn't seem to know who she was. . . . That this strange woman didn't speak to anyone or make any sound at all, but she was crying into her hands over the young girl who was sick . . . crying over Yvonne Tsosie . . ."

Sonny and the woman talk some more. Sonny looks at Push.

"I told her didn't neither one of us know this strange woman. And she says that's all she has to say, then."

And Birdy Tooclanny smiles up at Push and extends her hand once more.

"Thank you, Mrs. Tooclanny," Push says.

And the old hand-trembler turns away to gaze out at the activity in the arena. It is clear that she is finished talking about this or any other matter with Sonny Brokeshoulder.

"What did you make of that?" Push says, as the two men wind their way down out of the bleachers and across the arena.

"I have no idea. Maybe she saw a ghost in the hogan that day . . .

that, or she had herself a vision. I don't know, Push. Maybe I just misunderstood what she was asking us, is all.''

''Yeah, but did you notice something odd about the way she was looking directly at me when she was telling you about the dark woman with marks on her face?''

''Birdy Tooclanny's nearly blind, Push . . . she probably couldn't tell *who* she was looking at.''

''Well, I don't know about that . . . it's just that it seemed there for a minute that I maybe should know what it was she was talking about, Sonny . . . it was as if I was about to remember something, you know? Like I could almost see the face of that dark woman myself . . . could see her there crying . . .''

But just then, as if some word has been passed through the crowd, a strange hush falls slowly over the arena. This quiet does not come all at once, but when it has arrived, it brings with it an almost palpable stillness.

Sonny and Push have stopped dead in their tracks at this unexpected change in the whole atmosphere of the place. Without exchanging another word, the two men let their eyes follow the collective gaze of those gathered around them toward a place where they see that a group of men have just entered the arena and are standing together, surveying the scene before them.

It is a group of six Indian men who have drawn the attention of all those present. Five of these men are carrying boxes and baskets, the sixth one carries a melon cradled in the crook of one arm and several ears of corn.

And now Push begins to make out a single whispered word that is passing throughout the crowd . . . hears the word more clearly as it is repeated by those standing nearest to him:

''Kiis'áanii . . . kiis'áanii . . .''

''Kiis'áanii.'' Sonny says the word softly. ''Hopi Indians . . . Do you see them over there?'' And he purses his lips and only barely nods toward the six men. ''It's our friend Clifford Lomaquaptewa.''

The men begin walking slowly and deliberately across the arena—they walk with such a sense of purpose that Push wonders what it is exactly they are aiming for. The gathering of Navajo people fall back easily. Without anyone actually seeming to move, a path opens to make way for these Hopi men to pass. It is almost as though this parting of the assembled crowd has been planned . . . practiced, even, so smoothly and uniformly does it take place.

The six come to a halt only when they've reached the place near the center of the arena where there are three Navajo men sitting together on the grass. There is a very old and intricately woven Burnt Water–style rug spread out before them and upon this rug many objects have been neatly laid out: small medicine bundles, bull-roarers and bone whistles, prayer sticks, and other ceremonial paraphernalia. In the exact center of the rug there is a smudge pot in which a green braid of sweetgrass is smoldering.

"Those three men there are very important *hataałii,*" Sonny whispers to Push. "The one there in the middle is the husband of that hand-trembler we just talked to—the husband of Birdy Tooclanny."

Now one of the Hopis has begun speaking to the medicine men. He places the box he is carrying down beside the rug and stands off to one side as each of his companions takes his turn and offers the items he is carrying to the singers.

"Gifts from Hopi," Sonny says. "Corn, piki bread, candies and fruit . . . It's the tradition."

Then the Hopis sit down across from and facing the Navajo men—a pack of cigarettes is passed around, and each man takes one and lights it with the burning sweetgrass.

Sonny's voice is very low now . . . he is whispering to Push: "They say that *Hastiin* Tooclanny is one of only two or three singers left who remember how to do the Evil Way Form of the Male Shooting Chant. And that is a very dangerous ceremony. . . ."

Slowly now the people who make up the crowd in the arena begin to go back to their previous business—the noise of the conversation and the drumming is soon as pervasive as it had been before the Hopi delegation arrived.

"In the Evil Way Form of the Shooting Way they say that the singer actually calls for the sickness . . . summons the evil that is causing the problem in the patient and tells it to come into his own body instead,'' Sonny explains. ''He purposely invokes the badness and then dismisses it—tells it to go away. . . . Like I said, it's extremely dangerous to do . . . both for the patient *and* the singer. One little mistake and the medicine man will be left with the evil inside himself. . . .''

The two men continue to watch with interest the strange meeting that is going on just a few yards away from where they stand.

''I recognize all but one of those Hopi men,'' Sonny tells Push. ''Three of them are priests—which is pretty much the same as Navajo medicine men—and I'm pretty sure each one of them is from a different mesa.''

Although Push can't hear what's being said, it strikes him that the words that pass among the men seated together are likely being spoken in both the Hopi and Navajo languages—and that there is probably a good deal of translation being carried out among them.

''And I'm also pretty sure that the guy in the blue shirt sitting there beside Clifford is a headman from Hotevilla,'' Sonny says, ''which is a Third Mesa village. And since Clifford's from Mishongnovi up on Second Mesa, I'd say it stands to reason that the old man I don't know is from First Mesa—either Walpi or Sichomovi, most likely. Which would mean we're probably seeing a delegation representing all three of the mesas . . . and most probably six different villages.''

''Aren't you surprised to see them here?'' Push asks. ''I mean, Hopis at a gathering of Navajo medicine people?''

''I don't get it,'' Sonny says. ''But those men are too important to be turned away at the gate . . . they're outsiders, but it's not like they're tourists. They brought traditional gifts and apparently they've come to talk to the head medicine men . . . it's only proper that they be treated as guests.

''I still don't understand, though,'' Sonny adds, ''why they'd come.''

When about twenty minutes have passed, the nine men who've been talking among themselves get to their feet. Push sees that Clifford Lomaquaptewa has noticed something on the far side of the arena that has captured his attention. He watches as Clifford strides quickly away from the others and picks his way deliberately through the milling people until he comes to a place where there is a tall, thin man in a black hat standing alone and off to one side.

Because of the way the other man is facing—away from the arena—Push is unable to see his face, but he is able to tell that Clifford is saying something to the man. Push can see that the Hopi man's eyes are dark and deadly serious as he looks directly up and into the face of the other, and that his hands are balled into tight fists . . . he can see that Clifford Lomaquaptewa is angry.

And then Clifford turns abruptly and walks back to where his companions are shaking hands with the Navajo medicine men. He joins the others and the six begin to make their way toward the opening between the bleachers and the food booths, which leads to the exit from the arena. Although the path they are taking will lead them exactly past the spot where Push and Sonny are standing, Push can see that Clifford's eyes are fixed firmly on the ground before him as he walks—can see that this man will likely pass by without noticing him and Sonny. But then, just as he passes closest to where they are, Clifford stops beside them. He raises his eyes and looks directly into Push's face:

"I know what that one is up to," he says.

"What? . . ." Push says. "What do you mean?"

"That one over there . . ."

And when Clifford looks toward the spot where he had been speaking to the man in the black hat, Push sees that the man has turned his face toward him now . . . Push sees that the tall man in the black hat is Silas Slowtalker.

"There's a whole lot of strong medicine goin' around in this place today, Push Foster," Clifford says, and his eyes follow Push's to where Slowtalker stands watching them.

"But that one there . . ."—and he points with his lips and chin at the tall old man—"that one has two hearts. His medicine is bad."

And with that, Push watches as Clifford Lomaquaptewa follows the five other Hopi men out of the arena. And when he looks back a moment later, he sees that Silas Slowtalker is no longer standing there.

What the hell was that all about?'' Sonny says as the two walk across the parking lot toward Push's truck.

''I mean, that business about *two hearts*—did you know that's the way a Hopi talks about a *witch,* Push?''

''No, I didn't know that.''

''He wasn't saying that about Silas, was he?''

''I don't know,'' Push says. ''I was hoping you'd be able to tell me.''

''Man, I don't have a clue,'' Sonny says. ''Understand, I like Clifford Lomaquaptewa. We're pretty good friends, I'd say—and he's always been real straight with me. But I have to tell you, there's just some things about the way a Hopi looks at the world that escape me altogether. . . .''

HASHKÉ

On Monday morning as Push Foster walks into the front door of the Short Mountain Cafe, Yolanda waves to him from her place at the cash register:

"Say, Dr. Foster? I was hopin' you'd come in. . . . Can I ask you something?"

"I don't know, do you have health insurance?" Push looks perfectly serious as he says this and it takes the cashier a moment to catch on that he's making a joke.

She has been studying the newest edition of the weekly *Navajo Times,* which is spread out on the counter in front of her. There is an advertisement with a cartoon drawing of a vicious-looking rat that takes up a quarter of the newspaper's back page. The ad has large banner headlines that read MEDICAL ALERT and NEWS BULLETIN in bold type.

"I was wonderin' what you think of this 'Medic-Wash' that it says here you can order through the mail?" she says. "I mean, do you think it really works like they say?"

"Never heard of it," Push says. "Let's see, what are they saying?"

"Well, it says here that this stuff'll kill all the bacteria and the germs that are causing this hantavirus disease, for one thing. Then they also say it kills the TB and the herpes, and even the Hong Kong flu. They're saying this product will take care of all your health and cleaning needs."

"It's all bullshit, Yolanda—don't waste your money. Plain soap and water will kill everything on this list. This is nothing but a rip-off. . . ."

"Yeah? Georgia *said* it was a con job," the cashier says, shaking her head. "How can they get away with charging fifty-five dollars for a jug of disinfectant and a couple of mousetraps, anyway? See, it says to send them a money order and then allow four to six weeks for delivery—seems to me a person could just as well drive over there to Nevada and pick up her own Medic-Wash a lot quicker than that . . . you might just wind up dead if you have to wait six weeks."

TSÉGHÁHOODZÁNI

When Sonny Brokeshoulder walks into the Navajo Health and Human Services office that morning, Priscilla Yazzie is fuming:

''If you don't do something about these dead mice, I'm going to take my annual vacation early and go stay with my sister up in Utah and let somebody else deal with all this stuff. . . .''

''What are you talking about, Priscilla?''

''I'm talkin' about dead mice, is what I'm talkin' about!'' She points to a cardboard box on the floor next to the filing cabinets. ''Those signs you been havin' me take around telling people what all they should be doin' to avoid catching the virus have just ended up causing a lot of people to start acting very crazy,'' she says.

''Crazy how? What could our notices have done?'' Sonny asks. ''Aren't people getting the word about ways to help control rodents?''

''Oh, people are catching their mice in traps like we recommended, all right—but then these crazy Indians around here are putting their dead mice into grocery sacks and bringing them in or else mailing them in envelopes to our office because they think we can run a test to check if they got the disease. What are these people *thinking,* Sonny?''

''I don't know, Priscilla, but if you see anything that you even suspect is a dead mouse, you're to take and spray it or the envelope or whatever with Lysol disinfectant. Then you're to put it in one of those red plastic contaminated-waste bags I got for you so that I can have it burned or buried. Now don't get yourself worked up into a hissy fit, Priscilla . . . but don't you be shuffling those things around, either,'' he says. ''We sure don't want any kind of stirring around that might kick up the germs.''

Sonny has taken the large green can of Lysol and is spraying the cardboard box and its contents. ''And we're going to have to get the radio and newspaper people to start making it clear to people that they're not only not to handle dead animals themselves, but that they're also sure as heck not to take or send them anywhere.'' He is gingerly placing the box in a plastic garbage bag.

''We should probably talk to someone over at the post office, too—tell them they're going to have to keep a watch out for anything that seems like it could be infectious material and then stop it before it goes out on some postal worker's rounds. . . .'' And he sprays the outside of the first garbage bag before placing it in yet another one.

''Shit,'' he says, as he carries the double-bagged box of dead rodents out the door.

HASHKÉ

In the two days that have passed since the gathering of medicine people at the fairgrounds in Window Rock, Push Foster has been troubled by the nagging sense that he should go back and talk with Clifford Lomaquaptewa . . . to try and find out what it was about Silas Slowtalker that had so upset the man. Finally last night he'd called Sonny to tell him that he was going to take a run over to Mishongnovi first thing in the morning.

''It's like there's something pulling at me, Sonny,'' he'd said. ''I don't know what it is, but I almost feel like something's telling me I have to go up there and talk with him.''

''You need to listen to those voices whenever they speak to you,'' his friend had told him. ''I think it's on account of hearing them in the first place that we Indians have gotten so popular lately—it's like white people have got it into their heads that we're every one of us a bunch of holy men and New Age shamans and that for some reason or other we just naturally have all the answers. So I figure any time you hear a voice talking to you, you better listen to what it's saying . . . it might just be telling you one of those answers.''

There is a minute of silence on the phone and then Sonny begins to chuckle.

''Shit, Brokeshoulder,'' Push says. ''I can't tell but about half the time anymore when you're being serious and when you're pissing on my shoes. . . .''

MISHONGNOVI

The steady sound of drumming is louder now.

And when Push has made his way to the backside of one in a line of small houses facing the village center, he can see that people are gathered close up beside the wall in the alleyway leading into the plaza proper. Today there are clouds in the sky and the sun is not nearly so fierce as it might otherwise be this time of year, and yet the people—out of habit, he thinks—have crowded together by this particular wall in order to take advantage of what little afternoon shade it affords and still see the goings-on in the tiny plaza. Push stands just over six feet in height and so is a full head taller than most of those gathered around him.

There are people sitting and standing on rooftops, looking down into the village plaza. From his position between the rough stone-and-mud houses, Push can see mainly the backs of the many people crowded together. There are men in blue jeans wearing boots or tennis shoes; a few sport baseball caps, most are bare-headed—their coarse black hair cut in the Hopi pageboy style. And there are short, heavyset women draped in colorful shawls—many with umbrellas raised against a sun that beats down one minute and the next is hidden behind some offshoot of cloud-shadow racing now across the sky. Heavy dark clouds on the horizon are piling higher and lifting—roiling up into a towering thunderhead that is building from the southwest. Most of the onlookers are standing—stretching and craning their necks the better to see; some are squatting alongside walls, and some—mostly old women positioned around the edges of the open area—are seated in aluminum-framed green-and-white nylon-strapped lawn chairs. Except for the children darting in and out of the crowd—elbowing their ways among the legs of the adults, children with their hands filled and pockets bulging with candies and fruits—except for the children, all are watching with fairly rapt attention the activity on the plaza. It is apparent to Push that a dance has only just ended—one phase of some larger, afternoon-long dance, that is—for as he comes up he sees that the last half-dozen or so in a line of what would likely be fifty or sixty costumed dancers are just now shuffling, weary-looking, out of the plaza, filing down a pathway between two rows of houses, back toward what he imagines to be a kiva, where the men will rest and eat for a time and make their preparations for the next phase of this dance.

Push sees, too, that the five clowns that are a part of the dance have remained behind on the plaza. At first the clowns, covered with chalky white paint and naked but for breechcloths and odd-looking fur caps, amuse the crowd of onlookers by the outrageously exaggerated way in which they pantomime and mimic the dancers who have just departed. They engage one another in footraces and low-grunting wrestling matches and in boisterously loud, nonsensical conversation. And, as always, there are the skinny dogs. The dogs—and there are three that Push can see—mostly cower around the edges of the crowd, but then one will suddenly dash across the open area only to be chased and tormented mercilessly by the clowns, who whip and kick the poor, frightened animal. And then, watching anxiously the roiling blackness in the sky that has been steadily building and now bears down on the mesa, three of the clowns begin to point and gesture toward the clouds, all the while chattering loudly and with great excitement. And there begins now a low, almost palpable murmuring sound that passes throughout the crowd as the people look up toward the sky. Many of the men are pointing now, and Push notices that the women—as though at some signal—have gathered their shawls more closely about their shoulders. Mothers have gathered their younger children more closely about them, as well.

Suddenly there is a crash of thunder that is near-deafening in its intensity—and in just the instant that it takes the booming, rumbling sound to subside, the air has so filled with electricity that it trembles.

At the very moment of the crash, all five of the clowns have fallen to the earth as though they have been struck dead—felled, it seems, by the earthshaking boom of thunder. Push thinks for a moment that the clowns may actually have been stricken by some bolt of lightning that he has not seen, so immediate and so final-appearing has been their reaction. And now a palpable wall of fierce wind slams, pounding-screaming, into the mesa-top: Skin-stinging sand and dust and all manner of debris—swirling scraps of multicolored trash of all sizes and shapes; flying hats and scarves. And suddenly there is an incongruously soaring aluminum folding chair flanked precisely by two brightly colored umbrellas, swirling and flying, missile-like, climbing and twisting as though they are being lifted and thrown by some invisible hand—or pulled by some incredible force, even—into the clouds. And all of a sudden now the clowns come back to life—leaping to their feet, they run helter-skelter out of the plaza—bolt headlong down the path and toward the burrowlike kiva where the dancers have retired. People cover their eyes . . . they bend or squat low as they try to turn their backs to the buffeting wind. But the wind, like the black wall of cloud that accompanies it, roils shifting and swirling . . . changing in velocity and direction.

Ah, but it is maddening, this storm. A blinding, ragged streak of blue-white lightning scribbles its way across the sky to the north and immediately there is another peal of thunder—this one louder even than the first one had been. Children are clinging wide-eyed and frightened to the legs of their parents. It is remarkable how suddenly dark the sky has grown and how loud the wind now moans and wails. And raindrops have begun to fall. Startlingly cold and wind-driven, the drops at first are large and make distinct and individual plopping sounds where they strike the dust, faster and faster . . . and there is an increasingly rapid banging sound where the pelting drops find the occasional corrugated roof—it sounds as though dozens of iron hammers are striking the tin. And still the rain comes, faster and faster, until it is falling-whipping down and around in torrents—sheets of water carried, lifted and now driven by winds—spumes of muddied cold water pouring deafeningly from rooftops and rushing down over the sides of sheer mesa precipices. The narrow path leading up from below is at once a churning, boiling brown river of mud and trash—pop cans and plastic wrappers, corncobs and bottles hurtling along and down. The people—and they are, curiously, smiling now, out of breath and laughing mostly—have made their ways into houses or have huddled together where there are overhangs and crude awnings that afford at least a modicum of protection. The water has come too fast even to begin to soak into the hard-packed earth of the plaza—it is fast pooling now, in a widening lake of foaming brown liquid. A single dog—yellow and one-eyed, bone-skinny and mangy, lame in its off-hind leg—is making its way frantically across the plaza-lake where the churning brown water forms eddies and swirls as the dog splashes sodden-coated and madly yipping toward higher ground.

And then, suddenly, when only a very few minutes have passed, the rain stops abruptly and the wind subsides, becoming an intermittent breeze, cooler now than before, and the sounds of the pouring runoff—from rooftops and over the sides of this place—are louder even, magnified now that there is no competition with wind noise.

And then the storm walks on north and east and the top of this Hopi mesa is once again almost frighteningly still.

Along with several other people, Push has sought out what protection from the driving wind and rain there is to be found beneath the pitch of a low lean-to shed crudely built off the wall of one of the houses—built, he imagines, to serve as the summer cooking and eating place for one of the village families.

Looking out at the blackness of the fast-moving rainstorm as it makes its way off the mesa, toward Low Mountain in the general direction of Chinle and on toward Canyon de Chelly, he is startled when he hears his name spoken.

"Hello, Push Foster." The voice is that of a short, dark figure wearing a bright green Army-surplus rain poncho with a hood. "So, how do you like our summer showers up here on Hopi?"

"Oh, hello, Clifford. That was some shower—it was what my family back home would have referred to as a 'toad strangler.' Certainly did cool things off. I just hope the dancers aren't discouraged—I was looking forward to seeing them dance."

"But why should they be discouraged? 'Cause it rained? That's the whole reason why they were doin' that particular dance in the first place." And Clifford Lomaquaptewa smiles and winks at Push. "You know . . . that's how come we Hopis call it a *rain dance*."

"Oh . . . but of course . . . it was a rain dance." Push glances quickly toward the other man. He is remembering what Lomaquaptewa had told him on the day they'd first met—how he'd said it would rain soon—and now he wonders if his leg is being pulled. Probably not.

Clifford stands looking at the storm moving north. ''You know whenever you see them clowns tormenting the Kachinas during some of the dances?'' he asks. Push nods. ''Well, whenever they do that it has a tendency to make the cloud spirits very angry. . . . Oh, boy, I mean to tell you it can really piss them off.'' He motions toward the black sky. ''And when the cloud spirits get all worked up and angry like that, they usually send some rain. That's how come they do it, you know.''

''Well, it certainly worked this time, I'd say. I was hoping that I'd see you here today, Clifford.''

''Yes, I know . . . that's why I sent for you.''

''Sent for me?'' Push says. ''You say you sent for me?''

''Of course,'' Clifford says simply. And because he says nothing more, both men stand silently for several moments—bathed in bright sunlight, watching the storm as it recedes across the barren, cloud-darkened Hopi landscape and on toward Navajoland.

When finally he speaks again, Push says: ''Clifford, I wanted to ask you about what went on at the gathering of medicine people the other day. . . . I was wondering if you would maybe talk to me about those men you were with. . . .''

''Those were headmen from the different districts,'' Clifford says. ''We traveled over there to talk with those Navajo *hataałii* about what all's goin' on with this thing that's been causin' people to die.''

''I wanted to tell you that the doctors at the big laboratories in Atlanta have come up with some answers that help explain what the sickness is. They've determined that it's a virus that affects the lungs and that it's spread by coming in contact with mice.''

Clifford looks hard at Push. ''Do you believe that, Push Foster?''

Push is taken off guard by the question. ''Well, sure,'' he says. ''I mean, we know that viruses can . . .''

Clifford tugs the hood of his rain poncho down off his head. He is looking directly into Push's eyes.

''You just think you know these things, my young friend,'' he says. ''But I have to tell you that sometimes you don't know shit.''

''But . . .''

"No, you should listen to what I tell you now. . . . There was an old man over there at Window Rock that day, a man they call Slowtalker. . . ."

"Yes, I know him . . . or I've met him, anyway," Push says. "And I know you were talking to him and that you seemed to be upset."

"This Slowtalker, they say he used to be *hataałii*—used to do good for his people—but then something evil got ahold of him somehow and now he does the Bad Way."

"You said to me as you were leaving the fairgrounds that Silas Slowtalker has *two hearts*. . . . Sonny Brokeshoulder tells me that is the Hopi way of saying a person is a witch."

"Only a person with two hearts would disturb another person's grave." Clifford is quiet . . . he seems deep in thought.

"Do you know that trader from up there at Little Springs? The one whose woman died from this sickness?"

"Travis Austin . . . yes, I know him."

"Did you know that he came to see me awhile back?" Clifford continues. "He came to tell me that there's a white man who has been digging up Hopi town sites over there by Wepo Wash, and that this white man has got his hands on something that belongs to the Hopi people . . . something very important and very powerful that was stolen from over there at Hotevilla a long time ago."

"I see," Push says. "But what does Silas Slowtalker have to do with it?"

"I believe that Slowtalker is in cahoots with the white man who has the Hopi tablet. . . . I believe that it was Slowtalker who gave it to him in the first place, or else told him where he could find it."

"This is all very serious and important to your people, I know, Clifford. And maybe I'm missing something here, but I still don't see what any of this has to do with the problem we're facing with Navajo people getting sick and dying. . . ."

"Of course, you wouldn't understand. . . . It wasn't supposed to be the Navajo who got sick, Push Foster—it was supposed to be the Hopi. The wrong people are getting sick on account of the witching power went all wrong. It was Slowtalker who brought this terrible thing down on the heads of the Navajo. That's why we went over there to see those medicine people—to warn the *hataałii* that Silas Slowtalker has two hearts . . . that his medicine has gone bad . . . terribly bad.''

Clifford stands silent for what seems to Push like several long minutes—gazing out across the land. When finally he speaks again, he says: ''And now I think that things are getting worse—that Slowtalker's medicine has gotten completely away from him and he can't even control it anymore.''

''What do you mean by that, Clifford?''

Without answering, Clifford steps out across a shrinking puddle of brown rainwater and begins to make his way toward his house.

''Come on, Push Foster,'' he says over his shoulder. ''Let's go and see if Mary Esther has some of her good strong coffee for us to drink while I tell you why I sent for you.'' And Push follows.

When she has poured steaming cups of coffee for both men, Mary Esther Lomaquaptewa pulls the hem of her shirt down taut so that the lettering is more easily read.

"How do you like my new T-shirt, Push Foster?" she asks.

The writing on the shirt reads Don't Worry, Be Hopi.

"I like it, Mary Esther. It's very clever."

"This picture here is of the Hopi symbol for rain," she says, looking down and pointing at the cloud with the diagonal lines beneath it. "I thought that wearin' it might help to bring the rain today," and she laughs. "I think it worked."

And then, like before, Mary Esther Lomaquaptewa busies herself on the far side of the room, leaving the two men to talk in what passes in such a small space for private.

"Did you enjoy seein' the dancers, Push Foster? Were you there long enough to see all three of the sequences?"

"No," Push answers. "They were heading back down toward the kiva when I arrived, I'm sorry to say."

"Do you know why it is that the dancers always do three sequences—why they dance on just three sides of the plaza?"

Push shakes his head. "No, I guess I don't, Clifford."

"It's because they know that they have to leave the dance unfinished. That if they complete the cycle—that is, if they was to face all of the four directions—it would finish up the dance." He looks directly into Push's eyes. "And then if the dance was over it means that the world would come to an end."

Push is taken with how matter-of-factly Clifford Lomaquaptewa says that the world would end if the dance cycle were ever to be completed.

''I guess it's sort of like what the old people used to tell us back home in Oklahoma,'' he says. ''They used to sometimes say that as long as the people dance, the earth will live.''

''Same kinda thing,'' Clifford says as he blows on and then sips his coffee.

''About this sickness that's been goin' around over there?'' Clifford Lomaquaptewa is speaking low now as he hunches over his coffee cup, stirring more sugar into the already sweet black liquid. ''Are you telling me that your white doctors are sayin' that it's caused from some germs that the mouse people spread around?''

''Well, I guess that's one way of putting it,'' Push says. ''It's a hantavirus—a viral infection that affects the lungs and is spread through exposure to rodent nests and their droppings.''

''I don't know,'' Clifford says, rubbing his hand across his chin. ''That sounds pretty superstitious to me . . . blamin' it on mice and some germs that you can't see.''

''It's the best science we've come up with yet, Clifford,'' Push says.

''Have you ever heard about the Hopi Prophecy, Push Foster?''

''I've read some about it. . . . About *Pahaana,* mainly.''

''Yes . . . *Pahaana* . . . Elder Brother. Okay, then maybe you know that the Hopi are taught that Elder Brother will come back to judge and punish the people of this world someday—that all the people will be judged according to how well they have kept to the Hopi Way and maintained the ceremonies and kept righteous and not forgot things. And the Prophecy goes on to say that not just the Hopi will be judged, but the Navajo, too, and . . . and that they'll be judged according to if they've done right to the Hopi and not stolen our lands or any of our sacred objects. . . .''

Clifford sits awhile, sipping coffee and staring out the open door into the bright sunlight. The air smells fresh and clean from the rain.

''You know,'' Clifford says, ''whenever things go wrong, it's because someone's heart is not right . . . and the punishment for that comes down as sickness or sometimes maybe crop failure.''

"So this sickness among the Navajo is punishment?" Push asks. "Is that what you're saying?"

"I believe that's right. Of course it's not always easy to figure out the ways of the Holy People," Clifford says, and he shrugs his shoulders. "But I believe we can probably take some kind of comfort in knowing that the Prophecy also says that one day Elder Brother will come and cut the heads off all the witches."

"Pretty strong punishment, all right," Push says. "You know, Sonny Brokeshoulder told me that the Navajo believe that witches who aren't found out and punished will eventually just get struck by lightning."

"I think that them Navajo are maybe a little bit too tenderhearted," Clifford says, smiling. "At least when it comes to punishing witches, they are . . . don't you agree?"

Clifford gets up and goes to the stove for the pot of coffee. He fills both cups before sitting down again. As he spoons sugar into his cup, he says: "I think maybe it's not just Navajo people who are catching this sickness anymore."

"Oh?" Push is startled at what Clifford is saying—how he seems to have changed the subject entirely.

"Yeah . . . because now there's a dead woman at a place over yonder," and Clifford Lomaquaptewa points vaguely with his spoon in a northerly direction. "She's a white dead woman, too. . . . I guess you could say she's been dead for several days now." He takes another sip of the hot coffee. "I thought you would want to know about her."

"What do you mean?" Push is completely taken aback now. "*Where* is there a dead woman?"

"At a place I can show you," he says, getting up from the chair and starting toward the door. "It's not far from here, but it will be better if we go in your truck."

FIRST MESA

Push has turned off of the highway and stopped at the small store in the First Mesa village of Polacca at a place where Clifford has indicated to him that he will likely find a working telephone.

He has called Sonny Brokeshoulder's office in Window Rock to tell his friend what he's learned from Clifford.

"No, I haven't seen the body yet, but I'm willing to bet that we're about to encounter our first non-Indian case of the hantavirus, Sonny," he says. "I doubt we'll have to worry too much about getting the state's attention now . . . nothing seems to spark as much official interest as white folks beginning to figure out that they're vulnerable, too."

Sonny tells Push that since the body is presumably on Hopi lands, he'll need to get in touch with the Keams Canyon Indian Agency and arrange to have Hopi tribal authorities meet them at the site that Clifford has described. "And I'll let Leslie know about it, too," he adds.

''You should also ask her to get whoever it is they plan on sending for the body to bring along some extra latex gloves and surgical masks and some disinfectant solution,'' Push tells him. ''I'll get back to you as soon as I've got something more to report.''

Back in the truck, Clifford directs Push to a rough blacktop road that heads north, toward the village of Hard Rocks. ''We'll turn off at the place where there's that gravel road that goes on up to Piñon,'' he says. ''The spot we're heading for is about halfway over to there.''

''So you say it's a woman who's died, and that she's white. And you're not sure how long she's been dead, Clifford?'' Push is trying to sort it all out as he drives. ''But you've seen her?''

''It's the white woman, all right—the one who's been digging over there at Wepo Wash.''

''Wepo Wash? That's where the woman archeologist Dr. Blair told me about was working,'' Push says. ''I think Leslie went over there to look around the excavation site last week. . . .''

''That's where we're going now. This woman is the one who goes around with that white man who's mixed up with Slowtalker . . . and I can tell you that she died because she was fooling around with Hopi things—sacred Hopi things that she shouldn't ought to have fooled with.''

''What do you mean? What kind of Hopi things?''

''The things I was telling you about back up there . . . things that she shouldn't have been messing with.'' Clifford Lomaquaptewa's voice is beginning to rise in pitch—he sounds agitated . . . angry, even. ''What kind of business do these white diggers have, anyhow? Coming around here and robbing the people of things that have been a part of our world for as long as there's even *been* a world?''

''Are you saying she was in on the theft of the tablet you told me about?''

''Her or the guy who stays over there with her. It's the same thing, either way. It don't matter which one of them took it . . . it made for trouble.''

''So let me get this straight, just because she knows a man who you say stole something from the Hopi, she was killed as punishment? Is that what you're saying, Clifford?''

''No, no,'' and he shakes his head in irritation. ''It wasn't no *person* that killed that woman. It was the power of the thing that she stole that caused her to die . . . it was the Holy People who caused her to die.

''That woman was messin' around where she shouldn't ought to have been—messing with dead people . . . messing around their houses and with their personal stuff.''

''The Navajo would say that if she was digging around gravesites then she might have stirred up bone dust . . . the powder that they say witches use.''

''It doesn't matter either way,'' Clifford says. ''It was her own actions what caused this woman to wind up dead.''

Push is trying to make some sense out of what he's hearing and thinking when Clifford points to a spot up ahead. ''Start slowin' down . . . you can go in up where you see those tire tracks heading off between the bushes. We're just about there now.''

As he steers off the paved surface, Push brings the Chevy to a stop and climbs out. He tears a length of bright orange plastic ribbon from a roll behind the seat and ties it onto a bush where it can be clearly seen from the road.

''I just hope the Tribal Police will know enough to follow us in here.''

Without ever leaving his seat in the truck, Clifford Lomaquaptewa has been studying the landscape that surrounds them. And as Push begins to maneuver the truck into the brush and around scrub oak and piñon branches, Clifford says: ''We're lucky that the big rain we were having back up there at the mesa awhile ago didn't reach all the way over to here. This Chevy of yours probably wouldn't have made it if there was a whole lot of mud like we sometimes can get around here after a good rain. I think the wash would have been running waist deep, for sure.''

When they've gone another half-mile or so—slowly picking their way around large stones and across sandy arroyos—the two men crest a low rise and Push brings the truck to a halt and switches off the engine.

Spread out before them is the draw that makes up this portion of Wepo Wash. At the bottom of the wash they can see the two blue dome tents and the blue nylon tarp that provides the shade arbor—can see that the tarp is flapping in the breeze. Surveying the scene, Push can distinguish a single set of tire tracks leading off toward the north. A couple of hundred yards farther up the wash, he can make out two distinct sites where recent excavation has evidently taken place. In spite of the tents and the tire tracks, the site looks now to be eerily deserted. Except for the tarp that moves in the breeze, it is very still.

Push drives slowly along the rim of the wash for another quarter of a mile before discovering at last a way down.

As he makes his way toward the campsite, Push studies the movement of the blue tarp. When he is satisfied that he knows for certain the general direction in which the light wind is blowing, he maneuvers the truck to a spot some fifty yards upwind of the tents and comes to a stop. He opens the driver's-side door and steps down onto the sandy soil. Clifford Lomaquaptewa makes no move to leave the truck. Rather he sits staring straight ahead.

Push takes a medium-sized red metal fishing-tackle box from behind the driver's-side seat. Placing the box in the bed of the pickup truck, he opens it and takes out a paper surgical mask and a pair of latex surgical gloves and puts them on. By now the campsite is deep in late-afternoon shadow—he reaches once more behind the seat and brings out a flashlight.

"Where is she?" he asks.

Clifford nods, but does not look, in the direction of the sleeping tent.

"This won't take long," Push says. "If the Tribal Police or whoever they send ever does show up, try not to let them come barging in there—or at least start honking the horn so that I'll know they're here and can maybe try to keep them back out of the way." Then, without another word, Push takes the tackle box and the flashlight and walks straight toward the two blue tents.

• • •

As he nears the tent that Clifford has indicated as the one containing the body, Push can hear the low, steady buzz of the flies. And even through the layers of filtering mask material, the putrid stench of death is nearly overpowering in the late-afternoon heat.

No, this certainly won't *take long,* he thinks, as he stoops to enter the darkened interior of the sleeping tent.

"Oh, *shit*!"

A wave of nausea passes over Push now as his eyes adjust to the darkness and he is able to make out the body of a woman lying on a low cot. He is not unused to seeing corpses, but *this* one—this one is different. For even in the faint light of the stinking and buzzing room of the small tent, Push can see that the woman's head is missing from her body. But then he sees that it is not actually missing from the room, for now he begins to comprehend the incomprehensible: That the head is lying there beside the body on the cot—that the severed head has been positioned hideously in the crook of the woman's right arm.

The swollen and distorted features of what had once been the woman's face are turned toward Push . . . and what had once been her eyes are staring now, dull and unseeing, at the exact spot where he is standing.

Little more than a quarter of an hour has passed when Push hears the honking of the truck's horn.

As quickly as he has recovered from the initial shock of what he'd come upon, Push has set about his grisly task. He has just finished placing several small Ziploc tissue-sample bags into one larger plastic bag. The smaller bags contain the swabs with which he has methodically taken samples from the dead woman's mouth, ears, and nose as well as from her eyes. It was quickly apparent to Push that the woman's head had been severed only after she'd been dead for a period of time—such an horrendous wound, had it occurred even in the final moments of life, would have resulted in an enormous volume of arterial blood loss, and there was simply no evidence of massive blood flow. In fact, the only blood of any significant amount was black and thick—and it was minimal . . . obviously it was blood that had pooled in and near the woman's neck. Clearly there had been no circulation at the moment of the decapitation.

And so he has gathered samples from the same sites as he would have had the body been intact. Even before an autopsy can be arranged, if there is a viral infection, the lab can use what he is gathering to start identifying whatever it is that killed her.

Too, he has forced himself to take note of what else there is in the tent: the half-empty cup of tea, the overturned pencil container and the scattered pens—and Push is particularly interested in the spiral-bound notebook that is lying beside the dead woman's cot, and the neat, precise notes and photographs that fill its pages.

. . .

The truck's horn sounds again and Push steps out of the tent and into the failing light of dusk to see that a boxy and sun-faded orange-and-white Hopi Tribal Emergency Medical Services van is parked beside the spot where Clifford sits in the Chevy. Two Indian men are standing beside the van and looking toward Push. Leslie Blair is walking toward him. He motions for her to stay where she is as he carefully removes the gloves and mask that he has been wearing and places them in first one, and then into a second, red plastic Biohazard-disposal bag. Leaving the red double-bagged and sealed waste beside the entrance to the tent and carrying the tackle box and the bagged swab samples, Push walks directly back toward Leslie and the waiting vehicles.

"Oh, goddamnit, Push!" Her face is pale and her eyes are wide. "It's Sabine Vogel, isn't it? And she was all alone, wasn't she?"

"You don't want to go over there, Leslie," Push says. "She's been dead for some time . . . and in this heat . . ."

"But I told her I'd come see her last Sunday, and then after I was up all night with Lizbeth Austin . . . well, I just blew it off. How long's she been there, Push?"

Push sets the tackle box and the specimens on the ground and places his hands gently on Leslie's shoulders. "It's not clear, Leslie . . . she may have had the disease, but . . ."

"But *what*? What is it, Push?"

"But I just can't tell what it was exactly that killed her . . . because of her condition."

"Oh, Christ!" Leslie sinks to the ground and sits there with her arms clasped around her knees. "Shit, but it's just so awful to think about her being out here all by herself . . . when I'd told her I'd . . ."

Push kneels beside her. "Take it easy now, Leslie. We need to get her back over to Gallup—Ed Pierce has got the facilities there to do a post-mortem."

"I know, it's just . . ."

His thoughts are moving ahead now. "Listen to me, there are some things I need to check on. Is there a radio in the EMS van? I need to try and get hold of Sonny, or maybe the police. . . ."

"The *police*? What do you mean?"

"I just need to talk to Sonny, Leslie . . . trust me on this."

"I think there's a two-way in the unit, but clear out here things don't always work like they should." She looks around toward where the van is parked.

"Bennie!" Leslie calls out to the driver, who, along with his partner, is squatting beside a scrub juniper, smoking a cigarette. "Dr. Foster here needs to contact the dispatcher over at Keams. Can you help him out?"

The man stubs out his cigarette and hurries over to the van. "I don't figure we'll be able to get a good enough signal to get outta this wash, Dr. Blair," he calls out. "Probably have to drive on up there to the high ground, and even then they might not be able to hear us very good."

"I'll go sit in the truck with Clifford," Leslie says. "Bennie'll show you about the radio . . . if he can raise them at Keams the dispatcher can try and patch you through to whoever you want to talk with."

When they've reached the rim of the wash, Push waits while Bennie repeatedly tries to make contact with the base station at Keams Canyon. Push is about to give up and tell the man to drive him back down when the faint crackle of a woman's voice comes over the static hum. Bennie adjusts the squelch and then he and the voice exchange words in Hopi.

"Ask if they can possibly get me hooked up with Sonny Brokeshoulder at his office over in Window Rock," Push says.

Bennie relays Push's question in Hopi.

"Piece of cake," the voice replies in English.

Once the connection has been made, Bennie leaves the van and walks off a distance and lights a cigarette. Push is relieved that he can speak freely with Sonny. He doesn't have the slightest idea about how this sort of a radio-telephone hookup works, but he hopes no one is listening in to the conversation at Keams.

"Sonny? This is Push . . . can you hear me at all?"

"Hold the mike a little farther away from your mouth, Push. You sound like you're talking through a pipe."

"How's this? Is this better?"

"Yeah, I can almost understand you now . . . go ahead."

Push tells Sonny what he's found—including the condition of the white woman's body.

"I figured that since there's been mutilation, there'd probably need to be some kind of a police investigation before we move the body . . . you know, a coroner's report or something?"

"Ah, hell, Push." Sonny's transmission is breaking up in the static of the relay. *"This is not Atlanta or 'Hill Street Blues,' you know. If the tribal cops had gotten out there first they'd have most likely taken one quick look around and then called the EMS guys to come haul the body over to where some* bilagáana *doctor could take over. You've just saved them making the call, is all. Besides, who do you think is the coroner for the Navajo region that's closest to where you're sitting at the moment, anyway? It's yours truly is who it is. And the Hopi district doesn't even have a medical examiner . . . they would've just called on Leslie Blair."*

"Leslie's here . . . she came out with the EMS van."

"See there? So if there're two real doctors at the scene then the tribal cops will sure enough figure their asses are covered."

"So I take it you want me to . . ."

"Have them take her on over to Gallup. I'll call Earl Tso as soon as we get off the air and tell him what you've told me . . . then he or somebody from his office will probably want to be there when the body arrives, but they're not likely to want to actually view the remains. I can guarantee you they'll be only too happy to take your word for it that the woman died of something or other and then they can send somebody out to Wepo Wash tomorrow to have a look around in the daylight."

"Okay, Sonny. I'll get things moving here, then."

"Yeah, just tell Bennie and them to deliver the body to Ed Pierce at the IHS. And then how about if you stop by the office here at Window Rock and pick me up. That way you can fill me in on all the gruesome details on our way over to Gallup."

"Okay, Sonny . . ."

There is a long moment of static-filled silence on the radio before Push hears Sonny's voice again:

"Push?"

"Yeah?"

"You're supposed to say 'over and out.' "

And for the first time in several hours, Push Foster is smiling as he switches off the radio.

Because he cannot imagine the response that the Hopi EMS attendants might have to seeing a headless body, Push tells Bennie that the regulations for transporting a fatal case of possible viral infection of an undetermined nature require that only a trained virologist is allowed to place the corpse into the body bag. It is all bullshit, of course, but Bennie and his partner are only too happy to stand aside. And only when he feels certain that they won't be able to discern the true condition of the body does Push have the two men help him to load the remains into the van for the trip to Keams Canyon and then on to Gallup.

Leslie has watched from Push's truck, where she's been sitting beside Clifford Lomaquaptewa while the body bag has been loaded. She tells Push that she intends to accompany Sabine Vogel back as far as Keams.

"I'm sorry I wasn't more help, Push," she says as she climbs into the EMS van with the attendants. "I feel like such a baby. . . ."

"Not at all," he says. "What do you say I stop by your place for a little while after I take Clifford home . . . would that be okay with you?"

Leslie smiles at Push. "I thought you'd never ask," she says.

The sun has set and darkness has settled in as the orange-and-white EMS van makes its way slowly up and out of Wepo Wash. Almost two hours have passed since they first arrived at this place, and still Clifford Lomaquaptewa has not left the pickup.

"I'll take you back to your place now, Clifford," Push says as he turns the key in the ignition. "Then I'm going to need to get on over to Window Rock so that Sonny and I can be there when they bring her in. We have to figure out exactly how to proceed from here . . . this has just gotten even worse than it was."

Push looks directly at Clifford Lomaquaptewa. He makes every effort to keep his voice steady and calm.

"Clifford," he says. "What happened to that woman?"

"You're the doctor . . . my guess is that she died."

"Clifford, the woman's *head* has been cut off, for godsake!"

Clifford Lomaquaptewa's eyes widen. Push feels as if he's been punched in the stomach—he'd assumed that Clifford had known the condition of the woman's corpse from the very beginning.

"Do you mean to say you didn't *know* about that?" Push says. "That's not the way she was when you saw her?"

Clifford lets out a long breath. "I didn't see that woman, Push," he says. "Not after she was dead, I didn't see her. And I sure didn't have any idea that her head was missing. . . ."

"It wasn't missing," Push says. "It was lying there beside her. It looked to me like it had been cut off after she'd been dead for quite a while, too."

"Then it was a Navajo who did that thing," Clifford says.

"Why would you say that? Do you know who did it?"

"No. Just that it was a Navajo. That's how the Navajo people got the name 'Head-Pounders'—on account of they sometimes used to cut the heads off of their enemies. And the Hopis weren't their only enemies, you know . . . they never did have much use for white people, either."

"And so you think a Navajo would have done this thing?"

"I don't know of anyone else who could do such a terrible thing. . . . Unless . . ."

"Unless what, Clifford?"

"Unless that white woman back there was a witch."

"I don't understand . . . what do you mean?"

"That's what I was telling you about up there at my house earlier . . . the Hopi Prophecy: That Elder Brother will come back someday as 'Purifier' to help the Hopi people out of their troubles by goin' around and cutting off the heads of all the witches and the other evil people." And Clifford stares toward the blue tents in the now-darkened campsite.

"You know, I didn't figure that woman to be such a bad one. . . . I thought she was strange, that's for sure. . . ." And Push sees that Clifford Lomaquaptewa looks very old and very tired now—exhausted, even.

"But I didn't figure her to be no witch."

SECOND MESA

Even though the asphalt road is potholed rough and jarring, it looks to Push as though Clifford Lomaquaptewa is sleeping. He hasn't spoken a word since they left the Wepo Wash campsite, and his eyes have appeared to be closed every time Push has looked over at him. Push has been going over in his head again and again what it was he'd seen at the archeological site: The white woman lying dead and decapitated on the low camp cot, the broken pottery scattered about the otherwise neat and orderly worksite. And what if the Navajo notion that it was bone dust that had killed her in the first place was actually correct? What if it was dust from a disturbed gravesite that had infected the woman with the lethal virus? After all, that wasn't out of the question—it had early on been established that field archeologists run a very real risk of exposure to some long-dormant disease when they uncover the remains of someone who's died from that disease. The anthrax virus, for example, had been shown to survive in a dormant state for years. Smallpox, too. The stuff of horror movies surrounding the "curse" that Egyptian mummies put on those who disturb their tombs was really just the result of early observations of the deadly risk of grave robbers contracting viral diseases that thrived, or at the very least survived, in the cool darkness of those tombs.

What had the white woman come across at Wepo Wash? Was it the hantavirus? The same thing that had killed Greyeyes and Tsosie? And the others?

Push is jarred from his musings by Clifford's voice: "You know, the lights on this truck of yours are pretty dim."

"Yeah," Push says to Clifford. "Lots of things on this machine have started losing their luster. I'm not even sure how much longer this old heap will keep running. Sonny's always telling me I should get one of those new Ford three-quarter-ton trucks and stop embarrassing him by driving around in this rattletrap."

"Maybe you just need to wipe off the glass that goes over the lightbulbs—there's lotsa bugs flyin' around out there in the air, hittin' on the glass. Bug splatters can make glass pretty dirty, you know." Clifford is leaning forward in the seat, his eyes trained on the dimly illuminated semicircle of roadway ahead. "I never could figure out how come Navajo people to be so partial to Fords, anyway," he says. "Myself, I've always favored General Motors products."

Funny, Push thinks. It hasn't occurred to him that this Hopi man might have an opinion on automotive matters. Try as he might, he can't picture Clifford Lomaquaptewa driving a vehicle. And how is it that he can be thinking of such mundane things after what has just occurred?

"I believe it's true what they say, you know," Clifford continues. "That 'Friends don't let friends drive Fords'—at least that's what I saw written on this fellow's T-shirt that time when I was over to Phoenix."

Again, there is a long silence. And then it is Push who speaks: "Clifford, I have to ask you, if you didn't actually see her, how did you come to know about the dead woman back there?"

Clifford says nothing.

"At your house this afternoon you said that she'd been dead for a couple of days,'' Push continues. ''Did someone else *tell* you about it, or what? I mean, it's important that we know who might have come in contact with her, so that we can watch for signs of the sickness in them . . . the man who was staying out there with her and anyone else.''

Still, Clifford Lomaquaptewa remains silent. Push can hear the frustration building in his own voice.

''Do you know about viruses, Clifford? Viruses are tiny, microscopic disease-causing agents that depend on living cells to get along. And even though something mutilated her body, I think that it was a virus that actually killed that woman back there . . . and I think that it was the same virus that's been killing Navajo people. Viruses can be passed around in many different ways, Clifford, and it's important that we know if anyone might possibly have contracted the virus directly from the dead woman. . . .''

''No good person would have touched that dead woman.'' He speaks and then Clifford Lomaquaptewa is silent again. His eyes are fixed on the road ahead—it is clear from the finality in his tone of voice that he intends not to pursue the subject further.

After a while Push takes a different tack: ''You know, I can't get over the expression that was on her face, Clifford. I mean . . . she looked so surprised.''

As soon as he's said it, Push feels foolish. Clifford is quiet for a long time before he replies: ''I figure it must've been a real surprising thing that happened to her. She probably hadn't never been dead before in her whole life.''

Push looks over at the other man. Clifford Lomaquaptewa is clearly not going to tell Push how he came to know about the white woman's death. And his eyes are closed once more—it is as if he's about to fall asleep.

''She was a strange woman, anyway,'' he says finally. ''And she's dead now because her heart was not right.''

Just then the road curves sharply to the left, skirting a low hill. Push slows slightly to negotiate the turn. As the headlights swing around in an arc, Push sees for a moment in the lights the figure of a lone man walking among the scraggly brush and cactus just off the paved surface—the man is walking in the same direction as Push and Clifford are traveling. Instinctively, he begins to slow the truck even more. ''What's anybody doing way out here?'' he starts to say. But before the words are fully formed, Push is startled by Clifford's voice:

''Keep going!'' And he shouts with an urgency in his voice that is alarming to Push. *''Don't stop!''*

Push looks across the seat at Clifford. The man is hunched forward on the seat, both of his hands palm-down on the dashboard, as though he is bracing for an impending collision. Push does not slow down further, but rather steers the truck through the curve and past the man walking beside the road. The walking man doesn't look up.

As the highway straightens out again, Push glances into the rearview mirror to see only the empty, moonlit asphalt strip behind—the walker, he imagines, would by now be back around the curve, out of sight and so hidden by the hill.

''What's the matter, Clifford? I don't understand—do you know that man back there?''

In the yellow glow of the light from the instrument panel, Push can see that the Hopi man sits transfixed—can see that there is a strange look on his face . . . a look of real terror. His arms still stretch forward—his hands are still braced against the dash. And his eyes remain fixed on the road directly ahead.

''Clifford!'' Now it is Push who speaks sharply. ''What the hell is going on?''

And then suddenly he sees—through the glass of the passenger-side window just past Clifford Lomaquaptewa's head—that there is something moving alongside them on the shoulder of the road, something moving at precisely the same speed as the pickup in which they are riding. Push sees that it is the man that they had passed—that he thought they had passed, rather—and that the man is apparently now running along beside the truck. He looks down at the speedometer: The needle hovers just past the fifty-miles-per-hour mark.

''Yap Pahaha!'' It is a Hopi cry of great fear that Clifford Lomaquaptewa makes.

"Jesus! . . . Clifford!" Push can see that his companion's dark face has taken on a sickly gray cast—and that, while he must surely be aware that there is something racing along outside the window of the speeding truck, his eyes are shut tightly now, and his body is arched and rigid. Push mashes his foot down hard on the accelerator pedal—the engine hesitates for a moment and then begins to surge. Glancing down, he can see the speedometer needle climb past the sixty-miles-per-hour mark—he can hear the carburetor sucking air and the high pitch of the truck's tires whining in the dry stillness of the night. And as he looks across and past Clifford—who is by now petrified . . . virtually paralyzed with a horror that Push struggles to comprehend—he can see that the running figure is keeping a steady pace with the truck as it gains speed. He watches as this thing—and Push is not at all certain that what he is seeing there in the darkness beside the speeding vehicle is in fact a man—turns its head and looks directly into the cab of the truck. Push could swear that there is a smile on the thing's face—a terrifying grin, really—as it looks first at Clifford Lomaquaptewa and then focuses its gaze on Push. The hair on Push's neck bristles and he feels a blast of frigid air and his skin crawls with the horror of what he is witnessing. And he has no idea, really, what it is that he is witnessing, except that there is something horrifyingly familiar about the face on whatever it is that he has seen outside the truck—something he can't put his finger on. It is as though he should know that face—as though it is a face of someone or something he's seen before . . . somewhere. . . .

And then, as quickly as it had appeared, the thing beside the truck is gone. And the air inside the cab of the speeding pickup is once again warm and dry.

And at the very moment that the apparition vanishes from Push's sight, Clifford Lomaquaptewa lets out a great, loud, gasping sound. The kind of sound that a panic-stricken man might make who has been too long under water and who, having just broken the surface, is frantic to fill his air-starved lungs all in a rush.

Push looks into the rearview mirror and sees in the pale light of the road behind that there is a large dog—or more likely it is a coyote that he sees running—following the truck in which the two men are riding.

Push jams his boot down hard on the brake pedal and at the same instant jerks the steering wheel a quarter-turn to the left to swerve toward the opposite side of the deserted road. A cloud of swirling dust envelops the truck as it slides screeching to a halt partway off the paved surface. Clifford has been slammed hard against the passenger-side door with the force of the braking and as the vehicle comes to rest, he slumps over toward the driver's side as if he is unconscious . . . or dead.

"*Shit!* This is not happening!" And Push is scrambling out of the truck and standing, looking hard back up the road before the choking dust has begun to settle.

And in the pale moonlight—not thirty-five yards away from the spot where he now stands weak-kneed . . . his chest heaving and his heart pounding—Push can just make out the skulking shadow of what he thinks is a coyote as it stands panting, its head low in the middle of the roadway . . . can make out that the animal is standing exactly in the center of a pair of curving, parallel tire marks where, but a moment before, the truck had begun its skid across the roadway . . . can see, too, the eyes of the animal reflected yellow-bright in the glow of the moon. Push watches as the coyote turns and trots easily off the pavement to disappear into the brush.

And as he turns back toward the truck, Push is startled to see that Clifford has left the vehicle and come up behind him. That he, too, is standing watching the place where the coyote has melded into the night.

"What in the hell is going on?" Push says.

Clifford Lomaquaptewa is nearly overcome by what has just taken place. He reaches out to steady himself against the hood of the pickup. He rubs a hand across his eyes.

"*Iisaw* . . ." he says. And then: "Two Hearts."

"*Iisaw?*" Push says. "I don't understand . . . what is *iisaw*?"

"*Iisaw* is the coyote." His voice is weak and trembling.

"And you said Two Hearts again, Clifford . . . *Two Hearts*? . . . a *witch*?" Push can see that the other man is deadly serious. "Are you telling me that what we just saw back there was a witch?"

His face still deathly gray, Clifford sinks to his knees in the dirt beside the truck. Even in the relative cool of the evening he has begun to perspire profusely and his hands are shaking. Push thinks that the man is maybe about to collapse altogether—that he may be having a heart attack or at least that he is about to be sick to his stomach.

''Are you okay?'' Push kneels beside him. ''Come on, Clifford—let me help you back into the truck,'' he says, taking the other man's arm and helping him to his feet. ''Let's get out of here.''

And at the exact moment that he turns the key in the ignition, Push Foster is struck nearly dumb by the chilling realization that the face of the thing he's seen—or that he *thinks* he's seen—running alongside the truck looked very much like that of the old Navajo singer he'd first met at the meeting in the trailer annex. . . . Looked very much like the tall man that he'd seen Clifford Lomaquaptewa speaking to at the gathering of medicine people in Window Rock on Saturday.

Push realizes that whatever it was outside the window back there, it had looked like Silas Slowtalker.

"No," he says aloud to himself. "It *couldn't* have been him. . . ."

KEAMS CANYON

Hey, Push . . . come on in.'' Leslie Blair is standing barefoot in the doorway to her house at Keams Canyon Indian Agency.

''Listen, I'm really sorry for acting so silly out there. . . . I don't know what you must think of me. . . .''

''Leslie . . .''

''No, I can't help but feel guilty that I didn't go out to see Sabine Vogel on Sunday, like I told her I would, but that's no excuse for me to lose it like that. Still, the idea of her being out there all alone—with no way to leave and no way to get hold of anyone . . . and all the while thinking I was going to show up . . .''

''Well, you can't be beating yourself up over this—we're all doing the best we can.'' Push sits down at the kitchen table. ''Listen, can I get a drink of water or something?'' He puts his head in his hands.

''Push?'' Leslie leans down and looks at him more closely.

"Push, you look just awful . . . are you okay? What on earth is wrong?"

"I feel a little twirly, is all. . . . I'll be fine. This has not been a particularly good day for me, I'm afraid," and he looks up at her and smiles weakly. "And I swear to god that if you say I look like I've seen a ghost, I'm liable to throw up."

"You do look a little pale and drawn. How about a beer? It's a lot better than our water out here. And yeah, I *know* we're not supposed to have alcohol on the rez," and she rolls her eyes. "But there's just so much of life I'm willing to give up just to be on the federal payroll." She takes two bottles from the refrigerator and sets them on the table. "Are you sure you're okay? Tell me what's wrong."

Push takes a long draw on the beer bottle. "Okay, but if I'm going to tell you about this, you might want to sit down . . . there's more to it than just that a body had been lying out in the desert heat awhile."

"Come on, now—I explained to you that I was not being my normal tough self out there earlier. I'm a doctor, for Christ's sake! Tell me what's got you so boogered."

"Well, it turned out to be a little more gruesome than I let on to you. I told you that the woman had been out there dead for quite a while, but that wasn't the worst part about it. . . ."

"Oh, yuck . . . *What?*"

And Push describes to Leslie all that he's seen at Wepo Wash.

"Goddamnit!" And her reaction is more than just the shock and even the horror that Push might have expected: Leslie Blair is angry. "That really pisses me off," she says. "As if there's not enough creepy shit that goes on out here without some ghoulish sons of bitches cutting up dead bodies! *Jesus Christ!*"

And she's gotten up from her place at the table and is pacing back and forth in front of the sink. "Now let me get this straight—you don't think it was the trauma that killed her? You still think she died of a viral infection . . . of the hantavirus?"

"She was already dead when it happened, Leslie . . . that much was clear to me. And Clifford Lomaquaptewa knew she was out there and that she was dead—he led me to where she was. But it was obvious he *didn't* know that she'd been beheaded.'' Push drains the last of the beer from the bottle and wipes his hand across his mouth. ''It's not going to take Ed Pierce long to determine if respiratory failure was the actual cause of death.'' He looks at his watch. ''Your guys should have delivered the body to him by now—let me use your phone. I'll call and see if there's any word yet.''

''The phone's there in the living room.''

Push gets up from the kitchen table. Leslie puts a full bottle of beer into his hand and then goes back into another part of the house.

Push has just hung up the telephone when Leslie comes back into the kitchen—she's wearing shoes now. He's standing in the doorway to the kitchen as he tells her that Pierce is just preparing to make his examination of the body and that he's promised to call there as soon as he has some preliminary findings he can share.

He slaps his forehead in mock frustration: ''I guess I wasn't thinking clearly—I sort of let it slip my mind that the EMS attendants didn't know the actual condition of the body. . . . Anyway, Ed wasn't exactly prepared for what was staring up at him when he unzipped the body bag. I must say, he's a little bit irritated with me. . . .''

''I can see his point,'' Leslie says, arching her eyebrows.

Push sits down at the table. ''And do you want to hear something else? Something *really* strange?''

''I don't know . . . with the way things are going tonight do you think I'm up to it?''

And then he tells her about what he and Clifford have seen on the road.

''This is *way* too much. I mean, I've heard stories about these things, but they've always been secondhand stories . . . somebody telling about how they knew somebody *else* who saw one. But you're the first person I've heard who claims to have actually seen one himself! And you're sure enough the only person other than a Navajo or Hopi that I've ever heard of seeing one!''

''Does that mean you know what it was Clifford and I saw out there?''

"And you don't? I'd say it was a 'skinwalker' . . . or whatever it is they call those things."

"I remember Sonny saying once that a Navajo would never use that word, *skinwalker*—that they'd be more likely to say wolf, maybe, or even witch. But never skinwalker."

"Well, whatever you want to call it . . . it's creepy, is what it is . . ."

"It's way more than that, Leslie." Push is pressing his fingertips hard into his temples. "I mean, all the time I was growing up I listened to stories about ghosts and magical creatures. They were called Little People, and sometimes they were good and sometimes they were bad. And I gave them about as much importance in my day-to-day world as I did Santa Claus and the Easter Bunny—which is to say, they were something I just naturally grew out of. Do you understand what I'm telling you here? The older I got—the more experience I had in school and the more I learned about how things work in the world, the more I came to believe that these were really just quaint stories passed down by imaginative people as ways of teaching moral lessons or of keeping unruly children in line.

"But what am I to think now . . . now that I've seen this? How am I supposed to think about what I saw out there on the road with Clifford?" He looks directly into Leslie's eyes. She makes no reply. "How am I supposed to ever think about anything in the same way again? Am I going completely crazy, Leslie? How am I to see the world now?"

"I don't know what to say to you, Push . . . except that nobody around here is going to think you're crazy. Like I said, everyone around here's got stories about these things—I've never heard anyone claim to have encountered one himself, just that he knows someone who has."

"But if no one admits to actually seeing such a thing—if it's all secondhand? . . ."

"Don't take that as evidence that these are just *stories,* Push. The people hereabouts are not inclined to talk about such things to outsiders . . . and when they do they'll always describe an event as having happened to someone else—that way the onus is not on the teller. But that doesn't make them any less a fact of the Navajo and Hopi Ways. . . .''

Push can feel his heart pounding in his chest. ''But you and I are doctors, Leslie . . . we're trained as scientists, for godsake. If anyone should have a notion about the way the world actually works, it ought to be people like us . . . but now all of a sudden there are too many things going on even to begin to make sense of it all. Too many strange things for me to make sense of, anyway. Myths—or at least what I learned to think of as myths a long time ago—and facts—or what I've been taught for twenty-some years now to believe are facts—are exploding right before my eyes!''

Leslie reaches across the kitchen table and places her hand gently on Push's arm. The two are quiet for several long minutes. Then Leslie sighs and says: ''And you know something else? You were right . . . finding a body without a head does not make for a particularly good day. Not on top of everything else. And especially not when it's the body of someone who's most likely died from a contagious viral disease.''

Push feels calmer now. He even manages a faint smile when he says: ''And don't forget that a seemingly intelligent man who lives in Third World conditions in what is probably the oldest continually inhabited community in the country has told me that it was either some ghoulish Navajo or else the Holy People of Hopi Prophecy who chopped off a white woman's head because she was probably a witch. . . .''

And Leslie smiles back at him as she adds: ''And don't *you* forget that it wasn't just you, but that that same intelligent man was right there beside you when you were being chased down a deserted road by something that the both of you saw shape-shift into a coyote!''

Just at that moment a very large gray cat jumps up and onto the kitchen table, startling the both of them.

''Oedipus!'' Leslie says. ''You get down from there . . . we have company.''

''I'd say *he* looks healthy enough,'' Push says.

''I've been keeping him locked in the house all day and all night—he's not particularly happy with me, but I don't know what else to do to keep him from bringing in mice.''

''No, I suppose he wouldn't be too happy about that.''

The telephone rings in the living room and Leslie goes to answer it.

''Ed Pierce says that Sabine Vogel's lungs were saturated—completely filled with fluid,'' she says when she comes back into the room. ''He says he'll do a full autopsy and get all the lab work started, but that there's just no doubt in his mind that it's hantavirus.''

''What about? . . .''

''You were right—Vogel's head had been cut off sometime after her death. *And* Ed says that she was beheaded with a single and remarkably clean cut . . . said to tell you it was the kind of cut that he imagines a sharp guillotine might make.''

''God . . .'' Push runs his hands across his face. ''Listen, I'd better get on the road, I promised Sonny I'd come by his place to fill him in. . . .''

Leslie reaches across the table and takes Push's hand in hers. ''What do you say you just go in there and call him, Push? It's getting late.'' She is looking directly into his eyes. ''You want to know what I think? I think it's a good night for you to stay here. . . .''

Push stands and then reaches out and brushes Leslie's cheek gently with his fingers. He looks at her for a long moment and then bends down and lightly presses his lips against hers.

''I'd like a rain check on the offer,'' he says. ''I really would.''

And Leslie takes hold of the front of Push's shirt and, pulling him toward her, kisses him long and hard on the mouth.

''It very rarely rains out here, Dr. Foster,'' she says, smiling. ''But you do have that rain check . . . just don't wait too long to cash it in.''

''That's a deal.''

Leslie takes hold of his arm as she walks Push out to his truck. They stand together in the pale moonlight for a minute before Push opens the door and sits down behind the wheel.

''You be careful, now,'' she says. ''On top of everything else today, you've had two beers and you've been boldly propositioned just in the past hour. Besides, there are all sorts of weird things on the road between here and Window Rock. And I'm not just talking about skinwalkers, either.''

''I'll keep my eyes wide open,'' he says. ''And thanks for the beer . . . and especially the bold proposition. I hope my tales about headless archeologists and shape-shifting witches don't keep you up all night.''

''I doubt that I'll sleep much,'' she says. ''But it won't be because of witches. I'm not one to be all that surprised by witches, you know. To tell you the truth, I didn't think there was much that *could* surprise me out here anymore. But that was before you showed up . . . seems you've been more of a surprise to me than all this other business put together.'' She's smiling down at Push.

He is smiling back at her. ''I know what you mean.''

Push starts the engine and puts the Chevy in gear. He leans his head out the window: ''Hey, Leslie?''

''Yeah?''

''You know how I told you this was not a very good day for me? Well, it certainly has taken a turn for the better.''

She smiles. ''Me, too, Push.''

I-40

Travelers on Interstate 40 near the New Mexico–Arizona state line on this hot afternoon will more than likely take notice of the school bus.

It is, after all, colorful. Wildly festooned with bright-painted flowers and sixties-era peace signs, the bus's whip-antenna masts trail nylon streamers and tie-dyed flags and Day-Glo dragon wind socks. And it is closely followed by three similarly decorated vans: two Volkswagens and a Ford with dancing-skeleton Grateful Dead decals on all the windows. This gaily outfitted little convoy is moving more slowly than the other traffic—certainly more slowly than the overloaded 18-wheelers . . . more slowly even than the behemoth motor homes named after midwestern Indian tribes.

The slow movement of the caravan is not by design—indeed, the occupants of the four vehicles are in a great hurry to leave this part of the country—rather the slowness is the result of a rebuilt school-bus engine that is able to attain a top speed of fifty miles per hour only under the best of circumstances.

And the gusty wind that is blowing out of the southwest on this day does not make for the best of circumstances.

Perhaps an especially attentive traveler—if he or she were to happen to look directly into the windows of the bus and the three vans in passing—might notice, too, that the drivers of all four vehicles, like all of the passengers inside, are fitted with disposable surgical masks and plastic gloves purchased at a veterinary supply store in Gallup. Might notice that, even though the day is quite warm, all of the windows on all of the vehicles in this curious caravan are tightly closed.

On the other hand, even the most attentive passerby will probably *not* be aware that inside each of the vans and inside the bus, a gray-blue fog of pungent incense-stick smoke hangs heavy in the still, trapped air, and that mixed with the smell of incense there is the sharp medicinal odor of Lysol disinfectant. Neither will the passing motorist be aware that inside the slow-lumbering school bus, a woman whose New Age name had been chosen just weeks previously during a late-night session with a Ouija board in Santa Fe, and who sports a single gold earring piercing her nose and two others in her left eyebrow, is making her way unsteadily up the center aisle, stopping briefly beside each row of seats. She is pulling the green filter-paper mask away from the face of each young passenger momentarily so that she can smear a dab of Vicks Vapo-Rub on the child's upper lip.

"Oooh! That stuff smells *awful*!" complains a barefoot, towheaded boy of six or so who wears designer-label bib overalls and sports a bright orange-and-green flower stenciled on his cheek.

"Yes, Dylan, I know it smells strong, but this nice Mentholatum mustache is going to help kill all of the bad poisonous germs that are present in the ozone." The vacant-eyed woman speaks in a singsong, hypnotic voice.

"Now then, what do you say we all sing a happy song together while Sister Tarazahani plays the finger cymbals. You all know that we're going back to Sedona, children . . . these poor Indian people out here are getting very, very sick and we don't think it's such a good idea to stay around them anymore.''

And to think—only a few days ago this ragtag little tribe was hanging out with their newfound Navajo brothers and sisters—singing and dancing and preaching love and peace and sweat-lodge shamanism.

But of course, that was *before* the news began to spread that there was something terrible going around on the Navajo Reservation: Healthy young Indian people getting sick with what at first seemed like flu . . . many of them dying and no one seeming to know just why. And these New Agers—like nineteenth-century ''Friends of the Indians'' before them—don't really want to press this friendship thing *that* far.

Especially not now that the word has begun to spread that a white person has died from this thing. And so this odd little band is taking their drums and their crystals and their smudge-stick incense and scurrying back down to the red rocks of Sedona for a while. Where it's safe.

At least until this ''Navajo Flu'' business blows over.

TSÉGHÁHOODZÁNI

It's late afternoon—a little past five o'clock—and Push and Sonny have been standing together behind Sonny's desk, studying the big map that is dotted with the red and white push-pins, when they hear the main door slam close and a man's voice talking loudly in the outer office.

It is a red-faced white man with a close-cropped beard and wearing a baseball cap who's making all the commotion.

"They told me at Kykotsmovi that the woman I work with was taken away in an ambulance from our dig up at Wepo Wash." He is standing, leaning over Priscilla Yazzie, shouting at her in a loud and anxious voice. "They acted like they didn't know any more about it than that . . . told me I'd have to come over here to Window Rock and see somebody in this office named Brokeshoulder if I wanted to find out what happened to her. . . ."

Priscilla Yazzie looks bewildered—her mouth is open, but, uncharacteristically, there are no words coming from her. Sonny comes out of his office and places himself between the man and his besieged administrative assistant. "*I'm* Dr. Brokeshoulder," he says firmly. "Now, why don't you just come in and try to calm yourself down a little, so that we can talk about this."

Sonny tells Priscilla that she can go on home as he closes the door to his office.

Push has been listening to what the man has been saying to Priscilla. "Is your name Peter Campbell?" he asks.

"That's right . . . and who are you?" The man looks angry and defensive. "What's this all about? And how is it that you know my name? . . ." He is agitated . . . but at the same time he seems frightened. He rambles on: "What the hell happened out there at Wepo? My campsite's been ransacked . . . stuff has been smashed . . . and it looks like . . ."

"I'm Dr. Foster, Mr. Campbell . . . and I'm sorry to say that it's worse even than what you've apparently been told. Your partner was found at your campsite . . ."

"*Found?* What do you mean, she was found?"

"I mean that she was found dead, I'm sorry to have to tell you."

"*Dead?* But how can that be . . . Sabine's dead? You're sure it was Sabine Vogel?" Campbell sinks into a chair. He takes a pack of cigarettes from his pocket and lights one.

"Mr. Campbell, Sabine Vogel died from complications brought on by a viral infection that has stricken a large number of people in this region."

"It was a virus, you say? What sort of virus?"

"It's something we haven't seen in this country before," Push says. "It's an extremely virulent and fast-moving infection that attacks the respiratory system—the lungs. More than a dozen people have died from it in just the past couple of weeks."

"Are you saying she had that thing I've been hearing about on the radio and seeing in the papers?"

"I'm afraid so."

"But everything I've heard or seen says it's just Indians that have been dying from that—the papers are even calling it Navajo Flu."

''The papers have been wrong,'' Sonny says. ''It's not just Indian people who are at risk.''

''Do I understand that you've been in Santa Fe for the past week or so, Mr. Campbell?'' Push says.

''Is there anything you *don't* know, Foster?''

''There were some notes left by Miss Vogel. . . .'' Push feels uneasy telling this man that he's read Vogel's journal notes. ''How have you been feeling . . . how have you been feeling physically, I mean?''

''I feel okay. Why?'' His eyes narrow for a moment and then they widen. ''It's contagious, isn't it? And you're asking because you think I might have caught the virus that killed her, aren't you?''

''We don't know that it's contagious—or if it is, we don't believe it's highly contagious,'' Push says. ''But like I said, this is something we haven't seen before.''

''When was the last time you were in contact with Miss Vogel?'' Sonny asks.

''It's been just over a week—maybe ten days. I had some business to take care of in Santa Fe—but Sabine was feeling fine when I left on Saturday.''

''It appears that she died just a day or so later. So you can see, the progression of the illness is extremely rapid. It's what we've been seeing in the other victims, as well. So you probably are okay . . . we don't know why, but some people are affected by the virus and some are not.''

''Good luck, maybe.'' Campbell is rubbing his eyes. ''But who tore the place up out there? Why would someone smash everything like that?''

''We don't know.'' And Sonny's voice has taken on an edge now. ''We'd hoped you might have some idea.''

''What are you getting at? You think I would trash the place—break up my own artifacts?''

''There's a headman from Second Mesa who says you've somehow gotten your hands on an object that's very important to the Hopi tribe—a very old religious tablet that was stolen from Hotevilla some years ago,'' Sonny says. ''Is that true?''

''Where'd he hear that? That I had such a thing?''

''He said the trader who operates the Little Springs post had told him about it—that you'd apparently shown the piece to the trader.''

''Austin, huh? I might have known. Well, it's not something that came from the Wepo site . . . in fact, it didn't even come from the Hopi Reservation,'' he says. ''Besides, what would that have to do with Sabine getting sick and dying or with the site being vandalized?''

''The Hopi believe that just the fact that the tablet's not where it belongs may be behind a good deal of the misfortune we're seeing,'' Sonny says.

''What? It sounds to me like somebody's trying to get you to believe there's a curse attached to the tablet or something. *Jesus,* what is *with* these people? Don't they know this is the twentieth century, for godsake!''

''I don't know how much you know about the ways of Indian people, Campbell,'' Sonny says. ''But I've never thought it wise to discount *any* people's strongly held beliefs.''

''You say this tablet didn't come from Hopi,'' Push says. ''Where did you get it, then?''

''I picked it up in a trade with a Navajo.'' Campbell is eyeing the two men suspiciously. ''I told Austin that . . .''

''Listen, Campbell, there's something else you should know . . . when we found Sabine Vogel out there, her body had been badly mutilated.''

Sonny stares at the floor when Push brings up this troubling aspect of the woman's death.

''Mutilated? . . . Mutilated how? What are you saying?''

Push takes a deep breath and clears his throat before he answers: ''Her head had been cut off.''

''Oh, *shit!* What the fuck is this? At first you say she's died of some disease . . . and now you're telling me she was murdered?''

''No . . . no, I'm not saying that at all. In fact, that happened after she'd already been dead for some time,'' Push says.

''Jesus Christ! Who would do something like that?''

''It's been suggested to us that it may have been a Navajo who did it,''

Push says. ''And now you're saying you got the tablet from a Navajo. . . .''

''Oh my god . . . this is too fucking much. There's no Indian trinket worth this kind of trouble . . . I don't care how old it is.'' Campbell's face has drained of all its color. As he fumbles for another cigarette, his hands are shaking almost uncontrollably.

His words tumble out all in a rush now: ''The stone tablet I took in to show Austin came from over around Chinle—at Canyon del Muerto—from a place a little ways up from the Massacre Cave overlook just off the road that goes north to Tsaile. It was a Navajo who'd told me it would be there—told me that an old medicine man had it . . . had had it for a long time, he said. When I went to the old man's hogan to try and buy it off him, I found him dead . . . and he'd been dead a long time . . . I mean, the guy was all dried up and shriveled, you know? Like a fucking mummy?'' Campbell puts his head in his hands. ''The tablet was in a medicine bag tied around his neck. I figured there wasn't anybody going to go near that place—any Navajo would be too scared to go inside a place with a dead body in it, anyway—so I just took the medicine bag, that's all.''

Push and Sonny are watching Campbell. His eyes dart about nervously as he stabs his cigarette into the half-inch of coffee that remains in a cardboard cup on the desk and then immediately lights another.

''Man, this is all just way too crazy,'' he says. ''I'm getting the hell out of this fucking country.''

He looks up at Push, wide-eyed. ''Say, isn't there some kind of injection you should give me? You know, as a precaution to keep me from maybe getting this virus, I mean?''

''So far there is no vaccine against the hantavirus,'' Push says. ''About the most we can do at this point is to tell people, if they get to feeling like they have the flu or start feeling feverish at all, they're advised to get to a doctor or, better still, a hospital, as soon as possible.''

''Will you be wanting to arrange for the disposal of Miss Vogel's remains?'' Sonny says. ''She's over in Gallup at the county facility there. You're not her husband, I take it?'' Campbell shakes his head. ''Then maybe you know how to contact her next of kin?''

"No, I don't know anything about her family," he says, and he stands up abruptly. "Listen—I don't want anything more to do with any of this," Campbell says, and starts for the door. "And I can't tell you anything more, either. This is all just too weird." Then he stops with his hand on the doorknob.

"I can tell you one thing more," he says. "I can tell you that I'm getting as far away from here as I can, as *fast* as I can."

Push and Sonny follow him outside as he hurries across the road to where his vehicle is parked.

"Wait a minute, Campbell," Sonny says, and he puts his hand on the man's shoulder. "The Navajo who told you where to find the tablet? There's a chance he may have been trying to get it back from you . . . he may even have had something to do with what happened to Sabine Vogel after she had died. . . ."

Peter Campbell shrugs Sonny's hand away and climbs into the Land Cruiser. He fumbles the key into the ignition and pumps the accelerator. The still-warm motor sputters and then coughs to life.

"Slowtalker," he says over the loud noise the machine makes as he races the engine. "All I know is, his name was Slowtalker."

Push and Sonny look at one another. "And what about the tablet?" Sonny says. "Do you still . . ."

But it's too late—the two turn their faces away from the exhaust and dust and spraying gravel as Peter Campbell speeds away into the dusky light.

OAK CREEK CANYON

Peter Campbell looks down at his watch in the faint glow of the light from the dashboard.

It's a few minutes before ten o'clock—he's been driving for nearly four hours. He swallows the last of the tepid coffee he got at the Quick Stop in Flagstaff when he filled his tanks with gas. He tosses the empty Styrofoam cup out the open window and then reaches behind the seat and feels for the cooler—he flips open the lid and fishes a beer from the cold, icy water. He expects he'll be in Phoenix sometime after midnight. He'll find a motel, and then in the morning he'll begin contacting Indian-art dealers in Scottsdale.

Lots of money in Scottsdale, he thinks . . . amateur collectors who wear outlandish bolo ties and flash big rolls of greenbacks and don't have much in the way of know-how or scruples. Now that Sabine's gone, he doesn't feel himself bound by any constraints to try and locate a museum buyer for the tablet. Not that he ever really did.

It's nothing more than habit that's caused him to take the two-lane highway out of Flagstaff that heads south through Oak Creek Canyon to Sedona . . . the "scenic route" rather than the four-lane Interstate that runs directly to Phoenix. Nothing to see this time of night, certainly, and it will add probably half an hour to the trip—but he's buzzed and driving is better than sitting alone in an empty motel room. He won't be sleeping anyway—not with all that he's got on his mind.

The road is twisting and narrow—it follows Oak Creek as it meanders between high canyon walls and past spectacular red rock formations. There are forest-service turnouts and popular camping areas all along the road—the traffic at this time of night is light, however, and he's making good time until he finds himself stuck behind a slow-moving Ford Econoline van that is the last in what looks to be a line of three cars. They're moving very slowly, these cars, and Campbell can feel himself growing increasingly impatient. For several miles he's forced to follow—and he watches anxiously for a place to pass.

He's able to see in his headlights that there are pale images of top-hat-wearing skeletons dancing across the rear window of the van. He's thinking about Sabine . . . about the fact that she's died so suddenly. And even though he finds it repulsive to do so, he can't help imagining what Sabine must have looked like without a head.

And now he's thinking about the virus. There's an odd ringing in his ears and a pricking sensation on the skin of his chest and on his back . . . he's wondering if perhaps he's beginning to feel achy and slightly feverish himself. Surely he's imagining all this, he thinks. Still, he's growing more and more anxious by the minute.

"Fucking hippies!" He says this out loud. And he pulls partway over the centerline of the road, leaning forward over the steering wheel and straining to see his way clear to pass. The night is pitch-black . . . the darkness in this canyon is total.

He can make out plainly the red taillights of two cars ahead of the van. At last he tightens his grip on the wheel and mashes his foot down hard on the accelerator. He can feel the surge of power as the engine downshifts into passing gear and he steers across the centerline and around the first van.

As he speeds past the next vehicle in this slow-moving line, he sees that it, too, is a van—a Volkswagen bus with flowers painted on the side.

Campbell lays on the Toyota's tinny horn as he overtakes and passes the third vehicle—this one another Volkswagen. He shakes his fist angrily and glares back over his right shoulder as he swerves back into the southbound lane . . . purposely coming as close as he can to the VW bus.

"Bunch of assholes!" he yells.

And he is still yelling and still shaking his fist at the driver behind him when the Land Cruiser's heavy iron bumper clips the rear of the flag-adorned, multicolored school bus that has all the while been wending its way up the road ahead of the three vans.

A single small electrical fuse has burned out a couple of hours earlier—somewhere between Winslow and Flagstaff—and so there are no operating running lights on the rebuilt bus.

In that split second just before he jerked the steering wheel hard to the right, Peter Campbell may well have caught sight of the huge pink-granite boulder that lay a few yards off the paved surface of the road—may even have seen reflected in his headlights the silver *X* spray-painted there to alert nighttime drivers such as himself to the big rock's presence. But before the sound of crumpling metal and steel and shattering glass has stopped echoing its way up and down the canyon, Peter Campbell is dead.

And when, the next morning, the state troopers have completed their routine investigation and the county road crew has finished clearing the twisted metal and other debris from the crash site—spreading sand where fuel has spilled from the ruptured tanks—it's unlikely that anyone will have noticed one more small slab of stone lying there in the midst of the limestone and granite talus that covers the shoulders of the Oak Creek Canyon road. . . .

A small stone with strange markings on it.

TSÉGHÁHOODZÁNI

The phone on Priscilla Yazzie's desk is ringing as Sonny walks into the office. It's not yet eight o'clock, and his assistant hasn't arrived for the day.

''Brokeshoulder.'' It is a statement that the voice on the other end of the line makes, and not a question.

''Yes? This is Sonny Brokeshoulder. . . .''

''Brokeshoulder, it's Tso. I thought you'd probably want to know that the morning report from the state trooper headquarters over in Flag says that your man Peter Campbell bought the farm night before last.''

''Bought the farm?''

''Oh yeah, I forget, you're an Indian, aren't you? Let's see now, how should I put this? How about, Campbell has made his final journey to the Happy Hunting Grounds?''

''Okay, Earl . . .''

''He apparently ran his vehicle off the road and into something that didn't have much give. I understand the boys down there had to pretty much scrape what was left of him up off the highway."

"This was in Flagstaff, did you say?"

"Little ways south of there. The incident probably should have made it into yesterday morning's report, but you know the way those state cops do business—they're too goddamned busy drinking coffee and practicing their quick draws to do much paperwork."

"So, Campbell's dead. . . . *Damn*. Well, thanks for calling, Lieutenant."

"You're welcome." And the line goes dead.

Josephine Manygoats has just brought Push and Sonny their dinners at the Navajo Inn when Priscilla Yazzie comes into the nearly deserted dining room looking for them.

"I'm sorry to interrupt your dinner, Sonny—and you, too, Dr. Foster—but there was a call for you over at the office just as I was locking up—it was Mary Esther Lomaquaptewa from up on Second Mesa, she said that she was calling from the pay phone at that convenience store at Polacca."

"Funny that she should call like that—especially at this time of day. Is something wrong over there, did she say?"

"She said she was worried about Clifford—that he was very upset and that he took off out of there and told her he was going to go and find Silas Slowtalker."

"Find him where?"

"I guess at his place up at Chinle."

"Clifford was going to go to Chinle?"

"I think so. . . . She sounded pretty worried, like I said. And Mary Esther is always such a cheerful person—I never knew her to seem so serious, Sonny. She said it was important that I find you . . . that you'd want to know."

"How was he going to get to Chinle?" Push asks. "Did she say?"

"I expect he'd be going up there in his truck, Dr. Foster," Priscilla says.

"His *truck*? I didn't know he had a truck. . . . I didn't even figure he knew how to drive."

"I don't like the idea that Clifford's going looking for Silas Slowtalker after what all Campbell told us, Push."

"Did you tell Clifford everything Campbell said about where he'd gotten the tablet? The part about who had told him where to find it in the first place?"

"I felt like I had to," Sonny says.

"Yeah, I suppose you did."

Sonny looks at the plates of green chile enchiladas and shakes his head.

"I guess dinner can wait. It was right of you to come looking for us, Priscilla . . . thanks. I know where Slowtalker stays over there at Chinle, and I can't help but feel responsible if Clifford's going up there in a huff. I should probably go try and see if I can't maybe keep them from starting some new Indian wars."

Sonny is counting out bills for the check. "Priscilla, don't think of this as a date, but I'm buying your dinner tonight. Can't let these enchiladas go to waste, and if on top of everything else Gilbert back there in the kitchen sees a plate of his food come back untouched, he's liable to get so depressed he'll take a bread knife and cut his wrists."

"Yeah," Push says, putting a bill of his own on the table. "And see if you can't find someone who'll eat mine, too, Priscilla. I imagine our friend Dr. Brokeshoulder here could use some company."

CHINLE

The night sky is flashing brilliant white light from an electrical storm to the north and east of Chinle when Push and Sonny approach the town from the south. The wind has started to whip trash and dirt across the road that runs past the high school and the tribal government buildings.

''Slowtalker's place is over there . . . sort of behind those Head Start buildings,'' Sonny says. ''There's a couple of rows of those crummy HUD houses . . . they all look alike to me, but I think I remember which one is his.''

And the house *is* crummy. There is an old car without wheels in the yard—its windows have all been broken out. The yard is hard-packed dirt, and cans and broken bottles and other trash is scattered about. There is a stained and broken-down couch propped against the house next to the entrance—there is no porch, only a stack of cinder-block steps leading from the dirt to a door on which the screen has been ripped half off.

The door stands open and there is the flickering blue light

from a television inside the room. Somewhere a child is crying. A disheveled woman in a shabby housedress and men's slippers peers wide-eyed out at the truck as Sonny and Push climb out.

''We're looking for Silas Slowtalker,'' Sonny says when they reach the door. ''Is this where he stays?''

The woman turns and angrily yells something into the house. The crying stops abruptly.

''He's not here,'' the woman mumbles.

''Are you *Hastiin* Slowtalker's wife?''

''Why, do I look to you like I'm his wife?'' The woman's voice is low and edged with sarcasm.

''We'd just like to talk with him, is all,'' Push says. ''Can you tell us when you might be expecting him?''

''He went up there,'' she says, and motions with her arm toward the northeast. ''He went up there to *`Ane'é tséyi'*.''

''Canyon del Muerto? He went down into the canyon?''

''No . . . no, he went *up,* I said. Up on top of there. Like I told that *kiis'áanii* who was here awhile ago . . .''

Sonny looks at Push. ''So, that means Clifford's already been here and gone.'' He turns back toward the woman in the doorway.

''Did the Hopi man who was here go to look for your husband?''

''Maybe he did. . . . But he better hope he don't find him, is all I got to say. Sometimes that old man gets mad and then he talks rough. He was pretty mad when he left outta here. . . .''

''Let's go, Push, maybe we can catch Clifford.''

As they start back toward the Dodge, the woman at the door calls after them: ''He ain't my husband, you know.''

''Excuse me?'' Push turns to look back at her.

''Silas Slowtalker. He ain't my husband . . . he's my daddy,'' and the woman smiles around blackened teeth. And when she turns and goes back into the house, Push can hear a child has begun again to cry, and there is an odd, high-pitched giggling laughter.

In the truck Sonny says, ''*Damn* it! I was afraid of that . . . that she might be his daughter. Clifford's been so all-fired certain that Silas does the Bad Way, and now there's all that stuff Campbell told us about him. . . .''

''But what's his daughter have to do with it? She just seems a little retarded, is all.''

''The Navajo believe that witches commit incest—that they will have relations with their sisters or with their own children even. And they say that if a child is born of incest it won't be right . . . that it will be insane. And they say that that's one of the ways you can tell if someone is a witch. . . .''

As the two men drive out of the town, across the Chinle Wash and past the dark entrance to the Canyon de Chelly Monument Headquarters, Sonny is leaning far forward in his seat—peering into the blackness of the night. He tells Push: ''We'll take the fork that goes to the left up here. I've got a feeling that we ought to check the Mummy and Massacre Cave roads first.

''It's starting to rain. . . .'' Sonny switches on the windshield wipers and watches as the swiping blades smear dust and road grime across the glass.

''Keep a sharp eye out for animals on this road,'' Push says. ''And don't slow down if you see somebody walking on the shoulder. . . .''

ANE'É TSÉYI'

The rain is coming down in sheets and the wind is howling as it blows in gusts through the trees. Clifford Lomaquaptewa sits for a long time staring at the lone car that he'd found parked in the deserted lot when he'd driven slowly in. He pulls the green Army poncho on over his head and adjusts the hood before stepping out into the driving rain.

He walks directly up to the battered old car and places his hand on its hood. The metal is cold. It must not have been driven recently . . . it may even have been abandoned and left here days ago. Might not even be Slowtalker's car. Clifford doesn't know what sort of vehicle he's supposed to be looking for.

Should have asked that strange woman back there, he thinks.

The lightning comes frequently, though, so that he is able to see in flashes the trees and the brush that surround the parking area—is able to see where the trail begins that leads down to the overlook. The hair on the back of his neck is standing straight out. The pricking sensation that he feels throughout his body—is it the electricity-charged air, or is it fear?

Clifford gathers himself and starts off down the trail.

The smell of rain is strong, yet above even that there is the faint odor of burning wood—of piñon and juniper smoke in the air. Twice Clifford stops as he makes his way along the trail. And twice he is drawn to look toward the north. The third time he stops, there is an especially bright flash of lightning and Clifford can see that there is a rough path that leads off through the thick brush to his left—and he feels compelled to take that way for no reason he could explain.

The smell of the burning wood grows stronger now, and the rain lets up some. A booming crash of thunder explodes overhead and still he makes his way through the wet brush.

Clifford pushes on until he comes to a clearing, in the middle of which there stands the dark conical shadow of a hogan—and he instinctively understands that this is the abandoned hogan that the white man Campbell had described to Sonny Brokeshoulder. In the next burst of light, he can see that there is thick black smoke coming from the smokehole in the roof of the hogan. And as he moves slightly to his right—to where he knows the entrance to the structure will be—he can see that there is a faint yellow glow spilling from the door of the place—can see that the door is partway open to the black rainy night.

It is a frightening thing . . . to be here, alone and in the dead of night, at a place that he's heard described as one where there is a dead man.

But Clifford gathers his courage and moves quietly and quickly toward the open doorway and, reaching it, peers inside.

At first he can see only the flickering fire and hear the sharp crackling of the sap and pitch of the sweet, hot-burning wood. The smoke that rises from the flames is oily-looking and black—the knots of burning wood are heavy with pitch. Then, in the dancing light, Clifford can see that there is a figure of a man sitting, facing the fire, his back toward the door, and that alongside this figure are the shriveled and dried-out remains of what had been a human being.

The sitting figure is swaying slowly back and forth. It is singing—chanting—but the words are muffled and Clifford cannot make them out. The words are muffled because the thing that is singing is wearing a mask that covers its head—a mask that is more like a hood, really, by the way in which it covers the head and neck like a helmet rather than only the face. It is a Kachina-like mask, fashioned from heavy canvas material with triangular-shaped eyeholes and a long and pointed dark-colored snout. There are vertical stripes of blue paint, and there are tall feathers—striped white and black—rising upright out of the top of the mask to form a headdress. Large rectangular-shaped ears marked with *X*'s are attached to the sides of the mask. In the thing's right hand it grasps a huge knife—more than a knife, really. It is more like a machete.

The whole scene there before him is loathsome—the eerie light from the fire revealing a mummified corpse and the low, muffled chant coming from the horribly masked face of an ogre with black eyes. . . . Clifford feels a wave of nausea come over him—the room begins to spin as he feels himself about to lose consciousness.

But then the chanting stops . . . the thing there has somehow sensed his presence and has turned toward the door and is glaring full into Clifford's face. Clifford raises his hand and takes hold of the doorframe in order to steady himself. With his other hand he points at the thing there by the fire.

"Adiłgą̨shii!" Clifford cries out the Navajo word for "witch." His mouth has gone all dry from the abject terror that he feels welling up into his chest, and his voice trembles: "No good person would go near such a thing . . . I know you . . . I know who you are and that your medicine has gone all haywire and that you have lost your ability to do good. You are filthy and you are evil! . . ."

The masked figure scrambles to its feet, and raising the gleaming blade of the huge weapon threateningly, lets out a shrill, screeching noise and lunges toward the doorway where Clifford stands nearly paralyzed with the horror of what is happening.

It requires every bit of strength that he can muster just for Clifford to step back and into the darkness. The footing is muddy now from the driving rain and he slips and falls to the ground. The monster is standing over him in an instant and he feels a sharp burning sensation as the blade strikes a glancing blow off the arm that he has raised up to ward off the attack. Kicking his feet savagely now at the thing as it raises the blade to strike him once more, Clifford rolls to his right and struggles to his feet. He dives headlong into the darkness . . . into the wet, tangled brush beside and behind the hogan.

His lungs are burning now as he dashes slipping and falling, clambering to his feet and blindly pushing on through the heavy growth of pungent black greasewood and slick wet snakeweed. He cannot feel the wound from the razor-sharp blade—is unaware of the blood that flows from the gash on his forearm. He is only vaguely aware of the slap of pine branches across his face and the sharp, piercing needles of cactus as he plunges on into the blackness—blackness that is punctuated only by the sporadic flash of lightning.

Clifford Lomaquaptewa is nearly overcome with the horror of what he's seen at the hogan—terrified by the awful thing he believes to be following him now.

Just as he bursts out from the jumble of brush and trees and onto a shelf of smooth, slick rock, there is a brilliant flash and an earsplitting crash of thunder. And in that white-blue flash that lasts only a moment, Clifford can see clearly that his nearly mad rush has brought him finally to the very edge of the cliff—that he has reached the place where the earth falls away into the deep chasm that is the Canyon del Muerto.

As he stops and turns back toward the direction he has come, only now can he feel the sharp pain in his arm and at the same time he can see coming toward him in a burst of blue light the horrible specter of the masked thing with its deadly blade raised high above its hideous head.

The thing itself is not running, but rather it seems to be moving slowly toward the rock ledge where Clifford stands paralyzed. . . . It is as if the thing is able to see him clearly, even in the darkness.

It makes no sound now, as it moves—the only sounds that Clifford is able to discern are the rumblings of thunder as the storm moves across the canyons, and the quick gasping noise of his own tortured breathing. He is holding his bleeding arm and inching backward slowly now. Inching back until he can feel that his bootheels have come finally to the very edge of the steep cliff. Now fist-sized stones break away from the ledge beneath his feet and he can hear them as they tumble and crack against the jagged face of the wall beneath on their way to the canyon floor some eight hundred feet below.

In another flash Clifford sees that the masked ogre is closer now, nearly upon him—that it is swinging the huge blade in a widening swath . . . hears that the shrill, shrieking noise from beneath the mask has begun anew.

Clifford looks frantically about him for some weapon—he is searching for something with which to ward off the razor-sharp blade that passes now within inches of his face. He is desperate for anything . . . a large rock or a tree branch. . . . There is nothing. . . .

And now the monstrous thing grasps the hilt of the knife with both its hands and raises the blade high above its head. The shrill noise rises up until it is a piercing, maddening scream. Clifford can see that the thing intends to strike him in his neck—that it aims to strike his head off.

Clifford Lomaquaptewa closes his eyes . . . he can hear the pounding of his own heart and a faint sound of faraway singing, and he recognizes that what he is hearing is a death song. And it comes to him that he is likely hearing his own voice singing . . . that he is himself singing his own death song. . . .

"Silas . . . No!"

The masked thing turns toward the sound of the voice that has cried out.

It is Sonny Brokeshoulder—and he is standing with Push Foster at the edge of the trees—some thirty feet back from the ledge. He holds a flashlight, its beam trained on the two figures poised there at the edge of the cliff. For a moment the hooded attacker lowers the blade until it rests on its shoulder.

"Silas . . . Stop! What are you doing? Come away from there!"

And then Sonny and Push look on helplessly as the monstrous thing turns back toward Clifford Lomaquaptewa and again raises the blade. It is clear that it means to strike the Hopi man a deadly blow.

But at that very moment the two hear a strange, high-pitched keening sound. It is the high, sad sound that is the ancient and traditional death song of a warrior. For a brief moment, Push and Sonny believe that it is Clifford who has begun singing. But then, in a terrific burst of light that is very nearly blinding, so near to them has been the bolt of electricity and power from the sky, they see—or rather *think* they see—a dark figure that charges shrieking out of the shadows and straight toward the thing wielding the deadly blade. . . . They see that it is the figure of a woman, and they watch as she hurls her full weight hard against the masked attacker. And before the flash of lightning has dimmed, they look on in horror as the two plunge down, over the side of the sheer stone precipice.

Clifford Lomaquaptewa—alone on the ledge now—is trembling uncontrollably . . . his legs give way and he collapses onto the wet ground.

Sonny and Push—stunned by what they have witnessed—make their way to Clifford's side.

Sonny Brokeshoulder peers over into the pitch blackness that is the Canyon del Muerto. There is only darkness . . . and there is only the low, rumbling sound of thunder—distant now as the storm that was but a moment ago directly above the canyon walks on toward the south.

At first light, Push and Sonny meet Lieutenant Earl Tso and two of his Navajo Tribal Police officers at the Canyon de Chelly Monument Headquarters building. The five men drive slowly up the wet sand riverbed that is the canyon floor until they reach the place that lies directly beneath the Massacre Cave overlook. . . . There, some two hundred yards farther along—at a spot where there is a jumble of large rock debris and fist-sized talus—they come upon the broken, lifeless body of Silas Slowtalker. And not far from the corpse they find a large knife—its heavy, three-foot-long blade bent, but not broken. And though the five men search the area painstakingly, there is no sign of a blue kachina mask.

And neither is there to be found any evidence of a second body . . . no sign whatsoever of the woman that three men believe themselves to have seen push Silas Slowtalker over the side at *Adah Aho'doo'nilí*.

TÍDÁÁCHIID

It's the third weekend in June and Sonny Brokeshoulder is standing at the edge of a large, grassy field where a dance is in full progress. His head bobs gently with the beat of the drums and the high-pitched sound of the men's voices as they sing. He is smiling broadly as he watches from the darkness the solemn-faced couples who snake their way slowly around the brightly blazing fire. The dancers move double file, side by side, the women holding on to the men by their belts.

"I'll bet you there have never been anywhere near this many people in Tídááchiid at one time before," he says.

"Except maybe that time when they say all those TV reporters came up here askin' questions." Mary Esther Lomaquaptewa is chuckling. "I heard that the people who live around here were gettin' pretty mad about all the intruders and the busybodies who were snoopin' around."

"That's true, Mary Esther . . . I guess it got pretty hectic there for a while. But that's why they decided to hold these big doin's here now, to clean up this place and to chase out the sickness once and for all. The people usually come from all over the district whenever there's a Squaw Dance being held, but this one here has turned into a reservation-wide event. I guess everybody's so relieved that the worst seems to have passed and things are beginning to get back to normal.''

There are just a whole lot of people in Tídááchiid tonight. The atmosphere is festive . . . there are green Coleman stoves set up on the open tailgates of pickup trucks around which women are laughing and chattering as they patty-cake and stretch the sticky white dough into pancake forms for frybread and tend to black-iron cauldrons of boiling lard and extra-large blue-speckled coffeepots. There are children running into and out of the shadows and the light from the fires and the butane lanterns. Young boys and girls are giggling—capturing june bugs in jars and drinking canned pop and eating shaved ice soaked in sweet, sticky syrup: red and green and purple slush in white paper cones. Cars and trucks and pickups with campers are crowded in together among the scrub oak and the piñon trees. Modern nylon dome tents have been pitched and crude brush arbors built . . . and here and there, incongruous Plains Indian–style tepees have been set up.

The larger ceremony that is taking place at Tídááchiid is the *Nda,* or Enemy Way—the ceremony that is meant to treat the sickness that comes about as a result of contact with the ghosts of non-Navajos . . . sickness caused by being around strangers too much, the old people would say. Enemy Way is the chant that has traditionally been sung over warriors returning from battle—ancient warriors or modern-day soldiers, from the raiding parties of the last century to Vietnam and the more recent Gulf War. According to the Navajo Way, warriors who are victorious in battle run a terrible risk of harm being done to them by the ghosts of their dead enemies.

The nighttime portion of the Enemy Way ceremony—the Squaw Dance—is an important social event for the People. It is a time to come together—to receive and to give news, to make and to renew acquaintances, to see and to be seen. Young people engage in traditional courtship at the Squaw Dance—Navajo girls, urged on by their mothers, invite eligible young men to dance with them while the women gossip and the men do sway-singing. Outsiders—non-Navajo and non-Indian alike—are welcomed at the Squaw Dance, are urged to join in the dancing even, and are often seen in attendance.

Sonny has been watching the dancers alongside Clifford and Mary Esther Lomaquaptewa.

"These kinds of gatherings can be dangerous, you know," Clifford says solemnly. "A person has got to watch out for witches any time there's a lot of strangers in one place."

Sonny looks over at Clifford. He's glad that this Hopi man and his wife have come from Second Mesa to Tídááchiid for the ceremonial dance . . . he knows that it takes a great deal of courage on Clifford's part to put aside the events of the past few weeks.

"Not to worry, though," Clifford says. "I got me some strong medicine here this time," and he smiles up at Sonny and pats the small brown leather pouch attached to his belt. "Everything's getting back in the right order now, I believe . . . at least the world is still turning around."

"Yes it is," Sonny says. "That's what this night is really all about, isn't it Clifford? *Nda* and the Squaw Dance are the Navajo way of seeing to it that balance is restored—or as we Navajo say, *hózhǫ́*. These ceremonies are to help the People get back into harmony with the world—after something bad has happened. And bad things are bound to happen, you know . . . it's inevitable."

"Where's Push Foster, Sonny?" Mary Esther asks. "He didn't have to stay down there at Hashké, did he?"

"No, Mary Esther. He's got the whole weekend off. It's a good thing, too, because it's come around to his turn to go over to the Lukachukai clinic again . . . on Monday." Sonny is thinking to himself how Push's first turn at Lukachukai had marked the beginning of a bad sequence of events—he's thinking how he hopes nothing out of the ordinary happens *this* time.

"I expect he'll show up here pretty soon now. He told me he had some business to attend to on the way up, but that he'd be here before it got too late."

"Oh good." Mary Esther laughs. "I hope his business was that he's picking up something especially good for us to eat."

Sonny laughs. "I don't know about that, but now that you mention it, I *am* kind of hungry. I believe I'll go get me some of that good frybread I keep smelling. . . . I'll see you both a little later on."

And as she watches him disappear into the crowd of people, Mary Esther says to Clifford: "I'm real fond of Sonny, you know. I think he's a very nice man . . . especially for bein' a Navajo."

"Sonny Brokeshoulder's more than just a nice man," Clifford tells his wife. "He's a *good* man. He acts as though everyone is his relative."

Sonny has just finished the frybread and honey he's gotten from the food stand set up and run by Sampson Billy and is blowing on a cup of scalding-hot coffee. He is swaying to the drumbeat as he watches the singers and the dancers . . . someone taps him lightly on his shoulder.

"Hey there, Dr. Brokeshoulder . . . this *is* a Squaw Dance, isn't it?" Leslie Blair is standing beside him in the warm night air. Sonny is struck by how attractive this woman looks in the light from the fire.

"I thought the tradition at a Squaw Dance was for single ladies to flirt a little bit. If none of these young Navajo girls out here are showing enough good sense to invite you to dance, then maybe you'd like to go around a time or two with a mature white woman? . . ."

"You bet I would, Dr. Blair." Sonny grins broadly and then looks over both his shoulders as if he's afraid someone might be eavesdropping: "Just as long as some jealous Choctaw Indian doesn't come looking for me with his scalping knife out." He winks at the woman. "Speaking of which, have you seen our friend Pushmataha?"

"I most certainly have. . . . I'm the one who convinced him to come to this soiree in the first place. Of course, I told him that if it was to be a proper date he'd have to stop and pick me up and give me a ride up here."

"You guys are on a date, huh? That probably means Push took a bath and maybe even sprinkled on some toilet water." Sonny smiles. "Seems like every time I try to get hold of him lately the duty nurse at Hashké gets the giggles and tells me he's over at Keams."

Leslie feels her face flush slightly. "Well, he's around here somewhere . . . said he was going to get some coffee."

"Don't you go get all flustered, I'm glad to see you two enjoying one another's company. To tell you the truth I wasn't all that sure my friend was cut out for life on the big rez when he announced he'd signed on with the IHS. But now that I'm getting used to having him out here, I'm worried that he may go into a blue funk now that your tour of duty's about up. It'll be just our luck that your replacement will turn out to be some ugly old boy with a mustache. . . ."

"You mean Ed Pierce hasn't told you?" Leslie is smiling up at Sonny.

"Told me what?"

"That I've put in the paperwork to re-up for another two years at Keams?"

"Is that right? Well now, I'm delighted to hear it, but I'm surprised at you, Leslie. . . . I thought you were all ready to hang out your private-practice shingle in rural Alabama."

"Believe me, no one's any more surprised than I am, Sonny."

"Surprised at what?" Push says as he walks up to where the two stand talking. He hands Leslie a steaming cup of coffee.

"I was just telling Sonny how I've decided to hang around a couple more years . . . see that you two don't get yourselves into any more trouble."

And just then a new round of dancing begins . . . again the drum begins to play.

"Okay now, how about that dance I heard you inviting me to do? It's been a long time since I had a chance to show off a good-looking woman in front of a big crowd like this." Sonny begins to pull Leslie out into the firelight and toward the line of dancers. "And don't you worry about him." He nods toward Push. "He's not going to feel left out—in fact, he's probably relieved that you're not insisting he go out there with you." And Sonny laughs out loud: "Most white people think all us Indians are natural-born dancers, but the fact of the matter is Choctaws are not blessed with that instinctive sense of rhythm that the rest of us are so well known for. I remember seeing a bunch from the Mississippi Band of Choctaws one time who were supposed to be demonstrating some of their traditional dances. It was downright embarrassing . . . not one of them was in step."

Push is smiling broadly as Sonny takes the coffee cup from Leslie and hands it back to him and the two move off toward the line of dancers.

"You know, Clifford and Mary Esther came all the way over from Second Mesa," Sonny calls out over his shoulder. "And Priscilla's around here somewhere. . . ."

"A*héhee'lą́ą́,* Pushmataha . . . Thank you, my friend. And don't start being a stranger,'' Sonny is saying. The two men are standing beside Push's pickup. ''Just because you have a sweetheart at Hopi doesn't mean you can't come to Window Rock every now and then. . . . I think Josephine Manygoats has a big crush on you and a fellow never can have too many girlfriends, you know.'' He winks down at Leslie Blair, who is already sitting in the passenger's seat of the truck.

It is dawn at Tídááchiid, and the sky is brilliantly clear. The smell of the creosote bushes mixed with that of smoldering wood fires and boiling coffee is sharp and good. People are folding their tents and preparing to return to their homes. The Enemy Way ceremony is ended.

''That road goes both ways, you know,'' Push says. ''So maybe you could come around to Hashké once in a while, too. I've been thinking that it's time I get myself a new truck—maybe even one you won't be ashamed to be seen riding in.''

''Sounds real good to me . . . we could cruise around the rez with the windows partway open like in the old days . . . holler out Indian words at the tourists . . .''

Push climbs in behind the wheel and starts the engine. He looks up at his friend.

''You know, Sonny, I don't know that we've learned anything from all this. . . . I mean, we still don't have a clue as to why some of the people who got sick survived and some of them died. And we still haven't come up with anything we can do for anyone who contracts the virus . . . other than offer them supportive treatment and maybe try to relieve their anxiety.''

''That's true, Push. I can't help but remember how Silas Slowtalker told us one time that we doctors don't know shit about curing people—remember that? I guess he was maybe right about that, at least . . . we sure enough don't seem to know much about this thing.''

''But then I don't know that anybody else does, either,'' Push says.

''Even the traditional medicine people don't know what to do. And if it comes back . . .''

''*When* it comes back, Sonny . . . because it *will* come back, you know . . .''

''Well, then I figure about all we'll know to do is to make people as comfortable as we can. To the Navajo way of thinking that means getting back into balance, *hózhǫ́*. And to our formal Western medical training it means respirators and whatever else we can do to make them comfortable and less anxious. At least until someone comes up with something better . . . a cure maybe, or at least a vaccine.''

Push looks up at Sonny and takes his friend's hand in a long, gentle clasp. ''Yeah, and *hózhǫ́* or hypodermic needles . . . who's to say which is the better way, really?''

''I guess I'm what you might call a real cautious individual, Pushmataha . . . I prefer to keep all my options working. You know, I get my flu shot every year, but if I can't shake off a bad cold or I feel like I'm coming down with a fever, I'm liable to go see Birdy Tooclanny . . . just in case.''

Push Foster is smiling broadly now as he engages the clutch and puts the truck in gear. ''I've always liked the way you think, Brokeshoulder. . . .''

And so Sonny Brokeshoulder stands watching, his hand raised in goodbye, as the Chevy bounces off across the field and onto the dirt road. He is still watching as the truck tops the low rise above the wash, trailing a billowing cloud of red dust, and then disappears from sight.

Push slows and steers carefully past the scraggly flock of sheep and goats that are moving slowly down the road. A sullen old woman on horseback is following the animals . . . three scruffy-looking dogs amble along beside the woman's horse.

As they drive past a hogan where a thin ribbon of dark smoke escapes from a black metal pipe rising up out of the center of the roof, they can see in the open doorway that a woman is standing, holding a baby. The woman shades her eyes from the bright morning sun as she watches them pass by. Push raises his hand in greeting. The woman turns and disappears back inside the darkness of the place.

"Are you sure you're not too tired to drive all the way down to Keams?" Leslie asks. "After being up all night, I mean."

"I'm just fine," Push says. "After all, I didn't dance all night like some people I know," and he is smiling as he looks over to where she sits gazing out the open window at the countryside.

"What did you think of your first Squaw Dance?" Leslie asks as they turn north onto the blacktop road that will take them to Shiprock, where they'll turn west toward Teec Nos Pos and Mexican Water in their long loop back to Keams Canyon.

''It was wonderful, seeing all those good people there together like that. This place is magic, Leslie.''

Leslie lays her head against Push's shoulder and closes her eyes.

''You know, I thought I'd lost you there once during the night,'' she says. ''What happened to you?''

''I got very tired and went off to sit by myself for a while so that I could listen to the singing. I think I must've fallen asleep for a couple of minutes, because when I opened my eyes there was someone standing there watching me.''

''Who was it?''

''I don't know . . . I couldn't see all that well—it was very dark. Just that it was a tall woman with long hair who was standing there.''

''Uh-oh . . . Some pretty young girl wanting you to dance with her, huh?'' Leslie says.

''No . . . no, it wasn't like that. This woman was different—there was something about her . . . she wasn't a young girl, but it wasn't like she was all that *old,* either. I don't really know how to describe it. Anyway, when I stood up I could see that she was motioning for me to come with her . . . to follow her. She went over to the edge of that big field—sort of off to the side, away from where there were any other people—and then she very gently took hold of my belt and my hand. And we danced.''

''*You* danced?'' Leslie sits up—an incredulous look on her face—and stares grinning and wide-eyed at Push.

''Yeah, well, I'm not a total klutz, you know,'' and he laughs in embarrassment. Then his voice becomes serious: ''Her hand was very cold, I remember, and there was an odd smell about her—not a bad smell, but just strange . . . you know?

''She didn't say anything until the drumming stopped. And then she just stood there, looking at me for a long time. . . . I think maybe she was crying, Leslie. But her face was in the shadows and I could hardly see her.''

''She never spoke to you? Didn't say anything at all?''

''Just once she said something . . . it was right before she turned around and went off back into the darkness. She said that I should keep dancing. . . .''

''That was it?'' Leslie says.

''Yeah, funny, isn't it? That was the only thing she said to me . . . *''Keep dancing . . .''*

Epilogue

Listen . . . baa ha'aldéé.

I've been here for a very long time—going on two hundred years—so I probably shouldn't get too surprised when I see all the commotion that's always happening in the world where the Walking Around People are still going about their business.

I suppose I should be used to it by now, after so many years have passed. But it's not an easy thing. . . . I don't really know how it is that I'm able to see all that's happening, but I can *see it, just the same . . . and so I'm able to tell of terrible things that have gone on. Like about the bad business that started when some soldiers with hair on their faces came with long guns and big knives to rub out all of the People.*

I can tell about it because I was there that day.

As it happened the strong fighting men from our village were away taking care of other business at the time and it was just some of the old men and a bunch of us women and of course our young children who were left there. And so when we saw that those soldiers were coming we all gathered together and climbed way up there in those rocks and were trying to hide ourselves and our children. I can still remember how frightening it was to look up and see that first soldier coming over the edge there . . . see how he looked all mean and ugly . . . it was plain to me that he had it in his mind to rub us all out. When I saw that, I went crazy and started singing my death song like the Warrior Woman that I am . . . and then I took out my good sharp skinning knife and I ran hollering and screaming right toward that soldier and threw myself hard up against him. And when he saw me coming at him like that, he changed from looking mean and brave to seeming all scared and big-eyed, like he was maybe going to get sick or start running away. Except that there was no place for him to run. . . . And so we fought, that soldier and me. And I can tell you that I was very strong in those days—my war name is Baa′nééz, *which means "Tall Warrior Woman"—and so in my struggle I was able to pull him down over the side of that high place along with me. Oh yes, I rubbed him out, all right. But the moment we stopped falling—when we hit the earth down there at the bottom of that place—I knew right then that it wasn't just the soldier who was killed, but that I was killed, too—even though I didn't feel any pain that I can remember.*

And it was all very strange, because even before the dust had settled, a magical thing happened . . . and just like that, in the blink of an eye almost, I was somehow carried back up to the very top of that canyon wall and I realized that I was then watching while the rest of those soldiers shot and stabbed and beat the People until they were all dead . . . every last one of them.

I saw one of those devils take hold of my child—he was my only child, and he was not yet old enough to stand alone even—and I watched as that one bad soldier took hold of my baby by his ankles and lifted him high up over his head and threw him down hard against those rocks. He never cried out, my brave boy-child, but I can still hear how the force of him hitting those jagged rocks made such a terrible sound. . . . And I can tell you that still, after all these years, that sound echoes up and down in the canyon—or maybe it just echoes inside of my head . . . I don't know. But it causes great pain to rise up in my breast, pain that is nearly more than I can bear, and my heart cries out still.

Oh, and when that happened I can tell you that I wailed and I cried and I tore my hair to see such a thing—but no one could see me . . . or hear me, it seemed. And even now, after all these years, I'm still able to watch things happening, and still most people can't see me, or hear me, even. I say "most people" because there have been some people—very old people, mostly—who now and then it seems can see me and who will even hear me speaking to them. People who, if they're not too frightened, will sometimes speak to me. I think that maybe these are the people who haven't forsaken the traditions, and who are mindful of saying their prayers to the Holy People. It is as though these good people can see everything—including me—more clearly because they still hold to the Old Ways.

Yet always I can see things—and I want you to know that I have seen many things since that day I fell off. But I will tell you this: that I don't believe I will ever *see anything so terrible as what happened to the Navajo people on that day.*

And I only regret that I did not somehow manage to rub out every one of those soldiers.

And not just that first one, either. . . .

Endnote

Hantavirus Pulmonary Syndrome is a recently identified disease carried by rats with a high mortality rate among humans. An outbreak of the disease in the summer of 1993 in the Southwestern U.S. led to its identification. It is not known how rats acquire hantaviruses.

—The Lancet
16 March 1996
Vol. 347, no. 9003:739

A total of 131 cases of Hantavirus Pulmonary Syndrome have been reported in the U.S. since the disease was first recognized in 1993 . . . half the people affected have died.

—Centers for Disease Control and Prevention
Journal of the American Medical Association
May 8, 1996
Vol. 275, no. 18:1395

Atlanta, June 16 (AP)—A hantavirus outbreak killed 11 people and sickened nine others in Argentina last year in the first known case in which the respiratory illness spread from person to person, United States health officials have reported.

Scientists had previously thought that hantavirus pulmonary syndrome could sicken people only if they inhaled microscopic bits of rodent urine or feces containing the virus.

—The New York Times
June 17, 1997

Acknowledgments

It is no easy thing to write a novel. And without the encouragement and support of family and friends, I can't imagine how anyone could do it.

I am indebted to my friend and agent, Sharon Friedman, and to my editor, Beverly Lewis—more deeply indebted, in fact, than I care to admit. Together these two extraordinary women are the agent and the editor that most writers only dream of having. Believe it.

The Amerind Foundation early on afforded me access to its outstanding collection and a quiet and beautiful place to write in southern Arizona's Dragoon Mountains, and for that I am grateful.

And then there are Panki Bok and Joe-Babe. No matter whether they are dozing under my writing desk in Tucson, or barking at sheep from the back of a pickup bouncing across washboard roads on Navajoland, or smuggled into bordertown motel rooms—always they are enthusiastic and eager partners in this dance.

To all of you, *hózhǫ́*

Of mixed ancestry—Choctaw, Scot, and German—Ron Querry is an enrolled member of the Choctaw Nation of Oklahoma, a descendant of the Sixtown Clan (Oklahoneli). He has a Ph.D. in American studies from the University of New Mexico and has taught English and writing at several universities. He received the Southwest Book Award and a Regional Book Award from the Mountains and Plains Booksellers Association for *The Death of Bernadette Lefthand.*